NO CERTAIN HOME, the fictional retelling of the life of Agnes Smedley, the controversial, extraordinary American radical, is Marlene Lee's fifth novel. Her first, *The Absent Woman*, was published by Holland House in 2013 to much acclaim, with Ella Leffland writing 'I couldn't put down *The Absent Woman*. I relished every scene, every word. It's one of the most compelling novels that I've read in many a moon."

No Certain Home

MARLENE LEE

Caerus Press
An imprint of Holland House Books

Copyright © 2016 by Marlene Lee

Marlene Lee asserts her moral right to be identified as the author of this book. All rights reserved. This book or any portion thereof may not be reproduced or used in any manner whatsoever without the express written permission of the publisher except for the use of brief quotations in a book review.

Although based on real people and events, this work is presented to the world as 'fiction' not as a factual account. Any resemblance to living persons is purely coincidental. Any characters denoted by government office are not based on any current official, appointed or elected.

Paperback ISBN 978-1-910688-00-7
Kindle 978-1-910688-01-4

Cover design by Ken Dawson
www.ccovers.co.uk

Typeset by handebooks.co.uk

Published in the USA and UK

Holland House Books
Holland House
47 Greenham Road
Newbury, Berkshire RG14 7HY
United Kingdom

www.hhousebooks.com

To Bill, With Love

Acknowledgements

I wish to thank Stephen R. MacKinnon and the late Janice R. MacKinnon for their biography *Agnes Smedley, The Life and Times of an American Radical*. Without their book I would not have known about Agnes Smedley and could not have written *No Certain Home*. Their help and kindness is greatly appreciated. Quotations in the last chapter come from the MacKinnon book and from the Agnes Smedley papers housed in the Hayden Library Archives, Arizona State University, Tempe, Arizona.

I cannot thank Ella Leffland enough for her encouragement and time spent reading the manuscript. San Francisco Writers Workshop deserves special thanks as well as the following people and libraries: Vincent Payez; Marisa Milanese; Lavetta and Glen McCune; Robert McCutcheon; Betty and Victor Cochran, and Mary Ellen and Lonnie Courtney of Sullivan County, Missouri; Ann Brandvig; Jan Elvee; Lois Maharg; Aino and John Taylor of Ojai, California; Kyle Meredith of Boca House, Historical Society, Trinidad, Colorado; Trinidad Public Library, Trinidad, Colorado; University of Colorado Library, Special Collections, Carol Klemme, Librarian; Hayden Library Archives, Arizona State University, Pat Etter, Librarian; University of California, Berkeley, South and Southeast Asia Library; Det Kongelige Bibliotek, Copenhagen; Svendborg Bibliotek, Svendborg, Denmark, Lemming Pedersen, Librarian; Sinnet and Lars-Olaf Liljestrom of "Torelore," Thuro, Denmark; Professor Zhi Gui Wei and Family (Shanghai and San Francisco); Xiao Ying Wang and Family (Xi'an and San Francisco); and Susan Finlay for pointing me to Holland House Books.

My editor, Robert Peett of Holland House, has earned my deep respect and gratitude for his professional insight and for the faith he has shown in my work.

Marlene Lee
September 2015
Columbia, Missouri

1
China 1937

"Your father," the American woman said, getting to the point of the day's interview. "Tell me about your father."

Dark and stocky, Commander Zhu De got up from his small table. The burning candle illuminated his smile and sharpened the creases of kindness around his almost simian eyes. Like the woman, he was wearing army fatigues. The only concession to the late hour was soft slippers in which he padded about the dirt floor of the cave as he listened to her inadequate Chinese.

"Was he a good father?" she persisted.

Zhu De turned his face away from the candle and did not answer.

The American woman, too, lived in a cave. Hers was next to that of several lovely young actresses who belonged to the Red Army theatre troupe. No longer young and lovely, she had already spent eight years in China. Now she had come to Yan'an to live with the Red Army and to send out a constant flow of articles to the Western press from the remote headquarters.

"Did he love you?" She pushed her cap back from her high forehead.

"Father not a happy man," Zhu De finally answered. He simplified his Chinese so that Agnes was able to understand. "Cruel temper. Violent habits." He rubbed his eyes. "Very poor. Half our grain went to Landlord Ting. We went hungry, yet on holidays we gave up chickens, eggs and pig. We called landlord 'King of Hell.' All tenants hated him. My father grew tobacco but he was too poor to smoke one pipeful himself." Zhu De stared into the dark at the back of the cave. "Love did not enter our thoughts. We tried not to die."

Lily Wu, a beautiful actress with expressive eyes, entered the general's cave. Her hair was parted in the middle and hung to her shoulders like thick silk. Progressive women of China did not wear queues; they did not bind their feet.

"Ask him about his mother," Agnes said in English. With Lily present to translate, the interview went more smoothly. But Mao Zedong had seen Lily enter the cave and followed. Each evening he interrupted, ostensibly to discuss America and world politics, but really more interested, Agnes felt, in asking Lily Wu oblique questions about love and relations between men and women. Agnes disliked these interruptions. She disliked Mao. He was spiritual, remote, lascivious. Zhu De, on the other hand, was a plain man like her own father. A man of the earth.

Zhu De's face settled into repose. "My mother was too poor to have a name," he said. "There was no food. My mother drowned her last five children at birth."

Agnes gripped her pencil. Tenderness for the mother and dead babies overwhelmed her. Imagining childbirth made her feel ill. She swayed on the hard-packed dirt floor of the cave until Zhu De moved his straight chair from the table and insisted she take it. He waited for a sign to continue.

"My mother sang to me," he said. "I picked wildflowers and fished in the stream. I did not know we were poor. I often stood at the great road that passed through our village, the great road that ran from the south of China to Xi'an and northeast to where the Empress Dowager, 'The High,' sat on the Dragon Throne. I watched merchants, and salt coolies carrying salt, wedding processions and funeral processions. I stood at the edge of the great road and China passed before my eyes."

When the day's interview ended, Agnes Smedley returned to her cave and began typing up notes on the portable typewriter that rested on a table, covered with a cloth to keep out the yellow dust from the loess hills. It was in these hills of Yan'an that the Chinese Communists ended their Long March. It was here Mao Zedong, Zhou Enlai, Zhu De and his army dug in to rest and regroup after *the beating they had taken from Chiang Kai-shek.*

She frowned in the candlelight. She knew exactly what she wanted to say and how to say it, but small things still tripped her up, like the spelling of a hard word, or a confusing bit of grammar. She felt her lack of knowledge bitterly.

2
Missouri 1900

"By God, this is a fine way to start off the new century!" Father shouted.

Agnes looked through the sunflower stalks at the man in the fancy buggy waiting outside the cabin. Two bluebirds flitted from an oak to an elderberry bush; a woodpecker, quick wooden clapper in the bell of summer, rapped on the trunk of a walnut tree. Inside Mother was crying.

"You've been busy while I was away! Who is he? Who's the father? Just tell me that! Everyone's wonderin'!"

Agnes ran to the well and pumped a stream of water into the tin cup that hung on the post. She wet her face, then dried it with the floursacking of her skirt. Sometimes when she and Father stood here after supper he would point to the Missouri hills rolling one after another, like waves on an ocean, he said, and when she asked if he'd seen the ocean he said no, but he didn't need to. He already knew what it looked like. He told her about his Indian blood which he'd passed on to her, then spit with contempt at the Rallses, Mother's people, farmers and church-goers who would always be poor.

The Rallses didn't bother to think about what was beyond those hills, he said. The Smedley line was different. The Smedleys, now, they had some imagination. Some spunk. And Father would tell about the opportunities farther west, how you could jump on the Chicago, Milwaukee & St. Paul and be out of Missouri before you knew it. Farther west there was a fortune to be made in any number of enterprises.

The man in the buggy hadn't moved. In one hand he held the reins to Father's fine white team and listened to the shouting in the cabin. He was a doctor, Father said, and he was teaching

Father to be one, too. Agnes replaced the tin cup on its nail. Mother's people would perk up their ears when they heard about a doctor in the family, and they wouldn't feel sorry for Mother anymore. All the Rallses in Sullivan County would see the long line of sick people coming from Osgood out to the Smedley cabin and raise their eyebrows the way people do when they're interested in something. The line would stretch from the depot in town, across the tracks, over Medicine Crick, along the road, up the hill, all the way to the cabin door. People would be limping on canes and crutches, they would be carried on stretchers, like in pictures Agnes had seen in the church at Campground where a man in a long white dress with a sissy face and big blue eyes put his hand out to feed a crowd with just three little fishes.

When the team suddenly stamped the ground and started for the barn, the man in the buggy nearly fell backwards. He yanked on the reins and swore. Agnes laughed and he swore at her, too. He didn't look or act like a doctor. Agnes tried to picture him helping people, but couldn't. She went back to her dream about Father being a doctor in a doctor's office, say, next to Milsteads' Mercantile. In fact, she and Father might move to Osgood by themselves and live over his office the way the station agent lived over the depot. Every Saturday she and Father would drive out home, bring food and clothes for Mother and the children, then drive back to Osgood late at night under a moon that showed the rolling hills as far as anyone could see. He would cover her with a lap robe and put a pretty foot-warmer on the floor beside her like one she'd seen in town that slowly burnt little blocks of coal all night without a blaze. And while he loosely held the reins of the finest team in the state of Missouri, he would talk about the future, about far-away places, about train trips, horse races, gold mines — and Mother would be nowhere around with her sad eyes that Agnes could not bear.

"There's stories goin' around!" Father's voice was ragged now. He'd lost ground. His temper sputtered out and his words fell

5

like flies on the first cold day. Agnes crept to the cabin door.

"Oh, Charles, speak the truth!" Mother said, and fell forward. Father caught her, and then they were hugging and crying and kissing each other, Mother wetting Father's throat with her tears. Beside the door Agnes cried, too, and hid her confusion behind her hands. Father wheeled around.

"Agnes! Take the young 'uns outside!" Agnes' face burned. Father and Mother were going to go to bed in the daytime. It was like this sometimes in the middle of the night, too, only worse because she couldn't get away. She would be woken by sounds, animal sounds, coming from their bed. Next day Mother acted like nothing had happened in the night, and went back to whipping Agnes for lying.

Agnes half-carried the younger children across the wagon path up to the barn where she waited until Mother and Father were finished. Finally Father stepped around the corner of the cabin and came walking toward the buggy. From the south side of the cabin Agnes could hear Mother working the pump at the well.

She took off at a run. When she reached her father she threw herself against him.

"Here!" said Father, trying to disengage himself. He grasped her wrists and pulled her arms from around his waist.

"You can't go to St. Joe!" she shouted into his fancy belt buckle. There was a strange smell of bleach between his legs.

He pushed and twisted until he held her at arm's length. "Go back with the other children!"

Mother came around the cabin, hesitating and fiddling with her hair that straggled out of its bun. Agnes suddenly sprinted in her direction, then stopped halfway between her parents.

"You can't go away again!"

"Maybe we'll all go," her father said. He gave an odd, sideways glance at the doctor.

"I won't go!" shouted Agnes. This time she ran and didn't stop until she stood beside her mother. "We won't go with that man! He's not a doctor!"

Mother jerked her by the arm. Agnes grew quiet and ashamed.

"How old's your little filly there?" the man asked.

Agnes scowled. "I'm eight!"

He picked up the reins. His lip curled. "Better stay with your women folk, Charles Smedley," and he "gee'd" father's horses. They made a wide turn, re-entered the wagon path, and set off downhill toward the road that ended up in St. Joseph. Kansas City. Farther, even.

Agnes gave Mother a fierce hug that threw both of them off-balance. Mother moaned, grabbed Agnes to steady herself, then pushed her away.

"Such a selfish girl," she said. "Such a talker." And she marched into the cabin. Agnes ran to her father where he stood in the wheel ruts. She started to say something, tell him how happy she was he was staying. But when she saw his face, angry and hopeless, she turned, walked toward the storm cellar, and lay down under the sunflowers. Hugged the ground. Pressed her face against the earth. It smelled of dirt. Spicy weeds and grasses. Tough, green sunflower stalks.

3
Kansas and Colorado 1904

"Close that window, Agnes," Mother said, squinting against the stream of dirty smoke and soot blowing past from the engine. "Your pa's the one who wanted fresh air and he's gone to the smoking car again."

Agnes settled back on the plush seat facing Mother, who doled out bread and ham to the younger children. The only time Myrtle, John and Sam sat still was when they chewed. In the silence Agnes watched the flat landscape move backward in the window, miles and miles of wheat and milo fields, with a stray cow here and there grazing too close to the track. Occasionally she could see farmhouses in the distance, not forty acres apart like the farms in Missouri, but more like forty miles, lonely specks trying to populate the empty horizon.

The clicking of the wheels lulled Sam to sleep in the corner beside her. Earlier, to the conductor's disgust, he'd been sick in the aisle. But he wasn't the only child to be sick. The train was full of immigrant families going to the mines, and more than one thin child with enormous dark eyes had been rushed, pale-faced, up the aisle to the lavatory at the end of the car.

They hit a rough section of track and Sam stirred. Mother half-stood, ready to hold him up to the window before he could throw up on the beautiful seats. Myrtle handed him part of her sandwich.

"He hadn't ought to eat any more ham," Agnes said. Like the younger children, her eyes were large, though from excitement rather than illness. And they were blue, vivid, large-pupiled, darting from person to person, thing to thing. Sam bellowed, but stopped when Agnes gave him a piece of the hard candy Father had bought her in Kansas City. In the seats behind them

Agnes heard a strange language being spoken.

"Italy-an," Mother said. Agnes asked how Mother knew.

"Because they eat meatballs morning, noon, and night," Mother said. She put her finger to her lips and whispered, "They're Catholic. The old lady rattled her beads all night long."

"What's Cath'lic?" asked John. He stood up to peer over the back of the seat. Agnes grabbed him by the leg and pulled him down on her lap.

"What are 'beads'?" she whispered. "What do you mean, 'rattling her beads'?"

"So many questions," said Mother. "Ask your pa."

Agnes looked for a long moment at her mother and felt something unpleasant, something like a dough ball stuck between her throat and stomach. Mother could scold Agnes, shake her, but she didn't know how to answer her questions, and she didn't like it when Agnes told stories to make things more interesting, the way Father did: lies, Mother called them. Here in the train, traveling to their new home in the West, Agnes realized her mother didn't know much. She almost pitied the helpless ignorance, the wisps of hair falling in Mother's face, the rough, red hands that picked nervously at the children's clothes. Pity was harder to bear than anger. Agnes could not swallow the lump stuck just below her throat.

Nellie, swaying with the motion of the train, returned from the platform between cars where she'd gone to stand, less to watch the country go by, Agnes thought, than to look for boys. Myrtle stood up.

"Where are you off to, young lady?" asked Mother.

"To wash my hands."

"You just washed them."

"She likes the gold handles," said Agnes.

"Nellie gets to wash her hands whenever she feels like it," Myrtle pouted. "I want to wash the ham off."

"Take Sam with you," Mother sighed, "and wash him up, too." Nellie moved so they could get by. At the same time, she looked over her shoulder in the direction of the loud party at the far end of the car.

"They're talkin' about the Exposition," she explained.

Mother sniffed and closed the lid on the shoe box of food. "They play cards," she said, tying up the string. "I saw them last night."

"What's the Exposition?" John asked. He laid a piece of ham on the arm of the seat. Mother picked it up and wiped the red plush with her handkerchief.

"It's the World's Fair in St. Louis," Nellie said. "The 1904 World's Fair."

Agnes leaned forward. "We're headed the wrong way." She was proud of her directions. "We're goin' west. We'll miss it."

"Father says—" Nellie began.

"What does Father say?" asked Father himself, back from the smoking car. He took the empty seat across the aisle.

"That the St. Louis Exposition has got nothing on Trinidad, Colorado," Nellie said smugly.

"Trinidad"—Father paused to re-open the window, cross one leg over the other, and smooth his glossy mustache—"has people from every spot on the globe." He grinned at the children and flicked away a cinder thrown up from the roadbed. Across the aisle Mother's thick, red hands fiddled with the string on the shoe box.

"Italy, Germany, Russia, England, France, Brazil," Father enumerated, and would have gone on if he hadn't run out of countries.

"Canada?" asked Agnes.

"Canada," said Father, "and Mexico, and other countries too numerous to mention." The children looked at Mother who gave a small, apprehensive smile.

"God, woman!" Father said. He recrossed his legs the other direction. "Everybody in the world wants to be in Trinidad. That's where the money is."

"Are you hungry, Charles?" Mother asked.

"Nah," Father said. He was in a happy, magnanimous mood. The smoking car was also the drinking car. He rose. "Think I'll take a stroll."

"You just got here."

"Then I've just left." He stood and walked back along the aisle, his rolling gait as much a part of the train's sway as the train itself. At the end of the car he pushed open the door. The clatter of wheels on rails, the shriek of the train's whistle swept through the car like a wind.

At midnight the Smedleys stepped down onto the Trinidad station platform. In the dark, passengers milled around them, a pushing, shoving weight of shouts and strong-smelling bodies. Foreign babble flowed out of more cars than Agnes dreamed could be hooked up to one engine. The train hadn't been this long, she was sure, when they left Kansas City.

"Where'd all these people come from?" she asked Father, who was pushing ahead into the crowd.

"Denver!" he called back to her. "They come from Denver! And before that, Chicago and New York. Every spot on the globe!" Agnes stayed right behind him, calling back to Nellie and Mother who might get lost among the foreigners in the dark.

They slept in a boarding house that night. Agnes dreamed about Trinidad and their very own home, but when Father showed it to them that afternoon—"It's close by," he said, "no need to hire a wagon"—and they'd carried their grips across the railroad tracks, it wasn't a house at all, but a tent. Still, Father had nailed up a "kitchen" he called the shed, and once you were inside this kitchen you only had to dip your head a little to get into the tent where Mother and Nellie were already spreading blankets on the plank floor.

"We'll have featherbeds before long," Mother said gamely, and when she stood, her face was pink and pleased because Father had planned well and soon there would be enough money for a house.

Daylight ended early in Trinidad, shut out by the Juniper-covered crags of Fischer's Peak and the high mesas and foothills. Agnes crossed the ditch and climbed the embankment, Myrtle behind her. Following Father at a distance—he'd told Mother he was going to town "on business," but they all knew he was going to the saloon—they began picking up pieces of coal dropped from the trains' fireboxes onto the tracks. By the time they dragged the gunny sack, heavy and lumpy with coal, back to the tent, a cool and purple stillness had fallen over the shanties along the track; over the town of Trinidad and the Santa Fe Trail flowing through its center like a river.

Agnes set the gunny sack near the stove and looked Mother in the eye. "I'm invited to a birthday party," she said.

"How come?" asked Mother.

"All the girls in the class are invited. Everyone has to take a present to the birthday girl."

Mother disturbed a few embers in the stove, blew on them, and jabbed a short-handled shovel into the gunny sack. "They live on the hill," she said. "They already have nice things. What are you going to take?"

"Three bananas."

"Three?" Mother acted like she'd never heard of such a thing. "You'd take bananas from your own brothers and sisters so you can give them to a rich child on the hill?"

"Three," Agnes said firmly.

"Such a selfish girl," Mother said, and slammed the stove door shut.

Agnes was the first one at the party. She'd worn her best dress, the one she'd had her photograph taken in, a pinafore with a wide, ruffled yoke.

She climbed the long flight of steps leading up to the fine house and rang the bell. The little girl's mother came to the door. She looked at Agnes, then at the bananas, amazed at such a nice gift, and told Agnes to go in the parlor where the little girl was arranging a circle for "musical chairs."

"H'llo," said the birthday girl. "Where's your present?"

Agnes bobbed her head in the direction of the front door. "Your mother put them on the table."

"'Them'?" said the birthday girl. "More than one?"

Agnes grabbed a straight chair from the corner. "Does this here go in the circle?"

"Oh, we already have enough chairs," said the girl, and turned away to tighten her hair ribbon. The doorbell rang. Agnes remained holding the chair while the lovely little girl skipped to the entry hall. She was gone so long that Agnes set the chair back down and went out to stand near the round table. Other lovely little girls were setting their gifts on the lace tablecloth that hung clear to the rug. The presents were wrapped in colored paper and bright ribbons, all except three bananas.

She stared at the dark, woody stems and yellow skins beginning to turn black. A snake of doubt uncoiled in her stomach and slithered up her backbone. She took a step toward the door. Its beveled glass admitted light but shut out tents and railroad tracks. She considered hiding on the porch where it turned the corner and ran alongside the house. By now the entry and front room were full of noisy children. The little girl's mother hurried between the door, the gift table, and an inner room where Agnes could hear the soft chink of china and silverware against a background of women's voices.

When the piano in the parlor started up with a loud, fast song that had lots of fight to it, Agnes decided to stay a minute longer. She went in to stand behind the birthday girl sitting on a round stool at the piano. Patent leather shoes peeked out from her long, velveteen skirt. The girl twisted around to see who was watching and lost the beat.

"Go back with the others," she hissed.

"I'd rather watch you play," Agnes said softly. "Can I watch you play?"

"No! Can't you see you made me lose the beat?"

"Don't sound to me like you lost the beat," Agnes said. "It's beautiful."

"Wouldn't you like to join the circle?" said the little girl's mother. By now the children were stalking something in the middle of the parlor. Suspicious, Agnes stepped into the ring and followed the line around and around a lot of chairs. Suddenly the music stopped. There was a great crash as the children threw themselves onto the chairs. Agnes stepped back, shocked at rich people's manners. The little girl's mother came up and gently tapped her shoulder.

"You're out," she said.

"What?"

"You lost your chair."

"I never had one," said Agnes. Everyone in the parlor grew still

"The point of the game," said the little girl's mother, "is to find a chair."

Agnes went over and picked up the straight chair she had earlier put beside the velvet curtain. "I can set in this one," she said.

By now the children were tittering. The music started up and they stalked chairs again. The song was choppy and getting choppier. Each time it stopped, hell broke loose. Others joined Agnes on the sidelines, and she realized they, too, were out. Finally there were just two people circling one chair. Agnes turned away from such a stupid game.

After the winner was declared the mother said they would play it one more time, "now that everyone knows the rules." Again chairs were set in a circle. Agnes decided not to go home just yet. She'd hunted more quail and squirrel than anyone here, and she could damn well locate a chair.

The piano began again. A different piece. Slower and prettier. Agnes considered going out the first time around so she could stand by the piano and hear the music. This song needed quiet listening to, not dashing around a durn fool circle of chairs.

The music stopped. Agnes lunged for a chair and landed on

someone's hand.

"Ow!" screamed a short boy.

"It's the rules," Agnes said fiercely, and held her seat. Soon she was stalking chairs again, around and around, and she could see that the mother had placed them so that whoever was at one end of the lopsided circle would lose out. Each time she reached the end, she held back until she could make a dash for the chair on the other side.

"Now, Agnes," said the mother when Agnes was hanging back at the end of the lopsided circle, "move along with the rest of the children." Agnes glared at her. The music stopped and Agnes threw herself in the nearest chair, which sent some silly girl crying to the side of the room, sucking her hand.

After a bit they were down to three chairs. This time when the music stopped, Agnes leaped up sideways and landed where a chair had been a moment ago. But one of the girls moved it at the exact moment Agnes needed it.

"She moved it!" Agnes bellowed from the floor. "I seen her do it!"

"Now, now," said the mother, "let's all get along nicely." Agnes was out. But this time she didn't go over to the piano. She didn't even hear the music. She watched the cheating girl like a hawk. And when the girl started to throw herself into a chair, Agnes reached over and pulled it quick-like toward the short boy whose hand she'd sat on earlier, and when she moved the chair she also pushed him into it, so that the cheating girl stood red-faced, out, and ready to spit. She turned to the mother and cried,

"She's not playing according to the rules!"

"You hadn't ought to cheat!" Agnes shouted back. "I seen you before! You moved the chair!" The mother motioned for her daughter to play louder and stepped between Agnes and the cheating girl.

"Now, girls, it's only a game. We're ready for our refreshments. Won't that be nice?"

Agnes watched everyone troop through the double doors and thought just maybe, before she left, she'd take a bite of whatever it was people ate at birthday parties. She followed the others into the dining room. The first thing she saw in the center of a long table was a bowl of fruit, and right on top was a bunch of the most beautiful bananas she'd ever seen. Six. And not one black spot.

The three blackening bananas sitting on the gift table filled her with shame. So, too, did her tent, the kitchen shed, the railroad tracks. For a long moment she did not trust her family or herself. Then a strong, fresh feeling climbed up her spine where the snake had uncoiled before. She turned and walked out of the dining room toward the front door. On the way out, she grabbed her bananas. Descending the stair steps to the street, she held her head high. In case anyone was watching, they would not see her cry. She'd left early because she wanted to. She'd planned it all along. She hated birthday parties. She would never go to another birthday party in her life, no matter how many times she was invited.

4
China 1937

At dusk Agnes stood on the terrace near her cave and looked across the valley at the ancient walls of Yan'an. Beyond the ruins of the old town the Yan River snaked off to the east. Closer, at the foot of the loess hill where she stood, Red Army soldiers were racing their horses on the drill ground, a flat piece of land soon to be converted to an airfield. Agnes sometimes took her pony, Yunnan, captured in battle against the Nationalists, and galloped him across the clay-packed field, Yunnan's ears pinned back, her own short brown hair flattened by the wind. Zhu De had given her the pony as a gift. Second only to her portable typewriter, Yunnan was her most cherished possession.

"Good evening," Zhu De said in Chinese. He had come from his cave to join her. "It is a beautiful early evening."

"Beautiful evening," Agnes repeated in Chinese. Her accent was poor. Zhu De stood scanning the sky. In a single sweeping gaze he contemplated the ancient pagoda on the cliff; then studied the river itself that curled off into the distance where it would meet the Yellow River, "China's Sorrow"; then returned to the horse races on the field below. Zhu De's eyes and mind were never still.

"You are not racing Yunnan?" he asked, making a small joke.

Agnes' face, with its strong, pleasing bone structure, could suddenly break into a wide grin. "I will let others win today." A shout went up from the soldiers in the field below. Zhu De raised his arms and clapped. These were the same young men and boys he taught in the Red Army Academy, renamed the Anti-Japanese Resistance University. He dropped his arms to his sides. "It is a good army," he said. The sun sank, brilliant red, in the haze of dust hovering above the dry and dusty region. Zhu De turned from the sunset toward Agnes who had opened her notebook. He smiled.

17

"You are eager to work." She was already writing. He began:

"At the Lunar New Year when I was a child, we put wild honey on the lips of the Kitchen God and burned his picture in the courtyard that Heaven might receive a good report of our family." He paused until her pencil stopped moving. "We believed the stars made us poor and unlucky. We hated Landlord Ting, but it was the stars, we thought, that made us poor. The stars made us eat kaolaing gruel and vegetables from a common pot. The stars gave us a black cake of coarse salt over which we rubbed the wet vegetables. Only on very special nights did we burn a candle: cotton in a dish of rape seed oil.

"Famine came. Our family broke apart like a fallen fruit. I went with my uncle and aunt who had no children." Zhu De's face settled into a stoic mask. "Our world changed. We planted opium. The famine made it necessary. Now the family was split, you see." He gripped his hands together, then tore them apart to augment the simple Chinese he used with Agnes.

"It was decided I should continue in school. My schoolmaster was Hsi Ping-an, a good teacher. He believed in Western, scientific education, but he was too old to understand the mathematics and science. He taught us to inquire. Still, our curriculum was the old Confucian ethics."

Zhu De broke his monologue with a smile that began in his eyes, played out on his seamed face, and returned to rest in his eyes. "You are comfortable in your cave?" he asked.

"I am comfortable enough," Agnes replied. "I am not here to be comfortable."

"You have trapped all the rats in Yan'an?" He laughed outright. The Chinese thought her compulsion to kill the rats overrunning the caves was amusing. Similarly, they did not understand her interest in cleanliness and something called germs. However, Mao had put the weight of his authority behind her anti-rat campaign, and traps begged from her friend Edgar Snow in Beijing were cocked and ready to spring shut all over these loess hills.

"Rats carry disease," she stated, and the general did not disagree.

They stood in silence. Shadowy hills and plateaus stretched away into the dusk.

"In the days of my childhood," he continued, "the Old Weaver traveled through Szechwan villages each winter to weave cloth from the cotton thread my mother and the other wives and daughters spun.

"He fought in the Taiping Revolution of 1847 and wore the red jacket and carried the red flag. The Old Weaver told stories about the opium wars and foreigners' plunder of China. The Empress Dowager, he told us, taxed the poor to pay foreign victors."

Agnes needed her interpreter, Lily Wu, but if she called for her, Mao Zedong would see, even in the dusk, and follow her here to the terrace.

"There is much change in the world," Zhu De went on. "In China we live in the heart of change. During the Taiping Revolution, Marx and Engels were writing their works, India had a great rebellion, and soon your country would have a civil war, north against feudal south. I have lived in a time of confusion. I, myself, was confused. When I was nearly forty I cleansed myself of confusion and self-indulgence."

Agnes stopped writing and listened.

"I had grown addicted to opium. It was very pleasant. I thought my life should be pleasant. I grew confused and indolent." Zhu De shifted his weight on his strong, stocky legs and stopped talking.

"The wealthy say you are a bandit," Agnes prompted.

Zhu De did not smile. "I am a poor peasant. If it becomes necessary, I am a bandit. My life is work, walk, and hunger."

"The people of China call you 'Zhu-Mao' because they think you and Mao Zedong are one person."

Zhu De did not answer directly. "It is necessary that many people become one to achieve life for the poor," he said.

"In my country," said Agnes, "the government sends the militia to help the mine owners control the miners. Sometime I will tell you about the massacre near the mining camps where I lived as a girl."

"The wealthy always want more," said Zhu De. "The poor of the *world are one family."*

Lily Wu had heard their voices and approached from her cave.

Zhu De smiled. "It is Saturday," he said to the two women. "Tonight we dance."

Agnes had asked her friend Margaret Sanger to send a Victrola to Yan'an for the Saturday night dances. Even before the hand-wound phonograph arrived, Agnes taught the Central Committee, the Red Army officers, and the actresses from Shanghai to square-dance in the Date Garden, a flat, clay-packed area near their living quarters. It was in keeping with the new China; with the new equality between the sexes. Still, the Chinese wives remained at home. Plain, unadorned women who had made the Long March with their husbands, they had little in common with the imported actresses and the western woman who laughed freely and spoke directly. Modernization was one thing, but dancing with their husbands was another.

"Yes, there will be dancing tonight," Agnes said. Zhu De was an enthusiastic dancer, Zhou Enlai was graceful and inspired, but Mao Zedong moved with mechanical correctness as he pushed his partners up and down the dirt floor in determined circles.

While Zhu De and Lily Wu remained on the terrace, Agnes returned to her typewriter to transcribe her shorthand notes of this evening's conversation. At the entrance to her cave she turned back and saw, aiming for the terrace, his large head pointed toward Lily, Chairman Mao emerge from the twilight.

5
Colorado 1908

In the mining camp near Trinidad, Mother did laundry for the schoolteacher, a red-headed young woman full of energy and ambition. The first time Agnes delivered clean clothes to the teacher's boarding house half-way between the company store and the schoolhouse, the woman invited her in for a cup of tea.

"What are your plans for the future?" she asked.

"Plans?" No one ever asked her about her plans. She didn't have any. She didn't want to marry, and for a girl with no money for schooling, there were no plans.

Almost every week through that winter the red-headed school teacher poured boiling water over tea leaves in a china pot and asked questions as the steam rose around her. Agnes thought she was a silly, snooty woman; a bore. But Agnes wanted to have plans, so all through the winter she drank tea out of a hand-painted cup. She held it on her knee and watched the tea leaves drift through the liquid until they settled at the bottom.

"What do you like to do?" the woman would ask.

"Ride," Agnes would say. "Hunt squirrel. Read."

"What are you reading?"

"Nothing," said Agnes. "No library up here. No speakers at home."

"People who go to school say 'books,' not 'speakers'."

Agnes covered up her humiliation by draining the teacup. The teacher refilled it.

"Do you sometimes get down to the library in Trinidad?"

Agnes nodded. Whenever tea slopped over the edge of her cup and into the saucer, she was handed a linen napkin. She figured the more napkins she used, the more pieces of laundry she and Mother could charge for.

"What do you like to read?"

"Thick, dark books."

"Dark books?"

"With small print." Much of what she read she didn't like, but she forced herself through difficult pages because she would learn more that way. She looked around the room. Above a cloth and silk flower bouquet hung a picture. She set down her cup and saucer and stood to get a closer look.

"Is that a picture of Mary and Jesus?" Under Mary's feet, sticking out of some clouds, were two Cupids. She wasn't sure if it was a Bible picture or a Valentine.

"Yes," said the teacher. "It was painted by an Italian artist, Raphael, a long time ago. Do you like it?"

"Don't you have any pictures of animals?"

The teacher rose and opened a desk drawer. From it she withdrew a postcard and held it out toward Agnes. On the front of the card a horse pawed the ground while a cowboy crept up from behind with a lasso.

"That's better," said Agnes. "My father has broke lots of horses." She turned the postcard over. It was addressed to Miss Ramona Edmonds. Agnes thought it a most beautiful name.

"Dear Ramona," said the postcard. "You don't know how much—" but Miss Edmonds took back the postcard, put it away in the desk drawer, and returned to take up her cup and saucer again.

"Have you ever thought about teaching school?" she asked.

Agnes snorted. "I only went to fifth grade."

"How old are you, Agnes?"

"Sixteen."

Miss Edmonds tilted her head back and half-closed her eyes in contemplation. "In New Mexico you don't have to graduate from high school to be a teacher," she said. "You can take a test."

Agnes swallowed some tea, weak brown water that wasn't as good as the boarding house coffee she was used to. The room around them developed a beat, the beat of stillness and thought.

"What kind of test?"

"Reading, writing, arithmetic, history," said Miss Edmonds. "I can help you prepare for it." Agnes shifted on the straight chair with the embroidered upholstery. She wanted to get all objections out of the way, so that if the plan—for it was already forming itself into a plan inside her head—was impossible, the disappointment would be fast and she could forget about it.

"I don't have good clothes."

"You can borrow a skirt and blouse from me. We're almost the same size."

"I can already read," said Agnes. She tightened her grip on the cupful of cold tea. "And I can write."

"What about arithmetic?"

"Can't do much with numbers."

"Two plus two."

"Four," said Agnes.

"Next time you deliver the laundry I'll have some word problems ready for you," said Miss Edmonds. "We'll work them together."

Agnes stood up from the fancy chair and pointed to the laundry bag leaning against the door. "Throw in some extra pieces," she said. "No charge."

Before she and Mother even started on the next week's laundry, Agnes rode her horse up to the big stone schoolhouse resting against the foothills of the Sangre de Cristos Mountain. She didn't have to wait long for the recess bell. Miss Edmonds stepped outside with a line of children behind her.

"Hello, Agnes."

Agnes lowered her eyes, then raised them. "Do you want to go riding?" she asked.

Miss Edmonds turned once to survey the children still behind her. "I don't have a horse," she said.

"I can get one for you."

"Thank you. It would be a pleasure."

"I'll bring the laundry Saturday," said Agnes. She glared at Miss Edmonds' skirt. "Wear something to ride in."

The next Saturday they followed the creek up into the canyon. The water murmured in its rocky bed, clear and cold from melting snow higher up, no silt to muddy the reflection of the blue sky. On one side of the trail cactus grew at the base of boulders that seemed to hang, suspended, over the two women. On the other, cottonwoods, willows and box elders, their roots crawling underground toward creek water, shaded a long, thin strip of canyon floor. While Miss Edmonds chatted, Agnes kept an eye out for horned toads or rattlesnakes sunning on the rocks.

"Do you ride up here often?"

"Yup."

"It seems dangerous to be here alone."

"I ain't alone," said Agnes. "I got my horse."

"What time do you think it is?" asked Ramona after a silence.

Agnes squinted up at the sun. "Half past noon," she said.

"Would you like to stop for sandwiches?"

Agnes shrugged. "Not hungry yet." They rode on, single-file. When the canyon widened, Agnes held back so Ramona's horse could come up alongside.

"When do they give that test in New Mexico?" she asked, surprised the canyon did not ring with the pounding of her heart.

"In April," said Ramona.

Agnes pulled a thin book out of her saddlebag. "That gives me a month to study."

When they stopped at a broad place in the canyon, Ramona spread a tablecloth on a flat rock and set out the picnic. Agnes began thumbing through the arithmetic book.

"Here's where they lost me," she said. "Fractions."

"You won't find that difficult," Ramona said. "Look here." She set four half-sandwiches in a row across the cloth. "How many sandwiches?"

"Whole or half?" said Agnes.

"Precisely." Ramona moved the sandwich halves together to form two whole sandwiches.

"What kind are they?"

"Minced ham, but that's not the point. Look here. One sandwich plus one sandwich equals two sandwiches."

"Two minced ham sandwiches," said Agnes.

"And if I want to divide this sandwich between you and me—"

"You can have the whole thing," Agnes said. "I'll take the other one."

"—then I simply divide it in two. " Here Ramona pulled the sandwich apart. "Now I have two halves."

Agnes watched guardedly.

"So one-half plus one-half equals—" began Ramona.

"—one whole sandwich, " said Agnes. "That's easy. But fractions aren't that easy, leastways not how I learned them. "

"If you're afraid of fractions," Ramona said, "then you didn't learn them." They ate the lesson, then put their backs against the warm rock and began to study the book Agnes had stolen from the school in Trinidad.

On the third Saturday in April, Agnes told Mother she had to do some work for Miss Edmonds that would take the weekend. With the first sun touching the tops of pines and aspens on the west rim of the canyon, she tied her horse to the porch rail and carried fresh laundry up the stairs of the boarding house. Ramona was waiting for her with a skirt and blouse which Agnes folded and carried back down to her saddlebag. Ramona waved to her from the upstairs window. Agnes remounted and set out in a southerly direction for the state border and the teachers examination.

6
New Mexico 1908

Far back in mesa country stood a little schoolhouse that the District kept open from May to September.

"You'll have to find another job in the fall," the superintendent said to Agnes. His expression cast doubt on her examination score and stated age —eighteen. Still, she had passed the test and he needed a teacher for the school on the mesa where no one else wanted to go. "Snow gets too deep back in there for a year-around school. And I warn you, the people are rough. Miners and laborers." He gave her another appraising glance. "You'll have to build your own fire and cook your own meals."

"What's so hard about that?" said Agnes.

The superintendent turned her test results face down on his desk. "You'll do," he said.

Agnes moved into the little room at the back of the adobe schoolhouse. The mesa was as level as a rock table, its edges studded with boulders set on end as if to prevent the red dirt from breaking up and crumbling onto the plain below. Above timberline, it baked in the sun and lay flat for lashing rainstorms that swept over the mountain range.

Alone in the classroom late one afternoon, Agnes was studying the next day's lesson when a curious mother dropped by to meet the new teacher. She gave Agnes a copy of McCall's.

"You need something to do in such a lonely place," she said.

"I'm not lonely," Agnes replied. "I have my work, my horse, and the mesa."

But that evening she took the magazine to her little room and read the stories. In back, behind articles on how to talk to a man, how to dress for a man, how to cook for a man, were ads for pen pals. An ad from a Mr. Robert Hampton caught her eye. This Mr. Hampton lived in a cultured eastern city: Columbus, Ohio.

She wrote him a postcard and he responded with a letter. Robert Hampton was finishing high school, a lofty achievement. He sent her some of his old textbooks. Agnes studied them, made notes, and sent them home for her sister Myrtle to read. She propped his letters up on her desk in the classroom at night and copied his handwriting; the rough edges of her own hand began to take on his elegant ovals. He was her secret handwriter, secret ideal, secret love whom she would meet some day because she intended to go to him. The words Columbus, Ohio were beautiful to her: she intended to travel there. Every week she wrote him, nearly as proud of her endless supply of paper and ink as of her new teaching position. Even without the forty dollars a month she made in salary, Agnes felt wealthy each time she went to the cabinet stocked by the school district and took out the lined sheets of writing paper, purple ink bottles, pencils, and erasers the color of the adobe earth outside. She wrote letters home in which she exaggerated her responsibilities — lying, Mother would have called it — self-conscious at expressing her thoughts, at having the leisure to write at all.

"Write me back," she told them, and was surprised that the only person who did was Mother, her letters tucked inside the clean laundry done up and shipped to Agnes by train and wagon from the mining camp where the family now lived in the mountains above Trinidad.

"Your father is hauling goods," she wrote Agnes. "I guess the wagon is good for something besides moving us from place to place. Thanks for the textbooks. I read slow. Maybe you can teach me something when you get home."

Annoyed, Agnes took the letter outside and walked toward the burn can. She didn't want to hear from Mother. She wanted to hear from Father. A flush crept up her neck. Along with irritation at Mother's weakness and pity for her ignorance lay something that frightened her: longing.

Above, the sky glowed purple-black with an oncoming storm. The wind tore apart a thundercloud and for a moment the sun illuminated rose-colored sandstone and shale in gold light, more brilliant because it could not last. The first raindrops fell, sending up little clouds of pink dust where they hit. The world smelled of wet dirt and wet rock. The dark sky blossomed with bursts of light; split along a jagged seam that ended at the rim rocks behind the schoolhouse. In the midst of a thunder roll, when she had just spread her arms and lifted her face to the rain, the world cracked open. A bolt of lightning hit the mesa and threw Agnes to the ground. She lay motionless. Water running down her face brought her round. Her riding pants were soaked; her mother's letter smeared.

Agnes crawled into the schoolhouse. By stages she reached her cot in the back room. Hours later, when she rose in the dark, built a fire, made coffee, she had the strong impression that Mother was standing beside her. She felt surrounded by Mother's presence, cradled by a stubborn, glum, wordless love that was anything but weak. For days after, the recollection of Mother, life-giver, despised one, split Agnes as lightning splits rock. It struck her as a storm strikes the mesa, and left her flattened.

Colorado 1910

September came and Agnes had to find another teaching job. There was a school in a canyon above a mining camp called Primero. Her superintendent gave her a warning look.

"It's not New Mexico," he said. "It's Colorado. You're supposed to have a certificate from the normal school." She gazed at him. "But since you have experience, and it, too, is a primitive school"—he cleared his throat and adjusted his pince nez which seemed an affectation in mesa country—"I have recommended you."

It was there one day in February, 1910, in a canyon above Primero, where her landlord, Mr. Herrera, pushed through the snow drifting in front of the schoolhouse door and came straight up to Agnes who was at the blackboard teaching Mexican and Indian children the Pledge of Allegiance.

"Your mother very sick," he said. "They say you come."

Agnes laid down the chalk and moved mechanically to her coat and hat hanging in the corner. Without dismissing the children or saying a word to her landlord, she walked out the door. Mr. Herrera came running after.

"The train from Trinidad reach Primero two o'clock," he said. "No time. You wait. Tomorrow I take you in wagon."

"Where's your wagon now?"

"Timber." He waved his arm toward the top of the canyon.

"What time is it?"

"Eleven."

"I'll walk," said Agnes. He shrugged and dropped back. Agnes reached the Herrera house, strapped her gun under her coat, and said good-bye to Mr. and Mrs. Herrera.

"Too dangerous!" Mrs. Herrera called from the doorway, but Agnes did not reply. She set off up the canyon road and turned to take the short-cut across the divide. Snow came up to her thighs. Eventually she followed a path tramped to a thin layer of ice by herds of sheep. The wind bit into her lungs. She slipped often and pulled herself up by grabbing the tough scrub oak rooted in the frozen ground.

At the top of the divide she stopped for breath and looked far down at the smoke curling from the chimneys of Primero. In the thin, crisp air she could hear coal being emptied from ore cars. Without a thought of the train, of the cold, of breathing, without even a thought of Mother, she set off down the slope at a slow trot. She fell down and got up as matter-of-factly as if she crossed the divide every day. She pushed her body. Her mind was empty. She gained her second wind. Primero might have been far, might have been near, it made no difference. She could run to Primero, Secundo, Tercio; she could run to Denver, Kansas City, St. Joe.

With her breath deep and steady, she entered the coal camp, reached the company store, and turned to run past the mouth of the mine. She heard the train before she saw it. Sprinting the last few yards, she jumped onto the station platform and stepped up into the passenger car. Not until she had paid the conductor and thrown herself onto the plush seat did she notice her exhaustion. All the way up to Tercio she stared out the window at the white and featureless landscape. Home was at the end of the line. This is what all the striving comes to. Agnes leaned her head against the glass and, dry-eyed, grieved.

7

China 1937

"Failure. It was failure again and again," said Zhu De. Agnes sat opposite the Commander-in-Chief, the small table with its single candle between them. *"We studied the failure of the Taiping Revolution. Although the Taipings divided up land, freed slaves and women, outlawed opium, they failed."* His face, unsmiling now, was lit from below by the short candle. *"Their Kingdom of Heavenly Peace lasted fifteen years until they began to fight among themselves. They grew corrupt. At the same time the British and French waged the Second Opium War of 1858. Three-hundred thousand Taiping civilians were slaughtered in Nanking."*

Lily Wu, who sat on a straight chair close to the table, lifted her hand. Zhu De paused while she translated.

"In 1895 China failed again. China lost the war to Japan. I was a nine-year-old student. Our village and all other villages in China were taxed so that war indemnities could be paid. Rice-rioters prowled the roads for food. All China's blood went to foreign victors. China bled continually.

"The Reform Movement of 1898 failed, also. The Young Emperor ascended the Dragon Throne. I was twelve years old. My hair was allowed to grow in and my queue was cut off. China was to be industrialized like the West. But the reforms benefited only the merchants and rulers. The peasants were untouched. And without the peasants, backbone and heart of China, reform cannot succeed." He looked about the cave before his eyes returned to the candle flame. *"Thus did we learn from failure."*

Agnes laid her pencil on the table and flexed her hand. The General stood and walked into the shadows at the back of his cave. He returned with a broken shard of pottery that he held near the candle. Agnes and Lily Wu bent near.

"I have saved this to remind me of the bowl. It is from my family."

"It is broken," Agnes said.

"It came from a perfect bowl," said Zhu De. "We labor to make another bowl. It is the shard that reveals the bowl's perfection." Zhu De laid the shard on the table.

"The bowl is broken," Agnes insisted, and picked up her notebook and pencil.

"China was disturbed by foreigners' spheres of influence," Zhu De continued without disputing her. "She was drained of land and resources. Russia took Manchuria. Britain took the Yangtze River Valley and Kowloon Peninsula across from Hong Kong. France took provinces near Indo-China. Japan took Fukien Province near Formosa. Spain, then America, took the Philippines. All robbed China." He picked up the pottery shard and turned it in the candlelight. Its crazed surface gleamed. Gradually his expression freed itself from pain, his eyes warmed, and his generous lips relaxed.

"Again China struggled out of feudalism," he said. "Revolutionaries formed a society. They called themselves Boxers." He looked at Lily Wu. "It means 'Righteous Harmony Fists.'" Lily We looked at Agnes to see if she understood. Agnes nodded.

"Again they failed. The Yellow River flooded. Again rice-rioters took to the roads of China. The court diverted righteous anger from themselves to the foreigners who easily defeated the Boxers. Many years later when I lived in Germany I saw Chinese art treasures in comfortable homes. I saw vases from China, paintings, carved furniture, and I knew that my country had been looted." He put his palms together on the table.

"Foreigners profited from China's sickness. Cheap Western goods replaced Chinese goods in the markets of every small village. No longer did the Old Weaver come and weave cloth from our cotton. We used western nails in place of Chinese nails. Foreign kerosene was cheaper than seed oil from our own crops. Chinese reformers longed to imitate the West. 'We must study modern methods,' my old teacher said, though he himself was unsure how to do so.

"One day a traveler left a small book in our village. Mr. Hsi brought it to school. He dismissed our regular classes and we spent days studying this book of science."

The General's voice dropped. His face twisted. "It was a pamphlet from a Cleveland soap factory, simple drawings of machinery that we took to be basic science." Agnes wrote rapidly and did not look at his embarrassment. Silence fell. Agnes and Lily Wu stood. Zhu De roused himself, picked up the pottery shard, and watched them go.

The next day Agnes and Lily Wu went to the library at the Communist Headquarters in Yan'an. Lily helped Agnes find a Chinese reference book. They read what Marx had said in 1857 when he was the London correspondent for the New York Tribune. China, the oldest empire in the world, he had written, was in its death struggle.

In another part of the book they found a letter from Mark Twain to the New York Sun *on Christmas Eve, 1900*. He criticized the payments that Christian missionaries exacted from the Chinese government. The next day Agnes took the book to the General's cave and asked Lily Wu to translate for Zhu De.

"Who is this Mark Twain?" he asked, and Agnes explained, surprised by feelings of pride and homesickness, that he was an American writer who, like herself, had spent his childhood in Missouri.

8
Denver 1910

Failure. Agnes had failed. Sitting in the train car, she fed her infant nephew when he was hungry and jiggled him mechanically when he cried. Since Mother's death in the mining camp and Nellie's death in Oklahoma, life had gone out of everything Agnes touched. She'd shipped Mother's body to Oklahoma for burial beside Nellie, then quit her teaching job to look after Father and the children. But Father drank, the children ran wild, and Nellie's baby sickened.

At the Denver depot she handed down the baby through the train window, almost as if she might stay on the train herself and go right on through Denver. As soon as Aunt Tillie reached up for the bundle, the young life in its dirty blanket began to wail. When Tillie looked into the wizened little face, the baby looked back. For the first time in weeks its desperate gaze locked into place, as if it knew this woman possessed enough strength and comfort to help a baby stay alive.

"Didn't know if you got my letter," Agnes said after she'd gotten off the train and followed her aunt along city streets to the bus stop. People on the sidewalks—white, Indian, Mexican, European—were as swarthy and spicy a mix as she'd lived with in Trinidad but they held no interest for her. The world used to be a round, spicy place. Now, since Mother's death, it was flat.

"Here's where we get off," said Tillie after a long, silent ride on the street car. Carrying her valise, Agnes followed Tillie down Colfax. Horses and buggies and an occasional motor car rolled past.

"I don't have enough room for you and the baby," Tillie said, transferring the child's weight to the other shoulder.

Agnes thought of the mesa and the adobe schoolhouse; of the empty schoolroom at night where she had read and written Robert Hampton and improved herself. She thought of it and then stopped thinking of it.

"We don't take up much space." She followed Tillie through an iron gate set in a high brick wall. Like the wall, the house Tillie lived in was brick, and big as a hotel. From the wide porch furnished with two hanging swings and wicker furniture, they entered a hallway. Agnes glanced into the parlor at a piano, wing-back chairs, a fireplace with marble mantel.

"Is this a hotel?" she asked.

"Not exactly," said Aunt Tillie. They went to the back of the house and up some stairs. Tillie's room was on the top floor.

"You get your exercise," Agnes said. She let go of the valise handle and leaned against the wall. But Tillie wasn't listening. She'd made a crib for the baby, a basket that rested on two straight chairs pulled together to face each other.

"Should we change his diaper?" Tillie asked.

Agnes took a clean diaper from the suitcase.

"I set a wash basin in the bathroom," Tillie said. As Agnes peeled off the diaper, a stricken look crossed Tillie's face. "I forgot to buy powder."

"You don't need it unless he's got a rash," said Agnes. "I just wash him up good." She had dropped her schoolteacher diction and was back talking the way she always had.

She went down the hall to the bathroom, the finest one she'd ever seen: white tile floor, long porcelain tub, toilet with water tank and chain. She put the diaper to soak and returned to Tillie's room. By now the baby had fallen asleep in its basket.

Tillie stared out the window before she removed her hat and laid it on the four-poster. "When are you going home?" she asked. "I don't have much room here."

Agnes nodded toward the sofa. "I can sleep on that," she said, and knelt to unpack.

"My landlady doesn't like me to have overnight guests," Tillie said uneasily. "You can stay for a few days. Then we'll decide what to do." She looked away. "What about the children?"

Agnes' expression dulled. Her voice flattened. "Father beats the boys. He tried to beat me. Mother stood for it, but I won't."

"If you're not going back," Tillie said in a constricted voice, "what will happen to Myrtle and John and Sam?"

"Myrtle's hired out. Sam and John left for Oklahoma." She had sent them to Nellie's husband, sent them all off when Father was up in the camps. Before he could get back, she left with the baby. She had not told him where she was going.

Her family was her body. She had not known that Mother was the heart of her body.

"Charles Smedley has this coming," Tillie said bitterly, "stealing my sister's money from her trunk the minute she died. He took the last little bit from her… ." Tillie let herself go, and sank onto the sofa. Her cries woke the baby. The baby began crying, too.

Agnes crossed the room. Distracted, she jiggled the baby basket, then ran to the woodburning stove at the end of the hall; ran back for hot pads; returned to pick up the hot kettle; carried it to the bathroom; poured boiling water over the diaper in the tin basin; added cold water; scrubbed the diaper with a bar of soap; wrung it out over the basin; hung it on a towel rod to dry; ran back to Tillie's room; sank down beside her aunt. At last, realizing she was afflicted, she broke into sobs and tried, without success, to stanch her tears with the heels of her hands.

Agnes got off the street car at the Colfax stop and began walking. Her term at the stenography school in Greeley, paid for by Aunt Tillie, had ended. Shifting her suitcase to her other hand, she looked up at Tillie's window on the top floor. The baby was gone, taken back by its father to Oklahoma. Before he left he'd asked Tillie to marry him, but Tillie had refused.

"He would never be able to forget how I earn my living," Tillie had written Agnes at the stenography school. Agnes realized that her aunt had made up her mind about men. Made up her mind about the parlor house in Denver; about her room and what went on there. Made up her mind about her body and her money. Tillie had decided what was hers and what wasn't.

Agnes entered the house. In the parlor off the hall a woman sat at the piano singing "I Dream of Jeannie With the Light-Brown Hair." Agnes stopped outside the door and listened, her valise in her hand.

"Borne like a vapor—" The woman turned on the piano stool. She wore heavy make-up and looked shrewd. "What do you want?" she asked.

Agnes backed out of the doorway. "I was just listening," she said. She had heard that sweet, sad song somewhere in her childhood. Not in the mining camps of Colorado, but earlier, in the green and rolling hills of Missouri. Mother's people had sung those sad and sugary words.

"Where are you going?" The singer came out of the parlor and squinted down the corridor, an aging woman trying to look young. "Who are you?"

Agnes looked back over her shoulder at the corseted body hour-glassed in front of the window at the far end of the hall.

"I'm Agnes Smedley!" she called back. "I'm visiting Tillie Ralls!" She was not Jeannie with the light-brown hair, and she was not Annie Laurie, either, the song that soon began drifting in fragments up the steps behind her. She was Agnes Smedley, visiting her aunt, Tillie Ralls, a prostitute who had saved herself but could not save Mother any more than she or anyone could save the Jeannies and Annie Lauries and all the beautiful, sad women of poetry and song who do not save themselves.

Aunt Tillie was waiting for her at the top of the stairs. Agnes lifted her valise over the last step.

"Have you finished the term?" Tillie asked. Agnes nodded. Inside the room they looked at each other warily. Agnes set the valise on the floor and knelt beside it.

"I got a letter from your brothers," Tillie said. She held out a

37

single piece of paper toward Agnes.

Agnes shrugged.

"John and Sam—" Tillie began again.

Agnes bent over her few belongings. "I don't have time to read it." Pivoting on her knees, she emptied everything she owned into the bottom bureau drawer.

"Your sister and brothers need you," Tillie said. She began to pace about the room. "My landlady won't let me keep overnight guests."

"I don't see why not," Agnes growled. "There's a lot of coming and going in this house."

Tillie shot her a glance. "I make a living here," she said. "It pays the bills." She returned to the bureau and looked at herself in the mirror. Gingerly she touched the dark circles under her eyes. Then she picked up a tortoise-shell comb and slowly, rhythmically, began to comb her hair.

Agnes got to her feet. She felt no gratitude. "This house is noisy," she said. "It's hard to get any sleep." But since she needed a place to stay, she would have to ignore the nighttime laughter of men and women and the music from the bar drifting through hallways. She wished she could consider Tilly's line of work. But men's sex terrified her. Without being certain of what exactly her aunt did to earn a living, Agnes knew she, herself, could not do it.

"You can stay one night," Tillie said. "Longer than that, and I lose my place here."

Agnes stood biting a fingernail. "I have to get a job," she said. "I'll get a room somewhere."

"I can call a friend of mine. He's a newspaper man."

"Maybe he needs a reporter."

"I just sent you to stenography school!" Tilly snapped. "You're trained to be a secretary. If you're not going to take care of your brothers and sister, then you're going to be a secretary!" They glared until, moved by common memories of a frail, sad-eyed woman, they reached for each other. Agnes clung to her aunt as they stood teetering in the middle of the room. After a bit Tilly took Agnes by the shoulders and shook her gently.

"Take care of your sister and brothers," she said. "I'll support all of you as well as I can."

"I can't take care of them! I can't!" She did not know how to be a mother; she could not be a mother or act like a mother. Mother had been a mother at great expense. There was grave danger in being a mother.

Tilly stroked her niece's hair and kissed her cheeks. She led her to a chair, but Agnes refused to sit.

"I'll be a secretary," she said. "And then," she added in a low, rigid voice, "I'll be a newspaper reporter."

"I'll rent a room for you," Tillie said. "Go talk to the editor."

Agnes went for the interview.

"What sort of experience have you had?" asked the editor.

"Teacher. Stenography school in Greeley," Agnes answered. "But I don't want to be a secretary. I want to be a reporter."

The editor laughed. "Have you worked on a newspaper before?"

"No," said Agnes. "But I read a lot. I work hard. I'm a fast learner."

The editor gave her an appraising look. "Let's talk about it over dinner," he said, and took her to the Windsor Hotel on Larimer Street. Although the editor said the hotel had grown seedy, Agnes thought it splendid. She felt distinguished beside the tall, educated man whose fine head of hair was just beginning to gray at the temples.

"My parents brought me here when I was a boy," he said. "There were skylights in the ceilings then, and a gas-jetted chandelier right above where we're standing." Beneath heavy lids his eyes roamed the lobby. "Ask your aunt about the old Windsor." He took her arm and guided her toward the dining room. "She knows all the best hotels in Denver." Agnes glanced up to see if he was insulting Aunt Tillie. "Knows all the best people, too," he added seriously.

At dinner he told her what fork to use. The fricasse was delicious, whatever "fricasse" meant. The editor had ordered it, so it must be an elegant dish. He said her dress set off her slimness, and the gray set off her blue eyes. Gray added an interesting smoky effect, he said. He spoke smoothly and listened well as she talked about the schoolhouse on the mesa.

"Why don't you get another teaching job?"

Agnes shook her head. "My certificate's expired."

"Held any other jobs?"

"Domestic work."

The editor put his elbows on the table and leaned forward. "Tell me about the stenography course."

"It was a waste of time and Aunt Tillie's money. I don't want to be a secretary. I want to be a newspaper reporter."

"Maybe some day I'll let you write for the society page." He leaned back and wiped his mouth with a linen napkin.

"I'm not experienced in society," she said. "I'd rather write news."

"You have to learn the newspaper business before you can do that," he said. "You have to write and write and write."

Agnes stopped chewing. Since she'd quit her teaching job, she hadn't written much. "I took English at the stenography school," she said. The term in Greeley might be useful after all. "I work hard," she repeated. "I'm a fast-learner. If you give me an assignment, I can do it."

"I'm sure you can," said the editor. "What do you like to do in your free time?"

"Read," said Agnes. "But I don't have much free time. I clean house for Tillie's landlady every day."

The editor looked amused. "What are you going to do with all that money?"

Agnes picked up her fork and played with the food on her plate. She longed to tell the editor about John, Myrtle, Sam,

Father.

"My father— "

"Have you been to Elitch's Gardens?" the editor interrupted. His heavy-lidded eyes grew dreamy. "I saw Sarah Bernhardt at Elitch's. I used to ride the roller-coaster when I was young. They call it the helter-skelter now."

"I don't have time for such things."

"Time!" said the editor, throwing back his head. "Time? My dear girl, you have all the time in the world!"

Agnes said nothing. He was educated and rich, and Aunt Tilly hadn't told him about the Smedleys and Rallses, about the poor Missouri farm and the mining camps around Trinidad.

"Your aunt is a remarkable woman," the editor was saying. "One of the most beautiful women in Denver. She has a wide acquaintance in the city. You're a fortunate girl," he added, "to have her help."

Agnes laid her fork on her plate. This stranger didn't have to tell her about her own aunt. Irritated, she cast a sharp eye about the room. Suddenly she hooted.

"Look at that hat!" she exclaimed, pointing to a woman diner on whose head rested a collection of quivering flowers and fruit. "Is that what you want me to write about in the society page?"

"Forget about the newspaper business," the editor said, annoyed. "Buy yourself some nice clothes and find a husband."

"I don't want a husband."

"You don't know what you might want."

After dessert they climbed a broad staircase to a parlor on the second floor. The editor seated her next to him on a red velvet sofa and ordered two brandies. "So you want to write," he said. He laid his arm along the rich carving behind Agnes' head. She felt a stir of nervous pleasure.

"I could write book reviews," she said, and hitched herself closer to the edge of the sofa. "I could write a better book review than the ones you print now."

"You need to learn about life if you're going to be a writer."

He held his brandy glass close to his chest and leaned toward her. "You're still young. Life will teach you to write." He smelled subtly of shaving lotion and tweed. Her wish to rest against his shoulder alarmed her.

She stood. "I'd better get back," she said.

The editor stopped swirling his brandy. "We just got here. What's your hurry?"

"I have to go," she said. She handed him her glass and headed for the staircase. On the landing she halted, astonished. A midget, his face old and lined, hopped toward her up the stairs. Agnes remained motionless. At the top of the flight the old man turned back and laughed. He reached as high as he could, grasped the newel post, hauled himself up the last step, then threw back his head and laughed once more. Agnes laughed, too, a loud, free sound.

"It's not polite to laugh," said the editor, catching up to her. He took her arm and ushered her down the stairs and out onto Larimer Street. "H.H. Tammer owns a circus. He puts the performers up at the Windsor. Midgets, giants, fat women … ." He spoke with arch amusement.

Agnes felt a blast of kinship for the freaks of the world. She knew, without being told, that the little old man had arthritis; that he climbed stairs with a sideways gait to ease his small joints. She felt an impulse to go back into the hotel and talk to the short people, tall people, fat people, thin people. But the editor was propelling her forward. They turned the corner and passed saloons and brothels along Market Street.

"Does your aunt know you live down here?"

She turned to face him. "It's nobody's business where I live."

The editor was silent for the length of a block. "Come to work next Monday," he said when they stopped in front of a run-down house where Agnes rented a room. "You can start off as a magazine agent. Later we'll see about book reviews."

"You won't be sorry," Agnes said.

"Thank your aunt," said the editor, and kissed her on the

lips. "That was for life," he said when he'd finished.

Agnes entered the rooming house. "That was for a job," she murmured, and wiped her lips hard with the back of her hand.

Texas 1911

"Where are you off to this week?" Tilly asked.

"New Mexico. Texas."

"Can you stop off and see your sister in Raton?"

Agnes shrugged. She always shrugged at the question, as if she weren't sure train schedules would permit. In fact, she did not want to see Myrtle. She did not want to see John and Sam, either. She did not want even to think about them. If at night, falling asleep, Agnes felt Mother stir somewhere in the darkness and question her about the children, Agnes grew defensive and angry. Half-asleep, she would lift her chin and retort; her retorts were sharp, and she woke up exhausted.

Agnes had grown to know the conductors and porters on the Denver and Rio Grande; the Atchison, Topeka and Santa Fe; the Southern Pacific. She met the traveling salesmen who criss-crossed the Southwest by train. Often they invited her to the dining car for a meal; even bought subscriptions from her because she was so young and spunky. Her slender body, intelligent eyes, bold face, her infectious laugh and unaffected grin worked well with the men on the train, and worked well in the hotels and cafes along the tracks where she peddled a variety of reading matter. But Agnes was not successful with women.

"Could I interest you in a subscription to McCall's?" she would begin, standing on someone's front stoop and holding out a free pen that said, 'What is black and white and read all over? Our fine publications everywhere.' She would try to make eye contact with the housewife behind the screen door. "Are you interested in cooking and fashion?" Squinting to see through the screen, she might add, "Do you sew?" But the women in their gingham house dresses did not like to see this young girl striding through the streets selling. Their daughters belonged in school or at home, and so did she. They distrusted Agnes, and Agnes distrusted them.

Tascosa, Texas was a half hour's walk up a canyon from the train tracks. Agnes passed a cemetery, the local boot hill. As she climbed the dusty road, her valise in one hand, a cowboy rode toward her. His tired horse picked its way downhill.

She stopped and pushed the damp hair off her forehead. "Where's the telegraph office?"

He pointed with a single, plain gesture toward the string of adobe buildings ahead, and rode on. After several more minutes of climbing, switching her suitcase from one hand to the other, she left the dry, caked ground for planking and stepped up onto the porch of the two-story hotel. Cowboys sat in the shade, their boots and spurs resting on the porch rail. They paused in their tobacco-chewing to assess her.

"I'm expecting a wire," she said to the tired-looking clerk behind the desk. He watched her with weak and watery eyes.

"No wire come today," he said.

"But there should be a wire and some money waiting for me," she insisted.

"No wire come."

She glared, then stepped back in the small lobby and counted her money. Just enough for one night in the hotel if she didn't eat any meals. She paid for a room. The clerk gave her a large key on a string and she climbed the staircase to the second floor. As soon as she was inside Room Six she took a piece of paper from her valise, sat down on the edge of the bed, and drafted a wire to the editor.

"I am stuck in Tascosa, Texas. Stop. Need money. Stop. Wire me care of Exchange Hotel. Stop. A. Smedley."

She sent the wire collect and waited through the hot afternoon, but no money arrived. She went to bed hungry. The next day she hung about the lobby again, casting anxious glances at the clerk and trying to ignore the smells of food from the dining room. Now and then she stepped out onto the shaded porch, but the idle cowboys eyed her between tobacco juice squirts over the rail and she returned to the lobby where ceiling fans circled and flies droned.

"Is there a wire for A. Smedley?" she asked again.

"No wire come."

Agnes felt hot and light-headed. She went up to her room and lay down on the thin mattress. After a bit she dragged herself down the hallway to wash her face and swallow some water. Back in her room, she fell into a fitful sleep and dreamed that Mother and the children were walking up the canyon from the depot, looking for her. They needed a train ticket. When they held out their hands for money, Agnes gave them a free pen each. When she woke, the sheets were damp with sweat. Once more she went downstairs to the lobby.

"No wire come," said the clerk. "You're past due to check out."

Agnes lifted her head. "My editor's wiring me money," she said. "Can you let me stay one night on credit?"

The clerk didn't say yes and he didn't say no. Agnes climbed the stairs to Room Six where she dropped into another numb sleep. Night fell. She did not hear the horses in the street below; the stomping and violin music coming from the saloon; the coyotes howling down the hot Texas night.

But when the key turned in the lock, she came wide awake. In the moonlight that half-lit the room she lay and watched the door open. Before she could even sit up, someone was on top of her. She tried to reach the little dagger she kept under her pillow, but the man had pinned her. His breath stank and his sweat stank. Rage and revulsion gave her strength. She brought one knee up hard and threw him off.

"Whore!" grunted the clerk. Agnes was surprised that such a weak-faced man could be so strong. He staggered back from the bed. Agnes braced herself against the headboard and tried to see into the dark corner.

"You let me stay here one more night and I won't tell your boss," she hissed. She felt about for the dagger. The room swam. "And let me have some food tomorrow. My uncle's coming to get me," she lied, "and if you help me, he won't bother you."

The clerk stepped out from the corner toward the bed. Agnes raised the dagger.

"Put that thing away," he soothed. "Keep me company tonight. You'll like it. You know you will." He lunged. Agnes slashed his arm from elbow to wrist. She crouched on the bed. He backed up to the middle of the room and caught his own blood in his cupped hand.

"You come any closer and I'll wake up everyone in this town," she promised. Locking her gaze onto his face, she forced him to stop glancing sideways. "My uncle's coming from Arizona to get me," she said. "If you bring me some food and don't ever touch me again, I won't tell him about tonight."

The clerk backed to the door and left the room. The next morning Agnes opened the door a crack and saw a tray of biscuit and eggs on a table in the hallway. She ate ravenously in her room, washed up at the basin, and went down to the lobby.

"I want to send a telegram to Clifton, Arizona," she said to the clerk. He did not look at her.

"What's the last name?" he muttered.

"'Buck,'" said Agnes, then added pointedly, "They know him all over Arizona Territory." Big Buck had worked with her father in Colorado before he went off to the copper mines in Arizona. She hadn't thought of him until she realized the editor was not going to send money.

Big Buck wired the money in time for dinner. Agnes ate, paid off the previous nights' lodging, and asked about the Southern Pacific connection to Clifton.

The clerk looked at her sideways and sneered. "What about your editor?"

Agnes didn't answer but climbed the narrow wooden staircase she'd been climbing these two interminable days. She entered her room, sank onto the lumpy bed, and reached under the pillow. There was a crust of the clerk's dried blood on the dagger. She knocked it off against the bed frame, hating the clerk, the editor, and Father, too. They snuck in your room to rape you. They left you stranded in a heat-blasted Texas town. They drank away the family money and robbed the savings from your mother's trunk. She was not sure of Big Buck, either, or what he might expect for his money.

She stepped to the single window. Northwest lay the coal camps of Colorado. Agnes, who had hated the camps, now felt a great longing for them and for her girlhood that seemed to have been almost happy by comparison to the present.

Dusk was seeping through daylight and changing it. She lay down on the bed and remembered how Big Buck had swatted her once for crying. He'd taught her to lasso; to shoot a pistol; to skin a rabbit. He hated Mexicans, Indians, and Mormons. And although he had gone to the whorehouses in Trinidad every payday, he possessed a rough gallantry and would have knocked down any man who looked crosswise at her.

Clifton, Arizona 1911

When she alighted from the train at the Clifton depot, a tall, broad-shouldered man with a big gut, big handlebar mustache, big hat, and big, imperturbable face stepped forward and took her suitcase.

"See you got the money."

"Appreciate it," Agnes said, striding along beside him. Accumulated heat from weeks of summer lay between the canyon walls rising straight up on both sides of Clifton.

"Nice day," said Big Buck. They stepped back for a passing wagon. "How's the family?"

"Mother died."

"No." Big Buck turned to look at her. For a moment his remote eyes showed feeling. "What was it?"

"Malnutrition." She'd looked it up after the doctor left. She would never forget the word, or how to spell it.

Big Buck maintained silence. He didn't ask about the children and who was taking care of them.

"How's your father?"

"Between jobs."

At the door to the hotel Big Buck bent down and said in a low voice, "I told 'em you're my little sister. Best that way."

Agnes stood motionless, on guard, then followed him up to the third floor. He set her grip down in the hall.

"I'll find work as a secretary," she said, unlocking the door to her room. "I know shorthand."

"First you rest and eat and get some meat on your bones," said Big Buck. "I won't have people saying I don't feed my sister." He put his hand behind his head, pushed his hat forward over his noncommittal eyes, and left her there.

When she'd cleaned up from her train trip she found him in the lobby standing under a sign that said, 'Any man who won't eat prunes is a son of a bitch.'

"Follow me," he said, and crossed the street to the Chinese restaurant.

"The Chinks worked for the railroad laying track," Big Buck said, fitting shovelsful of chop suey beneath his mustache. "Chink food is the cheapest grub in town."

During days while he was up at the Longfellow Mine, Agnes explored the canyons on a cow pony. Following, one day, the narrow-gauge railroad track over which the ore cars shuttled between the mine up on Chase Creek and the smelter at the edge of town, Agnes met a man riding horseback down off the mountain. He was young and wore a uniform. He stopped and watched her approach.

"Nice day, ma'am." He tipped his hat. Agnes shook the perspiration out of her eyes and continued riding.

"Are you going to the mine?" he asked. He'd turned his horse around and come up alongside of her.

"No," said Agnes.

"You're not lost, are you?"

"Do I look lost?"

"I'm the forest ranger for this district. If you have any questions or need help— "

"No questions," Agnes said.

"May I ride along for a quarter of a mile?"

Agnes shrugged.

"I haven't seen you in these parts," the ranger said.

"I haven't been in these parts." She turned and looked at him. "If you're the forest ranger, where's the forest?" She scanned the Clifton and Morenci landscape, bald hills laden with dumps of waste rock and slag.

The ranger looked sheepish and defensive at the same time. "Mining's hard on the land," he said. "They cut timber to fuel the smelter. Tailings and fumes kill the rest."

They rode on. The sun grew higher and hotter in the sky. To the north brooded black, stony mountains. Agnes and the ranger veered away from the ore car tracks, their horses' soft steps the only sound among the ajos and creosote bushes. Agnes wiped her face and neck with a handkerchief.

"You have family here?" asked the ranger.

"Just Big Buck," Agnes said. After a silence she added, "He's a mechanic at the mine."

"Are you married to him?"

"Nope," said Agnes. "He's my brother. Not married to anybody." The ranger pushed back his wide-brimmed, official-looking hat. He was a thin young man with a boyish smile; his eyes were hazel and his face smooth. "I can show you some pretty country," he said. "Back in the canyons there's trees. Lots of trees. Care to go riding on Saturday?"

"I don't mind," said Agnes.

Every weekend after that they followed the Gila River up into the mountains. Sometimes they explored Geronimo's trail and searched for arrowheads, or rode far up into remote mountain reaches where the ranger showed her ancient, crumbling cliff dwellings built into canyon walls.

"Seein' the ranger quite regular, are you?" Big Buck said one evening over his chop suey. Agnes didn't respond.

"Mormon, and thin as a billiard cue," he muttered to himself. Disgusted, he pushed his plate back from the edge of the table. With his thumb and forefinger he cleared debris from his mustache. "Suppose he's asked you to the dance in Morenci."

"What dance?" said Agnes.

"Arizona Statehood Dance," said Big Buck.

"He hasn't asked me," she said, "but if I want to go, I won't wait for an invitation."

"You're ridin' over with me," said Big Buck. "You ain't ridin' all the way to Morenci with a Mormon billiard cue."

At the close of the next Saturday's outing, as she and the forest ranger passed the copper works on their way down into town and the canyon wall threw its stored heat into the abrupt nightfall, he asked Agnes to the dance. "Will you go with me?" he asked.

Agnes dabbed at her neck with a handkerchief. "I'll dance with you once I'm there," she said.

He reached through the unmoving air pocketed in the canyon and pulled up on her pony's reins. "I'll come for you next Saturday." He leaned toward her and kissed her on the mouth.

Agnes softened. She shifted toward him on her pony, then stiffened and pulled back. "No," she said. "I'll meet you in Morenci."

By the time Agnes and Big Buck neared Morenci, stars salted the sky with millions of bright grains. They had ridden the high desert ridge and canyon in silence. Now as they drew near the town, Big Buck began to talk.

"Workin' every day in the mine," he said almost to himself.

"Up at four, breakfast, lunch, a Chink dinner, bed, and then the same thing all over again… " He rolled himself a cigarette and struck a match on his thumbnail. "I'd trade it all in for a yaller dog." The horses snuffled and the saddles creaked.

"Mining is no way to live," he added. "It's just digging. Been thinking of going down to Mexico." The glow of his cigarette came and went. "Fight in the Revolution." He glanced sideways at Agnes. "Pancho Villa."

"Like our forefathers!" She spoke urgently. "Like my great-great-great-grandfather in the American Revolution!"

"Yessir," said Big Buck, encouraged by her outburst. "I just may do 'er."

Agnes turned in her saddle. "I read in the library," she said, "where the Indians licked the Spaniards. It's called the Pueblo Revolt."

"Yup," said Big Buck. "Digging is for moles, and I ain't no mole. Revolution's the thing." He pulled his horse closer to Agnes. "Ever see a flash flood in the desert?"

Agnes said she hadn't.

"Well, first you see a dark cloud far off, kind of in long fingers, like the shape of the mesas underneath. The storm comes down but there'll be bright sun still shining above." Big Buck's voice deepened. "The air turns blue and gold and the rocks and yucca and cholla turn a queer color.

"Then you'll see rain streaks off in the distance, and you'll see lightning strikes"—he turned to look over his shoulder and jabbed a thick finger at several imaginary spots on the horizon—"all around you, all at the same time."

Agnes inhaled deeply, as if she could smell the wet rock and cactus and dampened dirt.

"Then the thunder rolls down the canyons and it starts to rain." Big Buck stopped talking.

"Is that all?"

"Is that all?" he said, offended. "You'll be riding along a dry wash and the dirt will get kind of sticky. Your horse will slip around a little. The stream bed beside you is still dry so you figure you've got time. If you cross a river it's just a trickle." Again he stopped talking. Agnes waited a decent interval.

"Are you finished?" she asked.

"Like I say, the river is just a trickle. Then, all at once you hear a roar. It splits your ears. Maybe it's a whole mountain caving in, and you think terrible thoughts about buried miners.

"You turn your horse and scramble up to higher ground, and you look up-canyon and see a wall of water slamming down the river bed with trees and rocks churning around and around." He concluded the story with a lesson. "Next time you see the dry bed you'll know why it's gouged out and scarred."

"Are you really going to join Pancho Villa's army?" Agnes asked after a respectful silence.

"Might. There ain't nothin' keepin' me here."

"I'll go with you."

Big Buck looked at her in surprise. "You will?"

"To fight for freedom."

"What about your Mormon billiard cue?"

"He's nothing special to me."

"He likes you," said Big Buck. Music from Morenci carried through the thin night air. As they drew nearer they could hear stomping and singing and violins, accordions, harmonicas. The glow of lanterns hung over the town like steam over hot springs.

Big Buck reached out and reined in both horses. "It's not that I want to go to Mexico exactly," he said. Agnes turned at the despair in his voice. "I'm lonely," he said. Her horse danced away, but Big Buck jerked on the reins. "I'm not much," he said.

Agnes leaned forward and stroked the hot, leathery skin of her horse's neck. "You're a lot," she murmured into the horse's mane.

"Marry me."

Agnes sat bolt upright in her saddle.

"I'm not much, but I'd be good to you."

Agnes didn't speak.

"If it's my age you're worried about," he said, still controlling both horses, "I'm only forty-two. Without this mustache I look a lot younger. And I ain't a Mormon who don't know which end is up. I'd take good care of you."

"I know you'd be good to me." She laid her head back and half-closed her eyes until individual points of starlight swam together. "You've always been good to me."

Big Buck took a long, audible breath.

"But I'm never getting married," she said.

He let go of the reins. "Why's that?"

"I'm just not."

"Got to be a reason." The horses moved forward, their breathing and footfalls loud in the still night.

"I'll fight in the Revolution with you but I'm never getting married."

His silence troubled her. "You'll always be a friend," she said. It was the best she could do.

They entered Morenci. With the music and lights and stomping, it seemed like the heart of the world. They tied up their horses. In the crowd the billiard cue found her. As they danced, Agnes looked over at Buck, his face solemn under the red, white, and blue lanterns swinging from lines strung between poles. Maybe she could marry him; maybe she should marry him. If he'd asked her to fight in the Mexican Revolution, she would have said yes.

"You sure like to dance," he said when they started on the ride home. Moving rhythmically with the horse's gait, he rolled himself a cigarette and looked up at the stars. "You've learned a thing or two since the coal camps."

"I haven't learned enough."

Big Buck lit his cigarette. A worm of fire burrowed into the tobacco.

"I talked to a girl who's been to teachers' college for six years."

Her voice held both contempt and awe. Big Buck listened. "But I told her nobody needs that much schooling."

Big Buck smoked and Agnes fell into a morose silence.

"Where is this school?" he asked.

"Tempe."

Big Buck flicked away his cigarette butt. "I'll stake you to one term," he said. "After that, you can come back and marry me."

"What if I don't want to?"

"Then it's a present."

She studied the sky for a long while. "Mother wanted me to get an education, but she didn't tell me to take six years doing it."

"Did Sarah Lydia die sudden?"

"No."

He left a silence that she could fill or not fill. It seemed to Agnes the night sky blazed up and died down. Pungent odors rose from the damp desert floor.

"I sat with her three days and nights." Beneath her the horse continued its steady gait. Big Buck rolled another cigarette. "On the last day Mother asked me to hold her." Agnes was crying. "Said I'd been a good daughter." The color of her mother's face had frightened her. Death is colorlessness. It is a body without weight. Agnes sobbed. "She was dried out. She was like something left in the field after harvest."

Big Buck struck a match on his thumbnail and grunted. "People get used up," he said softly. She turned to look at him. Tears were coming down his cheeks, but his hand holding the glowing cigarette was steady.

"I'd appreciate your help going to school," she said, wiping her eyes with the back of one hand.

He stared straight ahead and nodded.

"Where's your sister and brothers?" he asked after a bit.

"Farmed out."

"Farmed out!"

"John and Sam are at Leonard's in Oklahoma. Myrtle's in Raton."

Big Buck weighed the information. "Leonard's the one that married Nellie?"

Agnes nodded. "Nellie died before Mother." She was afraid he might tell her to go back and take care of her brothers and sister, that he might tell her he'd changed his mind about helping her with school. But he pulled close and touched her hair once with his big hand. Then his horse moved away.

Early the next week Agnes climbed onto a coach car of the Southern Pacific. Big Buck handed her grip up to her.

"Write," he said. "Don't be a stranger." Agnes had failed to hug him on the way to the depot. Now that she stood above him on the platform between cars, it was too late. The train started up sharply. Cars bumped in uncoordinated jerks and the great wheels began grinding slowly away from Clifton. Neither Agnes nor Big Buck waved. A whistle blast filled the widening gap. With a steady, expressionless gaze, they watched each other grow small and disappear.

9
China 1937

"My education was not as my family wished," said Zhu De.

He, Agnes and Mao Zedong had finished their lunch of boiled cabbage, millet and tea at a wooden table set on the terrace outside Mao's cave. Mao was looking off toward the ancient pagoda that for centuries had guarded this valley lying between the hills of yellow dust. Zhu De, seated near Agnes, watched her stack the small tin plates and clear a place on the table for writing. Still abstracted, Mao rose and set off down the terrace. His thin, large-headed figure made its way downhill toward a group of soldiers gathered on the drill ground at the foot of the loess hill.

When he was out of sight, Agnes opened her flat, black notebook, larger than her hand but not too large to fit inside the leather shoulder bag she always carried. Zhu De stretched his stocky legs under the table and began where the previous interview had left off.

"In 1905," he said, "after much persuasion from my old schoolmaster, my family allowed me to study at the modern school in Shunching. They had sacrificed much money for my education and wanted me to pass the State Examination so that I could be an official in the dynasty and add to the family income.

"I promised my family I would study for the Examination. Secretly, I also intended to study the modern subjects of science and physical education."

Lily Wu approached the wooden table and took the place Mao had vacated. She laid her Chinese-English dictionary beside the stack of tin plates and poured herself a cup of tea.

"I thanked my family," Zhu De continued, "and set out walking for Shunching. I walked for more than a day. I felt"—he looked at Lily Wu and pronounced the Chinese word.

"'Elated,'" she translated. "He walked to the new school and he

felt elated."

Zhu De gave the tin teapot two turns on the table.

"Unfortunately I was informed I could not study the new science and physical education if I intended to prepare for the official State Examinations. They permitted me only one extra class: Japanese language." He threw back his head in contempt. *"All China, you see, all Asia, was impressed by Japan's victory over Russia. At last an Asian country had become as imperialistic as the West!"*

Agnes' pencil lead broke. She reached into her shoulder bag and took another from the row of pencils inserted in loops; pencils held like a row of cartridges in a gun belt. Zhu De waited until she was ready to write again.

"I did as my teachers told me to do, though I wept from frustration. That summer I went home and worked in the rice fields and continued to study for the State Examinations given in Ilunghsien twenty-five miles from my village. When it was time to go, my family worried about me. They had never traveled so far. To them it was as if I was traveling to the far side of the world."

He stopped abruptly.

"Did you take the examinations?" Agnes prompted.

"Yes," he answered. *"I was the only peasant. All other students were from educated families."* He stared into his enameled tin cup.

"Did you pass?"

Zhu De looked up at Agnes. "I passed," he said. *"My family was very happy."* But sitting at the table, he did not look happy.

"And you?"

Zhu De spoke after a long silence. "I wrote to them that I needed money, a loan, to take the next level, the Provincial Examinations." He changed position on the wooden bench. *"It was a lie."*

Lily Wu looked at him suddenly.

"What did you do with the money?" Agnes asked.

"Against my family's wishes I had decided to study physical education, mathematics, geography, and military drill at the new government Normal College in Chengtu."

Lily Wu smoothed the long hair flowing down her back like

black silk and looked away from his shame.

"What did you do with the money?" Agnes repeated.

Zhu De spoke only to Lily. "First I walked twenty miles to see the new western machinery at the Nampu salt wells. There I found no modern machinery, but much sickness and disease. The salt workers were slaves."

"Indentured serfs," Lily translated for Agnes, though the conversation had become Zhu and Lily's alone. They grieved for their country, they sorrowed for young Zhu's disobedience to his family. Their Chinese-ness excluded Agnes.

"Except for loincloths, the men worked naked," Zhu De said. "They were jaundiced. They coughed and had running sores. They worked from morning until late at night."

These moments when Agnes could not be Chinese, yet no longer felt American, were painful. Her eyes darkened and she sat without moving. Zhu De turned again to include her.

"I saw a childhood friend from Landlord Ting's estate. I spoke to him but he hid his face in shame. I thought of my brothers, nephews, cousins, poor people who were expecting me to help. I was tormented by my decision and by my lie."

Agnes' pencil moved fast as she caught up to his words.

"In five days I walked through beautiful Szechwan, sleeping at the homes of peasants each night, bathing in the running streams. All day I looked at the mountains, flowers, trees, and smelled the fragrant fruit. I did not know I was bidding good-bye to my youth. Bidding good-bye to old China. I ran the last distance to Chengtu. Its ancient, venerable walls were cool to my touch. Chengtu! Chengtu!

"Chengtu was the center of culture and politics in Western China. It was once the meeting place of the old trade routes. Now the ancient ways were struggling with the new. Here the teachers shaved off their queues. Women students had natural, unbound feet. The science class had one glorious microscope, one human skeleton, and one globe of the earth. There were no textbooks. Teachers who had studied abroad brought back their notes and lectured from memory. Revolution was in the air. An official position in the dynasty became even more obnoxious to me. I was determined to study science, physical education, military drill. I hoped some day to enroll in the military academy. Yet I was afraid of what my family would say.

"Rumors ran through the school that certain teachers were members of the secret revolutionary society, Tung Meng Hui, and my heart beat faster. My friends and I went to factories in order to see western machinery. When we were denied admittance, we stood outside the factory walls and listened to the hum of the machines.

"At the end of the year I obtained a position as a teacher of physical education. Walking the long distance back to my village, I felt confident that my family would understand. After all, as a teacher I could now send money back to my village.

"When I arrived they stood in a long line and greeted me with bows. They had not enough food for themselves. They lived in a small house. Still, they fed me like a king and gave me a private room furnished with the finest comforts they could provide."

Zhu De's lips trembled. "They thought I was going to become an official under the dynasty, you see, and lift them out of poverty. They would not let me work in the rice fields. They did not want me to touch the earth. My hands and fingernails must be clean, the hands and fingernails of an official." Zhu De paused and looked into the distance. "You see, they were trying to prevent me from sinking back into the darkness of peasant life."

Agnes had stopped writing again. Her eyes did not leave his face.

"I finally told them I was never going to be an official. I was going to teach physical education in Ilunghsien. The effect of my confession was terrifying. My mother sobbed all night in her bedroom. I could read the faces of my father and foster-father: I was giving up an official position in order to teach boys how to throw their arms and legs about.

"I left for Ilunghsien. My foster-father walked many miles with me. 'We are simple country people,' he said, 'and do not understand many things. What is unclear today may be clear tomorrow.' He *wore threadbare clothes and rope sandals. When he turned back I wept."*

Agnes walked away from the table and stood at the edge of the terrace. She looked in the direction of the drill ground. But instead of young Chinese soldiers, she saw three children: her brothers and her sister. She saw a woman, old and ill: her mother. And she saw a young woman turn her back and walk away.

Zhu De had come to stand beside her. "One must often walk alone," he said. When she returned to the table, Zhu De and Lily Wu had gone. Agnes wiped her face, poured herself a cup of cold tea, and began entering the last of the interview in her notebook.

10
Tempe, Arizona 1911

The train aimed for a single butte thrusting straight up from the desert floor at Tempe. Most of the passengers were waiting for Phoenix nine miles farther on. In the late afternoon sun, orange going to red, Agnes and another student stood on the platform between cars and watched fields of cotton irrigated by the Salt River glide by. Cotton gave way to cabbages, cantaloupes, citrus orchards. The hypnotic clicking of the train's wheels slowed as the cars rolled by a Mexican village that had dug itself in against the butte centuries ago and appeared to be biding its time until the ages covered it over again.

The wall of sage and rock and cactus, touched here and there by bright nasturtiums, reared up against the train. Where the butte ended, a spur of track set out toward the river and attached itself to a cluster of buildings under a tall chimney stack labeled Hayden's Mill. A ferry, a small barge hooked to a cable strung across the river, approached the dirt bank, ready to disgorge a carriage and two horses onto the mill dock. The train veered south, rocking on its rails. Agnes leaned into the long, slow curve until finally the train ground to a stop in front of the depot, open valves shrieking.

"Are you a student here?" asked the girl standing beside her, preparing to alight. She was dressed in a long skirt and slim linen jacket.

Agnes nodded.

"Do you want to share a hired car?" Over a burst of escaping steam the girl pointed to a sign across the street: "Fikes Auto Livery."

Agnes stepped down onto the ground. "Which way's the school?"

The girl pointed east and Agnes set out for Tempe Normal.

"Classes don't start for two weeks!" the girl called after her, but Agnes paid no attention. When she reached the corner of Sixth and Mill she stopped to wipe the perspiration from her neck. She was hungry. She'd eaten a single roll for breakfast, another for lunch, rolls she'd brought with her from Clifton. She and the bread had sat up most of the night and both were stale.

The sun hung low in the sky behind her now. The girl in the linen suit had long since passed in her hired car. Agnes changed her valise from one hand to the other and turned where she'd seen the automobile turn.

Passing between rows of palms, leaves moving slightly in the hot breeze, she saw a brick building three stories high. "Old Main," said the engraved lettering over its front entrance two flights above ground. Agnes walked around all four sides.

"Not so grand," she said to herself, and tried a sniff of contempt. After all, she'd lived in Denver. She'd traveled throughout the Southwest. She'd worked for a newspaper editor. If she stretched the truth she could say she was a journalist who was unimpressed by a little school plunked down in the middle of the desert.

She set the valise on the sidewalk, wiped her neck again with the damp handkerchief, and began to embellish her life in Denver the way Father embellished his stories. Mother would have called it lying, but Agnes had no intention of living in Mother's drab world. Instead of a magazine agent, hadn't she been assistant to the editor? She picked up the valise, threw back her shoulders, and continued walking until she came to a street of comfortable, two-story frame homes. By the time she found the corner house with a sign on its wide porch, "Rooms to Let," she had become the editor's assistant; the editor's book reviewer; the newspaper's star reporter.

She peeled off a bill from the roll of money Big Buck had given her and paid for a room.

"Can I wash my dress?" she asked. "I'll use cold water." Before the landlady could hesitate, she added, "I'll do up your breakfast dishes for you tomorrow morning."

"All right, but you can't iron," said the woman. "I iron on Tuesdays, and I won't build a fire for one dress."

Next morning, wearing the dress she had tried to smooth and stretch as it dried the night before, Agnes washed dishes for the family of eight and three boarders before setting off to the college. Inside Old Main, cool, high-ceilinged corridors stretched into the distance. She passed empty classrooms, an office marked "The President," and a mailroom with small brass mailboxes lining the walls. In front of an oak door she stopped to wipe her forehead and neck. She could not prevent herself from looking down at her unironed dress. Ashamed and defensive, she lifted her chin, pushed open the heavy door, and entered the admissions office. She approached a long wooden counter and glared with the effort to make up a life.

"How much does it cost to go to school here?"

"You have to be accepted first," the woman behind the counter said, and pointed to a stack of catalogues and application forms. Agnes passed over the school's accreditations and turned to the "Costs" section. Big Buck's money would last just one semester, not counting board and room. She completed the application form. In the blank beside "Parents" she wrote "Dead.

"Father's Profession: Doctor.

"Guardian: Tilly Ralls.

"Method of Payment: Cash."

"The admissions officer will see you," said the clerk. Agnes followed her through a low, swinging gate built into the counter and entered the office of a man who was as smooth and white as a blanched almond. After lengthy questions about her past, he paused and drummed his clean fingernails on the top of his desk. He looked dubious.

"We have a test we administer to students like yourself," he said.

"I passed the test for my teacher's certificate," Agnes said. "I'll take any test you give me."

He showed her into an empty classroom across the hall and left her at a desk with test, pencil, and eraser.

"How much time do I have?" She took a pocket knife out of her purse and began to sharpen the pencil. She shaved the wood into a neat pile at one corner of the desktop.

"Three hours," said the man, eyeing the growing pile of shavings. "Someone will come for you." He turned to leave. "We have a pencil-sharpener on the wall," he pointed out from the doorway. But Agnes continued scraping at the lead. Without a word she scooped the shavings into her hand and emptied them in the wastebasket.

The test was easier than the teachers' examination she'd taken in New Mexico. She didn't finish all the problems in the mathematics section, but she answered most of the history questions, and she wrote a good long essay on Geronimo's trail outside Clifton, Arizona.

The admissions officer returned and said she'd used up her time. "Be back here tomorrow," he added, "to meet the admissions committee. They'll have questions for you."

Agnes wandered outside to stand for a moment under a pepper tree. Walking south, she came to a sign that marked the site of the original Territorial Normal. College, she thought, was like a little town devoted to learning. Remembering the cool stare of the admissions officer, she tried not to love the grounds and brick buildings; she was sure the pale man would reject her application. She fingered the small cloth purse pinned to the inside of her shirtwaist and missed Big Buck's suntanned face and direct gaze.

Three days after being interviewed by a committee of men who told her she was deficient in mathematics but that her knowledge of history and the essay on Geronimo's trail helped make up for it, she returned to the admissions office. She'd been poked and prodded with questions about her family, her schooling, her employment, questions which she'd answered in a daze, lying when she saw no other way to pass through the committee's minefield.

"The admissions committee has made its decision," the blanched almond said when she'd seated herself on the edge of a straight chair. "We think you have the capacity to enroll as an irregular student."

In an instinctive release of tension, Agnes gave him a wide grin.

"But," he said with a warning gesture, "we will supervise your work closely. If we are wrong in admitting you, you will be dismissed from Tempe Normal."

"You won't have to do that," Agnes said. "I'll work hard. I'll make good. You'll see." She jumped to her feet.

"Where will you stay?" He motioned for her to sit back down, but she remained standing.

"I've made arrangements," she lied.

"The college may be able to offer you some help," said the almond. A hint of color had reached his head. He got to his feet. "Follow me."

They climbed two flights of stairs to the top floor of Old Main where they went up one corridor and down another until they reached a large, sunny room with rows of desks and long counters with sinks.

"Frederick?" said the admissions officer. A dark-haired man with a fastidious mustache and clean, ironed shirt stepped out from a storeroom.

"Professor Irish, may I introduce Miss Agnes Smedley." The lean man came forward and rested one immaculate hand on the edge of a counter. In an aside the admissions officer said, "This is the one I was telling you about, the irregular student."

The professor, who was perhaps ten years older than Agnes, put both hands behind his back, bowed slightly, and gave her a moment's study. "Sit down, Miss Smedley." She took a seat in the front row. Professor Irish drew up the straight chair from behind his desk and placed it near Agnes. The almond, seated two desks away, took charge of the conversation.

"Tell us about your interests," he said, as if she hadn't already exposed every detail of her life to him and his committee.

"I already told you," Agnes said. "Reading. Horseback riding."

"What is your favorite book?" Professor Irish asked. His eyes were intense in his thin face. Agnes debated whether to make up something that sounded high-class and educated, or to tell him the truth.

"A book on Geronimo," she said, and tossed her head.

"Geronimo was a magnificent leader," Professor Irish said.

Agnes looked at him through narrowed eyes. "You know about Geronimo?"

"Of course. Anyone with any interest in this continent cannot help but know of Geronimo."

"I found his trail," Agnes confided. "Part of his trail is up in the canyon behind Clifton, Arizona. I've been back in the Indian dwellings," she added, and began to talk about the hot afternoon rides up beyond the mine where she and the forest ranger had entered abandoned rooms that honeycombed the crumbling cliffs. She repeated facts about the copper mine she'd heard from Big Buck, about how hard the early miners worked to find a process for smelting copper that didn't cost more than the ore itself.

She talked about the mines in Colorado and New Mexico, mines with names like Give-a-Damn, Great Relief, Neversweat, and Kreutzer Sonata. About the gallows frame, as the miners called the beam at the top of the shaft, and how miners got sick from fumes; how they died in explosions.

She told Professor Irish about a deserted mine she'd passed once when she was riding her horse in New Mexico, its dark, mysterious mouth entered by a set of iron tracks, the rusted ore car lying on its side overgrown by weeds. She told him how, in the Colorado coal camps, strikes flared, died, and flared again, the miners' discontent smoldering as surely as coal burns in an abandoned mine, smoke escaping through cracks in the earth.

When she finished talking there was silence in the room. Through the window Agnes watched the leaves of the orange and lemon trees move. The admissions officer looked suspicious.

"For a girl whose father was a doctor," he said, "you seem to know a great deal about mines."

Agnes looked him in the eye. "My father doctored the miners," she improvised. "He saved many lives." The admissions officer actually chuckled. Agnes started to elaborate, but Professor Irish spoke up.

"Perhaps," he said, "you explored the mining country of Colorado just as you explored the canyons outside of Clifton, Arizona."

"Yes. Yes, I did," said Agnes. "And I covered the strikes for the *Denver Post*, too," she added for good measure. She was just about to embark upon a long lie when the professor spoke up again.

"Have you ever worked in a biology laboratory?"

"No," Agnes answered, "but I'm sure I could." She cast a look around at the sinks and shelves of glassware, then raised her head. "When can I start?"

"Will yesterday be too soon?"

Elated, Agnes laughed a loud, free laugh that embarrassed the admissions officer. He made for the door, leaving her to Professor Irish, who took her to the storeroom and pointed out rows of petri dishes, pithing trays, flasks, and dissecting tools. He showed her a lined book that she would fill in once the students began their fall class. Each piece of equipment that left the storeroom had to be accounted for, he said. Agnes walked over to a large jar and looked at the snake coiled inside.

"Are you interested in reptiles?" the professor asked. Agnes tapped the glass. She had not been aware of such an interest, but as she studied the thick, stirring snake she thought there was nothing in the world quite so interesting.

"I've killed lots of snakes up in the canyons," she said. "They spook the horses."

Professor Irish looked down on Agnes' short haircut and high forehead as she inclined her head this way and that to get a better look. She turned the jar. "Where did you get him?"

"In the desert," said Professor Irish. "On a field trip."

"What's a field trip?"

"We camp in the desert," he said. "We take specimens. We record temperatures and relative humidity, watch for vertebrate and invertebrate life, and catalogue plants."

"I'd like a field trip," she said. She moved along the shelf from jar to jar.

"Let's walk over to the dormitory," the professor said. He took a straw hat from a hook on the wall and put on his suit jacket in spite of the heat. "You may be able to wait tables in the dining room. That would help pay for your room and board." He looked down at her; she was nearly as thin as he was. "You do eat, don't you?"

As they walked, Agnes let her gaze wander about the campus. She no longer felt an obligation to memorize everything. She would be able to look at it again and again.

In her eagerness to learn what she felt everyone else already knew, Agnes didn't pay much attention to other students. If girls greeted her on the stairs as she descended from her single room on the top floor of the dormitory, she said hello. But she never visited in anyone's room or invited anyone to hers. What was there to say to rich and pretty girls who talked mostly about hair styles, clothes, and men? Besides, she was always working to supplement the tuition Big Buck had given her. She waited tables, cleaned house for faculty wives, and assisted in the biology lab.

Still, as the semester wore on, she found herself watching

the girls in the dormitory each night dampen their combs at sinks in the community bathroom and set their hair in wet, conscientious coils all over their scalps. Agnes let her hair grow and practiced winding clumps of it around her index finger.

"Your hair looks nice," said one of the Mormon girls who met her on the stairs when Agnes had finished washing dinner dishes in the dormitory kitchen. Agnes stepped aside, wary, half-embarrassed by her curls. She hid her red hands, raisined by hot dishwater, behind her back.

The girl turned to lean against the banister. "Are you going to the dance?"

"What dance?"

"The Fall Harvest dance."

"I guess I will. I like to dance."

"Who are you going with?"

"Nobody."

The girl looked puzzled. Agnes climbed several steps and stopped.

"Do you have to go with somebody?"

"You go as a couple," the girl said from the lower landing.

"I haven't asked anyone yet," Agnes explained. The girl smiled politely and disappeared around the newel post.

Ashamed of her manners and clothes, Agnes failed to invite a dance partner. Nor did anyone invite her. She spent the Fall Harvest in her room reading a book Professor Irish had suggested, a book about a monk, a great botanist named Gregor Mendel who lived in a little town in Austria. Professor Irish said Mendel made important discoveries while he worked in his garden, discoveries that had been overlooked for thirty years and only noticed in 1900, when Agnes herself was old enough to be working in gardens.

She read the book as if it might be taken away from her at any moment. She was intimately acquainted with gardens and with the subject of Mendel's experiments: the common garden pea. When the book talked about stamens and pistils, she knew what they looked like. She pictured exactly how Mendel conducted his experiments in the monastery garden, transferring pollen with a fine paintbrush from a red blossom to the stigma of a white blossom. Cross-breeding, the book called it.

She understood how a man could be so busy earning his keep that he spent only nine years of an entire lifetime doing what was really his life's work. When she came to the part where he had to drop out of school and join a monastery because he was too poor and ill to do anything else, she read without expression, dry-eyed and tense. All of this she understood.

She was surprised, even heartened, by his failure to pass the teachers examination. Teachers examinations she understood.

But she grew uneasy when she pictured Father Mendel separating the two petals of the pea blossom, parting the calyx that protected the female reproductive organs, the book said. Scientific pollination was one thing, but reproductive organs was something else again. She could accept Father Mendel's experiments in pollination, but she rejected the idea that he conspired in the sexual process. She did not like to think of flowers as mating, nor of Father Mendel helping them along.

True, it was interesting that some people in the same family are short while others are tall; some have blue eyes while others have brown. Curious that some pea vines are normal-sized and others are dwarf. She'd noticed that herself. As she read she tried to confine her thoughts to scientific inquiry; to size and color and other benign characteristics. But it was difficult to evade the fact of sexuality.

She could not fail to notice, for instance, that if the lowly garden pea was sexual, how much more so was she. She had always made a point of ignoring physical stirrings in herself; the heartbeat between the legs. Gregor Mendel had been a monk and therefore he must have ignored the heartbeat, too, she reasoned. Ignored it in himself and found it, maybe, in his garden.

After the first rain of the season, Professor Irish had taken his biology class to the desert. They returned with their arms full of primroses, sunflowers, pale gold desert dandelions, yucca blossoms. The desert air after the rain rang like a bell you could not quite hear, and the rock buttes and outcroppings stood as flat as cut-outs against the blue sky.

Agnes had been enchanted by the vivid patches of desert bloom, so unexpected and short-lived. But back in the classroom and laboratory she recoiled at the words "breeding," "mating," "reproduction," and worst of all, "sexual" in connection with the flowers they had gathered. She wished plants and humans could reproduce asexually, like the single-celled paramecium Professor Irish had shown her once under the microscope. She considered her sexuality a loathsome burden. Motherhood was weakening, frightening, unthinkable. She would kill herself rather than endure pregnancy. Childbirth was outside the realm of her imagination, a strange, dark territory so alien and fearsome that when she saw a pregnant woman she turned away with a tinny taste of revulsion in her mouth.

Agnes closed the book about Gregor Mendel. Absently, in the margins and above the masthead of the school paper lying on her desk, she sketched plants she'd grown up with: hollyhock, tomato, rabbit brush, columbine. The sunflower, milkweed, and burdock she remembered from Missouri. Outside the margins, unsketched by her, beyond the circle of visible stem and leaf, petal and fruit, hovered an intense and disturbing world she was afraid to enter.

She stood up from her desk and went to the window. The dark campus lay spread below. She watched the tops of palm trees, just visible under starlight, stir in the night breeze. Formless hopes swirled in her mind. She wanted to understand everything. Do something important and good for Mother, Father, John, Sam, and Myrtle. For Aunt Tillie and herself. Redeem failed lives.

She took a jacket from behind the curtain hanging across her tiny closet and descended to the first floor of the dormitory.

With a cold eye, the housemother watched her sign the in-and-out book. Agnes stepped into the night and began walking toward the music. When she drew near enough to hear voices, she made herself small in the shadow of a hedge and watched couples strolling on the lawn. A slender girl in a beautiful long dress looked up at her escort; her quiet laughter was like a low melody. Agnes moved away from the shadows and set out for the edge of campus and the desert beyond. She supposed the lovely young women in their long gowns would not dream of walking out in the desert alone, and instead of looking up at a sky filled with planets and galaxies, worlds beyond imagination, they must spend the evening looking up into their escorts' faces. It struck Agnes that, in choosing the sky, she would never have a man's face for her universe. And she would never be universe to a man.

The night air cooled her skin as she left the campus behind. San Pablo, the Mexican town at the foot of the butte, glowed with light. Lanterns swayed gently in the trees. Agnes could see the little fires in their glass chimneys rise and fall. Here was another kind of music, plucked strings, murmured Spanish. Another sound, too. She had heard it throughout her childhood: a grunting, rooting, animal sound she despised.

She skirted the butte and walked out into the flood of cool silver light poured out by the pitcher of desert moon. She wished she could walk all night, past the seguaros standing guard, their spiked arms flung upward. Past the flowers, now closed, and the rocks and buttes, straight into the heart of the desert.

At Christmas time the campus closed. "Christmas vacation," everyone called it. To Agnes there was magic and careless good fortune in words like "Christmas vacation," "semester," and "matriculate," but she did not use the college words. She was a miner's daughter, and miners know nothing of such language.

The dormitory closed, too. She could not stay in her little

room. She packed a worn carpetbag and carried her dormitory blanket to the biology lab in Old Main. Professor Irish, she knew, would not mind if she spent her vacation in his classroom. While others exchanged gifts and ate Christmas dinners, she would be writing an article and a story for the newspaper, *The Tempe Normal Student*. In the carpetbag were books about the Indian tribes who had settled the Salt River Valley. Her article would have facts and information about the Hohokam, a remarkable people who arrived, the book said, around the time of Christ and built irrigation canals and created a flourishing culture. But she was not going to say anything about "the time of Christ." She felt it silly to measure Indians' time by a man they had never heard of.

The story, she would make up. Love between the races. The idea came to her one day when she was thinking about a Mexican-Indian boy she had taught in New Mexico. She remembered his well-modeled head. She remembered his wrists, brown neck, broad shoulders and narrow waist. What if an Indian man and a white woman married and had a child; a daughter, say, like herself? Because she, Agnes Smedley, was part-Indian. Father had often told her so.

And what if the mother was the kind of mother who explained things to her daughter; a mother who liked to discuss things? They might have a conversation about the Indian man. The mother would explain why she loved the girl's father and why she was glad she had married him, and the daughter would listen to every word, proud of her Indian father, proud of her blood.

Agnes turned to the picture of a Maricopa woman taken in 1900 and gazed so intently into the proud face and dark, disinterested eyes that she felt she was that woman looking out at the white photographer.

By the time she had written the first part of the article in shorthand, the sun had set. She got up from the desk, stiff from concentration, and unfolded the dormitory blanket. She swung it around her shoulders, shawl-fashion, and walked over to the long, narrow east windows of the third floor. President Matthews' brick house lay beneath her, bright and warm. Someone had lit the Christmas tree candles in their little red and green and yellow glass chimneys. They illuminated the bay windows of the fine house and threw points of color into the night.

The beauty softened her heart, but Christmas was for others. She turned back to her writing. In the dark, ideas flowed. She scrawled large, slanted lines. At last, tired and hungry, she eased herself out of the desk and went to her carpetbag where she took out two hard-boiled eggs and some cheese she'd snitched from the dormitory kitchen. There was cold bacon she'd placed between slices of bread and wrapped in a cloth napkin. With the blanket still hanging from her shoulders, she stood at a laboratory counter and ate her dinner in the dark. She considered yet another essay, trying to ignore the cold bacon grease that lined her mouth. She drank water at the tap in the lab sink and lay down in the corner beside Professor Irish's desk.

Next day she put down her pencil long enough to cook and clean for the faculty wife who hired her once a week. She made mincemeat pies for Christmas Day and cared for the children until late in the afternoon. Then she hurried back to Old Main, removed the wedge of paper she had stuck in the lock, and went up to the third floor where she worked feverishly on her article and story as long as the light lasted.

She tried to sleep through Christmas Eve. Instead, she lay listening to wisps of laughter and carols that drifted through the night. She heard the train pass along the foot of the butte, heading east toward New Mexico and the Colorado coal camps, riding through her heart.

She fell into a half-dream, half-memory: she, Myrtle, John, and Sam gathering coal from the train tracks. At the far-off shriek of a whistle, they drop their gunny sacks. Flirting with danger, they kneel beside the iron rail nailed to the earth.

They put their ears against the track. Pebbles and weeds on the roadbed look enormous as they lie with their heads near the ties, listening to the thin metallic whine, advance warning of a splendid danger approaching. Far down the track a pinpoint of light grows larger. It shimmers above the rails, a single eye of such power that everything moves out of its way. The whistle shrieks again, as if in pain from the hot ash and scalding steam in its inner boxes; in its tubes and valves and cylinders. They jump back, terrified of being swept up in the wind and roar of the great engine, thrilled by the last few rotations of the coupling rods and the noise of the steam shutting down.

Agnes struggled to her feet and went to the north windows. Catty-corner from Old Main, the stained glass windows of St. Mary's glowed, lit by candles burning inside the church. The bell began to toll. From her window she watched people arrive by foot, by wagon, carriage, and car for the midnight service. Singing wafted up to her. Outside the church, horses stood at hitching posts, as calm and imperturbable, patient and dumb, Agnes thought, as the cattle in the barn at Bethlehem.

She spent Christmas Day serving dinner and washing dishes at the faculty home where she worked. She took more of the Christmas goose than the professor's wife knew, wrapped bread spread with butter and cranberry sauce in a napkin, and returned to Old Main.

She entered the biology lab and came to an abrupt halt. Professor Irish was waiting for her. He had found her encampment. Agnes sat down in a desk and stared at the red wool scarf he'd tossed around his neck.

"Merry Christmas, Agnes," he said solemnly. She blinked.

"I don't usually come to my classroom on Christmas Day," he said. Agnes lifted her chin and continued to stare at the bright scarf. "Do you know why I'm here?"

Agnes shook her head.

"The janitor noticed that someone was coming in and out of the building. He kept finding the lock to the west door cleverly wedged open."

Agnes looked into his eyes. "I needed a place to stay."

"Did you want to stay here particularly, or is it the only place you could think of?"

"I could have stayed where I do housework," Agnes said, "only the children have to be looked after and I wouldn't have time to write."

"What are you writing?" he asked. She went to the carpetbag which rested on the folded blanket beside his desk and took out a stack of papers.

"This," she said. "An article and a story and the beginning of an essay. I haven't typed them up yet."

"May I ask what is so pressing that you must write through the Christmas vacation?" Professor Irish unwound the red scarf from his neck and laid it on his desk. He sat down in the swivel chair.

Agnes' color heightened. "An assignment for *The Normal Student*."

"A signed article?" asked Professor Irish.

"Maybe."

"Agnes Smedley," murmured Professor Irish.

"Ayahoo."

"I beg your pardon?"

"Ayahoo," Agnes said. "My new name." She put the papers back into the carpetbag and looked at him sideways to see what he would think. "I'm going to sign my articles "Ayahoo."

"Why will you do that?" Professor Irish turned his swivel chair first one way, then another, following Agnes as she paced back and forth in front of him.

"I am Indian," she said. "My father was part-Indian and I'm part-Indian." She lifted her head. "I would have fought the white man if I had been with Geronimo." Professor Irish nodded his head now and then. His eyebrows went up when she said, "The white man has driven us off our land, humiliated us, murdered us."

"You are white, too, Agnes," Professor Irish said. "You are Agnes as well as Ayahoo."

"I am no longer Agnes," Agnes said.

Professor Irish fell silent. He swiveled to face his desk. "How do you spell 'Ayahoo'?"

Agnes stood with her feet apart, her hands on her hips, and spelled her new name.

Professor Irish handed her a piece of paper on which he had written, "Ayahoo has my permission to use the biology classroom through the Christmas holidays for study and work. I am releasing a key to the building which she will return at the resumption of classes in January."

He signed his name and asked Agnes to do the same.

"Have you told your family about your new name?" he asked.

"I don't have a family."

"No one at all?"

"My aunt lives in Denver. I'll tell her when I see her."

"Does your aunt know you're in Tempe? Does she know you're enrolled in college?"

"She doesn't need to know," said Agnes. "My mother was interested in my education, but she's dead."

"I imagine she would be proud of you."

Agnes stood mute. Her people did not give compliments. "Talkativeness doesn't run in my family," she mumbled.

"Of course it does," said Professor Irish.

Agnes looked sheepish. "Except for my father," she amended.

"I've read your articles in the paper."

"That's not talking," said Agnes. "That's writing."

"Writing is written-down talk," said Professor Irish. "Tell me about the story," he said, glancing at the stack of papers beside her carpet bag.

Agnes blushed. "You can read it if you want to." She could not speak to him about the subject: a woman who had married an Indian, an Indian who looked very much as Agnes remembered her student in New Mexico, tall, with jet-black hair and soft dark eyes. His voice had been gentle and musical, and when his hands brushed hers, his skin was as smooth as it was brown.

Professor Irish picked up his red scarf from the desktop. "Did you read the Mendel biography we talked about?"

"I read it."

"Did it capture your interest?"

"It captured my interest." She shifted her gaze to the window. "I like plants. I like gardens."

"So did Mendel."

"But he looked into it too much."

"Is it possible to look into a thing too much?"

"Well … ." Agnes turned away from him, unable to express her uneasiness. She could not say the words "reproduction" or "breeding." She crossed and uncrossed her legs. "People and plants live and die," she said. "What's all the fuss about?"

"I, myself, sometimes wonder what all the fuss is about," Professor Irish said. Agnes looked encouraged. "Could you," he continued, "summarize for me what Mendel is fussing about?"

Agnes stared at her long skirt. "Heredity."

"Yes. It is a new scientific concept," said Professor Irish. "It will change the world."

Agnes sat straighter. "How can it change the world?"

Professor Irish's long, narrow face came to life. "When we can produce what we need when we need it," he said, "we can control nature." He ran the tip of his index finger over his small moustache. "We won't have to wait for whatever God has in store for us."

Agnes sat still straighter.

"Crops can be bred to withstand weather. Famines will some day be a thing of the past. We can eradicate disease. People may not have to die."

"Rich people will still take the food," Agnes said after a few moments of thought.

"Perhaps that will change, too. Perhaps everyone will be

rich."

"It's easier to pollinate plants than it is to change people."

Professor Irish adopted the vernacular. "Agnes," he said, "whether something is easy or not doesn't amount to a hill of beans." He threw the scarf about his neck, stood, and handed her the key to Old Main.

She took it and watched the thin figure disappear down the hall. Perhaps if he were more like Big Buck, more like the miners she had known as a girl in the coal camps, perhaps if Professor Irish had some of Father's outrageous humor, exaggerated stories, imagination, yes, even his habit of lying and embellishing the truth until it was something much better than reality, Agnes could have told the professor about the young Mexican-Indian she remembered; could have told him about her story and about herself.

But Professor Irish was a gentleman. Agnes sat down on the folded blanket by his desk and studied the large iron key resting in the palm of her hand. He was high-class and educated, but he was not strong and suntanned. He did not tell yarns and stay up half the night laughing at tall tales, drinking too much, stumbling to bed and rising early to a day of hard labor. College people could not understand miners and prostitutes and beaten-down women who died early, and children who were farmed out to strangers. They could not understand Agnes and her family. They could not understand Ayahoo.

Tempe, Arizona 1912

Thorberg Brundin watched the girl stride into the tiny dormitory room with a holster about her slim waist and a scalpful of pincurls. The young teacher lifted her blonde head off the pillow and pulled the blanket up under her chin.

"I'm Ayahoo," said the girl whose striking face, direct blue eyes, and wide forehead took one's breath. "You're using my room for the week."

"How do you do—'Ayahoo,' did you say?" Thorberg extended one pale, slender arm from the bedclothes. The intense young woman gripped it with a hard hand and gave an abrupt handshake.

"Thank you for the room," said Thorberg. She eyed the riding hat and Mexican quirt hanging on the wall.

"Don't mention it." The girl removed her holster from the waist of her long skirt, slung it over the bed post, and began to remove pins from her hair until curls stood out in all directions, only slightly tamed by the brush with which she lit into them.

"You sure do go to bed early."

"I was reading," said Thorberg.

"What are you reading?"

"Boas's *The Mind of Primitive Man*." Agnes eyed the volume lying on the bedspread. Thorberg buttoned the top button of her flowered flannel nightgown and sat up against the pillow. "I understand you're a member of the debating society."

"I am," said Agnes.

"Perhaps I will hear you in one of the debates."

"It's likely. I'm debating tomorrow. The topic is, 'Resolved: Woman's Suffrage Should Be Adopted in Arizona.' I'm arguing for suffrage. My position is that half of the human race has been subjugated by the other half. Women must acquire equality with men."

"I'm afraid I can't discuss the topics," Thorberg said in a well-modulated voice, though she looked interested. "I'm obligated to maintain neutrality." She'd been invited as one of the judges for the spring debating contest. In the mirror Agnes studied the cool blonde beauty, the patrician eyes. She gave a final swipe to her hair and turned to face the bed.

"Do you like ice-cream sodas?"

"I love ice-cream sodas."

"Then after the debates are over, before you go back to wherever you come from, I invite you to have a soda with me. I want to interview you for the paper."

"Very well," said Thorberg. "And I want to interview a woman who wears a gun and holster over her skirt and has the interesting name 'Ayahoo.'"

Agnes grinned. "Agreed." Once again she shot her work-hardened hand out to Thorberg, gave a vigorous shake to the cool, slender fingers, and strode out of the little room.

"Where are you going?" Thorberg called after her.

"Waiting tables at the diner," Agnes answered. "The night shift."

"Where will you sleep?"

Agnes was already on the steps. "My room is yours as long as you need it," she called back. "I'm bunking on the first floor while you're here."

In April Agnes' little room on the third floor was already too warm. Thorberg Brundin sat fanning herself on the edge of the narrow bed when Agnes came striding down the hall and through the doorway, removed her holster, and once again slung it over the bed post.

"Well, how did I do?" She rummaged through the closet that had been poked out of a space under the eave.

"Best possible," said Thorberg, forgetting to move her fan. "You're a strong debater. I gave you highest marks."

Unused to praise, Agnes looked away.

"You made your points clearly and efficiently. Your rebuttal was extremely strong. You were passionate in defense of women's rights."

Agnes despised the tears gathering at the back of her throat. Thorberg's approval was making her as weak as the women she'd defended. She turned to the closet, pulled a belt from a wall hook, and began fastening the worn cloth around the waist of her skirt.

"I see you're dressing for dinner," Thorberg observed drily.

"I don't have time or money for fashion," Agnes said.

Thorberg looked down at her own white blouse, crisp even in this heat and fastened at the collar with a brooch her mother had insisted she take out West with her. Her pointed boots showed from beneath the hem of her long linen skirt.

"You're not from around here, are you?" said Agnes.

"How can you tell?"

"Your speech and your clothes."

"Phoenix is my new home," said Thorberg. She resumed the fanning motion. "I'm originally from New York."

"I thought so."

"Again, why do you say that?"

"The way you talk. And you look rich."

"Believe me, not everyone in New York is rich. Neither am I." She glanced about the room. "How long have you been at Tempe Normal, Ayahoo?"

"Since September." In the mirror she fixed her eye on Thorberg. "I'm a special student. Never went to high school."

With an expression of pleased vindication, Thorberg studied the fierce girl standing before her. "You confirm my opinion that school is unnecessary for people who want to learn," she said. "I'm very disappointed in our schools. American education is antiquated, reactionary, and uncreative."

The little speech annoyed Agnes. She picked up a brush and attacked her short hair with quick, hard strokes. "You're educated," she said. "You can afford to be critical."

Thorberg continued her even fanning. "Are you going to teach when you graduate?"

Agnes placed the brush back on the shelf under the mirror. "I'll do whatever I have to do to stay alive. I don't have the money to finish school. I have to stop and work." She'd received a letter from Big Buck in early spring in which he'd written, "Seein's how I haven't heard from you, I hope the money done you some good in your education. As for me, I'm going to Mexico to fight in the Revolution."

Agnes plopped down on the foot of the bed. "Why did you

come West?" she asked.

Thorberg curled her legs under her to make room for Agnes. "My brother's here," she said. "He's a surveyor for the dam."

"The Roosevelt Dam?"

Thorberg nodded. She pulled up her legs and hugged her knees. "When he wrote to me from the Superstition Mountains, I had to come West. I had to see the Superstition Mountains."

"And what do you think of them?"

"Marvelous. This hot, dry country is magnificent." Thorberg picked up her fan again. "But I'm going farther west still. So is my brother. We're going to Berkeley, California. We're leaving as soon as my teaching term is finished."

Agnes spread her strong, brown hand on the dormitory blanket and studied it. To be able to say, "I'm going here" or "I'm going there" and to know ahead of time you would have the money for it seemed unobtainable bliss.

"You and your brother, are you friends?" Agnes asked.

"Oh, yes," said Thorberg. "We're great friends. Do you have a brother?"

Agnes nodded. "Two." She got off the bed.

"Where are you from, Ayahoo? Did you grow up in Arizona?"

"Missouri and Colorado." She stepped to the door. "I have to go to work now."

"Where do you work?"

"In the kitchen. I'll serve you your dinner."

"I've enjoyed visiting with you," said Thorberg.

"The same, I'm sure." Agnes paused in the doorway. "Can I interview you tomorrow?"

"I'm through at four."

"I'll be waiting for you." said Agnes.

Agnes and Thorberg entered Laird and Dines Drugs and slid into opposite sides of a booth. Agnes immediately moved the glass canister filled with long-handled spoons to one side and put her elbows on the cool, marble tabletop.

"Chocolate?"

"Chocolate. My treat," said Thorberg. She gazed about her as if she were in the habit of removing hat and gloves and had just noticed she wasn't wearing any. "I sometimes find myself marveling that I'm actually in Arizona," she said after her eyes had made an aloof circuit of the drugstore. From behind a row of apothecary jars lined up on the oak counter, the druggist was waiting on a cowboy. Agnes took out pencil and paper from a large pocket in her skirt.

"Can't you interview me some other time?" asked Thorberg. "Couldn't we just talk?"

Agnes grinned. " I've given myself an assignment." But she laid her pencil aside.

"What are your plans after graduation?" asked Thorberg.

"Maybe work on a newspaper." Agnes' jaw tightened. "I'll never marry."

"Nor I."

"Men don't know how to live as equals with women, in friendship," said Agnes.

But Thorberg sat taller. "My brother is my friend," she said, "and we are equal."

The sodas arrived. They each took a straw and long-handled spoon from the glass canisters and bent to business, one woman blonde, her skin smooth as porcelain; the other darker, rougher, with a quick, frank expression.

Thorberg straightened, wiped her mouth with her handkerchief, and leaned back thoughtfully. "You could do political work," she said. "You could be quite effective."

Agnes dragged on her straw hungrily. "I'd rather write for the papers."

"Journalism is ideal for political work," said Thorberg.

"What sort of political work?"

"Help the working class overthrow the capitalists. Women's emancipation. Birth control."

Agnes lowered her eyes and whipped her soda into a froth.

"Join the workers of the world," said Thorberg. "Help bring about a socialist world."

"What's a socialist world?"

Thorberg filled the shallow bowl of her long spoon with ice-cream. "A world in which all classes own the means of production. A world in which there are no rich and no poor."

Agnes tapped her spoon absently on the lip of the glass. "How do you work for that?"

"Help organize strikes."

"Is there any money in it?"

"Well, no. You don't do it for money. You do it for idealistic and political reasons. You make speeches. Write articles. As you say, write for the newspapers."

"They have socialist newspapers?"

"Certainly. There's *The Call* in New York City, and many others."

"I worked for an editor in Denver," Agnes said. She sucked up the last of her soda and stared into the empty glass. "Do you know anybody on *The Call*?"

"Not specifically on *The Call*. But Ernest and I have many friends in New York who are socialists, just as we are."

"Is Ernest your brother?"

"Yes. Ernest is my brother."

Agnes eyed Thorberg's shining hair, precise and refined features, well-cut dress. Her boots were real leather, of that Agnes was sure.

"How can you be a socialist if you're not poor?"

Thorberg's color rose. "The Socialist Revolution is blind to class values," she said. "Socialism needs all of our efforts. The capitalist classes will not willingly relinquish their power."

"But aren't you the capitalist class? If the Revolution comes, you won't have money," Agnes pointed out. "You're on top now. You'd be pulled down. You wouldn't have money to go to California or enroll anywhere."

Thorberg trailed a slender finger through the condensation on her glass. "I am only too ready to do my part," she said. "I can give up what few advantages I have."

Agnes looked skeptical.

"Have you heard about the strike of the textile workers in Lawrence, Massachusetts?" Thorberg asked. "The mill owners were forced to settle with the workers for higher wages. It was a great victory for the working class." She explained the relief work and the removal of the strikers' children to sympathetic families in New York where they were cared for until the strike ended.

"That's what we need in the coal mines," Agnes said. "A strike that sticks."

"Is your father a miner?"

Agnes spoke tentatively of the farm in Missouri, the move to Colorado, the poverty, coal camps, mine accidents. Slowly she approached the subject of her mother's death, skirted it, came back to it. Thorberg listened intently and handed over her handkerchief.

"I will never die the way my mother did!" Agnes looked at the clock on the wall and took in a sudden breath. "I'll be late to set tables." Thorberg paid the bill. Outside, they stopped at the corner to let a horse and wagon go by.

"Let's talk again before I go back to Phoenix," Thorberg said, catching up to Agnes who had stepped into the street without waiting for the dust to settle. Thorberg's steps were light and langorous in contrast to Agnes' sinewy stride. "I want to introduce you to my brother. He comes down from the dam every weekend."

Agnes did not answer until they reached the dormitory. "Fine," she said. "Tell me where to meet you." And without another word she set off for the kitchen entrance at the back.

The next Saturday Agnes and Thorberg waited at Laird and

Dines for Ernest to arrive from the Roosevelt Dam.

"What are your brothers like?" Thorberg asked.

"Younger than me."

Thorberg slowly swirled a straw through her chocolate soda. "Do you see them often?"

"No." She'd told Thorberg about Mother's death, but she could not say outright that her sister and brothers were farmed out in New Mexico and Oklahoma because she left home instead of taking care of them.

It did not surprise her that Thorberg had, in addition to parents, money, and education, a brother who was her friend. Thorberg was a goddess who moved gracefully through the world, untouched by trouble. Intellectual, langorous, passive, she was everything Agnes was not. Yet this goddess seemed entranced by Agnes and never ceased asking questions. Sometimes the questions were silly. Agnes began to see that, in some ways, she knew more than Thorberg.

A tall, gaunt young man entered the drugstore. He was darker and more weathered than his sister, and shyer.

"Ayahoo, may I present my brother, Ernest Brundin."

Agnes held out her hand. Ernest solemnly shook it and slid into the booth next to his sister. His face was lean, intelligent, courteous. Compared to him, Agnes felt crude.

She put her elbows on the table. "I've never met a sister and brother who were friends," she said.

Thorberg looked sideways at her brother as if to say, "See? What did I tell you?"

While Ernest studied Agnes neutrally—his eyes were deeper and bluer than his sister's—Thorberg filled the silence. "Ayahoo and I have discovered Laird and Dines chocolate sodas," she said. "We've told each other the story of our lives over this table."

"What's the weather like up on Superstition Mountain?" Agnes blurted out.

"Cool and pleasant," he replied. Then, like his sister, he looked over the drugstore. His eyes moved in the direction of the apothecary jars, the small brass scales resting on one end of the counter, and back to Agnes. Unlike his sister's cool circuit of the room, Ernest Brundin's gaze was private and equivocal. Agnes was not sure what he was looking at, much less what he was thinking.

The soda jerk came to their table, retying his white apron soiled from phosphates and syrups.

"Coffee," said Thorberg.

"Coffee and a ham sandwich," said Ernest.

"Coffee and a ham sandwich and another chocolate soda," said Agnes. She calculated that Thorberg would buy again, and that if she didn't, the brother would.

"I told you Ayahoo was like no one you've ever met," said Thorberg. She turned to Agnes. "You are an authentic Western type, you know."

Agnes bristled. "And you're authentically Eastern."

"We're not authentic yet," Ernest said quietly. "My sister and I are still part-European. Our parents are Swedish."

"Speak for yourself," Thorberg said languidly. "I am authentically American."

"You're not," he said.

"I am," she insisted.

Ernest turned to Agnes. "'Ayahoo' is an interesting name."

"It's Indian," she said immediately. "I'm part-Indian."

"Which tribe?"

"Apache." Father had never told her what tribe.

"I understand the Indians who settled this valley built canals," he said. The coffee arrived. He moved his cup and saucer to make room for the ham sandwiches.

"The Hohokam built canals," said Agnes. "If you're interested, I can show you an article I wrote for the paper about the Hohokam and Pima and Papago Indians. There's a library book"—

"Let's not merely read about the canals," interrupted Thorberg. The color rose in her fine-boned face. "Let's find them."

Agnes whipped her soda with the straw, thrilled with the idea. She glanced eagerly from Thorberg to Ernest to Thorberg again. "I'll ask Professor Irish," she said. "He'll know where the canals are."

Thorberg ignored her coffee. "We could meet next weekend."

"What's wrong with tomorrow?" said Agnes.

"Ernest and I have to catch the train for Phoenix this evening. In any case, we need time to plan the outing."

Agnes had never said "in any case" in her life. It had a fine ring. There was so much she didn't know how to say; how to think. She'd never met people like the Brundins. She actually had a falling sensation as Thorberg spoke of going away. Without Thorberg she wouldn't know about Socialism and journalism and New York or that she was a good debater and an interesting person. With Thorberg these past five days the world had opened, like the diaphragm in Professor Irish's microscope, and now it was closing again. Agnes wanted to plunge into the center of this opening that threatened to snap shut and force it apart again. Thorberg must not leave her behind in the backwater of nothingness.

Ernest broke into her thoughts. "I work with a fellow who lives on a ranch near here," he said. "We can borrow some horses next Saturday." He looked at Agnes. "Do you ride?"

Agnes finished off the last of her soda and licked the far end of the straw. "Of course I ride," she said.

Next weekend the three of them found one of the canals, a wide, shallow depression that led through barren desert to the Salt River. They walked their horses along the declivity dotted here and there by low clumps of stickery ground cover, as if a centuries-old water memory still had power to grow something.

"It took a lot of labor to keep these ditches open," Ernest said. He stepped into the middle of the broad, faintly sunken trough. Agnes watched him place his hand against the slight rise at one edge, as if he were giving a benediction to all those ditch-diggers of the past. This stirring she felt for him was mixed somehow with her emotion for the Indians.

The next moment she felt foolish. Like a river in its deep channel, Thorberg and Ernest would flow on west, leaving her and the Hohokam behind. Some day they might think of her: "Whatever happened to that strange, authentically Western girl we met one time in Arizona?"

The three of them walked for miles before they got back on their horses and followed the canal to the Salt River. At night, near the south bank, they spread out their bedrolls and tied the horses to a cottonwood.

Beneath hard, bright stars, the desert lay sinister and beautiful. It had softened only at twilight when they'd made coffee over a little fire. But not for Agnes the twilight loveliness, false promise of ease that could only make her unhappy if she believed it. She even resented the river and the Roosevelt Dam that Ernest was helping to build. Water weakened the strength of the desert, and subtracted from its barren loneliness and dry threat. Water and nourishment and plenty undermined reality.

She looked over at the two low forms near her, this sister and brother, woman and man, who were friends. Ernest treated Thorberg as his equal. Thorberg expected it. Sometimes she even dominated.

Thorberg shifted on her bedroll. "Tomorrow is Easter," she said. "All good Christians will be up at sunrise." She yawned. "Workers, owners, all go to church." Agnes stared up at the stars and tried to imagine a number large enough to count all the bits of bright material shining in the night sky.

"People would be better off joining the Socialist Party than going to church," Thorberg added. "You know what Marx said." Agnes didn't know what Marx said, and she didn't ask.

"Professor Irish told me about a Yaqui Indian settlement not far from here," Agnes said.

"We were going to surprise you and take you tomorrow for their Easter Dance," said Thorberg. "It's a marvelous ceremony. Ernest went last year." The murmur of the river was even and slow. Agnes forgave it for bringing water to the desert; such a small river, after all, barely enough for a narrow strip of green in all this rocky dignity.

"The Indians are Catholic," said Thorberg. "They dance in rows for hours and hours before a small cross and a likeness of the Virgin Mary until they drop from exhaustion."

"It's as sensible as kneeling," put in Ernest, "and better exercise."

"What do they wear?" asked Agnes.

"Loin cloths," said Ernest.

"Do the women dance?"

"No. Religion is for the men. The women have to stay outside." Agnes imagined the dancers, shiny with sweat, moving in rows toward a terra cotta Virgin Mary, then back; forward again, and back. She heard the rattle of gourds; smelled the sweet smoke of a fire and the musty odor of the women's swaying hair. She heard a soft, strange language, and looked into the eyes of people who looked back without emotion.

"… communicate more directly in a primitive society," Thorberg was saying. Agnes listened for a while, puzzled. She heard "society this" and "society that," and still she didn't understand. "Society" was a section in the newspaper.

"Boas says there is no basic difference between the way a primitive man thinks and the way a civilized man thinks."

"Who is Boas?" asked Agnes.

"Franz Boas, the anthropologist. He has made brilliant studies of societies based upon scientific measurement of their physical types and language structure, among other things."

Maybe this Boas was doing to people what Mendel had done to peas, Agnes thought.

"Boas says a close connection between race and personality has never been shown." Agnes marveled at Thorberg's knowledge and Ernest's patient listening. Thorberg never ran out of things to say. Sometimes it seemed that the woman made ideas up as she went along. Whatever she needed, she could just say it, and it was so.

"The interplay between heredity and what is learned from society … ." Agnes didn't like the word "heredity." Hers, she thought, was shaky. What you learned, not who you were born to, was the important thing. Then you had half a chance. She tossed on her bedroll, tired of Thorberg's talk in which she could not participate.

"Ayahoo?" Thorberg whispered after a long silence.

"What?"

"Are you asleep?"

"Yes."

"May Ernest and I visit you again after next weekend?"

Agnes opened her eyes. The moon had risen until it seemed straight overhead, a great, light face with vague shadows that gave it an expression.

"Oh, yes," she said. "Yes."

Every weekend in April and May the Brundins came to Tempe. Agnes expected every weekend to be the last, but every weekend they made plans for the next. She began to hope they would never leave for Berkeley, California. One Saturday and Sunday when Thorberg had to stay in Phoenix, Ernest came to Tempe by himself.

"My job won't last much longer," he said as he and Agnes rode horseback past the town limits out into the desert. He'd ridden from a friend's ranch, leading a mare for Agnes. "I was lucky to get work on the dam. But it's just about finished. I'll have to find something else soon."

"I thought you were going to school out at Berkeley."

"First I need a job. Thorberg's the student."

"What kind of job? Surveying?"

"I'll hang around an engineer's office until they hire me to do something. There's lots of work in California."

"What did you do before you came to Arizona?" A car passed by on the dirt road and Agnes' horse danced sideways.

"She's skittish," Ernest said. He leaned over to smack the mare once on the rump. "General engineering. This and that. I don't have a degree. I do whatever they give me to do."

"I thought you went to college."

"Thorberg's the one with the degree," he said without envy. "I finished Freshman year, but I had to drop out."

"Did you run out of money?"

"No. I contracted tuberculosis. I'm well now, though."

"A lot of the miners had tuberculosis," Agnes said. She began to disclose her private life to Ernest. She told him about her family. She told him about the money Big Buck had given her and how it had run out. How she admired Thorberg more than anyone else in the world. How she wished the Brundins wouldn't go away to Berkeley, California. How she would never forget them.

"Thorberg considers you a friend," Ernest said. He kept his horse alongside and spoke in his slow, courteous manner. "She thinks you have talent."

Agnes blushed, swallowed, frowned, and held back tears, all at the same time.

"Thorberg is the best friend I've ever had!" she burst out. The mare shuddered and wheeled. Agnes yanked on the reins but the horse broke into a gallop. Mane streaming, eyes rolling, he plunged ahead into the desert. Sage brush, rocks, cactus flashed by against a blurred background of yellow sun and blue sky. Agnes might as well have shouted "Whoa!" to the wind. Finally, when Ernest had almost caught up to her, she managed to bring the horse to a stop. She sat without moving in the saddle and kept her eye on the mare's twitching ears.

"Would you like to trade horses?" Ernest asked tactfully.

Pride made her say no. But even though the horse obeyed

her the rest of the day, nosing in scanty brush beside the walls of Indian ruins, Agnes felt shaken and unsure of both the horse and herself. In the late afternoon they started back for Tempe.

"Have you ever been to California?" asked Ernest. Agnes looked straight ahead at the Superstition Mountains in the distance.

"Nope."

"Southern California is a desert, as dry as Arizona." His blue eyes, keen and methodic, covered the landscape they rode. "The Colorado River has more than enough water for Los Angeles and the farming counties in the south, so they've started a great irrigation project."

"Are you going to work on it?"

"Maybe."

"You'll find work," Agnes assured him. And you'll both forget me, she thought. But I will never forget you.

It was long after nightfall when they neared town. Ernest was telling Agnes about New York, his parents, the University of Maine where he'd been a student, the chicken farm he'd worked on, when her horse changed rhythm, trembled, and came to a dead stop. Agnes tightened her grip on the reins and froze. For endless seconds the mare stood quivering. Then, with her ears back, she reared and broke into another frenzied gallop.

This time Agnes could not bring her to a stop. She shouted for Ernest who had already spurred his horse and was moving up alongside her, his hair swept back from his forehead by the wind, his profile sharp in the moonlight. The horses galloped neck to neck. He leaned far out, caught the mare's bridle with his right hand, and gave a tremendous jerk.

The mare reared again and again. Her lather gleamed in the pale light. When Ernest had brought her under control, Agnes slid out of the saddle and half-fell onto the desert floor. While he tied the horses to a clump of sage and stayed by the mare until her wheezing stopped, Agnes sank into the shadow of the brush. After a bit Ernest came and sat down beside her. When he took her in his arms, Agnes cried against his shoulder.

"Ayahoo," he whispered. "You might have been hurt. Next time I'll ride the mare." He continued to soothe her, as if the danger had freed him from shyness.

"There might not be a next time! You're both going away!"

He stroked her hair. "We don't want to leave you," he said, and kissed her. Agnes tasted salt. They drew apart, then together again.

"All week I look forward to seeing you," he said.

"Please don't go away," she whispered, and kissed him back. Ernest was the only man who could treat her as an equal and teach her about love. If only they would stay in Arizona, she could be a sister to both of them. She could be a Brundin.

"Make up something about a high school diploma," Thorberg said at the end of the semester when, like the mare, Agnes bolted from Tempe Normal to be near the Brundins in Phoenix. "Remember, you have a certificate from stenography school."

Agnes had forgotten. She began to carry the diploma with her to interviews, and found a job. Soon after, she moved out of Thorberg's Phoenix apartment into a boarding house near the tracks. But nothing gave her pleasure. Anxiety about losing the Brundins took over her life. In the few days before they were to leave for California, she developed a rash.

When Thorberg applied lotion and said, "You're far brighter than most teachers, and anyway, education isn't as important as you think it is," Agnes emerged out of her morbid sadness long enough to snap,

"You can afford to think so! You're educated!"

When they took her to the theatre to watch a socialistic play, Agnes waited and waited for music and dancing and jokes.

"I gather you didn't think much of the production," Thorberg said coolly as she and Ernest walked Agnes to her streetcar stop.

"It was all talk," Agnes said in a sulky tone.

"That's what drama is!" Thorberg exclaimed. "Talk!"

"Well," Agnes retorted, "I like some humor and singing and dancing in my drama!"

Ernest smiled. "We'll have to take you to the vaudeville."

Thorberg patted Agnes on the shoulder. "You're still an innocent," she said. "We haven't had quite enough time to work on you."

Even as she pulled away from Thorberg's touch and walked ahead, hating to be laughed at, she hoped the Brundins would "work on her" for the rest of her life.

"Ernest likes you," his sister said the day after they'd laughed at her taste in drama. Agnes felt her face redden. She liked Ernest, too, but she mistrusted men, and feared sex. She wanted to be loved, but she didn't want to get married. Marriage wasn't honest. It was an arrangement that benefitted men and kept women backward. Prostitution was more honest than marriage. Aunt Tillie made no bones about having sex for money, whereas Mother, a married woman, had been forced to have sex and still ended up with no money.

Agnes once admitted to Thorberg that she wished she were beautiful.

"But you *are* beautiful, Ayahoo," Thorberg replied. "When you are thinking or daydreaming, your face is soft and very pretty. When you speak, your eyes are direct. You're slender and quick and graceful in your movements."

Agnes was amazed that anyone would find her attractive. She wondered how she could live without Thorberg's encouragement. When the three of them walked in the park or attended a lecture, Ernest's arm was around her shoulder. Sometimes he walked her home and kissed her in the shadows of the boarding house. At such times she felt a grateful trust that she imagined was the same as love. Once during a kiss when he pushed his tongue into her mouth, she drew away. Ernest said nothing; merely kissed her again.

When he and Thorberg waved good-bye from the train

window, Agnes turned her back on them, emotionally emptied, dry-eyed. The next day when she went to clean Thorberg's vacated apartment as she had promised, there was a letter on the hall table to Miss Agnes Smedley, forwarded by the Tempe Normal mailroom in care of Thorberg. The address was scrawled and smudged. She thought Father had written her. The thought was just another cold weight for her to bear. She put the unopened letter in her pocket and set about cleaning. Only after she returned the bucket and mop to the landlady, took the cleaning deposit money, and walked back to her boarding house did she open the envelope.

It wasn't from Father. It was from her brother John. Big Buck had gotten word to Father about Agnes' whereabouts. Somehow John knew to write her in Tempe. On a single sheet of paper in a dirty envelope crudely addressed to Agnes at the normal school, he told her about the farmer he, Sam, and Myrtle lived with in Oklahoma. They were whipped, he wrote in the poorest of English. They worked twelve hours a day.

Agnes wadded up the paper and squeezed it hard. While she'd been teaching and going to school, learning to write pretty sentences in cursive handwriting, her younger brothers and sister had been laboring like farm animals. By her calculation, none of them had gotten past third grade. She lay down on the lumpy couch in her furnished room and turned her face into the cheap plush. It smelled of cigarette smoke and sweat. Instead of taking care of John, Myrtle, and Sam, she'd been putting on airs, pretending that somehow she could be a Brundin and forgetting she was a Smedley. She ground her face into the sofa, filled with self-loathing.

For days she went to work and returned home to lie on the sofa. She hardly ate. Mentally she drove herself to consider an unbearable course of action: take Mother's place. Get John and Sam and Myrtle from their foster homes and be a mother to them, she who despised and feared family life and motherhood.

The next letter Agnes received was sent direct, not in care

of anybody, and made her feel faint. It was a marriage proposal from Ernest. He had a job, he wrote; he could support both of them. Enclosed was a train ticket to San Francisco. He loved her, he wrote in his steady hand, without flourish. He missed her. He wanted them to be husband and wife.

Agnes laid the two letters side by side on the drop-leaf table in the corner. John's wrinkled letter looked like wastepaper, something she'd tried to throw away but couldn't. The letters canceled each other out. She experienced a strange moment of aloofness. Her mind hovered outside herself, watching someone called Agnes.

But the moment of dispassionate peace ended. She broke into a sweat and left for the bathroom down the hall where she was sick again and again. The basin of her body could not hold its fluids. Her stomach emptied and then her bowels. Heaving, cramped, she crawled about the bathroom cleaning up after herself. Finally she stood and began the return trip to the sofa where she slept as if she had died.

When she awoke it was dark. She sat at the window and took some water and dry bread. A sliver of moon hung in the black sky. If she concentrated, she could not only imagine but actually see the full moon, a phantom, not shining, but there, nevertheless. As the earth moved out of the way, Professor Irish had said, the sun's light would illuminate more and more of the dead moon until it seemed a live and glorious body in the night sky.

Strange, she thought as she lay back down, that something so beautiful could not give off its own light and heat. Strange, too, how sad the thought of Professor Irish made her.

Before dawn she rose and walked to the edge of town and out into the desert. She would, she knew, marry Ernest. He would help her out of her dilemma and she would come to love him. He would teach her how to be married. Once again she would abandon her brothers and sister. She could see no way to mother them. She could never be Mother.

It wasn't just book learning she longed for. She wanted to succeed in the world; she wanted enough freedom to succeed. Waking from a sleep so deep that it obliterated all pretense, she knew she loved her ambition more than she loved her sister and brothers. If she returned to a mining camp, a tenant farm, she would never advance herself. She would never go to another school or meet another Thorberg and Ernest.

She would rather be successful than good. The knowledge made her ill.

As she walked, the desert engulfed her. It lay beneath the night sky, too vast to have personality. In the darkness she imagined she saw John, Sam, and Myrtle; in the desert wind she heard the whip of their beatings. Her misery was so profound that it was almost a kind of peace. A bird, awake before the others, called. At the horizon there was a loosening of night, like a knife inserted under the edge of the dark.

As she walked, she gathered strength from the desert and from the almost luminous misery that lay at the foundations of her family; at the portals of her very self. In this amplitude of grief, of guilt, she began to see her way. With Ernest working and her working, there would be extra money for her brothers and sister. Perhaps some day they could come to California.

She turned back toward Phoenix. She walked faster. The sky was a glorious red by the time she reached the boarding house. She sat down at the drop-leaf table and wrote four short letters.

To Father she wrote that John and Sam must come back to Trinidad. He must see that they go to school. He was their father, and they had no other.

In John's letter she enclosed money, all she had, and told him to buy three tickets for Trinidad; that he, Sam, and Myrtle would be better off with Father than with a stranger who beat them.

To the farmer who beat them she wrote a short, passionate promise. She would find him one day and kill him.

And to Ernest she wrote an acceptance. She would leave for

San Francisco in two days. She would not let him support her, she wrote. She would find a job and the two of them would live, work, and study together as equals.

John's letter remained on the table, a reminder to Agnes that happiness is ephemeral and difficulty is what sustains.

11

San Francisco 1912

The first thing Agnes noticed in San Francisco was the white faces. She was used to Mexican and Indian faces lacing the white populations of New Mexico, Texas, and Arizona. In the Southwest, even whites were suntanned. But not here. When she arrived at the Southern Pacific depot in San Francisco, the lean man—no longer tanned but still sinewy and strong-jawed—who loped toward her on the platform was Ernest Brundin. He smiled one of his rare, brilliant smiles, so unexpected in a gaunt face, and won Agnes to him and to California. He picked her up and whirled her two full revolutions until her flying feet caught the suitcase of a stout man who stood reading his timetable. On the streetcar all the way down Townsend and then Van Ness, he held her hand. It embarrassed Agnes but she permitted it.

"Everyone's so pale," she said as they climbed down at the Hayes Street stop. "You wouldn't know it was July." Already tatters of fog were blowing in from the ocean, now hiding, now revealing Hayes as it climbed west. It was early afternoon in summer but she shivered. "Folks look pale and puffy and cold."

Ernest pulled the brim of her straw hat a tad lower over her eyes. "San Francisco summers are not like the summers you're used to." Her face showed no fatigue from the journey. He bent, kissed her full lips, and tipped her hat up again. A few curls landed on her high forehead. Agnes grasped the handle of the carpetbag she insisted on carrying herself and matched his long steps. She pointed to a pile of old boards and debris on a corner lot.

"The earthquake?"

"Piles and piles of rubbish still haven't been cleared," said Ernest. "Six years isn't long to rebuild a city."

They passed narrow, three-story frame houses with bay windows that hung out over the sidewalk.

"Thorberg is engaged," he said without warning.

"What?" Agnes came to a dead stop. "Thorberg's engaged?" She stomped her foot. "Thorberg was never going to marry!"

"She's changed her mind."

Agnes frowned. The blood rushed to her face. Ernest watched her with a guarded expression.

"She might have written me."

"Don't you want to know who it is?"

"No."

He switched his weight to his right leg. "*You're* getting married," he said in a low voice. "Why shouldn't *she*?"

"It's just that Thorberg is a—well, a Socialist," Agnes said. "She's supposed to have ideals." They turned down Octavia Street.

"His name is Robert Haberman," Ernest said, as if she'd asked. "He's more of a Socialist than Thorberg."

Agnes sniffed.

"He's a pharmacist who works in San Rafael. Jewish."

Agnes sniffed again.

"From Rumania."

She laughed out loud. "You might know your sister wouldn't choose someone ordinary."

"He's living with us," Ernest added.

"He's what?"

"There's plenty of room," Ernest said. They turned in at 624 Octavia. Ernest opened the front door and they climbed to the third-story flat. No one was home. Agnes made a quick tour of the two small bedrooms, sitting room, dining room, and kitchen.

"It'll do." She tossed her carpetbag onto the sofa. "Where's Thorberg?"

"In school," said Ernest. "She takes the ferry to Berkeley three days a week."

Agnes paced about the sitting room. It seemed strange to be so near Berkeley, the place she'd heard about, the place she'd hated because it was taking the Brundins away from her. "What's she studying?"

"Zoology."

Agnes thought of Professor Irish's biology lab and pushed her hair back from her forehead with a harsh gesture of erasure. "Where does Thorberg sleep?"

"They sleep in the south bedroom." Ernest's plain answer shook her. Thorberg, her friend, the woman she most admired, was sleeping in the same room with this Rumanian, participating in the profoundly dangerous and ugly sexual act between a man and woman. It left one bedroom for Ernest and herself.

"I won't have sex!" Agnes said, furious. "We're going to study and work. We agreed on it. That's what you said in your letter." She picked up her carpetbag as if to leave.

Ernest reached out and stopped her. "I'll sleep on the sofa," he said. "There's no hurry, Agnes. We're not married yet."

"Neither is Thorberg."

"That's her business." He moved closer. She saw that he wanted to hold her, but she could not bear to be touched just now, and she ran downstairs and outside. The fresh air cooled her. She sat doubled-up on the front stoop and ground her forehead into her knees. She had not bargained for Thorberg's betrayal or Ernest's desire.

He joined her on the porch stoop. "In Arizona, didn't you like my kisses?" He put things so plainly that there was nowhere to hide from his words, no way to pass off his questions. This gentle man was terrifying her with his maleness. He was no longer someone to imagine. He was real. And in spite of their long horseback rides through the desert where they'd talked about friendship, work, and study, now that she was in San Francisco, it turned out that he wanted sex. And Thorberg wanted sex. And this horrible Haberman Rumanian Jew pharmacist wanted sex. Agnes could not help but notice that all the world, people, animals, even plants, wanted sex, as if that was what everything was here for, just to have sex and make more people and animals and plants. And she, Agnes Smedley, could not. She clenched her jaw. Would not. She would work hard and earn money, pay Ernest back the cost of her ticket, pay her share of the flat. She wouldn't owe anybody anything.

"Agnes!" Thorberg came toward her up the walk, more golden and more goddess-like than ever.

"Hello," Agnes said, and burst into tears. She braced herself against the stoop, willed herself to stand, and laboriously climbed the stairs to her new home.

Agnes sat at the tiny table that served as a desk in the corner of her bedroom, writing about the Chinese of San Francisco. During a lunch hour away from her secretarial job, she'd walked north from Market Street and found herself in Chinatown. Enthralled by the foreign culture, she'd almost been late back to her job. When the editor of *The Tempe Normal Student* wrote and asked her for an article from San Francisco, she had no difficulty deciding on a subject.

"Chinese men bend over sun-flooded benches of vegetables," she scribbled at the small, shaky table. "Some have little stalls of varieties where they sell brown, glutinous ribbons of seaweed— "

In the background Thorberg and Robert's voices sounded from the dining room where they were reading the Sunday morning *Call* spread out on the table before them. Haberman's rapid, accented speech ran like a choppy river through Agnes' days and nights. He never stopped talking. Agnes wondered how Thorberg could stand the high, penetrating voice, the endless opinions.

"Look at this!" he said. "What did I tell you?" And he began to fulminate against the United Railroads and other corporations who had participated in bribery schemes. "They let the Union Labor Party take the blame," he exclaimed—his hair, Agnes knew, was standing on end—"and big business escaped Scotch free!"

"Scot free," Thorberg said. Just when Haberman seemed about to master the American idiom, he would ruin the effect. Agnes got up and closed her door. She looked out the window at the backs of new homes being built on Gough Street. The 1906 fire had stopped just before it reached Octavia; the four of them lived in a pre-quake house. No, not the four of them. Ernest had left to work on the All-American Canal project in Southern California.

She stared down at the acacia tree in the backyard. Morning fog moved through its branches and toothy-edged leaves. Living apart eased the tension between them, but the prospect of separation had frightened them. On the very day his train left for El Centro, they'd gotten married. They pretended it was a lark. On her lunch hour, August 24th, they met in front of the Pioneer Monument at the hub of Market, Hyde, and Grove. While she waited for Ernest, Agnes walked around the frieze and statues of gold miners, Indians, covered wagons. It was the history of America, the history of her grandparents who left Mississippi for Missouri, the history of her restless father. He would have liked to be one of those men bent over a creek with a gold pan, an enormous nugget in his hand.

She took a dislike to the statue and turned her back on it. When she saw Ernest walking toward her with his leather grip, she felt the sting of separation. "I only have till one o'clock," she said.

"Agnes, I want to talk to you."

She looked up at his thin, honest face. She loved the face, loved Ernest, but couldn't permit herself to express it.

"I'll miss you," she said. It was as far as she could go. Ernest took it as a declaration. He put down the grip and hugged her. His cheek against hers was clean-shaven and tender. Agnes hugged him back. When he spoke to her again his eyes were wet. His emotion worried her. They began walking.

"Don't let Thorberg and Robert boss you around while I'm gone," he said. They both pretended to laugh. Before they knew it they were in front of the temporary City Hall on Market Street.

"Let's get married," Ernest said.

Agnes broke into a sweat. "We should think about it," she said, her mouth dry.

"No!"

It was one of the few times she'd seen Ernest impulsive. His bony face was flushed, and there was a compelling light in his eyes. She stared at him and began to relent. She did not want to be forgotten when he was down in the Imperial Valley, and without him she had no prospects. "All right," she said. He kissed her and she kissed him back. He was leaving on the afternoon train, so at least they would not have to resolve the sexual question immediately.

"I have to be back at work by one," she reminded him.

Ernest pulled a marriage license out of his pocket. "It won't take long," he said.

"How much did it cost?"

"Two dollars."

"And how much does it cost to get married?"

"Five dollars."

Agnes opened her purse. Ernest waited. He took the three dollars and fifty cents she handed him. It was no time for an argument.

"I guess we'll need a witness," said Justice of the Peace A.T. Barnett when they appeared in his office on the second floor. He opened a side door beside his roll-top desk and bawled out a name. When the witness arrived he began the ceremony without preamble.

"Are you willing to take this woman to be your wedded wife?"

Ernest hesitated.

Justice Barnett sighed. "What's the matter?" he asked.

"You go about it so fast," Ernest said lamely. "I wasn't ready for you."

"Well, what are you waiting for? Do you want me to do the hula-hula?" He began to lecture them about the vicissitudes of marriage. Agnes memorized the word "vicissitudes." She thought it probably had something to do with sex. She would look it up in Thorberg's dictionary when she got home.

"I now pronounce you man and wife. You may kiss the bride." The short, red-haired witness watched with interest, but Agnes squeezed Ernest's hand and pulled away. She felt stifled and needed air. They signed their names in a large black book. Agnes dipped the pen in the ink bottle and signed, "Ayahoo Smedley, Age Twenty."

"Sign your real name, your married name," instructed the Justice. But Agnes had refused.

Now she turned back from the bedroom window. It was January and Ernest had visited her just once from El Centro. He'd slept on the sofa again, but he was less patient than before and she could not put off sleeping with her husband forever. The thought made her tired and headachy. Sometimes she had trouble breathing. She picked up her pen and began writing where she'd left off. After a few minutes there was a knock on the door. She got up and opened it.

"What are you doing?" Thorberg asked, gazing past Agnes' shoulder to the table in the corner.

"Writing an article for *The Tempe Normal*."

"Can I read it?"

Agnes invited her in. They sat on the edge of the bed, Agnes feeding Thorberg pages as she read. Robert Haberman passed by the doorway.

"What are you reading?" he asked.

"Agnes is writing an article about Chinatown," Thorberg replied.

"Ah, the Chinese." Haberman's revolutionary zeal ignited.

"Do you talk about the Chinese Exclusion Act? Have you described the exploitation? The struggles of China against Western imperialism? Have you—"

"She has walked through Chinatown," Thorberg said languidly, and read aloud: "'In the school, the same modern and sanitary conditions are to be found that are found in other sections of the city. The teachers all seem to be devoted to their work and say the pupils are extremely keen and alert.'"

Haberman snorted. "Do you mention that the Chinese children are not allowed in the San Francisco public schools?"

Agnes flushed. She lifted her chin and her eyes snapped. "This isn't an article about the schools. It's an impression of Chinatown."

"An impression doesn't convey the truth," Haberman said. Uncharacteristically, he dropped the subject, perhaps because of the warning look from Thorberg, who finished reading the article and praised it.

"It shows a fine awareness of cultures other than your own," she said. Haberman returned to stand in the doorway. "Ah," she continued, reading ahead, "I see you included some of Ernest's ideas about ancient Chinese engineering."

Agnes gave a curt nod.

"May I read it?" Haberman asked.

Agnes shot the article toward him. Thorberg looked worried. Agnes went to the kitchen, opened the broom closet, and took a dust cloth from a peg. While he read, she ran it industriously over the furniture and shook it out the window with a snap. No one spoke. By the time he made his first comment Agnes had swept the kitchen and washed the dishes that Thorberg had, as usual, insisted she would do and, as usual, had not.

"How much do you know about Chinese history?" Haberman asked bluntly. Agnes came out into the living room, soapsuds to her elbows.

"Not much."

"Here, where you say"—Haberman searched for the

passage—"'There was no hereditary aristocracy, and the only aristocracy recognized was the aristocracy of learning. While dynasties rose and fell and practiced their beliefs of commercial truthfulness and honor'—" he broke off.

"What's wrong with it?" Agnes asked.

"The Chinese Revolution arose because of the abuses of the Manchus. Have you heard of Sun Yat-sen?" Haberman began to talk about modern China. It was the only nation in history, he said, that had formed a republic without spilling a drop of blood. China would, he assured Agnes and Thorberg, adopt the tactics of the West and beat the West at its own game. His comments moved from continent to subcontinent, across Russia, across India. As the lecture expanded to include the New World and the Mexican Revolution, Agnes stepped into the kitchen, rinsed off the soap, dried her hands and arms, and came back to the living room where she sat at one end of the sofa and listened.

"Under Diaz almost all of Mexico's oil and mineral rights went to American and British corporations," Haberman said. His curly black hair stuck straight out from his head. "Why don't you write an article about Mexico? Whenever Mexico tries to strengthen its economic democracy, her two greatest opponents are the United States and the Roman Catholic Church... ."

Agnes got up from the sofa and went to the coat closet.

"Where are you going?" Thorberg asked.

"For a walk."

"We planned to take the streetcar to the ocean," Thorberg said. "Don't you want to go with us?"

"No." Agnes despised Playland at the ocean end of Golden Gate Park. Haberman and Thorberg went there so they could mingle with what they called "the common man."

"I hate carnivals," said Agnes. She buttoned her coat. "And I don't like the common man."

Thorberg's fiance jumped to his feet, cocked for ideological struggle. "And why is that?"

"The common man is vulgar and cheap and ugly," retorted Agnes. "The common man wants quick thrills and silly prizes."

"And why are people vulgar and cheap and ugly? What makes them that way?"

Agnes thrust her hands into her pockets and stood at the door.

"The system!" he shouted in answer to his own question. "The system makes them that way!"

Agnes opened the door. "I'm a product of the system!" she shouted back. "I'm your common man!" Slamming the door behind her, she strode down Octavia and turned left on Ivy, a narrow street lined with small wooden homes. The windows had flower boxes and curtains. It was a domestic alley, clean and pleasant. For a moment Agnes wondered what it would be like to live in one of these nice little houses with a husband and children. Books. Maybe a piano. But she could not. There was too much she had to accomplish. She must not fail like Father or be trapped like Mother. She had to get an education. With an education she would know history and wouldn't make mistakes in her writing. She would know about Mexico and China. If she'd had enough money to finish four years at Tempe Normal, she would have known about the Manchus. She'd have known about Sun Yat-sen. She'd have known that the world is in turmoil, as Haberman said, struggling to take power and money from the rich in an effort to spread it around. She would have known what Haberman knew.

She wouldn't have gotten married, even to Ernest.

Agnes fished in her coat pocket and found paper and a stubby pencil. At the corner of Ivy and Gough she stopped to write a phrase. She stopped again at Franklin before circling back along Grove to Octavia where she re-entered the apartment, went straight to her room, threw her coat across the bed, and sat down again at the shaky table in the corner.

She wrote, struck out lines, wrote again, until, coming to a stopping place, she went out into the living room to show

Thorberg what she'd done. But Thorberg wasn't there. In the kitchen sink was another round of dirty dishes. Agnes laid her article on the table, washed the dishes, then sat down and read what she'd written.

"It is to be regretted that the yellow race are slowly absorbing some Western ideas. It is interesting, however, to note they are building up a nation of science, art, history, literature, and military power that, when it moves, it will move the world, and when it speaks, the world will listen and obey." She shifted on the kitchen chair, pleased.

"China was once a nation which used gunpowder for obtaining valuables in the earth, but has been taught a new use for it. She is a vast nation, compact, united, harmonious, arming silently and mechanically, after the white man's methods. With the shrewdness and intelligence of the diplomat"—she stumbled—"in the second birth of their progress, she is using not only Western ideas, but is also adding her own racial endowments—her accumulation—of failures and successes—to make her the most powerful and intelligent nation in the world."

Agnes doodled in the margin, then added: "Yet we consider the nation inferior when it gained a republican form of government without shedding blood, something which never occurred before in the history of the world."

She left the article on the table, returned to her room, and fell asleep with her coat over her. When she awoke it was dark.

"We've fixed you some dinner." Thorberg stood over her, stroking her hair. In one hand she held the article.

"What time is it?"

"Seven-thirty."

Agnes sat up. "Where's Robert?" she asked.

"At the Socialist Radical Club."

"How come you didn't go with him?"

Thorberg yawned. "I've had enough meetings for one week."

Agnes took her Chinatown article from Thorberg's hand.

"Don't show him this," she muttered.

"Robert gets excited," Thorberg said, and dismissed him with a wave of the hand. "The important thing is that you've written a very long essay that is quite good. I congratulate you." Some of Agnes' old warmth for Thorberg returned.

Thorberg sat down on the edge of the bed. "What are your plans, Agnes? Do you mind my asking?"

Agnes tensed. She herself didn't know what her plans were.

"You and Ernest are married now," Thorberg said.

Agnes pretended to be still considering her essay. Without looking up she said, "Do you and your fiancé"—she spit out the word—"want me to leave?"

"No, Agnes." Thorberg's hair under the orange-ish light of the ceiling fixture looked like spun gold. Her skin was ceramic-smooth, except for a tiny network of lines, delicate tracery, around the cool blue eyes. With one pale, graceful hand she smoothed a wrinkle in her skirt. "Your husband is lonely."

Agnes hated the word "husband." She missed Thorberg's radical opinions on the subject of marriage. Haberman had made her tame.

"Ernest's my friend."

"Don't you miss him?"

Agnes crossed her arms, fixed her eye on one square of the quilt that covered the bed, and evaded the question. "We both want to study and work and get ahead," she said.

"Do you want children?"

Agnes jumped to her feet and wedged herself between the foot of the bed and the straight chair in the corner. "I never want children." She half-threw her Chinatown article on the small table. "Ernest knew that when he married me!" But Thorberg, instead of leaving the room as Agnes had expected, remained where she was.

"There are ways to prevent childbirth now," she said in a low voice.

Agnes glared.

"Birth control," Thorberg continued. "Robert and I use birth control. We have more choice than our mothers had. There is no need for a woman to have children unless she wants them."

Agnes felt her face grow hot. She could not bear to talk of sex and pregnancy. She could not bear to think of Thorberg doing it with Haberman. She did not know the details of birth control; she did not want to know, and she did not want Thorberg, her fallen idealistic friend, to tell her. She didn't like her woman's body. She didn't want to know anything about it

"It is very easy to use a pessary," Thorberg said, and proceeded to explain as if Agnes had asked her how. "You insert it in"—even Thorberg hesitated. "You insert it in yourself, and then when—"

Agnes shoved her arms into the coat sleeves. "I don't need birth control," she stated, and stepped to the door.

"Where are you going?"

"Out."

"Please, Agnes." Thorberg ran her hand over her face. "I must talk to you."

Agnes kept hold of the doorknob. "Did Ernest ask you to talk to me?"

Thorberg nodded her head miserably.

"Why can't he speak for himself?"

"He's tried. He doesn't think you love him."

Agnes reached over to the chest of drawers, took out a clean handkerchief, and began to polish the doorknob.

"Can't you ever stop working?" cried Thorberg.

Agnes sank down on the edge of the bed.

"I don't want children," she whispered.

Thorberg turned sideways so that she could look directly at her sister-in-law. "Ernest wants a family," she said. "He loves you. He wants you for his wife and for the mother of his children."

"I told you, I'm not going to have children."

"And I told you," Thorberg said, flaring up, "that you can have sex without getting pregnant." A long silence hung between them.

"It's not just babies, is it?" Thorberg finally said. "You don't want sex."

Agnes turned her back on Thorberg. She reached out and grasped the bedpost. "I don't want children," she said. "I don't want sex."

"Then why did you marry?"

Agnes did not answer.

"Did you marry my brother to be near me?" A hard edge came into Thorberg's voice. "Or for money?"

Agnes stared hard at the bedpost. She had wanted to be near Thorberg. She had wanted some money. She did love both Ernest and Thorberg: they were her friends; they were more than friends; they were her family. She stood up, shaken.

"Because, temperamentally, the two of you are poorly matched." Thorberg's expression was icy.

"I can't explain it to you."

"Please try."

"You're from a different world," was all she could think to say. She felt sick.

Thorberg took hold of Agnes' arm. "Sit down," she said, and pulled her to the bed. "You're pale, Agnes. Sit down."

Agnes did as she was told. She sat down and then she lay down. She turned onto her side, away from Thorberg, and drew her legs up into a curled position. It was too much for her. She could not do all she needed to do. She could not vindicate her mother's and father's failed lives. She could not save her sister and brothers. She could not get an education. She could not write. She could not be a wife to Ernest. She could not be a mother. The only thing she could do was lie on the bed. She could not even keep her hot tears from wetting the quilt. Thorberg covered her with the coat and left the room. Agnes lay watching a full moon that hung so low in the sky it might be just above Van Ness Avenue. She fixed her gaze on its bright face. It was like being in Colorado and looking up into Aunt

Tillie's beauty.

The moon was not Mother's face. Mother's face was never the bright side of the moon.

Agnes lay calm and passive while the light struggled with the dark. She hung between weakness and strength. When the night sky began to give way to dawn, when the moon was a pale chip somewhere else in the sky and she could no longer see it, Agnes got out of bed. She folded her few clothes and put them in the carpetbag. She had dispelled something dark in herself. The bright side of the moon had won. She fixed breakfast and told Thorberg good-bye, then went to her boss on Market Street and said she had a family emergency and must leave the city. He paid her a portion of her wages. She telegraphed Ernest, withdrew her savings from the bank, and climbed onto a streetcar that carried her to the foot of Market Street. There she caught the ferry to Oakland and purchased a one-way train fare for El Centro where Ernest was working. Her life was no longer in San Francisco. She did not know where she belonged, but it wasn't with Thorberg and Haberman.

12
China 1937

"The Commander is not available today," said Lily Wu, approaching Agnes along the frozen terrace outside her cave. "He suggests you interview Kang Keqing instead."

Agnes looked out over the cold barrenness of Yan'an. It was the commander she wanted to talk to, not his wife. She and Lily Wu filed down the terrace, two bulky figures in layers of winter khaki, their breaths forming small clouds of steam as they walked,

"I haven't prepared any questions for her," Agnes said. So far the only question she had was an impolite one: why would an independent woman in the Red Army want to be married? She did not want to meet this wife; she was disappointed in Zhu De for marrying. But she must write about him as he was, not as she wished him to be. Evidently he liked marriage. He had been married several times. His previous wife, she knew, had been tortured, then beheaded by the Nationalists. Soon after, he had married Kang Keqing.

Agnes followed Lily Wu past make-shift classrooms of Kangta, Anti-Japanese Resistance University, to the women's dormitory where wives of the Red Army officers stayed. Most of the wives were suspicious of her. They didn't like the western dances she taught their husbands, they didn't like the Victrola and records she'd had shipped from America, and most of all, they didn't like her public statement that China could not abolish feudalism until marriage, the most feudalistic of all institutions, was abolished.

Kang Keqing greeted them at the entrance to the dormitory, formerly a Catholic church. She was a young peasant woman, much younger than her husband. Small, grave, muscular, she invited them inside and led them back to the kitchen where she poured tea out of a plain tin pot into mismatched cups. Her face was heart-shaped and her eyes were intelligent. She, too, wore winter khaki in the cold dormitory. She invited them to sit at a table by the window.

Agnes took out her notebook. "When did you marry your husband?" she asked in English. Lily Wu translated and Agnes wrote down the answers.

"I married my husband in 1929," Kang Keqing answered politely.

Her lips curve like a ribbon bow, Agnes wrote. "Do you see him often?"

Kang Keqing shook her head. Zhu De taught military students, she added. She herself attended political classes and organized women into the new Women's Associations. They were too busy to see each other often. "I was a young farm girl, a farm worker on a landlord's estate," she continued, "until I fought with the peasant army under Zhu De." She picked up a notebook, several sheets of paper stitched together with thread, lying at one end of the table.

"Do you read and write?" Agnes asked.

"Now that I am a cadet in the Anti-Japanese Resistance University, I read and write."

Kang Keqing looked at the column on the first page: "Number one, primitive communism," she began slowly, her voice growing stronger as she progressed down the list. "Number two, slave society. Three, feudal society. Four, capitalist society. Last, socialist society." She looked up from the sheet. "Yes, I can read."

Stages of social development, Agnes jotted down. "Did you make the Long March?"

"Yes, of course. It is our life." Faint sounds of troops drilling on the parade ground carried through the cold, bright air. Kang Keqing pointed to the pagoda looking down on them from the cliff. "The temple watches over us." Agnes' gaze followed Kang Kequing's to the ancient tower ringed with balconies, nine rough stone ridges. Privately Agnes disagreed. She thought the pagoda looked down without interest, as it had for centuries.

"Tell me about your husband," she said quietly.

Kang Keqing's eyes narrowed. Agnes was aware that this

woman—all the women at Yan'an—resented the time she spent with their husbands, socializing and talking politics. She'd been told by a friend of Zhu De's that Kang Keqing, especially, disliked her for interviewing her husband day after day. "The women are jealous and suspicious of you," he'd said. "And they don't like the sound of your typewriter when you're in your cave working."

"But I'm writing a book about her husband," Agnes had objected. "She's being petty. I refuse to acknowledge these wives' jealousy. I'm proof that men and women can be friends and comrades."

"He is a loyal man," Kang Keqing was saying, no longer looking at Agnes. "Much integrity. He is without political ambition." Seriously, methodically, Kang Keqing listed her husband's traits, It was as if she spoke of a distant figure she admired greatly. Agnes liked the woman's assessment of the man. "He submits to civilian authority. He is kind and even-tempered. He loves his troops and his troops love him."

"And children?" Agnes asked. "Do you want children?" In the margin of her notebook she wrote, "Why marry at all?" But the earlier fierceness had left her. Kang Keqing's words, Lily Wu's presence, the simple table where they sat, the temple on the cliff, all quieted her.

"I like babies as an institution," the young woman answered matter-of-factly, "but I don't want any myself. I have to keep fit for my work in the army."

"And why did you decide to marry?"

Kang Keqing looked at Agnes thoughtfully. After a long silence she answered. "I am a woman. My husband is a man."

Lily Wu spoke in Chinese, too fast for Agnes to understand clearly. Something about a mother, a grandmother.

"Is your mother living?"

Kang Keqing nodded vigorously and smiled for the first time. "Very old woman," she said with pride. Watching her face, Agnes suffered sharply. Her own mother was dead. The word she remembered still stung: malnutrition. But worse than grief was the *guilt tightly coiled inside her always ready to spring. She had not loved her mother enough. She had not helped her mother enough. She had not cared for her brothers and sister enough. Watching the pretty, unassuming face of Kang Keqing as she spoke of her husband, Agnes knew she had not loved Ernest Brundin enough. For all of her life, she thought, she had not loved enough or done enough.*

Late that night at the small table she reworked her notes from the day. "Kang Keqing and Zhu De were peasants," she wrote, "as strong and elemental as the soil that had given them birth .... She had clearly learned a great amount from him and had depended upon his guidance, yet there was about her the tremendous independence of the new revolutionary women of China. At the age of forty-three he had found a life companion, a woman able to accompany him and share every aspect of his life for better or for worse. What they meant to each other, neither said—they took each other for granted, as well-adjusted married people do. And marriage, in China, is taken for granted."

13
El Centro, California 1913

Seeing Ernest at the El Centro train station was like seeing a stranger. For most of the night she'd sat open-eyed, neither dreading nor looking forward to being reunited with him. Her deadened feelings had matched the monotony of the clicking wheels and swaying car. Yet once, in the middle of the night near Santa Barbara, her feelings had flared, like sparks from the locomotive wheels. Thorberg had violated her. What was the quiz about sex and birth control, the two subjects Agnes could least talk about, if not a violation? Ernest may have prompted his sister to ask Agnes about their marriage, but surely not to bring up pessaries, surely not to describe how she and her Rumanian practiced birth control.

She turned toward the window and stared into the darkness. It was Thorberg who had opened her eyes to a way of life she could never have imagined on her own. It was Thorberg who had mouthed the fine ideas about equality for all people through socialism and the education of women. Yet Thorberg was allying herself with her brother. Thorberg wanted her to have sex with Ernest, have his children, make him happy. And Agnes didn't know how. Furthermore, she didn't want to know how. She didn't want to end up drained, dependent, mired in marriage and motherhood.

She shouldn't have gotten married. Ernest was a very good man, but she shouldn't have gotten married.

It was a relief to leave San Francisco, that wet, pasty place where she'd been forced to listen to Haberman and ended up doing the housework for beautiful, langorous Thorberg. It was a relief to return to the dry Southwest. She was, she realized, a Colorado, New Mexico, Texas, Arizona kind of person. Hard, dry, honest land suited her. She looked forward to El Centro and tried not to think about the marital bed waiting for her in the desert.

The train leaned into a curve. Agnes returned to the monotony of the train's movement; to the relief of no thought, no feeling.

She saw him as soon as she stepped down from the train. The straw hat didn't suit him. His face was tan again, the way it had been in Arizona, but when he gave Agnes a hug, their bodies felt large and sluggish in the heat and she pulled away. But she liked the automobile he'd borrowed for the occasion. It rolled over the wooden main street with a rhythmic "thunk" at each plank.

Ernest parked the car in front of the El Centro Restaurant. Agnes stepped up onto the boardwalk. Wiping her face and neck with a handkerchief, she looked around at stores with false fronts and unfinished frame buildings crowding the main street and unpaved side streets.

"Looks like a boom town," she said.

Ernest held the door for her. "They build around the clock. Houses for canal workers and hotels for the speculators."

Agnes preceded him into the restaurant. The din of horse-clopping, of wagon-wheel and automobile-tire bumping, subsided. Ernest hung his hat on the hat tree by the window and they sat at a table under the ceiling fan. Agnes set a white box on the table beside the salt and pepper shakers.

"Thorberg sent you this."

Ernest eyed the pale blue ribbon but made no move to open it.

"Don't you want to know what's inside?"

He opened the box of cookies and offered one to Agnes.

"She made them on quick notice. The kind your mother makes. Swedish cookies."

Ernest nodded and closed the box. "I'm glad you're here,"

he said in his plain and accurate way. Agnes tried to reacquaint herself with the voice and the man. "I've missed you."

Embarrassed, she reached for a menu lying on the corner of the table. "You didn't come back and visit much."

"It costs money," he said. "And I wanted you to come here."

Agnes ordered fried chicken and mashed potatoes. "Where are you staying?"

"At the canal site. I've rented a room for you at a boarding house in town."

No matter where they were—here, Octavia Street, Timbuktoo—sleeping arrangements was the question between them. The waitress passed their table with three plates of fried chicken lined up along one arm. The dinners looked greasy. Agnes had been hungry when she ordered, but now she didn't feel like eating. The fan above them squeaked at each revolution.

"You're out in the sun a lot."

"Can't avoid it on the canal." The deep blue eyes were steady and still. "Why did you decide to come?"

"We're married, aren't we? I don't belong with Thorberg and Haberman."

"Haberman got on your nerves, I bet," Ernest said. His slight Swedish accent colored the Americanism.

Agnes ran her fingers through her hair, squinted, and exclaimed in Rumanian-English, "Ze system! Vee got to tchange ze system!" She clowned until Ernest loosened up and laughed, but then she didn't know how to wind down without exposing them both to awkward silence. It was a relief when the door opened and three East Indians in white turbans entered the restaurant. Agnes' Rumanian-English faded as she watched the tallest of the three move into the lunchroom, cautious and threatening at the same time. The restaurant owner, a heavy man with a soiled dishcloth tied around his waist, came out from behind the counter where he'd been keeping an eye on both the cook and the cash register.

The Indian glanced toward the back of the restaurant.

Aiming for the first seat at the lunch counter, he moved without hurry, like a river. Like the Ganges, Agnes thought, proud of knowing the river's name. When he reached the cash register, the owner moved his feet apart, leaned forward, and slowly rotated his shoulders as if to activate a fighting instrument that hadn't been used in a while.

"Get out," he said. The other two Indians stepped forward, not to fight, but to talk to their friend. After a few minutes of nervous persuasion, the tall Indian allowed himself to be led away and the three stepped out into the hot sun again. The restaurant door closed behind them.

"Hindoos!" the owner snorted. He tied the dishtowel tighter around his waist. "Rag heads!" The diners turned back to their plates.

"Actually," Ernest said to Agnes, "they're not Hindus. They're Sikhs."

"He didn't have a right to turn them away!" Agnes said, her face flushed. "They weren't hurting anyone!" He touched her arm to quiet her but she jumped to her feet. "I won't eat my lunch here!"

Ernest looked around at the other diners who were watching. His face brightened with embarrassment.

"Cancel the chicken!" Agnes flung over her shoulder as she marched past the owner. "If you don't serve Indians, you don't serve me."

Ernest picked up the cookie box and followed. Outside on the boardwalk she stood with her head high, arms akimbo. Her ankle-length cotton dress was limp from the heat. Her short hair had lost its curl. But she looked up at Ernest with triumph in her blue-gray eyes. "We showed them!" she exclaimed.

They began walking. Ernest took the planking in long, silent strides, but Agnes' boot heels shook the two-by-fours.

"Let's go out to the canal," she said abruptly.

But Ernest didn't want to go to the canal. "We'll drive into the desert later, when it cools down," he said. At the car he knew better than to walk around and open Agnes' door for her. He seated himself behind the wheel. "Don't you want lunch?"

"We can eat Thorberg's cookies," she said. She opened the box and ate freely as Ernest drove. He turned a corner and pulled up in front of a rambling, two-story wood house. Carpenters were framing an added-on wing in back, and their hammer blows pierced the dry, hot air.

"On the train ride down, I saw lots of Indians working in the fields," Agnes said. She closed the cookie box but made no move to see her new home.

"They come from the north of India," said Ernest, absently adjusting the rear-view mirror. "They pick cotton and cantaloupe. Some of them own their own farms. They live communally and share their wages."

"Where?"

"In encampments out in the fields. They leave their wives and children back in India until they're established."

Agnes thought of the miners in Colorado who didn't have a union and didn't share wages. She thought of Mother and herself and her sister and brothers following Father from one mining camp to another. She would have told Ernest about the camps, but he was already out of the car. Besides, shame and anger silenced her. The Brundins and that idiot Haberman would be surprised if they knew how primitive she'd grown up.

She opened the passenger door, hesitated, then followed Ernest toward the front entrance. He carried her carpetbag for her. Her mind was on other things: on turbaned Indians, on Colorado coal camps, on the boarding house bedroom ahead of her.

The landlady who answered the door introduced herself as Mrs. McCutcheon. She had a Scottish name, she said, because her husband was Scottish. She herself was Irish, as they might guess from her red hair.

"I wouldn't have guessed it," Agnes said. "It's not very red."

"Oh, it's red all right," she insisted. "Isn't it ironic," Mrs.

McCutcheon continued, folding her hands over her soft stomach, "that with my fair skin I should end up in the desert with the sun beating down on me mercilessly. That's what Mr. McCutcheon says. 'It's ironic, Margaret,' he says, 'that with your fair skin …'" She brushed away the end of the sentence with a gesture of her white, plump hand and picked up a ledger book from the hall table. "Let's see. Mr. and Mrs. Brundin. You're paid up to the end of the month." She looked at Agnes. "We have high standards here."

Agnes looked back, level-eyed.

"Second floor, west end."

Mrs. McCutcheon didn't fool Agnes. Under all the talk about high standards was a woman who'd fought her way up from a poor family and landed in a boarding house. Agnes intended to land higher. Ernest was a finer man by far, she was willing to bet, than Mr. McCutcheon. Ernest was a finer man than most. Agnes knew that. But she must not depend on it. She must rise on her own. She must never be stuck like Mrs. McCutcheon, running a boarding house and quoting her husband.

The bedroom on the second floor at the end of the hall was the same size as the bedroom she'd left behind in San Francisco. Even the furniture looked the same: a bed, a gate-legged table in the corner, one straight chair, and one bureau.

She dropped her carpetbag onto the bed. "It's awful hot," she said. Ernest opened the transom above the door and crossed the room in four steps to lift the window higher. He sat down on the sill while Agnes took a blouse and skirt from her bag.

"I need to wash up," she said, self-conscious. The bathroom was all the way down the hall, on the right near the stairs. It wasn't half as nice as Tillie's bathroom in Denver. There wasn't any window and there wasn't any air. The light bulb above the sink gave her face a pasty look. She washed under her arms with soap and held her face under the faucet. But when she was finished she felt just as sticky as she had before the wash. In fact, she felt worse.

Maybe it was the train trip, or all those cookies she'd eaten. As she walked toward her room, the end of the hall seemed to recede. She grew short of breath and began to sweat. She might as well not have washed at all.

Pushing open the door to the room, she saw Ernest stretched out on the bed, her bed, in her rented room, paid for, she had to admit, by him. When she saw him there, she could scarcely have said his name or her name or where she was. A strangeness overtook her. She'd come to the wrong room. She belonged somewhere else but couldn't remember where. Mechanically she gathered up her clean blouse and skirt and started out to the bathroom again.

"You can change in here," Ernest said, his eyes still closed. He turned toward the wall. "After all, I have a sister."

Agnes stood where she was, struck dumb with disgust and dread. She could not possibly undress with him in the room. She lowered her arms until the clean skirt and blouse she held dragged on the floor. She stared at Ernest's back. It was long and slender and came to a V at the waist. His shirt had pulled out above his belt when he turned over. Always so well dressed, he now looked disheveled. His collar was rumpled, and there was a sweat stain that spread from under his arm into a wide semi-circle. The back of his neck glistened and she could hear his breathing. He looked so solidly present. To undress in this room with Ernest on the bed, even if he had turned to the wall, was unthinkable.

Her blood rushed in her ears when it dawned on her that undressing here, now, was much easier than what she would have to do later. She turned her back on him. Trembling, she unbuttoned her dress. Tears of humiliation dropped onto her chest and ran down between her breasts. She was surprised at how hot tears are. She stepped into the closet and tried to close the door, but the closet was shallow and the door wouldn't close with her in it. She heard the bedsprings creak.

Throwing herself around the closet door, hiding between it

and the wall, Agnes removed one arm from its soiled sleeve and quickly drew the clean blouse over her shoulder. She repeated the movement with the other arm and buttoned up the clean blouse. The bodice of her soiled dress hung down over her hips.

"Agnes?" Ernest said. The bed springs creaked again. Crying out loud now, unable to stop herself, she stepped into the clean skirt, pulled it up under the low-riding dress, buttoned up the placket by feel, and dropped the old dress in a heap around her feet. She leaned against the wall behind the closet door and slid to the floor.

"Agnes!" Ernest got off the bed. In his stockinged feet he crossed to the closet door and closed it, then crouched down in front of her and touched her hair. She seemed not to know he was there.

"Agnes. Agnes. You musn't. There's nothing to be afraid of." She quieted. "There's nothing to be afraid of," he repeated. But his face showed strain as he removed the soiled dress from around her ankles, folded it, and dabbed at her tears with the hem of the skirt. Then he sat down on the floor beside her, leaned his back against the wall, and put one arm around her. He cradled her head on his chest and rested his own against the flowered wallpaper. Much later he stood and asked her to stand with him. She complied, wiping her face and hugging the soiled dress to herself as Ernest guided her to the bed.

She lay on top of the spread and he removed her shoes. "Rest," he said. He pulled the window shades down. Through swollen eyes Agnes watched him grasp the stiffened edge of the shade and draw it up, down, up until the tension on the roller allowed it to stay.

It was late afternoon. The desert was beginning to cool. Light through the paper shades was pink now instead of yellow. Ernest came around the bed and lay down carefully beside her.

"I don't know how to be married," Agnes said in a flat voice. Ernest turned toward her. He started to pull back the spread.

"Don't," she said.

"Just for a pillow," he offered. But he gave up the attempt. Agnes wadded the dirty striped dress and put it under her head. It seemed to her that she was floating above the boarding house, watching herself and a man try to do something difficult. Beside her, Ernest's breathing was uneasy. He rubbed his eyes with the thumb and forefinger of one hand. Rubbing his eyes made him seem normal again. She struggled to hold onto the Ernest she knew, the quiet, gallant escort, the fellow worker. She tried to calm herself by picturing a young man and young woman working late, studying, making plans. She saw the woman marching at the head of some parade, she didn't know what or where. The man walked beside her and a little behind. Farther back a brass band matched their stride, and behind the band marched an army of people, all working for the same thing—she couldn't tell what—and moving to the beat.

That was what she wanted. Work. Parades. Music. Marching together. She did not want a double bed. She did not want the darkness of babies growing inside her; of putting things in herself so babies wouldn't grow inside her. She didn't want anything inside her; she would not be invaded; she would never be penetrated the way Mother was penetrated by Father.

She realized with alarm that Ernest was crying. He wasn't crying out loud. It was his moist, congested breathing that gave him away.

"Ernest?"

He turned his face full toward her, unashamed of his misery. Agnes touched his cheek and came away with a shiny finger. It stunned her that a man should cry.

"Ernest," she said. Looking into his eyes, she saw her own fright mirrored. He kissed her on the lips. She kissed him back at first, until his tongue was inside her mouth. She tried to draw away, but this time he insisted, and this time she could not control him. She leaned into him once and felt, for a wisp of a moment, the receptive power of being a woman to a man's thrust.

At the verge of enjoying his body near hers—for he was very close to her now, over on her side of the bed, all around her, his breathing heavy—she pulled back, terrified of losing herself. His tears stopped and a drama began. She had a part to play, a part that was necessary, essential, and she could not play it. He didn't bother to talk to her now or soothe her.

Once she whispered, "Ernest," into his hair while he kissed her neck and started to move down toward her throat, but he seemed not to hear her. He was shaking, she was shaking, and she wanted nothing more than to jump up from the bed and run to—to somewhere she could not remember well. She was ashamed as Ernest touched her blouse and fumbled at her breast. He tried to kiss her there. Horrified, she understood what it meant to nurse a baby. She tried to squirm to one side, out of his range, yet still not leave the bed altogether. Because, crying, moaning in terror and humiliation, she somehow must do what women do. After all, Aunt Tilly did it every day for money. Agnes felt a rush of pity for Tillie, for Mother, for her sister Nellie who had died in childbirth.

Then there was no time to think. She clamped her jaws together as Ernest, usually so refined, so modest, so gentle, disregarded polite behavior and began to take his trousers off in daylight. She struggled up on her elbows and began scrabbling motions to get under the bedclothes.

"Loosen the covers," she managed to say. Red-faced, they both peeled back the bedspread, thin blanket and sheet, bumping heads. Ernest drew his legs up. They were hairy and sinewy. Above his thighs, his pelvis had a much different look than her own. Her eye followed the rope-like muscle and bone around and down, down to an alarming mass of dark hair and a large, rigid organ which he tried to cover with the sheet, but which seemed to have a life of its own and rose up under the bedclothes. She could not imagine anything so unlike her little brothers' harmless bodies. This organ was so conspicuous, the dark hair ruffling all about it, and under it more organs and meaty tissue, that it looked as if it should be inside his body instead of out.

Ernest pressed against her and she felt the hardness of the swollen organ, and her mind went blank until Ernest's awkward jabbing between her legs turned into piercing, shrieking pain and she, like the pain, was shrieking. Ernest threw himself off her, covered her mouth with a sticky hand that smelled like bleach, and said he was sorry. He rolled onto his back and pulled his trousers up, bracing himself on his heels. Half-dressed, he lay beside her, then turned and sat up on the edge of the bed, his head in his hands.

Agnes lay under the sheet with her eyes closed. Something warm and liquid was spreading along her inner thighs. She was afraid she had wet the bed. Her bottom was a dark cavern filled with pain. She had been mauled. The mattress moved. When she opened her eyes, the man standing with one hand on the bedpost didn't seem familiar to her. She had married someone she didn't know. Beneath his trousers was undreamed of danger. She felt sick to her stomach. She sat up on the edge of the bed, then moved to the door and down the hall to the bathroom where she vomited. She dared not empty her bladder; her female parts were so raw that urine must not sting them. There was nothing to do but return to the room. She stayed close to the wall, for she needed something to steady her. When she re-entered the room Ernest was standing by the bed, his face white, while there on the sheet was a circle of blood. Agnes forgot about him and lifted her skirt to her waist. She bent down and saw that her drawers were stained, her thighs red and smeared.

She tried to call out, but no one heard.

She woke in the bed. The landlady sat on a straight chair beside her. Ernest stood at the window as if he were looking out, except that the shades were still drawn. The room, immobilized in dying light, floated and Agnes floated with it.

14
San Diego 1913

Ernest got off the streetcar at El Cajon and Normal, the car stop Agnes said was near her house. Even after his train ride from El Centro had ended, he felt as if he were still swerving, going upgrade and downgrade on a narrow pair of rails. Two blocks beyond the San Diego Normal, he stopped in front of a white frame bungalow, set his grip on the sidewalk, and took a slip of paper from his wallet. He studied the street number, replaced the wallet in his back pocket, and climbed the steps to the porch. The paint was peeling, and the windows needed putty. He peered into the front room. One sofa and one straight chair. The porch, with its pots of red geraniums, looked more livable than the room inside.

He knocked twice. No answer. He walked around the side of the house, a strip of stubby grass that no one watered. In back was a screened-in porch. Only when he saw the large garden was he sure this was the place: row upon row of lettuce and green onions, cauliflower, tomato plants tied up on stakes, squash with its trailing leaves. Agnes had written him about her vegetables. He sat down on the back porch steps to light a cigarette.

Full-time student. Full-time gardener. Part-time wife.

Down the block, children played through the last weeks of summer. For them, being promoted to the next grade was just another step in an endless childhood. He smoked thoughtfully. The flame threatened to go out once. It was a doubtful cigarette, a doubtful smoke, and it tasted bitter. In any case, to use his sister's expression, he was here. Thorberg had tried to dissuade him. She was angry with him for buying Agnes' train ticket to San Diego, paying her enrollment fees at the Normal, renting this house. She was angry with Agnes. "She'll leave you again and again, Ernest. Listen to me. She is not going to be anyone's wife."

Ernest ground the cigarette under his heel and replayed scenes from El Centro in his mind, as he did most days

"Don't call me Mrs. Brundin!" Agnes had shouted once to the landlady. "My name is Ayahoo Smedley!"

When Mrs. McCutcheon had telegraphed him at the canal site in the desert to come at once, his wife was ill, he'd borrowed a car and driven to El Centro in the cool darkness of the night, though he felt as hot as if the sun were beating down on him.

"She's been trying to get rid of her baby," Mrs. McCutcheon said when he'd arrived. He hadn't known anything about a baby.

"Has she seen a doctor?"

The landlady nodded. "But he won't abort her unless it's a medical emergency."

Ernest started toward the stairs.

"She tried to kill herself in the bathtub," Mrs. McCutcheon said, panting slightly. "I heard a lot of splashing and I ran upstairs." Her faded eyes came alive, glowed, and she whispered as one whispers about mortal sin. "She said she hated herself and she hated the child. She's taken poison this time. I called the doctor—"

Ernest shifted position on the porch steps and lit another cigarette. From near Agnes' garden a mourning dove called. He looked at his pocket watch. Three o'clock. He didn't know what time to expect her. She, for that matter, wasn't expecting him at all, as he hadn't told her he was coming. But she was his wife and he was paying the rent. Whether she wanted him or not, he belonged here. Thorberg's voice haunted him, cool and reproachful. "She left you, Ernest. She left you. She will always leave you."

In any case, Thorberg, I'm here. I've come off the canal project with money in my pocket. I've made my decision. I'll make a life in San Diego.

He stood, his long, lean body brown and hard from more than a year of work in the desert. He dropped his half-smoked cigarette in the burn can and returned to the front yard where he sat down under a eucalyptus that shaded the house. Leaning back against the white bark, he stretched his legs out in front of him and ran a hand through his light brown hair, high and wavy on top and parted in the middle. This might be his last quiet moment for a while; when Agnes got home it wouldn't be quiet anymore. That was one reason he was here, he supposed: life without Agnes was too quiet.

"She will never enjoy sexual intercourse," the Mexican doctor in El Centro had said. Ernest perfectly remembered the small, white moustache riding the dapper, nut-brown man's upper lip. The abortion had cost $100. Afterwards, in the doctor's back room, Agnes had cried hysterically, thrashing her head from side to side until he was afraid she would roll off the table. He'd tried to comfort her. He'd held her firmly and talked to her. But apparently he'd smiled once—he cursed himself, how could he have smiled?—because she yelled at him not to smile when she'd nearly died. A man has no idea of the danger a woman passes through just because she's a woman, she'd screamed at him. She would pay for the abortion herself. No man would buy her body.

Yet, Ernest thought, sifting the mulch of dead eucalyptus leaves through his long fingers, she let him pay for her school and train trip to San Diego, not to mention the rent. Her savings from secretarial work paid the doctor.

"You'll have to come to San Diego if you want to stay married to me," she'd said. So here he was in San Diego. The doctor in El Centro had smelled of hair oil as he leaned close to Ernest and said, "Some women are not made to be wives and mothers."

But the doctor was wrong. Time and love was what Agnes needed. Only Ernest knew the self-doubt she carried at her core, only he understood her bright cover of bravado. He would give her confidence. She would come to love him as he loved her.

A woman passed by on the sidewalk. She looked once at Ernest leaning against the tree, then walked on without speaking.

When Agnes still hadn't returned by four o'clock, he set off in a northerly direction until, to his surprise, he stood at the edge of a cliff overlooking mud flats far below. He couldn't see the ocean to the west, but he could smell salt and seaweed. It was unexpected, this abrupt ending of the neighborhood. He followed the rim of the bay for several city blocks, then turned back toward the bungalow.

She was outside on the porch with her back to him, washing the front window.

"Agnes?"

She wrung the rag out into a pail of water. "Hi," she managed to say offhandedly, but he could tell she was shocked. Color came to her face, perhaps because she was bent over the pail. Such a pretty woman, he thought. Such frank, receptive, wide-set eyes. In spite of her flinty spirit, she looked soft and feminine. He was just getting ready to tell her how beautiful she was, how much he'd missed her, when she said,

"They've made me supervisor of beginning typing, and secretary to the faculty." She stared at Ernest, then grinned. "They pay me to edit the alumni news. I'll be able to bring Myrtle out from Oklahoma pretty soon and pay you back for my ticket and the rent."

"You don't have to pay me back," Ernest said. "You're my wife." He watched Agnes wash the same window twice. *I've missed you,* he was getting ready to say. *Have you missed me?*

"Come see the garden," she said. She dropped the rag into the bucket and reached for his hand.

"I've seen it," he said. "It's a fine garden." But she pulled him through the side yard, her hand still wet, until they were standing at the back steps. She eyed the rows critically. "I planted late. Still, everything came up. You can take some tomatoes and peppers back with you."

"I'm not going back."

"You quit the canal?"

"I quit." He patted his back pocket. "I've saved money."

"I get paid every two weeks," she stated. A breeze came up carrying dampness from the ocean, lifting the curls from her forehead. Ernest touched her hair. He kissed her. For a moment she leaned against him, but then, as if aware for the first time that her hand was still wet, made a point of drying it on her skirt.

"There's a student recital tonight at the school," she said. "Do you want to come with me?"

"All right," he said.

They went to the concert and listened to three violinists, four pianists, and a tuba player.

"Come and meet some of the professors," Agnes said. Her folding wooden chair clattered to the floor as she jumped to her feet. Ernest set it right again. She took his hand and pulled him through the crowd. He noticed that people liked her bright expression and smile; that they, too, were uplifted by her quickness and enthusiasm.

At the reception she introduced him over and over again as "my husband."

In the bungalow that night she talked and talked, perched on the edge of the broken-down sofa in the living room. Later, drinking tea at the kitchen table, she still talked.

"When I went to Tempe Normal I was afraid of everything. Now it's different. Schoolwork doesn't scare me anymore. I've signed up to audition for a play. Shakespeare!" Her laugh was part hoot, part music. "Me in a Shakespeare play!"

"You'll be good," Ernest said. He'd seen her exaggerate, heard her build on a story until it was far more interesting than the actual occurrence.

"My father was a natural actor," she said. "He told wonderful stories. Mother always accused him of lying. Accused me, too." She stopped talking and lit a cigarette. "And you know what?" She shook out the match. "She was right. Father did lie, and so do I." She dropped the match in the ashtray. She looked forlorn.

"Wait here," Ernest said, not wanting to know about the lies. He brought his grip in from the porch and set it on the kitchen floor where it made both of them nervous. Agnes jumped up from the table and refilled the teakettle at the sink, not looking as he unstrapped the grip and felt around the edges of shirts, socks, and underwear. He found the bottle of wine and held it out to her.

"To celebrate," he said.

"Celebrate what?"

"Being together again."

Agnes took the bottle, set it on the table between them, and turned off the flame under the teakettle. "I guess I'll try some," she said. "I'm not much of a drinker. My father drank for all of us."

"Sit down, Agnes," he said. She took the other chair without speaking while he filled water glasses with red wine. He'd made up his mind. After months of being confused, he knew what to say and what to do. "I've come to live here."

She looked at him over the rim of her glass. "I know," she said, and took a swallow.

"I want to sleep beside you," he said. He felt steady now. The bedroom down the hall seemed to Ernest as real as a person. "But I won't touch you until you're ready."

Agnes lifted her glass and studied the color of the wine against the hanging light bulb. "I will never have a child," she said. "And I will never have another abortion." She set the glass down hard and picked up her cigarette.

"Never," agreed Ernest. He lit a cigarette of his own and blew the smoke toward the dingy ceiling. "I am very sorry about what happened in El Centro."

"I'm moving to a boarding house," she said. She tapped her cigarette against the ashtray. "A house is too expensive. I can wait tables for my meals."

Ernest straightened. "I'm paying the rent," he said. "Didn't you hear me? I've come here to live. We need a house. I don't want to live in one room and eat with a bunch of boarders."

"Even before you came I'd decided to move to a boarding house."

"Then why didn't you just move to a boarding house in the first place?" he snapped. Agnes said nothing. "That was when you thought you might still need me," he said quietly.

She ground out her cigarette. "I don't have time to be married right now."

Under the bare bulb she looked older than Ernest remembered. He laughed bitterly. "Whether you like it or not, you *are* married. Anyway, people don't marry or not marry because they have enough time."

He stood up from the table and walked to the front of the house. From the porch he had a good view of the moon. It was neither full nor new, sickle nor wedge. It was misshapen, spongy, and it was the first time in his life he hadn't thought it beautiful.

He returned to the kitchen. Agnes still sat at the table, drinking.

"I came here to live," he said. "This is where I belong."

She put down her glass and looked him in the eye. "I have a lot of work to do. I can't be cooking and cleaning."

"You don't have to cook and clean."

"Good! Because I don't intend to!" She left for the back of the house. Ernest followed. Without an invitation he found the bedroom and lay down on the bed, careful to keep his shoes off the spread. She turned out the light and he heard her undressing. She seemed to have lost her fear. A triumphant sense of having done the right thing began to warm him again. The mattress shifted as she pulled back the cover and slipped into her side of the bed. They lay without moving.

"What will you do if you live in San Diego?" she asked after a while.

"Look for a job."

"There's a filling station for sale on El Cajon Boulevard."

"I've never worked in a filling station."

"You could buy the station and hire somebody else to work the pump."

He considered the statement in light of Thorberg's and, to a certain extent, his own politics. "But that's capitalism."

Agnes laughed. He reached for her hand. While the shadows of the eucalyptus in the front yard wavered on the window shade, he slipped his arm under her head and urged her to face him. She hesitated, then turned beneath the covers. They lay that way for long minutes. She touched his shoulder. He took it as a sign and kissed her on the mouth, but it was too much. She gave a phony yawn, turned away, and imitated sleep.

Somewhere in the neighborhood a cat began to moan. The moan turned into a wail, edged with lust, absurdly human. Ernest could hardly bear to listen. He wondered how many weeks, months, years he would have to lie beside his wife without touching her.

His arm under Agnes' head had gone to sleep. His belt bound him. Even the elastic of his socks constricted. He got up and went into the bathroom. The bridegroom in his chamber, he thought. Satire at least prevented him from seeing how pathetic he was. Despising himself, he relieved his obstructed passion. Then he walked into the dark living room where he took off his shoes and padded to the window, his eyes damp from humiliation and anger.

Agnes was not the only actor in the house. He, himself, had play-acted well. He'd actually believed he could be married without sex. Now he knew he couldn't. Thorberg was right: this marriage had been a mistake. He cursed himself for his stupidity, for his fully dressed state in the middle of the night. Cursed himself for purchasing a one-way ticket to San Diego. He lay down on the sofa to wait for daylight. The ugly, lop-sided moon shone in through the window that Agnes had washed twice.

15
Fresno, California 1916

Ernest laid down the letter-opener and pulled out a single sheet. Agnes had started off in shorthand, scratched out the strokes, and started over.

"Dear Ernest, I'm arriving by train this week. I'm not sure when. I'll wait on your steps. Something terrible has happened. I've been fired from teaching at San Diego Normal. President Hardy found out that I am a Socialist. Agnes."

She arrived two days later, pale and nervous, her eyes red from weeping. She had not slept since Monday, she said, when President Hardy found her lost purse on the steps of the administration building, looked inside for a name, and found her pink Socialist card.

She stood in the middle of Ernest's rented room, her valise at her feet, and began to cry. "He called me into his office. He said they couldn't have a Socialist on the faculty." Ernest led her to his single bed where she perched on the edge and rocked back and forth as if she had a massive stomach ache. He sat down beside her and did not know how to comfort her.

"What will I do? I have no place to go! No job!"

"What about Myrtle?"

Through her tears, Agnes' face lightened. She'd brought Myrtle to San Diego and enrolled her in the normal school. It was the one bright spot in her general hopelessness. "Myrtle has a scholarship. She's in the dormitory now. She's going to be a teacher." But darkness put out the light. "People think there's political freedom in America," she muttered.

They went to bed that night without question, without awkwardness. Agnes let him make love to her and came close to responding. But he knew the difference now. A woman in

Fresno had taught him to know the difference. He felt a pull on the taut line between this other woman and himself. With her he wasn't left to throw out the line and then, alone, try to haul it in. At last he understood that Agnes held her sexuality in contempt and, in one form or another, would wage war against it all her life.

"Ernest," she said, "I want to be married now. I want to stay here. I can find a job in Fresno." She stroked his hair and his face. She reached for his hand. It struck him as strange and unfair that at the instant she wanted him, he no longer wanted her. It struck him as odd and remarkable and perfectly true that he should now know this and be able at last to say, "I will always love you. But we will never be happy together."

He said no more. Later they would get the divorce he wanted. He held her through the night as she cried, dozed, and cried again. But this time the blackness of night in their bedroom was not so deep, not so empty as it had always seemed to him. Now he felt himself drawn toward a faint light, a light of his own. Outside of his will, he felt himself moving away from Agnes.

16

Brooklyn 1917

Agnes could see the family resemblance in Mrs. Brundin's slender, bony nose and blue eyes. But the woman in the doorway untying her apron was only slightly taller than Agnes and had a stocky solidity about her. Mrs. Brundin picked up the valise and Agnes stepped into the house where Ernest and Thorberg had grown up.

"Thorberg said you'd be here sometime today. We've been expecting you." In her speech Agnes heard the Swedish inflection that she'd grown so accustomed to over the past four years. She was led into the parlor and introduced to the man who had been her father-in-law. Here was the height and slimness of his children, the blond hair and cool temperament. Mr. Brundin nodded once and said nothing.

"Thorberg will be here soon," said Mrs. Brundin, filling in her husband's silence. "She is eager to see you."

"I want to see Thorberg." Agnes' words sounded rough. Too strong and direct for this quiet house. Without looking at her, Mr. Brundin picked up the valise and carried it upstairs ahead of her.

"Thorberg will be here soon," Mrs. Brundin repeated when Agnes returned from changing her dress in the guest room.

"Where is she?"

"Greenwich Village."

Agnes sat down beside a small table that held cups and saucers and a plate of cookies.

"I thought you might be hungry." Mrs. Brundin poured coffee and offered cream and sugar, then settled into her chair where she fell silent and abstracted. Mr. Brundin's shifting weight on the floorboards above their heads made an uneasy background to the silence.

"Thorberg makes these cookies," Agnes said. "Swedish cookies." It was meant to be a compliment but didn't sound right as spoken.

"Did you have a pleasant trip?"

"I sat up for six nights."

It should have been a fine trip, seeing America sweep by, but the land had been hard and cold with snow, and she'd felt hard and cold, herself. Coffee and Swedish cookies could not warm her, not when her marriage to this woman's son had finally ended. Not when she'd been fired from her teaching job.

"Did you change trains?"

"I got off in Colorado and Ohio," Agnes answered. "And I changed in Chicago."

"That must have been restful."

Agnes snapped a cookie in two with her front teeth. Mrs. Brundin had no idea—no more than Ernest and Thorberg—how it is to stop in a mining town and see your father demented by alcohol and your ragged brothers who have worked since they were eight. No idea what it is to turn your back on them a second time.

The space between Colorado and Ohio had passed in a blur of sleeplessness and self-loathing.

"Did you have time to go sight-seeing?" Mrs. Brundin asked. Agnes shook her head.

She'd gotten off the train in Toledo to look up the pen pal whose handwriting she had copied in the schoolhouse on the mesa. He'd met her at the depot. Alighting from the train, she passed a short, fat man who stood behind the baggage cart. While she was searching for her educated, dashing pen pal, this little man came out from the shadows. He held onto the cart handle and introduced himself. It was another disappointment in a string of disappointments. After a cup of stale coffee over which he talked mostly about his mother and his Sunday School class, she thanked him for the books he'd sent her seven years earlier, said good-bye, and waited all night in the depot for the next train.

"Thorberg should be here soon."

Mrs. Brundin didn't ask her about Ernest. She probably didn't understand this marriage that was not a marriage, and Agnes had no explanations and no blame. She'd lost him. She hadn't wanted a husband, she admitted to herself. Today, however, she did. And she wanted a sister, but she was no longer confused about whose sister Thorberg was.

When they were younger, when the clear air and bright sunlight of Arizona had drawn them together and she'd followed—who had she followed? Ernest or Thorberg?— to California, she thought she had a sister for life. But she had no sister, no brother, no father and no mother, no husband, no pen pal: No one but herself. She popped the rest of the cookie into her mouth.

"I hope you'll be comfortable here," Mrs. Brundin said as she began to clear away the cups and saucers.

"Yes, ma'am." Agnes took the tray from Mrs. Brundin and carried it into the kitchen.

"Where's your soap?" she asked, and when Mrs. Brundin showed her, she began to wash the cups and saucers and went on to clean a pan that had been left to soak. She dried the last saucer and turned to hang up the tea towel. In the doorway stood Thorberg, tall, golden, a little older now, but Thorberg. Agnes dropped the towel and ran across the room.

"Thor!" Tears broke the ice floe behind her eyes. She hugged Thorberg and cried against her shoulder, oblivious to Mrs. Brundin. "I've been fired from my job!" She pulled back to let Thorberg see her misery and sank onto a kitchen chair. Thorberg poured herself a cup of coffee from the pot on the stove.

"It was my Socialist card!" Agnes wailed. In a broken narrative she described study groups led by the only Marxist lawyer in San Diego—"I don't even understand Marx!"—and dreary Socialist dances in a cramped little room over a pool hall with earnest single-taxers who stepped on her feet and talked interminably about a classless society.

"But you *are* a Socialist, aren't you?" Thorberg said. "I've told all my friends about you."

"I'm a Socialist, all right, but I don't like meetings. I'm for the poor!" She brightened momentarily. "I do like speeches! Emma Goldman ... ."

"Emma Goldman is an anarchist," Thorberg corrected her. "What do you mean, 'It was my Socialist card'?" She sugared her coffee and sat down at the table.

"I lost my purse and President Hardy found it on the steps of the administration building. Of all people to find a Socialist card!" Agnes pulled a large handkerchief from the pocket of her dress and blew her nose.

"You can carry your card in New York City without fear of reprisal," Thorberg said with a touch of smugness.

"And since I don't have a job," Agnes added, "no one can fire me."

Thorberg slowly lifted her mother's fine China to her lips. Agnes thought Thorberg and the cup both lovely, with something of the same translucent strength. From out of nowhere came a buoyant optimism. Agnes smiled. "I'm glad to see you again." She supposed Thorberg knew of the divorce; she supposed Mr. and Mrs. Brundin knew, too. Probably they had all known of the separations and Ernest's unhappiness. Whether they had guessed at her own, she did not know. She had not talked about her fears and inabilities and distaste for marriage. She had not known how to talk about such things but carried them with her, like a baby on her back which she managed while she worked.

"Ernest and I are divorced," she said.

Thorberg calmly swallowed her coffee. "He wrote us the news. It's time for you to lead your separate lives." She rose from the table in a languid movement. "Let's join Mother." But Agnes was reluctant to leave the kitchen. Though Mr. and Mrs.

Brundin were hospitable, as kind as their daughter and son, she wasn't sure they liked her.

"In a few days you can come and stay with me in the Village," Thorberg said under her breath. "I have a set of friends you'll like. They're very advanced politically. Don't say anything to Mother."

Mrs. Brundin sat in the living room working on a piece of white linen stretched between embroidery hoops. She had put on her glasses and looked peaceful.

"Where's Dad?" Thorberg asked.

"Upstairs." Mrs. Brundin's silver needle caught the light and glittered above the linen like a quick slant of rain. "Thorberg tells me you're a teacher, then," she said to Agnes.

"My certificate expired," said Agnes. She watched Thorberg cross to the stairway and disappear.

"You won't be looking for a teaching position, then?" Mrs. Brundin concentrated on her embroidery.

"No."

"What, then?" Agnes wondered if Mrs. Brundin always said "then" at the end of her sentences.

"A secretary."

"Do you like secretarial work, then?"

"No," said Agnes. "But I need a job."

Mrs. Brundin looked over her glasses. "Ernest says you brought your sister to San Diego from Colorado and that, without you, she would not be in school."

"My sister's almost ready to graduate and be a teacher. And she'll have a certificate and be able to take care of herself. Then she and I can help our younger brothers." The pride she felt in Myrtle surprised her.

"And where are your brothers, then?"

Agnes walked to the window. "In Trinidad, Colorado. Myrtle and I are going to help them go to school, my sister and I, and then they won't have to work for other people." She knew, as she spoke, that she and Myrtle had made no such plans. Mother would call it lying. Actually, it was a double lie, because it was already too late to help the boys as they needed to be helped.

"They're very fortunate boys to have sisters like you, then."

Agnes turned back to the room. Here the lying ended. "They're not fortunate boys. They lost their mother, their father is a drunk ... ." She stopped. *And their sister abandoned them.* "They are poor," she concluded. The murmured voices of Thorberg and Mr. Brundin carried downstairs.

Mrs. Brundin rested the embroidery hoops in her lap. "Ernest is very fond of you, Agnes." Ernest's mother was not going to cry; Ernest's mother held her emotion as in a deep bowl; the bowl would not break.

Soon Thorberg and Mr. Brundin came downstairs and entered the living room. Ernest's father was smiling. When he smiled he resembled his son. He took a chair near his wife and, for the first time, looked directly at Agnes.

"Agnes is going to find a job as a secretary, then," Mrs. Brundin said. "She needs a hat and white gloves for her interview."

And wearing the hat and gloves, Agnes found a job as typist for *The Graphic Magazine.* Shortly after, she moved in with Thorberg, who was no longer married to the Rumanian. It was a lovely apartment just off Washington Square, with a blue rug, a piano, fresh flowers, and diaphanous curtains that made the outside world look blurry and beautiful. At first Agnes sat in the corner chair listening to brilliant Greenwich Village people discuss their writing, their painting, their politics, their restaurants and tearooms, their relationships, their neuroses. Where did they find the time ? she wondered. Didn't they have to work?

When Thorberg's friends discovered that Agnes had grown up in mining camps, they sought her out.

"Did you live near Ludlow?" asked a young man, coming to

sit on the floor beside her chair in the corner. He stretched his long legs out in front of him, turned onto his side, and literally lay at her feet, his elbow braced against the blue carpet, his head supported by one soft, pale hand.

"I lived near Ludlow," said Agnes. She didn't bother to tell him it was the Dalagua coal camp where she'd lived. Dalagua would mean no more to him than the North Pole. Another young man who smoked a pipe joined the first young man, and then a woman with cropped hair who wore a sack dress and brown socks and sandals came to sit on the floor, and soon all three were firing questions at her and she found herself telling them that yes, she'd been in Colorado, very near Ludlow, in fact, on the day of the Massacre, when actually she hadn't been anywhere near Ludlow but was teaching typing in San Diego.

"John Reed took a trip to Ludlow to see the site of the strike and Massacre," said the first young man, shifting his long, lean body on the blue rug. "He gave a talk at the Liberal Club. He said even now, two years later, the damage, the charred ground, is positively devastating."

Agnes closed her eyes. During a strike in 1914 the government militia had poured coal oil on miners' tents and set fire to them. Women and children were trapped and burned to death. Thirty-two people died, people like herself and Mother and the children. Thinking about it now, her hard shell of work and will power disintegrated and she felt weak as jelly.

"Who's John Reed?"

"You don't know who John Reed is?" murmured the young woman in the sack dress.

"John Reed is a brilliant reporter, a Socialist, an activist," said the man with the pipe.

Suddenly Agnes blurted out, "I wasn't living in Ludlow at the time." The truth was important in this pretty room.

"But you said you were there," objected the woman.

"Well, I wasn't. I wasn't anywhere near. I was teaching typing in San Diego. But I did live in Trinidad and Dalagua and Tercio, and miners do spend their lives underground so mine owners can stay rich." Her passion seemed too strong for the room, too personal. Her speech was too western. There was a silence.

Half-interested, half-embarrassed, the man standing by her chair took his pipe out of his mouth. "Thorberg says you're working at *The Graphic*." At least he was still standing, the only one of the three not wallowing on the floor. Agnes nodded.

"You must come over to *The Masses*," said the one who was stretched out on the carpet. He looked as if he might fall asleep from superiority.

"Why?"

"It's a splendid paper," said the woman. "Socialist. They have the courage to speak out against the war. The government is forever hounding them."

"Are you in the editorial department at *The Graphic*?" asked the prone man lazily.

"I'm a—book reviewer," said Agnes, and she got up from her chair before the woman could ask what books she'd reviewed.

"Charming girl, eh?" she heard the man with the pipe say as she left her corner for Thorberg's room where she would wait out the party. She did not want to be charming. She had no intention of being charming. She didn't keep up her grueling schedule, typing by day, attending classes at New York University by night, to be charming.

On a Saturday she met Red, a seaman on shore leave, and felt a brief reprieve from the pressures of work and school. After he had taken her to dinner she invited him back to the apartment where Thorberg's friends asked him endless questions about his duties, his pay, how he was treated at sea. They crowded around him and clapped him on the back.

"This is better than Mabel Dodge's salon," someone said. Red made a great hit, a real man from the working class, right there in Thorberg's living room. He told them he was against the ship owners and the capitalists. But he knew and Agnes knew that he was saving his money to buy a hardware store, for he had spent all dinner talking about his dreams for the future, and those dreams had not included Socialism.

"Let's go to Polly Holladay's," someone suggested. Everyone agreed. Agnes and Red got their coats. But it turned out that Thorberg and her friends hadn't really intended to leave the comfortable apartment just yet. The talk turned to Freud and the psychological complexes Thorberg's friends were continually discovering in themselves.

"They think," Agnes remarked to her sailor as they left for the movies, "that when I've been here longer I'll achieve a complex, too."

Late that night when Red kissed her in the shadows of Thorberg's apartment house, Agnes kissed him back. She would miss this man she could understand. And since she did not have to marry him, she enjoyed his mouth on hers. When he asked her to spend the night with him, she grappled with the old fear, forced herself to consider sex, and finally said she couldn't spend the entire night, Thorberg might worry about where she was, but she wouldn't mind visiting him. She needed to go home first, she told him.

Thorberg had bought her a pessary. From the New Feminine Alliance, Agnes had learned more about her body than she wanted to know. Modern young women owe a debt to their mothers and grandmothers and their daughters and not least themselves, Thorberg said, to reject their submissive roles. There were no standards for men, she maintained, that a woman cannot adopt for her own. Agnes decided that Red was the man she would try out the new standard on. She didn't care to be charming, but she did want to be free. She gritted her teeth. If necessary, she could out-Greenwich-Village Greenwich Village.

Red went back to sea. Now Agnes no longer sat in the corner chair during Thorberg's evenings. She was invited to lectures and art shows and dances at the Liberal Club. Two young men, one short, one lanky, took her to see the building on

Washington Place where more than a hundred women workers at the Triangle Shirtwaist Company burned to death. A fire had started in the bolts of cloth, the short man told her, and the women died because they couldn't get out of the locked factory. That was back in 1911, added the lanky one, implying that things were much better now that it was 1917. Both men were relaxed and confident and seemed to have a great deal of leisure. The fire in the shirtwaist factory interested them, but Agnes thought the flames they felt were not hot; the women they heard were not screaming.

But even though the two young men seemed like children to Agnes, stunted and adolescent in some way, fancy in outward style, deficient in hard experience, she slept with them, one on one occasion, the other on another. She had been a child with Ernest, she knew now; not a woman. She sensed a great lack in herself and tried to make up for it. She began to practice sex in order to feel like a free and modern woman. She grasped at affairs in order to feel loved, for Ernest had loved her; she might never find anyone who loved her half so much.

17
Manhattan 1917

A tall man wearing a white turban stepped onto the stage. He seated himself in a high-backed chair behind the lectern. His face glowed like dark, polished wood. With his legs crossed, his expression contemplative, he gazed out at the audience and waited for the introduction to end.

"Ladies and Gentlemen," he began. "Friends of India. The Indians are a chivalrous people." His voice and accent moved like a deep river with a fast current. "They will not disturb England as long as she is engaged with Germany." He paused. "The struggle after the war—and make no mistake, the war will come to an end—might, however, be even more bitter and sustained."

He spoke of Indian villages deteriorating under British rule and of what it cost India to remain loyal to England. "The money-lender, who before the advent of British rule held an extremely subordinate position in the village community, has suddenly come to occupy the first place. He owns the best lands and the best houses and holds the bodies and souls of the agriculturists in mortgage." In his face was sorrow and a great purpose.

Unable to afford a ticket, Agnes had slipped into the auditorium by a side door and mingled with the crowd waiting to hear Lala Lajpat Rai speak at Columbia University on the subject "India During and After the War". Now, from a seat in the center section near the front, she listened to the Lion of the Punjab, aware of his height, his leanness, the scar on one cheek. She thought him so ugly that he was beautiful. Plunged into the river of his speech, Agnes felt that, until now, she had never understood anything. She breathed carefully, as if the air in the auditorium needed to be conserved. In her bones she knew what it meant to be looked down on. To be oppressed. The knowledge extended further back than herself. She was Mother, looked down on for a lifetime, not just by her husband, but by her own family. After her marriage, the Rallses held Sarah Lydia in silent contempt. Before she was ten, Agnes knew that Mother wasn't a Ralls any longer but had been penetrated by something strange and unlucky from Father's side. She knew why Mother's eyes were always sad. Mother was India.

It seemed that this man extended his muscular brown hand to Agnes, stronger and more beautiful than the pasty hands of the Socialists she knew. It seemed to her that he lifted his face with its high cheek bones, gleaming black mustache, and asked her to join him in helping India.

"You see," Agnes pleaded an hour later, "there is so much I need to learn about your country."

Lajpat Rai, who had half-turned away and started up the aisle in the nearly empty auditorium, turned back at the passion in her voice. He studied her face for a long, solemn moment. "I cannot say no to someone who wants to learn," he finally said. "I am at home on Sunday." And he handed her his card.

On Sunday Agnes walked east through Village streets, a stiff March wind blowing litter and leaves before her. She stopped at a door in a Lower East Side tenement. When Lajpat Rai opened it, she followed him into the kitchen-sitting room of a small apartment.

"Sit here," he said, pulling a straight chair up to a table. He went through a doorway into a tiny room that overflowed with books and papers, and sat down at his desk. While he worked, Agnes looked around her. The windows in the cramped sitting room-kitchen were high, narrow, and drafty. There was a sink and stove in one corner. A door led to a third room.

Lajpat Rai returned to the table. "May I offer you tea, Miss

Smedley?"

"No. I came to learn about India." She gestured toward the typewriter visible through the doorway. "I take shorthand and I'm a very good typist. I can do secretarial work for you."

The Lion of the Punjab smiled. "If you are not going to have tea, I, at least, am." His voice was melodic. The British English, colored by his native tongue, was music itself.

"When would you like to begin your studies?" He filled a teakettle at the sink.

"At once," she said. "Today."

Lajpat Rai threw back his turbaned head and laughed. "You are eager," he said. He stopped laughing and lit the gas jet that went out once in the draft. "You are as fast-growing and primitive as a weed, Miss Smedley," he said, and returned to the table.

"We will begin with the KOMAGATA MARU as she sails into Vancouver, Canada. It is July 1914. Aboard are three-hundred forty Sikhs, twenty-four Muslims, twelve Hindus, and a handful of Chinese and Japanese. Our ship comes from Calcutta, Shanghai, Kobe, and Yokahama. It is turned back by the Canadian authorities who have orders from Great Britain to declare the passengers vagrants. The Chinese and Japanese aboard will have help from their countries who will make official protest. From England will come no help at any time for Indians." The kettle came to a boil. Pausing, he brewed the tea, then poured it from a chipped brown teapot.

"Today England is engaged in a great war against Germany. India awaits the outcome." He spoke as if India were a person. He had endured prison and faced death for her, he said. When he spoke of her invasions, her empires, her rivers, jungles, purple hazes, the "cow dust" as his people called the sunset, bright saris of women, white garments of men, his gaze grew distant with longing.

He rested the teapot on an intricate brass trivet and took the chair opposite Agnes. He studied his tea and drank in silence before he spoke again. "Are you a student?"

Agnes told him about her night classes at the University, how ignorant she felt, yet how shallow the professors and students seemed, as if they had no experience in life. She was too unsure of herself to speak up in class. She did not know how to theorize, she said. Then she lowered her head and told him she'd been fired from San Diego Normal.

"And your family?" he asked. "Where is your family?"

"I have no family." When he pressed her for information, she removed two letters and a telegram from her purse. She offered him the first letter which he held in his dark, steady hand and read with quiet comprehension. When he finished he looked up.

"And who is this John?"

Her brother, she said, pointing to the letter. He had stolen a horse and was put in jail. He had written Agnes for money.

"I wrote him back," she said. Her voice rose. "I told him we were poor but we weren't raised to be thieves. 'You were taught better than to steal,' I wrote him. 'Why can't you be patient and wait a little longer until I can help you?' I was hard on him."

"And did you send the money he asked for?"

"Yes," said Agnes. "I borrowed it." Lajpat Rai put the letter down and took the telegram she held out to him. He scanned the four words: "John killed today. Sam."

"I was very hard on John," Agnes said dully. Lajpat Rai said nothing, but picked up the second letter from the table.

"John died of a broken neck," the letter said. "Dirt caved in on him. He was digging a sewer. Mud was in his eyes and mouth. The county paid Dad $50. I can't get ahead. I'm enlisting in the army. Sam."

Below his untidy signature, added in pencil, were two lines: "Don't blame John for trying, he stole a horse, he don't have an education like you."

Lajpat Rai stood and walked to the stove where he heated up the teakettle again. Agnes blew her nose.

"Since you have no family," said Lajpat Rai, pouring two

fresh cups of tea, "you must help my country. I will prepare you to teach in India."

She moved out of Thorberg's apartment and took a room on the Lower East Side to be near him, dropping out of night classes in favor of history lessons from Lajpat Rai. At the table in lamplight he sometimes looked old and tired, and when he spoke of being denied a passport by the British to return to his home, he brooded. Sometimes his dark eyes smoldered with anger, or grew cold and bitter. But when he taught Agnes, read with her, dictated his book to her, his eyes were warm and patient.

Sometimes he let her see him with his turban off. His hair was thick and long, with much gray among the glossy black. She would have liked to stroke his hair, bury her hands in it, rest her face against his. But he always grew distant when he sensed her adoration. And perhaps, after all, he did not like her very much. He had called her primitive as a weed.

"If America joins the war it will be hard on all of us," he said to her one evening at the close of their lesson. "You will not be spared."

"Americans are for India!" she exclaimed.

"Even sympathetic Americans will turn against us," he continued as if he had not heard her. "If America enters the war, England will increase its pressure on your government to arrest us."

Night and day he waged a scholarly war on two fronts: one against the British who wanted to eradicate Indian nationalism, and one against his own people who wanted independence immediately, war or no war.

"India will need England after the war. India must take her place in the British Commonwealth until … " He turned away and left the sentence unfinished.

"I'm expecting visitors soon," he said one warm evening in May.

It had been less than a month since America entered the war. Children played stick ball in the street; cabbage, curry, fish smells mingled in the tenements. "Two young men who think a world war is a minor impediment to Indian nationalism." He lowered himself onto a straight chair. "They think of nothing but revolution. Soon you will see another side of the Indian movement." Agnes made no reply. "They are Ghadars," he said with distaste. "They are going to undermine my work."

Although Agnes had heard of the Ghadar movement on the West Coast, she was not prepared for the fierce energy, only slightly masked by courtly manners, which the two young revolutionaries, Salindranath Ghose and M.N. Roy, brought to the apartment of Lajpat Rai. They prowled restlessly about the two small rooms, their single topic independence. They were both very handsome, she thought.

"England calls up more and more of our men," Salindranath said, pacing between the sitting room-kitchen and study where Agnes and Lajpat Rai were trying to work.

"Tell me, Miss Smedley," Salindranath said from the doorway, "what has brought you to our independence movement?"

Agnes inserted a sheet of paper between the rollers of her typewriter. "When I heard my teacher speak," she said in a low voice, "I knew I would work for India."

"He has won much support for the cause," Salindranath said half-heartedly.

"He is a very great man."

"He is a very great man," Salindranath agreed. Casting an impertinent glance toward the Lion of the Punjab writing at his desk, he added, "However, we do not all agree with his position." He started to say more, but Agnes turned back to the typewriter and began to type at a furious speed.

"May I walk you to your home?" he asked that evening as she placed the dust jacket over the typewriter. She did not answer but laid a stack of letters on Lajpat Rai's desk.

"I guess so," she said.

From the stove in the corner of the sitting room where he was beginning to prepare a meal, Lajpat Rai watched Salindranath open the door for Agnes.

She turned back. "I'll be here tomorrow," she said, as if there were any question.

Lajpat Rai bowed and remained facing the door even after Salindranath closed it behind him.

"He's tired tonight," Agnes said as they stepped away from the tenement and entered the stream of East Side foot traffic. It was twilight. A young man passed them carrying a bouquet of daffodils.

"The Lion of the Punjab is old."

"He's not old," said Agnes. "He's tired." Salindranath started to say something but changed his mind.

"My friend and I are going to Mexico," he said a few minutes later.

"Mexico! Don't you have enough revolution in India?"

Salindranath lowered his voice. "We were arrested the night you first heard Lajpat Rai speak."

Agnes shot him a glance.

"We— I believe your American expression is 'jumped bail.' We are hiding. Now we must leave the country."

"What are you charged with?"

"Violating neutrality laws. The British do not want Indian independence, and the Americans do not want to offend the British."

"The Americans offended the British in 1776," Agnes said.

"They were not allies then," Salindranath pointed out. "Neither were there Asian Indians in America in 1776. And if there had been, they would not have been working with the Germans."

Agnes stopped in the middle of the sidewalk.

"The Lion of the Punjab has not told you of the Berlin Indian Revolutionary Committee?" he said, amused. Agnes began walking again. She looked straight ahead. "I see by your face you do not know of the ties between Germany and our revolutionary movement."

"I know all I need to know to help the Indian cause," Agnes said. "I know nothing about—German ties." Her sharp tone could not quite compensate for the uncertainty in her face. She resumed walking and almost fell over three raggle-taggle children who darted in front of her. They reminded her of children in the coal camps, babbling in many languages.

"Don't worry, Miss Smedley," Salindranath said with a rare note of regret in his voice, as if he were tired of the great cause. "I will not trouble you with Indian matters further. Your teacher has invited us to leave and we comply." They approached her landlady's house. Agnes reached for the key and felt Sam's letter in her purse.

"My brother has enlisted," she said. "Americans are dying in Europe because of Germany."

"England's enemy is India's friend," Salindranath said. "Lajpat Rai does not agree. He has done great work for India, but he belongs to the past. His interests now lie with England. And with Indian landlords. He, himself, was a landlord for many years. He is too patient with England." Salindranath's eyes snapped. His turban was brilliant white in the dusky light of evening. "Incredibly, he believes India should remain in the Commonwealth." He was about to say more but Agnes stepped up to her door.

"I wish to speak to you further," he said, leaning toward her.

"I do not wish to speak to you further," she said and entered the building before she could see his deep bow and folded hands at his forehead.

Two days later he walked her home again. "You know of the arrests in San Francisco," he stated, turning his bronze face and turbaned head toward her. She felt disloyal to Lajpat Rai. She should not walk home with this man; she should not look up at him.

"I don't know about any arrests in San Francisco," she said. "What arrests?"

"The government is arresting Indians for violating the espionage laws of the United States. Because we do not support Britain, your government calls it a Hindu-German conspiracy."

"That's not Lajpat Rai's fault," Agnes retorted. "He doesn't work with Germany."

"He does not work at all except to write speeches!" Salindranath's full lips curled with contempt. "Meanwhile India's sons die for England." He bent to the sidewalk and picked up a dropped coin. "We are not all as sanguine as your teacher."

Agnes wondered what "sanguine" meant. The Indians she had met spoke with a courtly, old-world diction learned from British schoolmasters and Indian teachers trained by British schoolmasters. Sometimes in the middle of an ordinary sentence, a difficult, refined word would jump out at her and she would marvel at the Indians' vocabulary, yet wonder whether they had the usage quite right.

"Some day perhaps you will meet my friend Taraknath Das," Salindranath said. He handed the coin to Agnes. "He is presently in Japan passing time."

"What's he doing in Japan?"

"It is confidential," Salindranath said. "Smuggling."

"Smuggling what?"

"Guns. And men. To India."

In spite of herself, the stories Salindranath told her about exiled young Indians in every corner of the world, waiting like coiled springs to see who won the war, excited her.

All that summer and into the fall, Salindranath wrote her letter after letter from Mexico and she answered back. He had never kissed her, not so much as a brush against the cheek. The Indian men she met maintained a distance and treated her with respect.

They were her friends, her brothers. Indian men, Lajpat Rai had told her once, perhaps as a warning, reserve love for wife and family. It weakens a man in his work if he falls in love outside of marriage. Without purity, he said, a man cannot lead. And, he added pointedly, neither can a woman.

"Good," Agnes had answered. Her only love was India, she said, ignoring her teacher's smile.

"I have left Mexico," Salindranath wrote from San Francisco. "I am trying to escape arrest. I am working on a plan that will gain India's freedom. I need your help."

Agnes did not mention the plan to Lajpat Rai. It would not interest him. Or more accurately, it would interest him but he would not favor it. It was perhaps even unworkable—but she could not forever sit typing and waiting for the war to end. The speeches she typed sounded like the books she typed that sounded like the letters she typed. She didn't need the drafts Lajpat wrote out for her in his ornate, old-fashioned script; she knew what he would say before he said it. Lajpat, himself, began to seem ornate and old-fashioned. Agnes missed the young Ghadar activists prowling about the living room and study. What she wanted was action. Action was change, and change was what was needed.

The revolution in Russia, for example. She was electrified by newsreels she saw, the Communist flag carried through the streets of St. Petersburg while, in the darkened theatre, the organist played thrilling music that was foreign and patriotic and very loud. Everyone she knew was electrified. Everyone but Lajpat Rai. The revolution in Russia was just one more step, he said philosophically, looking up from his books and papers, in the progress of the human race. Its impact on India must be examined.

Wasn't a revolution exactly what was needed in India? Were Indians less courageous than Russians? The Russians had thrown out the Czar! Couldn't India throw out the British?

No. Conditions in the two countries were very different,

he said, returning his attention to the work table where he had begun a careful analysis of the Bolsheviks. Agnes began to think of him as old, unimaginative, ineffective. Definitely behind the times. He no longer seemed the same man she had begged to study with less than a year earlier. Elated by the revolution, by the plan Salindranath wrote of almost daily, she moved back to the West Village, to a tiny room on Waverly Place.

But leaving her teacher proved more difficult than she had expected. Seated at the work table across from him on a cold evening near the end of the year, Agnes' elation deserted her. Through the window she watched snow, fine as dust—was it "cow dust" he had called the sunset in India?—sift and whirl in the light from the street lamp. She forced her attention back to the lesson and her teacher. How pale and displaced he looked in wintertime. Winter did not suit him. Studying his face, she felt troubled, as if she, too, were in the wrong season. She felt as if she had turned her back on more than Lajpat Rai and history lessons. She was turning against a parent, a lover, a cause, youth itself.

"One must work and one must live," he said. His eyes, dark and heavy-lidded, never left hers. He touched her hand. "Our revolution is not easy. It requires strength and endurance."

"Strength, I have," she retorted, glad to fight grief with a flare of emotion. "Endurance, I have. But we cannot sit and wait for England to grant India independence. It will never be done voluntarily."

He released her hand. "You sound like a Ghadar," he said.

"My family were tenant farmers and miners!" she flared again. "If I were Indian I would be a Ghadar! If I were Russian I would be a Bolshevik!"

"Nothing precludes you from being either a Ghadar or a Bolshevik," he said. "I taught you to love India. Do not forget her." They stared at each other. Together they stood up from the table. He seemed stunned. She was appalled at what she was doing, yet she could not sink into comfortable lessons again, mindless typing.

"Good-bye," she said, and thought she heard a tearing sound. She turned and left the apartment. Once outside she walked fast beneath black tree limbs along which a thin, crisp fall of white lay precariously. A solitary motor car moved through the streets, following the two shafts of light from its head lamps. The sound of the engine was muffled by thick night busy with snow. Far ahead the car turned a corner and all was darkness and whirling white.

She answered a letter from Salindranath who was still in San Francisco. "I am not typing for Lajpat Rai anymore," she wrote, trying to think of things to say in order not to admit how the young Indian revolutionary had stirred her imagination and her lust. Only rarely did she reflect on how she, a girl from a Missouri tenant farm and Colorado coal mines, had come to live in New York City to work for a foreign revolutionary cause.

Before long, batches of blank paper began arriving through the mail, official-looking stationery stamped with the name of an invented Indian government. In the late afternoons and evenings, instead of studying history and typing Lajpat Rai's drafts, Agnes did as Salindranath asked and composed letters to embassies, consulates, even President Wilson. She signed with the name "Pulin Behari Bose," a fictitious officer of a fictitious Indian government in exile created by the Ghadars in San Francisco.

But the only people who took the letters seriously were investigators from the Department of Justice. Immigration authorities, military intelligence, and the Secret Service had been reading Salindranath's mail for months. They descended on Agnes for interrogation, with no lawyer present. Lajpat Rai's warning had not been frivolous. Only slightly daunted, feeling like a Bolshevik in Russia, on the righteous side of history, she was hauled off to the Tombs, then tried and indicted under the Espionage Act for fomenting revolution in India and falsely representing herself as a diplomat.

18
The Tombs, New York City 1918

Agnes did not cheer with the others when Kitty Marion came clattering down the corridor alongside the cells with her mop and pail.

"Three cheers for birth control!" Kitty shouted, and the women prisoners shouted back. But Agnes could not think of birth control or Socialism or the Russian Revolution or anything except one small black notebook. If she stared at the ceiling, the black notebook was there. If she stared at the wall, it was there, too.

Secret Service men had confiscated the notebook from her room. She had seen it in the pile of books and clothes in the office where they questioned her. No doubt they had already found the list of Indian names she and Salindranath had glued behind the binding the day he arrived in New York.

Her Indian friends would think she had informed on them.

"Three cheers for birth control!"

Agnes rolled her face into the thin straw mattress of her bench and breathed dust. She could hear the matron progressing down the corridor behind Kitty, unlocking cells. She got up and used the broken toilet in the corner where leakage still froze on the floor overnight, though it was already April. She wanted a pail of soapy water, wanted to get down on her hands and knees and scrub the floor, wished she could scrub floors and walls all day long. Anything was better than silence and inactivity. She bit her fingernails and tried, at the same time, to think, yet not think, of Salindranath, Lajpat Rai, the Ghadars, India.

"Every time I'm jailed I go in a spark and come out a flame," Kitty had whispered to her once when they met in a corner on their hands and knees, a bucket of dirty water between them.

For a moment Agnes caught fire from Kitty. "Every time!" Color came to her face and she scrubbed faster. But back in her cell, the camaraderie of prison life vanished and she relapsed into despair. No matter how hard she tried, she ended up at the bottom of the heap. Like Mother and Father. Worse. As far as she knew, no one in her family had ever been jailed, except her brother for stealing a horse.

She had been very hard on John. She spat out a bit of fingernail. How self-righteous she'd been.

Of course Father had occasionally been jailed overnight for public drunkenness, and at least she wasn't in jail for stealing or being drunk. Yet, sitting in her cell, the reason didn't seem to matter. She was still behind bars. Hearing Lajpat Rai talk about being jailed was quite different from being jailed yourself. What a fool she was. Her teacher had taught her about India and modern history, shared his ideals with her, and then she left him, as she had left her family. As she had left Ernest. Again and again she broke away, ripping out the seam that stitched her to others. She'd lost contact with Thorberg.

No one knew she was in jail. If it was up to her, no one ever would. She'd dropped all contact with Missouri and Colorado, and she hoped Sam, who'd enlisted in the Army to help his country, would never know that that same country had arrested his sister for treason.

Wasn't it her own fabric she tore? She was made of doubtful cloth.

Ayahoo! Indians were not her people. Neither were Americans. Once she had had people of her own, but she'd left them behind. Father had left his people in Missouri for something dubious: mining in Colorado. Mother had left her people for something even more dubious: Father. Always leaving people behind and gaining nothing.

A forbidden memory pushed at the back door of her mind, tried the lock, and turned the knob. When it shouldered through, she sank to the floor, holding onto the bars as if they were consciousness itself. She had slept with a man who possessed the same dark power as Father. Not Ernest, kind and gentle. Not casual young men in Greenwich Village who meant nothing to her. This had been something illicit. Overwhelming. There had been the same animal sounds she'd grown up hearing in the night, but now the sounds had come from her own throat.

She drew her legs up and pressed her face against her knees. He was a Ghadar, this man. Not Salindranath. His name was Herambalal Gupta. He had visited Lajpat Rai and learned where Agnes lived. He was not courteous like the other Indians. He had knocked on her door at Waverly Place and told her he had a message for her. He came inside and she made him tea. But he had no message. Instead, he tried to learn where Salindranath was staying. Agnes would not tell him, for Salindranath had come to New York secretly and given her a list of key Indian nationalists and their addresses all over the world. Together they'd steamed open the back of her black notebook and inserted the thin paper into the space before sealing it up again.

Gupta was not well-liked by the other Ghadars; he was not well-liked by Lajpat Rai; he was not well-liked by Agnes. But in the late night, the light from her small fireplace dancing on the walls, he had kissed her and in her hunger, her unexpected misery after leaving Lajpat Rai, she'd kissed him, too. Lying on the narrow bed in her tiny room, he'd removed his turban and he'd pressed his bronze body against hers. His long, black hair swayed above her, and when they were finished, he told her not to tell anyone because looseness with a woman, particularly a woman in the movement, would ruin his reputation with the revolutionaries.

While she lay on the bed, horrified at her pleasure, woman's pleasure that grips her and opens her, Gupta went through her books and papers without finding the secret list, and left.

Shamed by the sex act, shamed by her secret life and sexual desire, troubled by her future with men—for she saw that there would be trouble with men—she had turned on the jet under her hot plate. The landlady smelled the gas in time and turned it off.

Now she got up from the jail floor with an uncanny feeling that someone was with her. As if, while she'd been thinking of herself, she'd really been thinking of someone else. Someone unhappy. Someone mistreated. Mother, dead, endured.

Agnes lay down on the bench and slept. When morning came she no longer tried to avoid thought. America had put her in jail, not so much because she was helping India as because it appeared she was helping Germany. England and America were playing up the Hindu-German connection. It served their interests. She would be more careful about interests in the future.

Her head throbbed. She longed for a scrub brush and pail. She needed work. She needed pencil and paper. She would write about prison and the women prisoners she'd met. A sentence about Kitty came to mind. "When she had been forced to put on a striped dress of the convicted women, she looked at it and remarked, 'Ah! blue and white stripes! Now if there were only a few red stripes and some white stars!'"

But when the sentence ended, no other began. She could report Kitty's words but she still had no words of her own.

19

New York City 1919

"Why work for the Indians?" Florence Tannenbaum asked the intense young woman standing in her doorway. "There are plenty of causes right here at home that need help. I mean, there's birth control, Socialism, pacifism, feminism, labor. Why India?"

Agnes bristled. "England has no right to control India and no business meddling in America's affairs. They think they blend in with the American Secret Service, but I know an English sausage when I see one!"

"English sausage!" Florence laughed. Even when she laughed she could not take her eyes off Agnes. The woman was thin and pale from eight months in prison. She had short hair, badly cut, and a haunted expression. They'd been introduced at the Liberal Club, but Florence, the daughter of a wealthy merchant family in New York City who lived a Bohemian life as far as she was able, already knew Agnes Smedley from the newspapers. All of Greenwich Village knew about the coal miner's daughter who had gone to prison for helping Indian nationalists.

Now the woman needed a place to live. Landlords didn't want a political activist. But Florence needed adventure, and she could afford drama.

"Well," said Agnes, still scowling, "do you want a roommate or not?"

"Yes," said Florence. "For ten dollars a month you can sleep in the living room."

So at 184 West Fourth Street, Agnes sewed a chintz curtain and hung it around the couch in the living room. Florence tried not to notice when Agnes didn't come home some nights. She asked the psychiatrist whom her parents had been paying since she was eleven—she was twenty now—if she should pretend not to notice that sometimes Agnes didn't come home.

"What do *you* think?" he asked. "What do you think about this roommate staying out all night?"

"Well, I don't think she's out all night," Florence answered. She, herself, was still a virgin. She felt a red flush rise from her neck up into her face. "I think she's *in* all night with someone."

"And what do you think about that?"

"What do I think? I think I'll go with her. Then we can both spend the night in."

The psychiatrist removed his round eyeglasses. "And what will your parents think?"

"Oh, bugger my parents," Florence Tannenbaum said, and got up from the couch twenty minutes before the hour ended.

"Were you working late at the *Birth Control Review* last night?" she asked Agnes the next morning over oatmeal.

Agnes sugared her cereal without comment.

"Do you need someone to help you?" Florence asked. "If you do, I volunteer."

"Aren't you too busy visiting your parents and going to your psychiatrist?"

"I may be inexperienced, sheltered, even pampered, but I am not stupid, Agnes. And this is the last time I volunteer to help you." She picked up her oatmeal, took it to her bedroom, and slammed the door behind her. She set the bowl on the dresser and went to the closet where she ran through her dresses and jersey jumper suits at fierce speed. Finally she found what she wanted, a simple skirt and shirtwaist in the style that Agnes wore. She dressed, gobbled the rest of her cereal, and returned to the kitchen. Agnes stood at the sink washing the pan.

"That was fast."

"There's no point in wasting time when you have a busy day ahead of you," Florence said mysteriously. She left her dish for Agnes to wash, threw on her cardigan coat, and hurried out of the apartment. She walked in the direction of Fifth Avenue, her heels tapping the frosty sidewalk, her breath a quick cloud that dissipated just before the next one formed. She turned left. Only then did she stop to ask herself where she was going.

She resisted the temptation to take the subway uptown to Mummy and Daddy. After all, she was an independent woman who had already achieved a mild success in her translation of Maria Montessori's letters for *The Call*. The editorial staff knew her work. She had friends there.

"I have plenty to do," she said to herself, and set off for the public library where she spent the day writing poetry. Walking home in the afternoon sunlight, she laughed at her earlier fit of pique. All about her, people smiled above their bright mufflers and scarves. The war was over, and since August the nation had been happy and proud and optimistic—Florence had written a poem on the subject just last week.

As she approached her apartment house she shook back her mass of dark hair. There was so much in life to enjoy, what was the point of killing yourself to help a country across the ocean? What was the point of going to jail for an idea? Her new roommate was a tortured woman who enjoyed being pinned to a cross. Florence must not allow herself to be thrown off course by someone who couldn't even afford a room of her own.

"I've been asked out a lot," Florence confided to Agnes as they rode the subway back to the Village from her parents' home uptown where she'd introduced them to her new friend and tenant. "However, I am very choosy about men."

Agnes made no response.

"As a matter of fact, I'd rather spend an evening alone than go out with a man who has nothing to offer."

Agnes nodded.

"I think Mummy and Daddy were interested in your views," said Florence.

"That's one way to put it."

"No, really. You fascinated them."

"Your parents are very comfortable."

Florence bristled. "What's wrong with being comfortable?" But Agnes didn't respond.

As the train slowed for the next stop, Florence reopened the conversation. "I think work is more important than love, don't you?"

"I think they're both important," said Agnes. The subway stopped at Thirty-fourth Street. A group of men, a drinking party that smelled of liquor, entered the car.

"Have you ever been in love?" Florence asked.

"Probably not."

"You're not sure?"

"I'm not sure."

A burst of laughter erupted from the back of the car.

"I've been married," Agnes volunteered.

Florence looked surprised. "Who was he?"

"Someone in California."

In the overheated car, Florence's dark hair formed a glossy frame for her slightly flushed complexion. She unbuttoned her coat with the fur collar that set off her fine coloring and leaned toward Agnes.

"What's it like being married?"

Agnes studied Florence with a cool eye. The men in the back of the car swayed with the train's motion and began to sing.

"Have you ever slept with a man?" Agnes asked.

Florence drew back, shocked. "That's very personal."

"But you have no qualms asking me about my sex life."

"I didn't ask you about your sex life."

"Yes, you did," said Agnes. "It's overrated. You both take your clothes off, only the man doesn't like it if you just get undressed and hop into bed, which is what you're both going to do in the end, anyway. No. You have to spend the evening going somewhere or talking about something he's interested in because he'd be shocked if he knew you just wanted to sleep with him."

She watched Florence's face with amusement.

"But that's—cheap," said Florence. A woman in a brown hat who sat just ahead of them looked over her shoulder and frowned. Agnes made a face and continued louder than before.

"Men can do it with a prostitute. They pay money, get what they want, and leave. If I had money, I'd pay the man. Let him take the risk of getting pregnant. Let him clean up the bed afterwards. Let him raise the child for twenty years. Or get the abortion. I'll poke around in *his* body."

The woman got out of her seat and moved to the front of the car. Shocked, speechless, Florence tripped over Agnes' feet getting to the aisle. The train stopped at Sheridan Square and they left the subway.

"You wanted a good story," said Agnes as they walked toward West Fourth, "but you got the truth instead. Go to your psychiatrist to hear what you want to hear."

"I believe in love," Florence said tartly. "If I thought you were right, I'd kill myself."

Agnes shrugged. They turned onto their street.

"Why do you want to be the man?" Florence asked.

"Because they have power. Everyone, especially women, gives them power. Women wait on men, clean up after men, raise the children for men, listen endlessly to men—"

"I'll admit I sometimes wish I were a man," Florence said. Her voice dropped to a near whisper. "That is one of the things I've been working through all these years with my psychiatrist." She raised her voice again. "But then I ask myself if I could really run a business or make governmental decisions…" Her voice trailed off.

Agnes crossed to the inside of the sidewalk and looked directly into Florence's face. "Men are trained for it from birth. There's no reason women can't be trained. And what do men do? Get us all into wars again and again. Step on top of each other trying to get more money than the next person. Make sure there are plenty of poor people who will do the unpleasant work for low wages. Wealthy countries subjugate poor ones. Children go hungry while the rich spend money on trifles. Women could not do a worse job of running the world, Florence. It would be impossible to do a worse job."

Florence looked away from Agnes' intense gaze. In the street, cars and an occasional horse and wagon rolled by. Before daylight, smoke would be pouring out of factories on both horizons.

"This was once a pretty village," Florence said.

Agnes snorted. "And this is what men call progress." They began walking again.

"Women share the benefits, though," Florence said.

"At what price? Don't disagree with a man, or be disagreeable. Read the magazines and learn how to look, cook, talk to please a man. Blame yourself when you're not happy. Blame yourself when your husband isn't happy. Blame yourself when your children aren't happy." She gave Florence a penetrating look. "Spend thousands of dollars on a psychiatrist to learn what's wrong with you."

Florence flared. "Go to hell, Agnes." Her eyes narrowed. "I suspect, of the two of us, you'll be the one to fall hard for a man and be miserable, and I'll be doing the world's work, competent and contented." Their eyes locked.

Agnes ended the contest by laughing. "Miss Tannenbaum, in spite of your rich mummy and daddy, there is something about you I like."

Later, when they had both gotten into their nightclothes, Agnes lay on the living room couch. Florence sat in a wing back chair Mummy and Daddy had insisted she bring from home. "What do you think of my parents?" she said.

"The pertinent question is: what do your parents think of me?"

"Oh, they criticize most of my friends," Florence said. "With you, I think they were stunned."

"Why did you introduce us?"

"I keep hoping they'll look below the surface."

Agnes got up on one elbow. "Your parents and people like your parents are not going to look beneath the surface because the surface serves them too well." She lay back down. "Your parents are all right," she added, seeing Florence's expression. "Personally, they're all right. It's their class that's so awful."

Florence had turned pensive.

"You asked me what I thought," Agnes said. She got up on her elbow again. "Tell me," she said. "Why do you live in Greenwich Village in a tiny apartment when your parents would give you any accommodation you want?"

"I don't really know," Florence said. "I'm not like my parents. But I'm not as radical as my friends, either. I'm somewhere in the middle, but I don't know where." She lapsed into silence.

"Don't worry, kid," Agnes said. She reached up for the curtain and began to draw it around her couch. "Life will teach you. Not your psychiatrist. Life."

Florence reached out and stopped the curtain. "How?"

"Go to jail," she said. "Jail clarifies everything."

"How does it clarify everything?"

"When I went to jail I was confused and very unhappy. I'd foolishly cooperated with—" She stopped.

"With what?"

"With someone who used me."

"Who?"

Agnes didn't answer.

"Are you happier now?"

"No, but I'm not confused."

"*I'm* confused," Florence admitted.

Agnes opened her eyes. "Go to jail and you'll know who your friends are. People helped me because I suffered for a just cause. It wasn't really me they were helping," she added more gently. "It was justice."

After a rare and thoughtful silence, Florence said, "I've

spoken to some of my friends at *The Call*. I told them you've written some wonderful character sketches of women prisoners and that you need money."

Agnes half-listened to the prattle.

"I'll introduce you to the staff," Florence added magnanimously.

Agnes sat up. "In jail," she continued, "I had to ask myself why I was working for India, a country I'd never been to, with people who are so different from me and my upbringing." She glanced at her roommate. "People ask me that all the time. India was the first thing I suffered for from choice. I was not just reacting, trying to save myself from a bad situation. I was expressing my own self through work." The practical light in her eyes grew almost mystical. "I had chosen the work myself, you see."

"I'd like to work," said Florence. "I'd like to have a job."

"In fact"—Agnes swung her feet onto the floor and pushed up the sleeves of the old silk pajamas Florence had given her—"one of the mainstays of Western capitalism is the subjugation of Asiatic people."

Florence began absently twirling the ribbon on the bodice of her nightgown.

"India is the base from which the West dominates China, the Near and Middle East, and part of Africa. So I'm working for liberty in the West as well as for justice in the East."

There was a silence before Florence changed the subject. "I want to teach children," she said.

"What's stopping you?"

"Well ... ."

"Your parents? Your psychiatrist?" Agnes turned her back on Florence. "Make a decision." She lay back down, closed her eyes, and fell asleep without bothering to pull the curtain the rest of the way around herself.

"Where do you go?" Florence risked asking one night when they'd roomed together for more than a year, "on those nights when you don't come home?"

Agnes shot her a glance that held both secrecy and humiliation. "Working late at the FFI."

"But all night?" Florence pursued the subject. "Agnes, you have a boy friend, don't you?"

"Certainly not."

"Well, then—what?"

Agnes turned onto her stomach and buried her face in the pillow. The cast-off pajamas of light green silk gleamed in the lamplight.

"The FFI," she said in a muffled voice. "I'm at the FFI."

"What's that?"

"Friends of Freedom for India."

"I don't believe you."

Agnes lay very still. Florence moved over to her and perched on the edge of the make-shift bed. "You're tense," she said, and began to massage Agnes' shoulders. "These old pajamas are just the thing for you," she crooned. "They fit you better than they ever fit me."

"I'm not always at the FFI."

"Well, what?" Florence worked her thumbs at the base of Agnes' neck.

Agnes lifted her head. "Don't play psychiatrist with me," she said and lowered her head again. A fire truck's claxon sounded in the direction of Washington Square. "I used to be terrified of sex," she said into the pillow.

"I'm still terrified of it," Florence said.

"You can get over being scared."

"How?"

"Once you know you're not going to have a baby and you're not going to get married, it's not so bad."

Florence returned to her chair. "It's very modern to have sex."

"People have always done it, Florence."

"But now we can be open about it," said Florence. "Can't we?"

Agnes rolled over onto her back and drew up the covers. She closed her eyes and pretended to be tired.

"On those nights when you don't come home, you're out doing it," Florence declared. "You and all the other free and modern women in Greenwich Village. I'm the only one sitting at home alone, still a virgin at twenty-one."

"It's not because you haven't been asked."

"I just can't abide the thought," Florence said frankly. "I wouldn't know what to do."

"Oh, for God's sake, you don't have to do anything!"

"Love will show the way, I guess," said Florence.

"Lust will be even more helpful."

"Aren't you in love when you sleep with a man?"

"No."

"You sleep with men you don't love?" Florence asked, surprised.

"You have to be careful about love," said Agnes.

"Why?"

"If you're in love you might want to get married and have children."

"Is that a warning for me? Or for you?"

Agnes rolled onto her side so that her back was toward Florence. "Both of us," she said. "All women. I'm warning all women."

Florence remained in the wing-back chair. "Agnes?" she said after a lengthy silence. "Are you asleep?"

"Yes," said Agnes. "I'm dreaming that no one is bothering me."

"If you don't love him, what's the point of doing it?"

"I don't know."

"Because it feels good?"

"I hope you have sex soon so we can stop talking about it."

"When I do," said Florence, "it will be in my own bed, and

I won't keep it a secret and go slinking around in the dark of night and not tell my best friend."

Agnes slowly lifted her head. "I do what I do, Florence," she said. "And I don't have a best friend."

20
China 1937

Although the soldiers still wore winter padding in their ragged jackets, spring was coming on. Afternoons lengthened and branches of trees were knobby with buds.

"The men look rested," said Zhu De. "They are putting on weight. We have lived through another winter. We will live through many more." He and Agnes climbed the terraces that snaked up the loess cliff. Agnes wrote as she walked, pausing to complete a phrase, half-running to catch up to the short, strong commander who never hurried, never rested.

"You are teaching the 'little devils' to read," said Zhu De. "Little devils" were young boys who hung onto the shirttails of the Red Army, eager to become soldiers when they grew older. Many were orphaned in the civil wars that raged among the monarchist, Kuomintang, and private warlord troops.

"I am teaching Chinese, though I barely read it myself," Agnes said. "There is a saying in English, 'the blind shall lead the blind.'"

Zhu De threw back his head and laughed. "In China we express the same thought," he said, stopping in front of his cave. "It must be that throughout the world the blind are leading the blind." He stepped through the doorway, brought out one straight chair, and set it on the dirt terrace.

"You do not wish to sit?" Agnes said.

"The blind shall stand," Zhu De said. "You see, I make up a Chinese saying!" They settled into a comfortable silence. "Today I will tell you what I learned as a young teacher in Ilunghsien."

"The year was 1907. The school where I taught was hated and feared by conservative families in the town. We had only twelve students, all boys. They called us 'fake foreigners' for teaching science and politics and body training. The body was all very fine

for animals and peasants, they said, but the sons of gentlemen educated their minds."

The general squared his shoulders. "I made a speech in which I explained that China and all Chinese must become strong, stronger than the foreign countries that are trying to control us. But my speech did not help. Feudalistic forces in the town brought us to court. They accused us of treason against the dynasty. At the end of the year our school was closed and I made plans to enroll in the Yunnan Military Academy. My family was bitterly disappointed. I was not to be an official in the dynasty after all. I had betrayed them."

In a tree at the top of the cliff a single bird sang as if it, by itself, could bring an end to winter.

"I, too, was a teacher," Agnes said. "I, too, left my school."

"Was yours a revolutionary school?" asked Zhu De.

"Hardly. I was fired for being a Socialist."

"I see," Zhu De said with interest. "And did you develop confidence in the struggle against feudalism?"

"Not exactly. I developed confidence in the power of administrators to fire radical teachers."

"America is not China. America does not need you as China needs you."

Agnes met his eyes. "America needs me. America needs to learn about China."

"There is a saying," Zhu De said. "Eating Yunnan bitterness." It took Agnes a moment to realize he had resumed his narrative. "There, walking through Yunnan on my way to the military academy, I saw peasants with great goiters hanging from their necks. They lived with their sheep and goats and tended their poppies. Three-quarters of the population was addicted to opium. I believe they were the most miserable people on the face of the earth."

Sounds of women singing drifted up to them, Lily Wu and the theatre troupe rehearsing for the evening's performance.

"At the academy I joined the secret revolutionary society, the Tung Meng Hui. While I was waiting to be admitted— for I was

not a Yunnan native and at first was denied entrance— I read and discussed political matters with officers and students in secret."

Zhu De stopped and listened to the women. Then he turned and looked down at his soldiers exercising on the drill ground near the foot of the cliff. "But the Tung Meng Hui, though revolutionary, was made up of intellectuals," he continued. "They thought peasants were animals. They did not understand that peasants are the backbone of China."

"And were you admitted into the academy?"

"Yes," Zhu De said, "but I failed to progress in a straight line. I, like China, made mistake after mistake."

"What kinds of mistakes?"

"Mistakes."

"Yes. What were they?"

"The Canton uprising failed, and though our Yunnan revolt succeeded—the dynasty was so rotten that when we blew on it, it collapsed—we marched no farther than Szechwan, when we should have persevered to Wuchan."

"You were a soldier by then?"

"Yes. I had graduated from the academy. I was an officer, but for the next two years my duties were confused. I fought bandits hired by the French who were trying to occupy Yunnan."

"France, monarchists, Kuomintang, warlords"—

"China was nothing but hundreds of pockets of confusion," Zhu De said. "Everyone struggled to take control. I grew depressed. China signed Japan's Twenty-One Demands, attaching our country as a protectorate."

Zhu De disappeared into the cave and brought out a second chair. He sat down, back straight, hands resting on his knees.

"A teacher whom I greatly admired died, my wife died, a close friend died. I began to do official work that was tainted by the local warlord." He rubbed his knees. "I grew comfortable and well-to-do. I had a private library. I collected musical instruments. Still, I joined revolutionary study groups, hardly aware that I was splitting myself in two—a military man who was inactive, a revolutionary

who loved comfort."

Agnes did her best to translate his Chinese into English and then into shorthand. His flow of words allowed her no time to look into his face.

"I stuffed my brigade with relatives. I assured my parents who now lived with me that my brothers would be safe in battle. When they were killed, I too felt dead.

"My parents left my fancy house. They did not like the city. They longed for the country. But before they reached home, my father died." Zhu De stood. "Sun Yat-sen, father of the revolution, made alliances with one warlord, then another, trying to avoid the greater evil. Always he was betrayed." He turned and faced Agnes. "I saw that I was as confused and impotent as China itself. I decided to go to the West and find out why they could maintain independence and democracy while China could not. But before all else, I must conquer my opium habit.

"I made a plan. First, enter a hospital. Next, visit the centers of China I had never seen: Shanghai, Nanking, Beijing. In Shanghai I saw the great wealth of the few." He smiled a crooked smile. "I stared into space and daydreamed of leading a great army through the rich sections of Shanghai, killing and burning. I met Sun Yat-sen who offered me much money to organize the Yunnan army and overrun Canton, but I could not. I continued with my plan to travel to the West. I left for France."

"Did you think of going to America?" Agnes asked.

"No. America was too expensive."

By now the sun was a weak light low in the sky. Zhu De walked around to stand at the back of his chair. "I had been in France for a few weeks when I met students from my country who told me of a young Chinese man living in Berlin. He was in his mid-twenties. I was nearly forty. But by now I had no false pride." Zhu De picked up the chair and turned toward the entrance of the cave. "After talking with them I felt I could learn much from this person. And so in 1922 I set out for Berlin to meet Chou En-lai."

21
Berlin 1921

The short, muscular man with the head of thick gray hair, ears cocked at an angle, and a habit of lifting his face high when he spoke his lightning-fast, near-perfect British-Indian-accented English, looked at Agnes and said, "We have been eager to meet our sister from America. We have heard many good things of her."

Agnes studied this man, Virendranath Chattopadhyaya, who had rescued her from the customs officials at Danzig Harbor where she jumped ship.

"We can offer you accommodation here in Berlin while you look for rooms."

"I cannot pay—"

"There is no need to pay. Germany has provided us with a home in Berlin."

Agnes tried to smooth her hair. "I didn't sleep much on the trip over." She didn't expect to sleep in Berlin, either. Nearly-starved Germans creeping about the streets affected her deeply. It was impossible not to see the veterans with missing legs and arms who sat on benches and curbs in stunned dejection.

Chattopadhyaya put up one hand. "*Bitte* … ." He returned to his fast, articulate English. "Please feel free to rest. You are no doubt quite tired. I will cook curry for you when you are hungry."

As if she had slept in the pause that followed and was now rested, he leaned forward. "Tell me how matters go in New York. How is Taraknath? Salindranath? We read your news information service regularly. We follow your articles about India in other publications. Your work is splendid. I congratulate you."

"The British Secret Service reads my work, too."

Virendranath Chattopadhyaya held up his hand in a command, a plea. "I hope you will say no more. We do understand. I know what it is to be followed; to be interrogated." A shadow passed across his face. "It would be wise to find rooms as soon as possible. Our arrangement with Germany is no longer certain." The shadow lifted. "Did you have a difficult passage from America?"

"It was difficult," Agnes replied. "I was deck stewardess. For two weeks I did nothing but run here and there on command." She found herself speaking well with this intense man. "I'll have that curry now, Mr. Chattopadhyaya."

"Please call me Chatto." He stood up nimbly. "Come to the kitchen and we will talk while I prepare food."

"Tell me," Chatto said on the second day as they waited for the streetcar near the Hallensee U-Bahn. "What do you find in India, in us, to call forth such loyalty?"

Coming from him, the question did not annoy her. "I met a great Indian teacher. My friends are Indian. I love India." She looked him in the eye. "And I'm always for the underdog."

"The underdog," Chatto repeated. If he did not at first understand the expression, he soon grasped its meaning. "I am not an underdog," he said. "That must be understood."

"I am a fighter," she said. "That must be understood." The streetcar rolled toward them, its silent wheels locked onto its rails.

"It is only obvious," Chatto said.

Four days of talk confirmed their attraction. Finishing each other's sentences, interrupting each other, speaking in unison, they talked their way into bed. Though Agnes had not yet experienced sexual love, her Greenwich Village years had at least taught her how to go to bed with a man.

"I have something to tell you," Agnes whispered one night

in the darkness of their room. The steady pulse in Chatto's neck stirred against her lips. The icy coldness that had once gripped her when she was aroused, that spread from breasts to belly to genitals, no longer numbed her. Chatto was the sun. There was no possibility of frost. "I've been married before."

"Marriage is not a consideration to politically enlightened men and women," he said. She got up on one elbow to study his face. In the darkness she could not see him, but she felt his warmth, sensed his quick mind working, smelled his spicy odor that to her was the scent of India.

"Actually," Chatto said, pulling her back down beside him. "I, myself, am married."

"You're married?"

"The politically enlightened person draws no distinctions between the single and the matrimonial state," he said. "The freedom of the individual is paramount in all social arrangements."

Agnes jumped out of bed. "I'm not as enlightened as you!"

He followed her to the wardrobe where she began to dress. He was smiling.

"What's so damn funny?"

Chatto snapped to attention. "I am no longer smiling," he announced. "I will tell you about my marriage."

"I'm not interested."

"My wife is a nun," he said. "The Catholic woman left her Hindu husband and went to live in Ireland."

"In a nunnery, I suppose."

"Just so."

"Then you don't love her?"

"I don't love her," he said. "She doesn't like to talk."

"Or listen," Agnes said drily. But her eyes and mouth were not dry as she reached for him. Chatto took a very long time removing the undergarments she had just put on, yet no time at all in leading her back across the room to his bed.

In the weeks that followed there were long, intimate talks

and evenings with Indian nationalists who dropped in from all over the world. Her husband, for that is what she came to call Virendranath Chattopadhyaya, was a giant figure in exile, known to all Indians, the man who had persuaded the German government to support them, the scholar and activist from a great Brahmin family of Bengal. Her respect for him mingled with eroticism, and eroticism transformed itself back into respect. As with Lajpat Rai, she was overwhelmed by his brilliance, but this time she took her teacher for her lover.

When she glanced at the writing materials lying undisturbed on her small desk, she dismissed feelings of uneasiness. Chatto captured all her attention. She would never lose interest in this remarkable man. She no longer needed to write to prove she was somebody. She would never want to move on to see what kind of woman she might be in another context. Chatto was a magnet and her entire mind and body aligned itself to his field of force. In her letters to Florence she never admitted that her friend had been right: when she, the feminist, fell for a man, she'd fallen harder than anyone.

"Now that I'm in Berlin," she said to Chatto one day as they sat drinking tea in their room on West Falischestrasse—already they'd moved twice to avoid British agents who wanted both of them deported—"I can see that the independence work we did in New York didn't amount to a hill of beans. The leaders in India barely knew we existed."

"'A hill of beans?'"

"Of no significance."

"One can never be sure of one's own significance," Chatto replied tartly. As she began to see more and more of his dark moods, she realized he no longer felt politically significant; Germany had stopped subsidizing the Indian exiles in Berlin.

"When Germany lost the war," he told her, "Indian revolutionaries lost Germany," and he said no more. Without German support, he fed and housed, out of his own pocket, the steady stream of students and visitors who came to meet him. He still wrote letters on the letterhead of the Berlin India Revolutionary Committee, made a few speeches, took long walks with Indians, and brooded over the Third World Congress of the Communist International to be held in Moscow in March.

"In Moscow," he told her as they lay in bed, her head on his shoulder, "we will meet Lenin. It will be a coup for both of us." He kissed her. "I will regain leadership in the movement and you will publish an interview with the foremost Bolshevik."

Next day, silent and grim, he scooped rice out of the burlap bag they bought each week from the Indian grocer on Kurfurstendamm. Agnes stirred the pork dish he insisted on serving to their Muslim visitors. When the guests were Hindu, he served beef

"Many Indian traditions are foolish," he grumbled when Agnes questioned him. "A people who remain half-starved because they will not eat beef or pork when it is plentiful can never be free."

"I decline with thanks," said their Muslim guest that evening, a young man who persisted, even during meals, in wearing a hat he had found, a woman's straw hat with grapes dangling from the brim. Agnes withdrew the plate of pork and looked at Chatto uneasily. The student asked a question and Chatto responded in Persian, at the same time remarking under his breath to Agnes,

"He wears a hat with grapes but refuses to eat pork. Explain the logic."

Agnes laughed and turned her face away. The young man looked hurt.

"Please," Agnes said. She touched his hat.

Chatto spoke to their guest, then translated for Agnes. "I told him it is a summer hat for women, that he is a man, and that it is now winter." Chatto ducked his head and murmured something more in Persian, something effective, because the young man removed the hat and dug into his rice, although he still refused pork.

"I will help in your kitchen," their guest announced when the meal was finished, but Chatto urged him to linger over tea since the meeting of the Berlin India Committee would not begin until eight o'clock. Agnes, he explained, would wash the dishes and straighten the room.

Among those Indian men who, in twos and threes, silently climbed the stairs to the fifth-floor apartment was someone most unwelcome to Agnes: Herambalal Gupta. It had been nearly four years since she'd slept with him in Greenwich Village, but he still frightened her. Out of the corner of her eye she watched him seat himself on the floor. His face glowed in the lamplight. Under his turban, Agnes knew, his hair was thick and black. Once again, as in the firelight of her little room, it seemed to sway above her breasts. The old fear of arousal combined with a new fear: somehow Chatto and his friends would find out, not what Gupta had done, but what she had done.

Toward the end of the evening when Chatto spoke, she pulled her attention away from Gupta long enough to second her husband's opinion. "Chatto is right," she declared. "India's first task is to gain independence. Before ties with Russia, before Communism in India, we must shake off England." She pushed the hair away from her face. Her forehead felt clammy.

The men sat without speaking. From across the room Gupta stared at her longer than necessary. Chatto noticed and, with a short speech, brought the meeting to an end.

"The work in Germany is proving to be more difficult than it has been in the past," he said. "There have been many changes in the world, not the least within Germany itself. We must now look eastward for help. Next month in Moscow when we meet with fellow revolutionaries from around the world we will take the pulse of the movement. And we will personally speak to Bolshevik leaders."

As the men rose from their cross-legged positions on the floor, Agnes, too, stood to say good-bye. But Chatto stopped her with his hand, the command gesture, the plea that worked so well, and preempted her remarks. Gupta bowed low to Agnes. His touch of sarcasm did not go unnoticed.

"My dear young woman," Chatto began when the door had closed behind the last of the visitors, "in a roomful of Indian men you will gain more respect by a few well-chosen words than by—"

"Equal participation?" Agnes finished his sentence. Relief at Gupta's departure made her strong again. "You give lip service to independence, but I think you mean independence for men."

"Nonsense. If you are going to babble like a woman... " He began to pace about the small room.

Agnes picked up cups and teapots and set them down hard at the sink in the corner. "It is fine for me to cook curry for a small army of Indians every day of the week! It is fine for me to brew pot after pot of tea! It is fine for me to go without necessities so that guests may be treated well! But it is not fine for me to speak in a meeting! You are England and I am India!" She stormed to the far corner of the room where she knelt on the floor and began to unroll the bedding.

"You have a great deal to learn!" Chatto roared. "Not all the people I work with are as enlightened as I! They are not yet ready to listen to an American female tell them about India! You must work with me, not against me! It is I who must regain a footing in the revolutionary world! It is I who must find an alternative to working with Germany!"

She listened to him rail. Finally she lay down on the bedding and grew still.

"The work of India must go on," he said.

"Like the Ganges," she snapped. "Forever. Drowning you, drowning me."

He knelt and lay down beside her. "You are impatient, Miss Smedley," he whispered into her ear. "Individualistic. From the West you have learned to think of yourself and of comfort. It will not do for a revolutionary."

Agnes stared into the darkness. If the river of India flowed over Virendranath Chattopadhyaya, one of its own, how much faster did it flow over an American woman who never finished grade school. A woman who presumed to write. A low-class woman who had been loose with men. It seemed to Agnes that Herambalal Gupta lay in the bed between her husband and herself.

In a dream, canny and shrewd, she willed the river to roll over him, and the river obeyed. It trickled in from India, grew to be a ditchful of water, then a creek like the creeks running through Colorado coal camps. Gupta struggled in the water that flowed down the center of the bed. On the far bank Chatto still slept while the brown water, sluggish and inevitable, rose and spread onto the flood plain of the bed. Realizing what she had done, Agnes kicked off the covers and tried to stop the river as, crying, babbling in Persian and English, all three of them were carried along by the holy, dirty water.

Chatto grasped her by the arm and shouted "Swim!" He shook wet gray hair from his eyes and spat out Ganges water like a fountain. "We have an appointment in Russia!" he cried. "You are going to interview Lenin!"

The room was still littered with the boxes and bags Agnes had been too ill to unpack when they returned from Moscow. With his back to her, Chatto looked down at the traffic that passed the busy corner on West Falischestrasse.

"Your reputation hasn't helped," he said, as if speaking to the world outside their room instead of to her.

"It was a long time ago," Agnes whispered. Her throat, as so often happened these days, particularly in the afternoon, as if her body could get through only part of a day, tightened and constricted in painful spasms. The sick headaches brought on bouts of vomiting. She closed her eyes against the light coming in from the window and gingerly changed position on the bedding.

"I refer to the reputation you have today."

She opened her eyes but had to close them again. Ever since the summit meeting in Moscow where they didn't get to interview Lenin, where Chatto didn't regain the reins of leadership, where the Berlin Indian Committee had been referred to as "defunct revolutionaries" and "museum pieces," Agnes had battled physical ailments and depression. Now she waited to hear about her reputation, so ill that she felt herself slipping into agreement with Chatto, no strength to defend herself.

"People say you talk too much, you have too many opinions, you are not Indian, you have never been to India. That you give me bad advice and that I follow it." Chatto was pacing back and forth in their small room. "Indians don't like you."

She was too tired to say out loud, "I don't like Indians." But at least he was not talking about Gupta.

Chatto stopped pacing. He stood for a moment at the window, then whirled around. "Everyone knows you slept with Gupta! He talks about it openly! You have humiliated me!"

"It was years ago," Agnes said without inflection. "I'm not your property."

Chatto paled. The skin around his eyes grew mottled. Stepping over to the corner where Agnes lay, he bent down and struck her across the face.

Stunned, she struggled to a sitting position against the wall, braced herself, and then stood, wobbly on her feet. Chatto was gulping mouthfuls of air. He covered his ashen face with his hands. Agnes, unable to bear her pain and his both, set out across the floor. When she reached him he took his hands from his face and leaned against her until both of them nearly fell.

"Forgive me!" he whispered, agonized. "Please forgive me!"

She could not prevent herself from comforting him, from holding his clammy face between her hands, he who refused to wear a turban, he who questioned all things Eastern and all things Western. He whose worth others now questioned.

"Why is my reputation talked about, not Gupta's?" she whispered.

He put his hand across her mouth, this time gently. "Let us not speak of it," he said, and once more buried his face in her hair. Unable to stand, she returned on hands and knees to the bedding in the corner. When Chatto had left the room, she lay in a stupor. Mother seemed to hover over her with large, still eyes, thickened hands, a martyred spirit. Helplessness dogged both of them.

In the months that followed, Agnes had to force herself out of bed. Fearing a breakdown and not realizing she was already in the midst of one, terrified of an anonymous, early death, she spent a day here, a day there in panicky activity: gave an English lesson, typed out fragmentary pieces on her typewriter, looked for a job, though scarce jobs went to Germans, not Americans. Then either Chatto, or she, or both, would grow newly discouraged and, feeding off each other's depression, retire to their room to bicker and sleep. Chatto stormed out often, but he always came back.

"Your suffering sounds dramatic," Florence Tannenbaum wrote in the deepest, grayest part of winter. Gray streets and gray buildings of Berlin were indistinguishable from gray sleet, gray slush. Gray 1922. Gray Europe. "Since you're in Europe," wrote Florence, "why not drop in on Dr. Freud?"

Agnes was furious. "Why not advise me to drop into Heaven and have tea with God?" she wrote back. "It is far from possible, I assure you. Freud charges money; it also takes money to go to Vienna; and it requires a passport which I don't happen to have …"

"Enclosed is $25," Florence wrote back, "for psychoanalysis. I will send a check every month until you are self-sufficient again."

Holding Florence's check between her thumb and first finger, Agnes lay back on the bed. How could she accept such a sum of money every month? How could she not accept it?

There was a silk sari Chatto's sister had given her. She would send that to Florence. There was a broken strand of pearls, and she would send that, too. When she was well again she would give English lessons and write articles. She would pay back all the money she ever borrowed from Florence. And she would never again laugh at psychoanalysis, or at Florence.

She clutched the check. Her mind began to spin again in the same useless circles, always the same questions that could not be answered: how to live with Chatto? How to abandon a great man? How to abandon India?

She felt herself begin the familiar descent into semi-consciousness. Concentrating on the check in her hand, she got to her feet, crossed the room, vomited in the sink from dizziness, cleaned the sink and herself, and set out for the underground station, one foot placed methodically in front of the other. In the pocket of her coat she held onto Florence's check.

From reading the catalogue of courses given at the University of Berlin, she knew about the Psychoanalytical Institute associated with the school. Many of the analysts had studied with Freud himself. There were trainees who might agree to see a desperate American woman for a session or two.

At Unter den Linden, Agnes got off the underground train. Unaware now of the overcast sky, the grit and smell of coal smoke, the dirty snow along the sidewalks, even of the haggard people she passed carrying satchels of paper money for small purchases, she passed through the gate leading to a large, gray stone building. Inside she made inquiries of a man standing behind a counter. Three times he had to explain that the Institute was in a neighboring building. She retraced her steps toward the great front door. When she looked back, he was still watching her.

The receptionist at the Institute also watched her, but more in the way of study than disbelief. The woman opened a black book. "I will make an appointment for you to see Dr. Schmidtke three weeks from today," she said.

Agnes sank into a chair. "Is there someone I can see now?" she whispered, holding out the check. But the woman was already consulting the black book.

"Perhaps a short appointment could be made sooner," she said. Agnes wept with gratitude.

"Frau Dr. Naef can see you at three o'clock. Will that be acceptable?"

The sun broke through a cloud. "Even the weather knows," Agnes said. Her laughter was pitched too high.

Without a word the woman left the room again. When she returned she motioned for Agnes to follow her. "Dr. Naef will see you immediately. It can be only a few minutes today." They walked down a hall. She knocked on the door, then whispered, "Frau Dr. Naef is a doctor, not a trainee. She is very good."

A woman in her late forties wearing a dark skirt and white medical smock opened the door and invited Agnes into a comfortable room furnished with a patterned rug, two soft chairs, a small desk, and a couch. When the door was closed, Agnes sat on the edge of her chair. "I don't need the couch," she said.

Dr. Naef studied the new patient. "Your eyes are bright and observant even with tears," she said in accented English. "Come, let us talk about these tears."

But Agnes remained on guard.

"Tears can help us." Dr. Naef continued to study Agnes. "Tears are friends. They tell us what we need to know. They tell us about our feelings which are often difficult to understand."

Agnes was afraid to settle back in the chair, not because she didn't like this woman, but because she feared, once comfortable, she might never pull herself out of the softness.

Dr. Naef made her a cup of tea on a little hot plate in the corner of the room. At the end of thirty minutes Agnes had not spoken a word.

"Here," she said on her way out, and handed the check to the receptionist.

The woman looked at Agnes, shocked. "American dollars," she said. "This is far too much."

"Keep it for now," Agnes said. If she took what was left, she might spend it on food. Or Chatto would see it and want to lay in a supply of paper and envelopes and stamps, a request she would not be able to deny.

The receptionist unwound the string from two buttons on a brown folder, placed the check inside, and rewound the string in a figure eight. She entered the amount in a ledger. "This will pay for several sessions," she said.

"You can give me what's left when I'm finished."

"Most of our patients continue in analysis"— the woman searched for the right words—"a period of time, let us say."

"Not me," said Agnes. Still she remained at the desk.

"Good-bye, then," the woman finally said, and Agnes walked to the door. She put her hand on the doorknob.

"Can I come sooner than Tuesday?" Her throat went into another spasm and she coughed.

The woman looked in the black book. "Friday," she said. "One o'clock."

Agnes nodded and left the room. Outside, she did not notice the weather or the people she passed, only what she needed to see: the underground station, the ticket, the train seat where she could rest until she arrived at the Hallensee station. Once off the train, she would have to walk several blocks. It seemed impossible. But hadn't Dr. Naef said to her, "Don't look ahead. Think of the present. Get through one hour. That is a great accomplishment"? Agnes took a deep breath and studied her hands. They looked like Mother's.

"You're looking at your hands," Dr. Naef stated the obvious a few minutes into the second session. Agnes still sat on the edge of the large, cushioned chair. "You have done much work with your hands, I believe."

Agnes nodded.

Dr. Naef wore the same tailored skirt under the white smock. It was short and came just to the knees when she sat with one leg crossed neatly over the other. Her black shoes had a narrow strap across the instep. She wore silk stockings.

"You're not crying today," she observed, and added, "Would you like some tea?"

Agnes nodded. Her throat had seized up again. "I guess if I don't talk I won't get my money's worth," she whispered.

Dr. Naef turned around from the hot plate and laughed. "Agnes, that's amusing. And it's true."

"I used to laugh at my friend for going to a psychiatrist. Now she's paying for me to be analyzed."

Dr. Naef returned from the corner with two cups of tea. "Is it difficult for you to talk about yourself?"

"My throat gets dry."

Dr. Naef took a swallow of tea. In the silence she touched up her blonde-gray hair that was done off the neck in a loose roll, like a sausage. The front, too, was combed back from her face in a similar well-kept roll. Dr. Naef was neither young nor old, pretty nor ugly. She took another sip of tea and said something about the close relationship between the body and mind.

Agnes felt embarrassed. "I'm neurotic." She knew what "neurotic" meant. It meant you thought there was something wrong with you when there really wasn't. If she would just straighten up, think less about herself, help Chatto instead of lying on a sick bed, work unselfishly for India, forget about Western desire for recognition, publication, money of her own, she wouldn't need to be spending Florence's check on a psychiatrist.

"Why do you think you're neurotic?"

Agnes could barely hear Dr. Naef over Mother's voice. *Such a selfish girl.*

Dr. Naef didn't seem to mind when Agnes couldn't answer. This psychiatrist, Agnes decided, was better than Florence's psychiatrist. She liked the woman's lively blue eyes that showed personality. Her nose was long and aquiline. When she was especially interested, her nostrils flared into dainty triangles. Her attention never wandered.

Several weeks into the analysis, Dr. Naef's professional objectivity faltered. "But surely there were happy times in your childhood." She leaned forward and her nostrils flared daintily.

"I remember a few happy times," Agnes admitted. "But compared to the misery, they don't amount to a hill of beans."

"What is this 'hill of beans'?"

"'Of no significance.'"

Dr. Naef slipped into reflection. She might have been contemplating the figure of speech. "Perhaps the few happy times," she finally said, "can cast light. Yes. We will use it as a small torch. Its beams will dart about in the blackness and help us see."

Agnes crossed her arms. "I don't want to think about my childhood anymore," she said. "I just want a little advice from you."

"My dear young woman, ask your friends for advice, not your analyst. The purpose of psychoanalysis is not to give advice."

"What is the purpose?"

"To complete the formation of the personality."

Agnes glowered. "What's wrong with my personality?"

"There is more growth to be done. You, yourself, are dissatisfied with your personality but do not know what steps to take. And so, in confusion and grief, you grow physically ill." Dr. Naef looked at the clock. The hour was up. She stood, an imposing figure. "We will look into the past," she concluded. "It requires courage. I will be there to help you. When we are acquainted with the child Agnes, we will begin to know the woman. And when you know the woman, you will feel more complete."

Agnes walked out. Her headache was coming back. She didn't want somebody in a white jacket telling her she wasn't complete. She didn't want to know more about her childhood. She didn't even want a childhood. She didn't want to dilute her anger with pity, dangerous pity, that could dwarf you, turn you into a weeping, sodden mass, undermine you, show you up for what you are: a pitiful person held together by hard work, will power, and fury.

She canceled her next two appointments. When she returned she was thinner and paler than before.

Dr. Naef's expression was bland, almost without interest. "Hello," she said, and seated herself. But this time Agnes did not perch on the edge of the soft chair. She took a deep breath, crossed the room, and threw herself lengthwise upon the couch. Dr. Naef's nostrils flared with interest.

"I want more than advice," Agnes said. "Analyze me."

"First comes relaxation," said Dr. Naef, "and then we will talk."

"I'm relaxed," Agnes said, breathing heavily. "You talk. I'll listen."

Dr. Naef reached for a notebook and pen on the small table next to her chair. "Are you rushing into this, Agnes?"

"Yes."

"The past is a difficult and frightening place for you," Dr. Naef said. "Let us approach it slowly."

"I'm thirty-one years old," Agnes said. "I don't have time for a slow approach." Nevertheless, she lay quiet until her breathing was even. "I'm ready."

"A happy time. A rare, singular, happy time in your childhood," Dr. Naef said. "Put yourself back there, and when you want to tell me about it, speak."

Agnes thought for a few minutes. "I could tell you about the day we got molasses from the Westons."

"Very well."

"It wasn't all happy."

"Fine."

"Father came home from a business trip." She rolled her head toward Dr. Naef. "'Business' was carousing in St. Joe. He'd be gone for weeks at a time." Agnes closed her eyes but soon lifted herself up onto one elbow. "It's hard to talk about myself," she said. "I'll pretend it's a story."

"Fine," said Dr. Naef. Agnes lay back on the couch and began.

We need some sweetenin', Father said when he got home from St. Joe.

Oh, Charles, Mother said, it's going to be a hard enough winter without we spend money on molasses.

It'll be a harder winter if we don't get some sweetenin'. We're goin' to the Westons' for molasses.

Immediately I developed a terrible hunger for molasses.

Mamie Weston's my friend from school, I said.

Who's to say she'll remember you? Mother said. You haven't been to school since Grover was a pup. The Westons'll be busy what with everyone bringing in their cane. Don't be expecting too much, Agnes. You'll only be disappointed.

She began combing out Myrtle's hair. John and Sam were eating bread and butter on one of the rag rugs Mother braided. I wandered outside. The sun was bright, the air cool; the kind of a day, Father said, when a nice breeze blows from Kansas and Colorado. I saw Father wave from the barn and I ran back to the cabin.

It's time to go!

Mother sighed and picked Sammy up from where he was propped beside the sewing machine. John was old enough to walk by himself, and he came over to me with crumbs on his mouth. He had chubby little fingers that were shiny with butter…

Agnes faltered.

"You feel deeply about John," Dr. Naef said quietly. Agnes nodded and put the heels of her hands against her eyes to stop tears.

I cleaned him up. Mother and the children and I walked to the barn.

Goddam bridle's broke, Father said when we got to the wagon.

Mother looked worried in her resigned sort of way. Father cursed and fixed the bridle "just temporary." It was harder to get sweetenin', he said, than horse radish from a horse, but they could at least try, even if Mother did look sour as old milk and the children were more trouble than shoes on a chicken.

Agnes opened her eyes. They were clouded. "I'm adding a little bit here and there," she said.

Dr. Naef nodded.

At the Weston house Mamie's mother stood at a shallow, three-footed vat. Beside her, Mamie was taller than I remembered. She was throwing sticks onto the fire. As soon as Father stopped the team a ways off from the shed, I jumped down from the wagon.

Mamie!

Hush! said Mother. The Westons are busy.

But Mamie dropped the last of her sticks on the fire and began walking toward the wagon. When she got closer to me, she broke into a run and didn't stop until we were face to face.

You want some molasses? She reached for my hand and we walked back to the vat. It was steaming and bubbling.

Mamie's mother looked up from the rolling boil. So this is your friend.

It's Agnes, said Mamie, from Knob School. You coming to

school this year, Agnes?

Don't know. I scuffed a place in the dirt with my shoes. When does school start?

Mrs. Weston gave a final stir and leaned the long-handled spoon against the lip of the vat. She wiped her hands on her apron and set off for our wagon.

Don't know.

I leaned forward and looked into the vat at the glossy molasses. The fumes were sweet, like taffy, but there was a taint of something foreign, something interesting. It was a smell that sharpened the sweetness; added an edge of danger to the candy.

Mind the vat! called out Mother.

I stepped back.

It's going to be a hard winter, I said. I don't know if I can go to school this year.

I remembered the geography book at school; the blackboard and chalk on the north wall. You're a good speller, I said.

So are you.

It was hot there by the fire, with the steam coming off the sorghum. Mamie grabbed my hand and we ran over to a stack of cane where she broke off two pieces, one for her, one for me, and began to chew on the end. I did what she did. The tough fibers gave out the sugar Father had told us about; the sweetening he and I both craved.

Inside the Weston cabin there was a cane-backed chair by the hearth. There was a clock and sewing machine, chairs and a love seat, two separate bedrooms, and a real wood floor.

I'll show you something, Mamie said.

I looked. It's only a cloth doll! I said.

Her name's Madeleine.

Madeleine!

I'd never heard such a prissy name. She wasn't real. And people said I lied! This doll was a lie. Nobody is that pretty; that loved.

You got any good climbing trees?

There was too much of everything in the Weston cabin. Too much nice furniture. Too much peace and quiet. Too much love for a silly doll.

I like high trees, I said. Like to get up off the ground.

Once we were outside, I boosted Mamie up into the apple tree and followed. This isn't very high, I said. We sat on a bough almost bare of leaves. I don't know if I can come to school this year. I'm late now, anyway. No point starting.

Don't matter if you're late, Mamie said. I'll tell Teacher you had to help out at home.

You're lucky being an only child and all, I told her. But I can climb higher than you. I was ready to bust from the wish to go to school and from the wish to show Mamie I was equal. I shinnied up the trunk and reached a higher limb. But it wasn't any fun to race with Mamie. She didn't care if she was higher or not.

I looked down through what leaves still held to the tree. Already Mamie had started to climb down. I felt for footholds and came down, too. When we reached the grown-ups standing around a pail of sorghum by the wagon, I blurted out, Can I go to school again?

Mother squeezed me by the shoulder. Don't ask about that now.

Father laughed. What does a girl need school for? He looked up to share the joke with Leroy. But Mr. Weston had moved a little way off where he stood writing something in a pocket notebook. I was surprised to see someone carry a pencil and paper. He stopped to write something down the way you might pick up a stone or break a twig off a bush. I'd never seen anyone stop in their work to reach for a pencil or slip a notebook back into their pocket like it was as common as a tobacco pouch.

By now Agnes' breathing was slow and deep. Except for the wind blowing around the corner of the Berlin University building, there was no sound.

Dr. Naef ended the silence. "It seems as if you know this child Agnes very well. You are a gifted story-teller."

Agnes smiled and nodded, as if she were used to being wakened from a dream. She came to a sitting position and looked up, surprised. "I had my feet at the wrong end of the couch," she said.

Dr. Naef laughed. "Perhaps psychoanalysis works better when the feet are where the head should be."

"Being analyzed isn't so bad," Agnes said.

"Next week we will begin the hard work," Dr. Naef said. "We will talk more about this young Agnes who so badly needed sweetening."

"I thought we were finished with that story. Next week I can tell you a different one."

Dr. Naef said nothing but looked for a long moment into Agnes' eyes. With a touch of mystery, she said good-bye. Agnes hurried home, filled with energy. She wrote an article that she called "Starving Germany." The paragraphs on inflation, hunger, illness, suicides, splintering political parties, failed to depress her. She mailed it off to *The Nation* and began another. She canceled her next appointment with Dr. Naef and spent Florence's check on food and a new dress.

But by the time she received a letter of acceptance from *The Nation*, accompanied by a check for $17.50, she was sick again.

"I felt good after my analysis," she said to Dr. Naef in a stricken voice. "I thought I was cured. How long do I have to be analyzed? I should be writing. I should be earning my own money instead of waiting for Florence's checks. I shouldn't be depending on analysis!" She spat out the word, then burst into tears.

"It is common for patients to think they are well before they actually are," said Dr. Naef. "Perhaps the extent of your instability has not been clear to you. But it has been clear to me. Now we can begin the real work."

"I can't bear to be a cripple!" Agnes cried out from the couch. "I can't bear to come limping back here again and again!"

"Until now, your youth and strong will have carried you," Dr. Naef said quietly. "You were a child and now you are called upon to be a woman."

"I don't want to be a woman!"

"Let us talk about that," Dr. Naef urged. She got up, poured two cups of tea, and returned to her chair. "In Vienna, Dr. Freud has elucidated a theory which you may find interesting."

Agnes looked up, guarded. "What's the theory?"

"It is believed that when a little girl realizes she doesn't have a penis, she unconsciously feels that hers has been cut off. She feels as if she has lost something important. She feels that someone has taken something that belonged to her. She is plunged into grief. She is bereft, and she is angry, too."

Agnes stared at Dr. Naef, insulted. "I never felt that someone cut off my…" She could not say the word.

"We are talking about an unconscious process," Dr. Naef said. "The child is not aware of these thoughts and feelings. Nevertheless, she must live with the consequences of this knowledge."

"But it's just a theory. A man's theory."

"A useful theory."

Agnes sat in deep reflection.

"Can you share your thoughts with me?" Dr. Naef asked.

Agnes began to rub her forehead compulsively.

"I can't leave Chatto!" she cried out. "He gets sick when I leave. I tried it for a few days. I had to come back." She looked up. "Men aren't as strong as women! They want mothers! They suck away our energy! Marriage is a struggle for power and I'm losing!"

"Is it possible to share power and to share love?" Dr. Naef said.

But Agnes didn't hear her. "For instance," she rushed on, "I've been invited to give a speech on Gandhi to an English class at the University. Chatto says I can't do it because I don't know enough." She looked up, desperate. "I think I know enough. I think he's angry because they didn't invite *him*."

"Who invited you, Agnes?"

"A friend I met in Russia, Emma Goldman. She knows someone who teaches at Berlin University. Emma thinks it would be good for me to give a talk."

"You must give this speech."

Agnes picked up the pillow from the end of the couch and held onto it. Her throat seized up and she had to cough. She sank back onto the couch.

"I can't give a talk in a university," she whispered. "I never even finished grade school."

"You're very familiar with the Indian independence movement. You are a fine speaker. Sometimes you hold me enthralled, Agnes. You are quite capable of giving a talk on Gandhi." Dr. Naef looked at the clock on the wall and stood. "I will speak to your husband," she said in a brisk tone. "Perhaps Freud would not, but I will. He is depressed and fails to grasp the situation. Allow me to speak to him."

"When?"

"Tomorrow over lunch, if he is free. Perhaps I can explain what this would mean to your recovery."

"I think maybe he is afraid his—you know what—has been cut off."

"Do not be too sure," said Dr. Naef. "Easy answers can be wrong. But it is possible your success threatens him at this particular time."

"Maybe I should just stay sick," Agnes said. She stood up and reached for her coat on its hook.

"No," said Dr. Naef. "You will not stay sick. And neither will Chatto. Both of you must work through this difficulty."

At the door Agnes hesitated. "You're much better than Florence's psychiatrist," she said. "You're better than Freud himself."

Dr. Naef looked startled. "We do not all agree with Dr. Freud in every respect," she said. "I am perhaps less objective than he would like." She gazed at a spot above Agnes' head. "I believe the relationship between the patient and analyst is, in itself, healing."

Agnes reached out to Dr. Naef and the two women shook hands.

On the day of the lecture Agnes could barely haul herself out of bed.

"I can't give the talk," she said to Chatto who was dressing to go out. "I'm too sick."

Chatto gave up the attempt to tame his wiry hair and replaced the comb in his pocket. He shrugged. "It is your decision." He stared out the window glumly, then turned back and said with an effort, "I will be in the audience. It will be a disservice to all concerned if you cancel the speech."

Agnes glanced away. She knew how much it had cost Chatto to meet with Dr. Naef. When he'd returned home he'd even admitted to an interest in psychoanalysis, this phenomenon of the twentieth century, but he refused to discuss Agnes' case.

"The proof of the pudding is in the eating," he had said, pleased with the figure of speech. "If you regain your health I will have much respect for this psychoanalysis."

That night, the lecture hall was crowded. In his introduction the professor described Agnes' years of work for Indian independence. He mentioned Chatto. He listed her publications, more than she remembered writing. She had perched on the edge of the speaker's chair in case she decided to jump down from the platform and run. But instead of running, she found herself taking steps toward the lectern.

She held her shaking hands behind her back and began to read from the speech she'd typed on thin paper. After reading several lines she began to hear the words. By the time she reached the paragraphs on revolution in exile, she grew interested, herself, in the sweep of the movement. She had been so busy with small parts of the work that she had failed to see history's firm grip on the Indian subcontinent.

Eight or ten Chinese students sat in the back row, their faces impassive. Chatto sat directly in front of them, his gray hair standing out from his head. As she neared the end of the lecture, she sought him out. Strangely, although he was in sharp focus, his face began to grow small, as if she were seeing through the wrong end of a telescope. Fascinated, she watched him grow smaller and smaller until she could hardly see his face against the row of Chinese students behind him. She acknowledged the applause and answered a question from the audience.

Yes, she said, she was confident that India would gain its freedom. She was confident that history was moving, even at that very moment, to make other changes in Asia as well. As she spoke, Chatto appeared in actual size again, and with the return to normality, she realized, in a matter-of-fact way, that she was no longer of use to Chatto. In an anti-climactic moment of clarity, she knew he belonged to her past, and it occurred to her that time's flow can only be caught in occasional fleeting moments, like this one. That we are too busy to understand our lives and our work. That in those rare moments when we see ourselves clearly, we have already been used up, thrown away, and are being made ready for the next task.

We are thrown away, Agnes thought, so the world will get better.

She answered another question from the audience, and then she ended the evening with a question of her own: what will be the next massive change to occur in Asia?

She watched the Chinese students in the last row leave the hall. They did not look back. They had asked no questions and given no answers.

"I understand your lecture was a great success," Dr. Naef said at their next session. "In one generation you have leapt from frontier farm to European university."

Agnes closed her eyes. She could not remember ever feeling worse. Chatto and she had fought the night before. He was jealous of everything she did; everyone she met. He had now become a patient of Dr. Eitingon, the analyst who founded the Berlin Institute. But instead of contributing to his relationship with Agnes, analysis seemed to be driving the wedge between them ever deeper.

"We are both being analyzed and we are both miserable," Agnes said to Dr. Naef. "The only difference between us is that I pay for my analysis and Chatto gets his free."

Dr. Naef lifted her eyebrows. "Chatto is not paying for his analysis?"

"No."

"Why not?"

"Because an Indian who is such a wreck is interesting. But I'm just an American."

Dr. Naef smiled. "You are a wreck, too. That should give you some comfort." Agnes was too depressed to laugh. She covered her eyes with her forearm and lay without moving on the couch.

"The purpose of psychoanalysis is to develop understanding," Dr. Naef said. "Happiness is something else again." She waited for some kind of response, but there was none.

"Do you want to stay with Chatto?"

"No."

"Do you want to leave him?"

Agnes made no reply.

"In any case," said Dr. Naef, "you are profoundly sad. I have seen you in many moods, Agnes. I have seen you elated, despondent, and many degrees of feeling in-between."

Agnes nodded.

"But now I think you are facing the grief that is at your core. Falling ill, plunging into activity, anger, none of that will do now. You are strong enough to endure your sadness. It is a sadness you have earned. It is yours."

"I don't understand what you're saying," Agnes whispered.

"Your throat is constricted with unshed tears. I think when you have accepted your grief, your body will not work at cross purposes with your mind."

"Why must I be sad?"

"Do you know, yourself, why you must be sad?"

"Mother," Agnes whispered. "Father. The children."

"Your family has made you sad," Dr. Naef said after a bit. "Your own intelligence has made you sad. You have taken on burdens. They will not make you happy, but they are yours."

"There are burdens I should have taken on."

"You were not strong enough at the time."

"I wish someone would carry *me*."

"Chatto would carry you if you let him."

"But that puts me in a weak position."

Dr. Naef lifted her hands. "You are in conflict."

"Sometimes I feel I cannot live."

"You have lived more than thirty years," Dr. Naef said. "Why not tell a story about those thirty years? Tell it thoroughly until you understand yourself. You are a fine story-teller. In writing, I think you will find peace."

"Who should I tell it to?" asked Agnes.

"Who were you talking to in your speech the other night?"

"The audience."

"Who is your audience when you tell stories from your life?"

"You."

Dr. Naef sat in thought. "You need a larger audience than one," she said. "You can write a book. It will be a very good book, I assure you."

"For who?" Agnes corrected herself: "For whom?"

"For the world. You are interesting enough to hold the world's attention."

"For a moment, maybe."

Dr Naef smiled. "No one can ask for more than a moment."

22
Berlin 1928

Rain on the window panes blurred the houses across Holsteinischstrasse. Agnes fought back a rising desire to see Dr. Naef. She sat with the manuscript, *Daughter of Earth*, resting in her lap. With the intensity of a child who wants to show her mother, father, lover, God himself, what she has made, she longed to run through the wet streets of Berlin and deliver the manuscript of her book to her analyst.

Writing the book hasn't improved my personality, she would say right off the bat. You said it would cure me, but it hasn't. I still come running back to you.

It is a good sign, this passion for your book, Dr. Naef might reply. It has done its work. You are alive again.

Agnes had begun the book in Denmark three years earlier, with a young Indian lover established in a cottage adjoining the house of writer Karin Michaelis. On that small island separated from the mainland of Denmark by a narrow sound of limpid gray water, it was Bakar, not Chatto, who interrupted her work, called her to his cottage two and three times a day, not to mention the nights. But she would not tell Dr. Naef about Bakar. Dr. Naef liked Chatto. And Dr. Naef believed in marriage.

Agnes heard a question so clearly that she felt compelled to answer it:

Was Chatto in Denmark with you, Agnes?

Nope. He was back in Berlin. I couldn't have written if he'd been with me. I will never go back to Chatto, Dr. Naef. I will not commit myself to one man, deny myself sexual and creative freedom. Take Florence, for instance. Generous, silly Florence has gotten married.

Let us examine these feelings about Florence, Dr. Naef seemed to say.

I don't need to examine my feelings. I'm disgusted because she's abandoned her writing, her independence. She's caved in to convention and I'm disappointed in her. But then, she always was a ninny.

Would that have been a shadow passing across Dr. Naef's eyes?

A ninny, you say, except when she sends you $25 every month.

$25 is peanuts to Florence, Dr. Naef. I am not embarrassed to accept money from rich friends.

The rain outside her window had let up. Agnes lit a cigarette and shook out the match. But Dr. Naef's presence was not to be obscured by a small cloud of smoke.

What do your women friends mean to you, Agnes?

Agnes inhaled deeply and closed her eyes. Dr. Naef, she imagined, was leaning forward, the roll of hair at the back of her head shiny and in place, her expression of professional calm not quite hiding personal interest.

What is Tilla Durieux to you, Agnes?

Startled, then irritated, Agnes opened her eyes and tapped off the ash.

Tilla took me on as a friend and a project. For three years she supported me. I wore her elegant, hand-me-down clothes. I was driven here and there in Berlin, even on trips outside Berlin, by her chauffeur. People gossip, particularly some of Chatto's friends who are already against me for being Western and outspoken. They think I was sexual with Tilla. But let them talk. Without Tilla I couldn't have afforded to write the book. Wouldn't have had an introduction to my publisher. Eventually I grew tired of Tilla's wealth. The taste of upper-class life began to cloy. I felt terrible seeing beggars from the back seat of her Reis-Benz motor car. I liked Tilla, but I had no illusions. I accepted the friendship, money, training, connections. Now can we stop talking about the past?

Dr. Naef's face came clearly into focus.

You're in charge of this conversation, Agnes.

It had stopped raining. Agnes laid her manuscript aside, got her coat, and walked to the konditoria on Hohenzollern where she ordered coffee. Berliners, many of them back to their pre-war stoutness, had to have their cakes and *kuchen* every day. Agnes took only coffee. She found eating a chore, and endured stomach pains off and on. Her friend Käthe Kollwitz once sketched her in a hospital bed, skin and bones, the face of a refugee.

Käthe was one of the few friends Agnes had not borrowed money from. Käthe was poor, and in the presence of the great artist, Agnes had felt ashamed wearing Tilla's fussy clothes.

She'd been given money by Margaret Sanger, Karin Michaelis, and there were others. She knew quite well that she was a poor manager of money. She had a contempt for money which, she admitted, did not prevent her from accepting cash. Friends saw how poor she was and how hard she worked. They wanted to help her. She threw herself into tasks that they could not or would not do, and they paid her. Fine. It was one more tool a lower-class girl could use to get through life.

She drank her coffee. Absently she watched the waitress behind the counter move the last slices of cake from a soiled plate to a clean one, shuffle the sweets onto paper doilies, then wipe away the crumbs. All must be clean. All must be tidy. Germany. She would be happy to leave Germany.

And how is Chatto?

Chatto joined the Communist Party. He asked me to join, too, but I can't, no more than I can join in a marriage. I can't submit to anything or anyone. Besides, Communists don't understand the working class. They're not realistic about poor and ignorant people.

She finished her coffee and set the cup down decisively.

No more questions, Dr. Naef. I have something to tell you. I'm finished with Berlin. I'm going to China.

China? Dr. Naef's nostrils flared with interest. You've made up your mind?

Yes. I'm Shanghai correspondent for the *Frankfurt Zeitung*. Europe is tired, and I'm tired of Europe. The future is Asia. That's where a writer like me belongs.

Dr. Naef's eyes were a bright blue.

I'm going to write about China for Indian newspapers. I'm going to introduce Indians who live in the treaty ports to Nationalist Chinese. I'm going to work for revolution. England is done for. I want to be in Asia when the Empire dies.

Agnes paid for the coffee and put on her coat. For a moment she allowed herself to be pleased. She was burning brightly. If she didn't get sick, didn't get discouraged or depressed, she could burn on and on.

The door of the *konditoria* banged shut behind her. The wind was drying the streets. At the corner, she turned left and began walking at a brisk pace.

She was not going to see Dr. Naef. She had known it all along. The past was the past. It was over. Used up. Her work was the future. China called.

23

Manchuria 1928

Agnes pressed herself into one corner of her compartment and waited for the train to pull out of the Berlin station.

Everything she knew about China deserted her. Asia had become a continent not to be talked about, but to be lived. The other half of the world was as near as the other half of herself. It felt like a destiny which she now wished to evade. All that first night, upright and tense, she was aware of her heartbeat; felt, in fact, like a massive heart, herself, valves squeezing open and shut.

White ground rushed by the frost-patterned window. The train stopped often for snow to be shoveled off the tracks. At the Russian border, a solitary guard stood silent and watchful in his boots and great coat, rifle butt resting on the ground, fixed bayonet even with the red star on his peaked hat. He faced west as uncertainly as Agnes faced east.

Several side trips and six weeks later when she stepped down from the train onto Manchurian ground, a pack of fifteen or twenty coolies came running toward her. Behind them, wet, falling snow nearly obliterated the single light bulb hanging outside the Customs shed. The conductor shouted something in Russian and made a motion as if he were tossing coins from the train. The ragged clot of men scattered, then gathered again, fighting to get close to the foreign woman, to pick up her suitcase and portable typewriter. They stuck their open hands into her face for money and touched her clothes.

A blast of steam pierced the Northeast China night. The train that had carried her across the vast Russian steppe huffed, labored, and began to move. Agnes wanted to run alongside it, shouting to be let back on. Instead, she stood motionless and stared into the heart, not of 1928, but of the Middle Ages. She followed the coolies into the Customs shed where a powerfully built Mongol studied her papers patiently and without comprehension.

In Harbin she found an interpreter. He was slim and lithe and his black hair gleamed in the winter sunlight. He concentrated when she spoke, for his English was rudimentary.

"America," he said. "Too far."

They tramped in the snow past stores filled with hunting, trapping, and fishing gear. Lucrative retail trade centered around furs: squirrel, fox, Russian sable, Siberian bear, Korean tiger. Mongolian dogs were raised for their long silky hair. Her interpreter tried to explain that, since the spirits of human ancestors were housed within their narrow skulls, the dogs must not be killed but must be allowed to die naturally.

"Like coolies," Agnes said, but the interpreter did not understand.

He took her to a horse sale where Mongols from the Gobi Desert met to race their ponies. Agnes watched a buyer and seller strike a deal. They inserted their hands into each other's sleeves and pressed out a number without speaking.

"Price secret," said the interpreter.

Beggars stood, sat, lay in the streets. Agnes forced herself to look at the women who carried their dirty babies tucked in the fronts of their padded jackets. "Give!" they cried. They made her think of her defeated mother.

She pushed herself hard, walking by day, pounding out articles for the *Frankfurter Zeitung* by night. In the early morning hours she would crawl into bed beside the interpreter and go through motions of love that she craved but did not feel. Soon after daylight broke she hurried out to cable her article, for she needed both money and confirmation of her writing from the German editor.

"Send more character sketches," he cabled back. "Forget

Japanese in Manchuria."

She cabled back: "Article on Japanese aggression sent Monday."

Not only had she seen Japanese military swaggering down the streets of Harbin, but she had met a newspaper reporter from Vladivostock who told her the Russians were building airfields and underground shelters, and widening the gauge of all railroad tracks to accommodate military equipment. They expected war with Japan.

"Japan a threat in Asia," she cabled her editor again. "Print article," but he did not comply.

Insomniac, bothered by a stubborn cough, she went to bed, but sleeping powders could not silence the beggars' cries outside her window.

Her interpreter brought food and a rumor from the Consulate. "British say Miss Smedley no travel in China. Wrong papers."

Agnes roused herself from bed and began to pack. "An American passport isn't good enough for the British," she said, swaying on the bedroom floor. "We're leaving for Mukden."

"Every Chinese run sometime," the interpreter said, and steadied her with his fine-boned hand.

In Mukden they had to run again. "You run so fast as Chinese," he said.

Agnes tried to explain that, because of her work with Indian nationalists, she was a defendant, an absent defendant, in a trial taking place in India; that the British were afraid she might incite the Indian Sikhs in the treaty ports of China to political action.

"We run together," the interpreter said cheerfully, and reseated his frameless glasses on his small nose.

Eluding British agents in Manchuria, they fled to Beijing, Nanjing, and finally Shanghai. In the French Concession, Agnes met a German woman, a reporter from *China Weekly News*, who offered to share her apartment. Agnes and the interpreter moved in immediately. While Agnes shopped for food, he found a bottle of creme de menthe in a cupboard and drank it down. The landlady had discovered him on the floor having a foaming green seizure and called for help. When Agnes returned, a massive Russian doctor sat in the living room waiting for payment. Agnes paid, but that night she slept on the sofa. The next day she terminated the interpreter and went looking for another, finding an attractive man whom she liked; Agnes had swung as forcibly into sexuality as she had once forcibly denied it.

She moved from room to room, apartment to apartment, outmaneuvering the Shanghai police, who took their orders from Britain. Fanning Indian nationalism, reinforcing the subcontinent's drive for independence, she gave speeches to small groups of Sikhs in secret meeting places—"red heads," the Chinese called them because they wore official red turbans as they directed traffic from kiosks in the streets. She made contacts and friends, amused some people, offended others. She began to see her articles in print.

At the German bookstore on Soochow Creek, she met European leftists who lived in Shanghai.

"I'm Agnes Smedley," she told the man who introduced himself as Richard Johnson. "I'm a writer. What are you doing in China?"

But Mr. Johnson did not answer directly. They strolled along the water that smelled of fish and stagnant shore line and cook smoke from hundreds of junks tied to pilings and to each other. The name "Johnson" and his accent, which was hard to locate—Russian? German?—made Agnes disbelieve him. He was handsome, a rugged Nordic type with a strong, craggy face and, she was sure, plenty of craggy experience. He invited her to dinner and helped her into a rickshaw that an aged coolie pulled to the curb. The crowds, the shouts, the shuffle of a thousand wheels and a thousand sandals constituted a prolonged and dreamy traffic through which their rickshaw moved.

"What are your plans in China?" he asked when they were seated in a small restaurant on Nanjing Street in the International Settlement. He offered her a cigarette and they dipped their heads to the same flame.

Agnes blew out a cloud of smoke and reverted to her tough manner. "I told you. I'm a reporter. I write."

"You're American."

"A citizen of the world," she said. "I'm a freelance revolutionary."

Richard Johnson looked amused. Agnes assessed his handsomeness, confidence. She thought he was an agent for one faction or another in politically splintered Shanghai. They rested their cigarettes in the ashtray and wiped their chopsticks on linen napkins.

"What are you writing?" he asked.

"An article about a peasant woman in Manchuria."

Richard Johnson picked a shred of tobacco from the tip of his tongue and looked at her through smoke while she described an old woman in Mukden who fell on the ice. A crowd had gathered, laughing at the spread legs and bound stumps of feet.

"She cursed them," Agnes said, and half-closed her eyes as she quoted from the article. "She cursed the assembled men, all their ancestors back to the thousandth generation, and all the brats they would bring into the world in the future. She cursed them individually and collectively, up and down and around and about. She cursed systematically and thoroughly, working them over inch by inch."

"You have a good style," Richard Johnson said. The waitress set a plate in front of them. He offered her a preserved duck's egg in gelatin. "Are there other American writers in Shanghai?"

"If there are, I don't know them. I prefer the Chinese. Out here most foreigners are one-hundred percent boobs and all are one-hundred-fifty percent imperialists."

After dinner he took her home by rickshaw, their feet resting side by side on the carpeted footrest. Mounted oil lamps illuminated the shoulders and elbows of the coolie running between bamboo shafts.

"May I see you again?" he asked.

"How about tonight?"

Mr. Johnson showed no surprise, but followed her up to her room. He hung his coat on a hook beside Agnes'.

She poured them both a shot of whiskey, took a swallow from one of the glasses, and set it down hard.

"Jesus Christ!" she screamed, and averted her eyes from the wastebasket.

Richard Johnson bumped against the table, sending both whiskey glasses to the floor, and caught Agnes just before she fell. They gripped each other and stared into the wastebasket at the bloody face of an Indian Sikh.

"God! Christ!" Agnes wailed. Richard Johnson swore in German. Agnes moved toward the door and ran for the bathroom down the hall. When she returned, Johnson was standing by the wastebasket with another drink, his complexion greenish. Agnes knelt and began to pick up broken glass from the pool of spilled whiskey.

"Who … "

Agnes gagged. "I don't know." She got up from the floor, carefully holding the handful of broken glass, and started for the wastebasket. When she realized what she had been about to do, she backed up and laid the fragments in a tidy pile on the table.

"It's a message to mind my own business." She knelt again and mopped up the whiskey with a towel.

"A message," Johnson said drily. "Wouldn't it have been easier to send a letter?"

Shocked by his humor, Agnes sat back on her heels.

"A letter," Johnson repeated. He peered into the wastebasket. "Dear Miss Smedley … "

Agnes began to laugh. She got down on all fours and crawled toward the severed head. "This is to inform you," she said and, with face averted, squeezed the towel out over the wastebasket.

"Only in Shanghai … " said Johnson. Agnes got to her feet, hung the towel on a hook, and tottered back to stand by Johnson who had lit a cigarette. He offered her a drag. They sat down on the edge of the bed, traded the cigarette back and forth, and grew silent, as if being watched.

"The British Secret Service aren't the only ones I've upset," Agnes whispered. There might as well have been a third person in the room who shouldn't hear what they were saying. "Indian nationalists are a volatile lot."

Johnson stood and grasped the wastebasket. Holding it out from his body, he walked to the door.

"My speeches have stirred them up," Agnes continued. "I criticized their methods. I told them they're out of touch with India. There's been a violent argument and they've deposited the loser in my wastebasket."

Johnson put his hand on the doorknob and looked down at the head. "I'm going to remove it," he said, sounding tentative.

"It's already been removed," said Agnes. Johnson came back and fell onto the edge of the bed where he and Agnes leaned against each other, giggling, unstrung.

"Indians are an emotional—" Agnes began, but she was interrupted by Richard Johnson pulling her down onto the bed, followed by whispers, laughter, more whispers.

While he went to the light switch by the door, Agnes pulled off her sweater and slacks. Johnson looked into the wastebasket, shrugged, clicked off the light, and made his way back to the bed where he undressed and slid beneath the feather ticking Agnes lifted for him.

Far from inhibiting them, the head in the wastebasket made sex free and lusty. They laughed. They groaned. Over the next few hours Agnes fell in love with this Richard Johnson. Fell in love with the deep voice, the tender chuckle that cracked as it reached a higher register. Fell in love with the guffaw lurking at the edge of what she thought was his spy mentality. The horse laugh at the center of fatalism.

Had she known he was Richard Sorge, not Richard Johnson, she wouldn't have cared. What she loved was the way they talked as equals, she a working journalist, he a working— Agnes wasn't sure what. He said he was a correspondent for European newspapers, but he wasn't specific. Spies in Shanghai were as thick on the ground as slugs after a rain. He was a spy, she thought. That suited her fine. A revolutionary who had no doubt left a comfortable position in a European university—for he seemed intellectual as well as a man of action—to come out here and help build a new and better world.

That night, while this man who called himself Richard Johnson slept, Agnes crept out of bed, dressed, and walked to the wastebasket. Turning her face from the meaty smell, she opened the door and glided down the hall. Because informers often lounged around the entrance to her section of the building, she climbed the half-flight of steps to the flat roof, crossed it, and re-entered an adjacent wing. She exited at ground level, moved quickly along the street, turned a corner, and ducked into a lane where she emptied the basket onto a pile of rocks and debris in the dark corner of a construction site. She returned to her room.

"Where did you take it?" Richard Johnson asked.

How alert he was, she thought. Even when wakened from sleep, he chose the right language of all his probable languages: English. He'd known immediately where he was and he'd known exactly why she'd left.

"I would have taken it out for you," he added. She undressed again and lay close to him. When he turned and put his face next to hers, waves of tenderness washed through her. He kissed her deeply. Eroticism carried them outside themselves and this time there was no laughter.

The next day they walked along the waterfront together. "Do you know any Japanese in Shanghai?" he asked. "Japanese who speak English?"

"Certainly," Agnes said. "Ozaki Hotsumi is translating my novel." She described *Daughter of Earth*, its American and German editions, the depiction of her childhood on a Missouri tenant farm, the adolescent years in Rockefeller mining camps. She veered away from her own experience to talk about child laborers in Shanghai matchworks who slept in the factory and lived on millet gruel and salt. About landlords who collected taxes from peasant farmers years in advance. She talked about a China that few Westerners knew, then fell silent as they stopped to look at the British, German, French gun boats lying at anchor in Huangpu Harbor, ready to quell any uprising that might threaten foreign investments.

"Ozaki will interest you," she resumed, taking a cigarette from her shoulder bag. Richard Sorge struck a match for her. "He questions his government's actions"—she inhaled—"but he's not political. Yet." She knew Richard's politics. They had talked all night. Richard was German. He distrusted his own country, he'd told her. After fighting in World War I, he'd come to hate fatuous idealism. He was a Marxist.

Agnes watched him as they strolled between the harbor and the ornate, foreign-style buildings that lined the Bund: Hong Kong & Shanghai Banking Corporation; Chartered Bank of India, Australia and China; Chase Banks of New York; Jardine & Matheson's; Sassoon's, inheritor of the East India Company trade. Richard carried his leonine head high, and limped from a war wound. He was disillusioned.

"I believe no national leaders," he said.

The next day she introduced him to Ozaki. She went to a locksmith for extra keys so the two men could meet in her apartment, away from the eyes of British, Germans, Russians, Chinese, Americans. She shared their view that Japanese aggression was a greater danger to China than Chiang Kai-shek and the Kuomintang. Sometimes she joined them. Usually, however, they met alone.

24
Shanghai 1931

In wintertime Song Qingling worked at a small desk in what had been her husband's second-story study, but when the Shanghai spring arrived she moved to the adjoining sun porch. Even when her husband, Dr. Sun Yat-sen, was alive, she had preferred the sun porch. She liked the light. She liked looking down on her peonies and begonias as the breeze through the open windows played across her skin.

The American woman would be coming soon to help with the correspondence that accumulated each day. Song Qingling hardly knew what to say to letter-writers from around the world who paid homage to Sun Yat-sen. She missed her husband's leadership in political matters, not to mention the love that had illuminated her life briefly, then left a kind of darkness which, after the raw grief passed, puzzled her.

She moved gently, loyally, a little mechanically, from task to task. Her sister, Madame Chiang Kai-shek, begged her, then tried to intimidate her into joining the right-wing branch of the party that had strayed so far from her husband's original principles. But her sister could not persuade her nor could the Generalissimo imprison her. Her international prestige protected her from her brother-in-law's political thugs.

The door to the street opened and closed. She heard running steps on the stairs. Did the American woman never walk? Whether climbing or covering level ground, she seemed always in a hurry. And such light skin. The eyes were stunning, wide and blue-gray, but the forehead was too large, too white, and the hair was too thin. Of course, the writing and typing skills, the loyalty to China and to the revolution, proved over and over again so very useful. Nevertheless—

Song Qingling braced herself for Agnes Smedley.

"Song Qingling!" Agnes exclaimed as she rushed onto the sun porch. Song Qingling recoiled ever so slightly.

Agnes, for her part, made a conscious effort to control herself. She refrained from taking Madame Sun Yat-sen's hand. Trying to explain away Madame's coolness, she told herself that the Chinese were indirect—subtle. Since Madame was a woman of great distinction, Agnes should not mind her aloofness; since her own busy, productive life now overflowed with purpose and adventure, she should not mind being snubbed.

She reeled from happiness to happiness. From Richard at night, to fact-finding excursions during the day, to evenings pounding out articles on her typewriter. Every week she picked up paychecks at the American Express office, money from German, American, Indian, Chinese publications. When converted to 1930s yuan, her income was comfortable. She had wealthy Western friends, and although she felt guilty riding through the International Settlement in coolie-drawn rickshaws, rich dinners were pleasant. Singsong girls ran through songs from Chinese opera in a fascinating screech. Storytellers clapped their bamboo sticks, and charcoal braziers glowed under heated wine. She drank good liquor and smoked good cigarettes.

Until she met Richard Sorge, she'd had affairs, European, American, Chinese, to stave off loneliness and fill the night with something that approximated love. Now she had Richard. The mystery at the center of his personality made him so desirable that she sometimes could not bear the hours between dinner and bedtime when she waited for him to come to her. Occasionally she worried that she loved him too much. She was not accustomed to such happiness. She also knew that nothing in Shanghai—nothing in all of China— would last in its present form. Why, then, should the intimacy between Richard and herself last? And so she was able to fall back on impending unhappiness that, in an odd sort of way, made happiness acceptable.

"I have invited a friend for tea this afternoon." Madame's English was fluent and accurate. "Her name is Ding Ling. I want you to meet her. She is a writer."

Agnes tried not to sound enthusiastic and American. "I am familiar with her work," she said coolly.

The young woman arrived late in the afternoon. "I am Ding Ling!" she exclaimed in a most un-Chinese manner. Madame Sun Yat-sen, so reserved with Agnes, held Ding Ling's hand. "I know of you! You are Agnes Smedley, China's friend! I will take you to meet Lu Xun!"

Agnes offered an exclamation of her own: "Lu Xun!" She would have liked to take Ding Ling's other hand, but the look on Madame's face stopped her.

"I would be most pleased," she carefully rephrased.

Madame began speaking in rapid Chinese, too rapid to be understood by a foreigner. Agnes walked to the windows, a row of clear eyes for looking out on the world. but she put her back to them and turned inward to watch Madame assume the role of a mother. Ding Ling, the child, a dancing, brilliant flame, was arguing, so sure of Madame's love that she could actually thrust her muscular little body forward and point a finger near Madame's nose. Though Agnes was cold and shivering, Ding Ling was just warming up, trying, perhaps, to persuade Madame that the American should be allowed to meet Lu Xun, China's foremost writer. Sticking up, maybe, for the American who, though useful, was still a foreigner after all, and would always be.

Agnes looked for a chair and sat down, struggling there on Madame's sun porch to locate her own identity. And she tried to remember her own value, to recall it as a fact; she could not count on Ding Ling's natural, easy confidence.

Ding Ling stepped back and looked proud. She had won the argument. "Where do you live?" she asked.

Agnes stood up from the chair. "Rue Dubail."

"May I have tea with you today?"

Agnes looked at Madame's tea service.

"After tea with Madame, of course," Ding Ling said. She ran her fingers through her short haircut and smiled suddenly. "Two teas in one day!"

The following week they walked together to Lu Xun's birthday banquet. Agnes talked with brilliance and humor, wooing Ding Ling's friendship, wanting more than anything to be part of China's circle of left-wing intellectuals. It helped that she was an American reporter, a Westerner in a country where the avant-garde admired Western above all else. Swinging along the streets of Shanghai, dodging knife-sharpeners, rag-collectors, humans of all ages and nationalities, she listened to Ding Ling praise Flaubert.

Entering an alley where a rickshaw repairman had set up shop in the entrance of a building and women washed vegetables in tin tubs at the edges of the pavement, Ding Ling stopped talking. Walking around an old woman with bound feet who held her little grandchild under the knees, swing-style, while the baby dropped a turd through the split in its pants, Ding Ling looked left, then right, and made brief eye contact with a lean young man in a shadowed doorway. She motioned for Agnes to follow her into a restaurant owned, she explained, by a Dutchman who could be trusted.

They entered the restaurant's kitchen, darting around stoves, past cooks and cooks' helpers whose thick black hair was gathered up under white hats. Avoiding a rack of hanging, gamey-smelling ducks, they entered the dining room. Together, in step, they reached the far end of the Western-style room and stopped in front of the head table.

"Here is the American writer Agnes Smedley," Ding Ling said. Agnes looked into the quick, black eyes of a small man, handsome, charismatic, and, she learned later, tubercular.

"I'm not a real writer," she protested. Then, looking into

the face of China's conscience, she cringed at her disclaimer. Without speaking, he penetrated her self-criticism. He saw her hypocrisy and made her see it, too.

She loathed herself for the apology. She was a good writer. She knew that. Why had she claimed she wasn't? She could knock out an article with a minimum of fuss; knew how to take shorthand notes and organize them quickly; understood the thrust of a piece before she began; could execute it swiftly. In contrast to the dry and difficult years in Germany, there was never a month now that she didn't have several articles in print somewhere in China, India, Germany, England, or the United States.

What she'd meant to tell Lu Xun was that she wasn't satisfied with herself. She wasn't the writer she wanted to be. A real writer was someone with talent and at least one other thing: time. Time to plan and write a book. Book-length was what she wanted.

"I admire your work," she said simply.

The man before her was one of the few Chinese who, even before Sun Yat-sen's revolution of 1911, had understood his country in a new way. After looking hard at China's passivity and corruption, he'd looked equally hard at his own flaws, sacrificed his anonymity, then written about the rottenness he found. He'd electrified and infuriated his countrymen by the metaphors he chose for China: cannibals feeding on each other in *Diary of a Mad Man*. A stupid and pathetic peasant in *The Story of Ah Q*.

Before the banquet was served, several people at the head table stood and described prison conditions for left-wing artists. Ozaki Hotsumi came to sit at Ding Ling's table where he translated the Chinese for Agnes. She took out her notebook and wrote verbatim in flashing shorthand. She didn't have to be told why she was here: to report actual conditions in China to the West. She would write not only about the speeches, but about the lookouts in the alley, about the banquet guests whose wary eyes scanned the room for strangers who might be spies, about Chinese City, the section of Shanghai a few streets away where thousands of the poor crowded together, angry and restless. Prodded by revolutionary workers, they were beginning to stir and awaken from centuries-old sleep.

Someone stood and talked about the soviet in Jiangxi where revolutionaries named Mao Zedong and Zhu De had confiscated land from the landlords. Agnes had to ask Ozaki how to write their names in English. Wherever their ragged Red Army marched, it was said, they picked up recruits. Agnes wrote furiously until the last speaker sat down. While waiters brought chicken, duck's belly, steamed fish, green vegetables, beer, and rice from the kitchen, she sketched out a paragraph that conveyed the risks these left-wing intellectual guerrillas, as they called themselves, incurred in Chiang Kai-shek's China, risks from which her reputation as an American reporter protected her.

She put down her pen and picked up chopsticks. Reporting was a tame business. The people sitting all around her could lose their lives rejecting the remnants of old China—old China was not going to die alone, it was going to take many Chinese with it. But it would leave an American newspaper reporter safe.

At the head table, Lu Xun picked at his food. Agnes braced her notebook on her lap and described the handsome, suffering man: black hair that stood up from his head in a brush cut. Cream-colored silk gown with Mandarin collar. She described the vivacious company and the sudden silences that fell on the room when a door opened. Beside her, Ding Ling ate heartily and argued with Ozaki about the potential for war between Japan and China. Outside, a sudden Shanghai storm hit: The rain tore apart peonies and camellias in the parks. Aralias thrashed in the light from street lamps and threw tormented shadows onto wet, black streets.

When the dinner ended Ding Ling leaned toward Agnes. "Come with me," she whispered.

At the entrance to the alley she and Agnes, the novelist Mao Dun, and Lu Xun himself split up into separate taxis to be driven through the rain and dropped off in lanes near Shan Yin Lu, Lu Xun's street. From separate directions they slipped into the semi-foreign-style house at Number 9. A servant opened the door and led them to a ceramic bowl of heated wine in the Western-style parlor. Lu Xun sat in an armchair drinking and listening to the rain.

"I am too stimulated to sleep," he said in Chinese. His wife and son had already gone to bed. Agnes saw that his forehead was pale and moist, his face drawn. The silk gown may have fitted his neck and shoulders at one time, but now it hung loosely. He was over-stimulated, he repeated, and needed to lie down. They followed him upstairs to his study where he gestured for them to sit in the high-backed rattan chairs that flanked his desk while he reclined against pillows on the bed.

"There is much you can tell the West," he said to Agnes in German, their common language. He crossed his hands on his silk gown. The clipped nails formed light ovals against his dark fingers. Pausing to translate into Chinese for Ding Ling and Mao Dun, he described the Kuomintang's literary censorship that extended to anything remotely resembling events in China.

"Carmen, for instance," Ding Ling said, taking up the subject. "When Don Jose stabs Carmen, she speaks words which remind the censors of the split between themselves and the Communists, and they cancel the production."

Agnes was the only one who laughed at the paranoia. To cover the insensitivity, she pulled out her notebook.

Lu Xun lifted his head from the pillows. "You must let the West know of these things," he said, speaking again in German. "China requires help." He lay back on the pillows. His black eyes did not leave Agnes' face. "Many things must be translated. Your book, for instance, must be translated into Chinese."

"*Daughter of Earth* translated into Chinese?" She had never considered that her unheroic life might be of interest to anyone in Asia. She had not believed Dr. Naef in Berlin who said Agnes' writing would hold the attention of the world—hold attention for a moment, Agnes recalled. Perhaps this was the moment.

"It shows the necessary struggle of the poor," Lu Xun continued. "And it shows democracy to be more fertile than feudalism. Writers, cultural guerrillas, must bring this message before the people again and again until it is understood." His eyes moved to Ding Ling's face. "Ding Ling understands the importance of Europe and America for Asia."

"If my book is to be translated into Chinese," Agnes said, "Ding Ling's stories must be translated into English."

"Nothing like *Miss Sophia's Diary* has ever been written by a Chinese author," Lu Xun said. He motioned for someone to get Ding Ling's collection of stories from a pile of books stacked on the bureau. He began to read.

"When I think that in this precious, beautiful form I adore, there resides such a cheap, ordinary soul, and that for no apparent reason I've gotten intimate with him several times (but nothing even approaching what he gets at his brothel)! When I think about how his lips brushed my hair, I'm so overwhelmed with regret I nearly break down. Don't I offer myself to him for his pleasure the same as any whore?"

Ding Ling's color was high as she listened to her words read by Lu Xun. Agnes keenly felt the boldness of her writing.

"When they are feeling bad," Lu Xun continued reading, "talented women these days can write poems about 'how depressed I am,' 'Oh, the tragic sufferings of my heart,' and so on. I'm not gifted that way. I find I'm incapable of exploiting a poetic situation … I should make myself good with either a pen or a gun …

"I've lowered myself into a dominion of suffering worse than death. All for that man's soft hair and red lips …

"It was the chivalric European medieval knights I was dreaming about. It's still not a bad comparison; anyone who looks at Ling Jishi can see it, though he also preserves his own

231

special Eastern gentleness. God took all the other good qualities and lavished them on him. Why couldn't God make him intelligent?"

Lu Xun stopped reading and held the place with one finger. "A woman's honest thoughts," he remarked in the silence. "The exploited. We must translate *Miss Sophia's Diary*. We must translate *Daughter of Earth*. We must translate"—here he looked at Mao Dun—"your fine work, *Rainbow*. Art, in the end, will be a most effective weapon against …" He relapsed into silence and stared at a small, rectangular fish tank on his desk. A single cat fish moved slowly through the water.

Agnes broke the silence. "And you. What are you writing?" She asked the question in a journalist's mode. She never went long without thinking how her daily experience in China could be written up for publication. But Lu Xun did not answer as he would for an interview. Keeping his eyes on the fish, he spoke personally.

"I have long wanted to write a novel as you have," he said, "a novel drawn from my own life." Agnes was surprised at the regret in his voice, this finest of modern writers. She would have thought he was satisfied with his work. She leaned her head against the high rattan backrest and half-closed her eyes.

"My life is a symbol of modern China," he said. "There is a great deal I can say about my country indirectly through a life story such as my own. I know the details, and I can write it accurately and fully." He paused. "Of course, one is always trying to understand and capture the elusive self, even if for only a moment." He shifted on the pillows. "But I do not have time now," he added softly. "I must bring forward younger writers, writers who will have great influence on the future of China." Slowly he reached toward the bedside table and pulled his ashtray closer. A matchbox holder was permanently affixed to the saucer.

As she watched Lu Xun strike a flame with his small, deft hand, Agnes felt a return of the desire that attacked her from time to time: to write a novel. Perhaps here in China she could begin. She glanced about the room with dreamy, speculative eyes. Although she had no specific plot or characters in mind, the setting was all around her.

Late that night she returned to her room and recapitulated the evening for Richard Sorge who lay propped against a pillow, not unlike the position Lu Xun had assumed, and smoked while he listened.

"I don't understand Chinese as well as I should," Agnes said when she'd run out of descriptions. "I'm not Chinese. I'm not exactly American, either. Not anymore."

Sorge ground out his cigarette in the ashtray. "I thought you were a citizen of the world. A freelance revolutionary." His sarcasm caught her by surprise.

"I am a citizen of the world, though sometimes …" She trailed off, stung.

He turned away. "All of us wonder where is our home," he said, his English more accented than usual. She lay down beside him. Home? He was a revolutionary. So was she. Revolutionaries have no home.

The next day he moved his few things out of her room after announcing that he had found someone else, someone in addition to his wife whom Agnes had already known about. But if she believed in freedom between men and women, love when you love, love whomever you love, leave when it is over, why did she feel so dreadful when he left? She'd embarrassed herself by crying. She thought she could get over any man, yet she moped through the next weeks as if she believed in eternal love between two people. She was as jealous of the other woman as if she believed in sexual loyalty or—God forbid—matrimony.

She went through the motions of her life, writing articles, typing correspondence for Madame Sun Yat-sen, even putting on a long, Chinese-style gown and going to a garden party for

George Bernard Shaw held at Madame's house.

Ding Ling, who knew Shaw's plays, talked at length with the great Irishman. Agnes talked to him, too, without enthusiasm.

"Who are you?" he asked. "What are you doing in this part of the world?"

"Helping the Chinese," she said.

Shaw looked disappointed. "All Americans are missionaries."

"I am far from a missionary, I assure you," Agnes said. "I am a Marxist and I am fighting Fascism. It is as great a danger in the East as in the West." The fragrance of burning punk, a stick of finely ground, scented wood used against mosquitoes, wafted between them.

"I am fond of *Heartbreak House*," she said in a neutral tone. "It is my favorite of your plays."

"And mine," said Shaw.

"You remind me of Captain Shotover," she said. In his eyes Agnes read agreement. She thought she saw in him the contemplation of death. He seemed uncertain how to take her, and turned aside. Her eyes fell on Lu Xun, sunlight and breeze playing across his silk gown. She crossed the lawn toward him, consciously moving away from Shaw and the West.

Gradually, like an inevitable sequence of events, China tightened its hold on Agnes, narrowed her choices, and would see to it that she, like the Chinese she had come to live with, could not avoid suffering.

Because of money and political disputes, her relationship with the *Frankfurter Zeitung* was concluded as surely as her affair with Richard Sorge. There were other newspapers, but there were no other Richard Sorges. She did not rush to replace him. Her life quieted, her libido stilled, as if conserving energy for something not yet known.

One evening Ding Ling knocked on her door in the French Concession, darted inside, and closed the door quickly behind her.

"They have executed seven members of the League of Left Wing Writers!" she whispered, white-faced.

Agnes passed a hand over her own wide forehead. "Lu Xun?"

"They did not dare kill him."

The two women hugged each other, swaying back and forth. The swaying was new to Agnes. She was more accustomed to handshakes, grips, impulsive hugs, sexual positions, than to this timeless movement which does not alleviate grief but deepens it and helps make it bearable.

"You're in danger," Agnes suddenly said, lifting her head and pulling away. Ding Ling stared, seeming not to comprehend. "You must leave Shanghai at once."

Ding Ling scanned the room with wild eyes. She seemed her true age now, ten years younger than Agnes. "Where shall I go?"

"Xi'an," Agnes said without hesitation.

"I can't leave Lu Xun and Mao Dun and Madame—"

"You *must* leave them, and at once. It can be done." Agnes looked into Ding Ling's pale, frightened face and felt maternal. "We will all be escaping to the Northwest before we're through. I tell you this as an objective foreigner."

"I don't know how to live in such times." Ding Ling sounded childlike. "My mother did not have to run."

"Your mother's feet were bound," Agnes said. "She couldn't run. Stay here with me. Do not return to your flat."

In the early evening, alone, Agnes went to Ding Ling's apartment building. Two heavy-set Chinese loitered on the opposite side of the lane. She walked on. Stopping at the door of an acquaintance, she instructed him to create a diversion while she entered Ding Ling's building. She stuffed a few items of the young woman's clothing into a cloth sack hidden under her jacket, then stepped into a pair of trousers she'd brought with her. She looped a sash around the waist and rolled the cuffs. With her short haircut dampened and slicked back, she waited for darkness and the return to her apartment and Ding Ling.

Late that night, dressed as males, the two women climbed into a taxi.

"To the train station," Agnes commanded. But when the taxi slowed behind rickshaws choking the narrow street, Ding Ling touched the driver's shoulder.

"Turn back."

"No," Agnes said in Chinese. "Continue to the station."

"I cannot go in two directions at once."

Ding Ling grabbed Agnes' hand. "I can't leave! My work is here! My friends are here! I can't run like a frightened woman!"

Agnes jerked her hand from Ding Ling's. "This is no time for heroics," she snapped. Ding Ling's eyes watered. Agnes softened her tone. "I promise to join you," she said, as if a promise could be relied on or delivered in China in late 1931.

25
Shanghai 1931

Agnes stared up at telephone lines looping over roofs, dropping to the street, swaying in the winter wind like filaments of a destroyed spider's web. The smell of burning buildings and food, burning humans and rats, hung over Shanghai. She picked her way through jagged pieces of concrete that were once the street. A dead man lay bloated behind a wheelbarrow, propped unnaturally between a wheel and a stone wall. He sat naked, his chest slashed open. Someone had told her of seeing Japanese soldiers cut out a man's heart; how it had steamed in the January air.

Three Japanese soldiers sauntered out of an alley carrying scarves full of jewelry. The scarves were tied into silk bundles and looped through their fingers. The shortest of the three stopped and kicked out a window as casually as if he were greeting an acquaintance. Agnes kept a distance. Her western appearance, her press pass pinned to her coat like a corsage, had so far warded off attack.

She had not remained in the safe European concessions. With her notebook and pencil, she walked and ran with Chinese families as they evacuated, lane by lane, just ahead of the Japanese. In the background, bombs, gunfire, and sirens shook the city. Wearing slacks and an army cap, Agnes had stayed close to the Nationalist Nineteenth Route Army, dropping back a street when fighting erupted, catching up when the soldiers moved ahead. Nearly trapped once in gunfire, she ran into an apartment building that seemed deserted. Only after she'd crouched on the stairs for long, silent minutes did the building give up its secret: the rooms were full of people. A baby's muffled cry drifted down from an upper floor. Someone with a light step moved now and then above her head.

A short distance down the lane, Japanese machine guns erupted. Another alley full of Chinese soldiers and civilians was being cleaned out.

As she'd known all along, Japan, not internal dissension, was China's real enemy. For a short time she'd helped Ozaki Hotsumi and Richard Sorge inform Russian and Chinese contacts of Japanese activities. Now, as she passed the bodies of two dead Chinese children holding each other, the depth of her hatred for Japan nearly paralyzed her. When Lu Xun's neighborhood was bombed, she forgot about being a war correspondent and put aside her notebook. By rickshaw and foot she tried to reach his house, but the Japanese had sealed off the area. She located a friend who owned a car and military pass. When he picked her up in the French Concession, she climbed into the back seat. It looked official that way.

As they passed Japanese troops lining the streets of the Chapei district, the friend looked at her in the rear view mirror. "You're not taking notes?" he said. "You'll remember all this?"

Agnes only nodded. Her face in the mirror was still and white.

In front of Lu Xun's house, Agnes opened the car door and walked with a business-like gait to the front entrance. The roofless building next door still smoldered, three walls guarding the gutted core. In a vacant lot, Japanese military trucks sat parked while the drivers made tea over a fire.

Agnes banged on the front door, then each ground-floor window, but there was no answer. The back door, too, was locked, curtains drawn.

Two soldiers stepped around the corner of the house. One of them spoke to Agnes in Japanese, a short sentence that, itself, sounded like gunfire. Agnes pointed to her press pass and, walking around them, returned to the car. Poised, even detached, she got into the back seat behind the driver. Only when they turned the corner did she begin to weep.

"Is Lu Xun your lover?" the friend asked.

"No. No. Much more than that. He is—a father. A father for China." The statement consoled her. It would be days before she learned that Lu Xun and his family were safe with friends.

Even when the attack subsided and Chinese troops formed a defensive perimeter around the city, Agnes still had to watch carefully each time she stepped out of the European concessions and into Chinese City. She was not safe with either the Japanese or Chinese. The Shanghai police, attempting to carry out instructions of the British Secret Service, had wanted to arrest her on some pretext or other ever since she arrived in the city. Now they wanted her for hiding Communists in her apartment. Worst of all—worse, even, than the nagging worries about Ding Ling and Lu Xun—was the break that occurred between herself and Madame Sun Yat-sen.

Madame did not speak of it directly. Agnes heard nothing of it from Ding Ling, nor from Lu Xun. It was Mao Dun, gentle, conciliatory Mao Dun, the novelist, who haltingly conveyed the specifics when Agnes asked if he knew why Madame no longer wished to see her.

"It is a question of cultures," he said in Chinese, slowly, so Agnes could understand. "It is East and West."

"What do you mean, 'It is East and West'?"

"You are an internationalist," he temporized. "We Chinese are still isolated. Provincial."

"Why has Song Qingling never accepted me?"

"It is your incisiveness," he said. "Your thorough lack of feudalistic—"

"It is *you* saying these things, not Madame!" she snapped.

Mao Dun took a deep breath. "It is frankness," he said. "Chinese are not so frank as Americans."

"Frank!" Agnes said the word in English. "Madame should see me when I am frank!"

"I will be frank," he said. He cleared his throat. "It is money."

"Money? What do you mean, 'money'?"

Mao Dun looked off into space, as if he wished he had begun another way. "The money that she gave you for *The Voice of China* journal has been spent."

"That money was used for a good cause! That money supported Communists from Jianxi who hid in my apartment! And I have paid the editor of the journal! Never have I taken a yuan for myself!"

"You are not accused of stealing."

"The hell I'm not!" Agnes said in English.

"Madame is careful about money," Mao Dun said gently. He tried humor. "Politically liberal, financially conservative."

But Agnes did not smile. Tears threatened to overcome fury; then fury overcame tears. In the end the two canceled each other out. With a last prolonged look at Mao Dun, she walked off, already in the grip of a stony depression. Even in China, even in the heart of the Revolution, she could find no acceptance. It felt as if she had been rejected by a mother. Rejected by earth itself. A daughter of earth found wanting.

Money! She'd never been good with money. When a need came along, not for herself but for revolutionary friends who slipped in and slipped out of Shanghai, she offered it. Madame Sun Yat-sen with her orderly columns of figures didn't understand the risks revolutionaries take just living through an ordinary day.

It was her own fault. She'd put Madame, like Lu Xun, like Chatto, like the Lion of the Punjab so long ago, not on a pedestal, but worse than that: in the center of her heart. And Madame did not wish to be there. In spite of her hard work and the risks she took, she was an outsider. She was not Chinese and never would be.

26

China 1937

Agnes pumped the bellows and picked out "Streets of Laredo" on the small harmonium that had been transported by a Red Army truck over the mountains from Xi'an to Yan'an. From there, soldiers had carried it up the narrow, winding terrace of Army headquarters, past Zhu De's and Mao Zedong's hillside caves, on up to Agnes' cave one level above.

The bellows wheezed and the song ended.

"Play 'My Beloved,'" Zhu De said in Chinese. The end of daylight hovered outside the wooden door that had been fitted into an archway cut out of the hill. Inside, white-washed walls held onto the dying light. The Commander pulled a small, dog-eared song book wrapped in a piece of red cloth from his tunic pocket and turned several pages.

"'My Beloved,'" he repeated, and held the stitched sheets apart with one rough hand while Agnes leaned forward and squinted in the faint light. She hit a flawed chord and stumbled over the melody. Zhu De, after waiting a courteous period of time, began to sing, ignoring the harmonium.

> "My beloved! I say farewell before our bed
> And tell you not to love me.
> We must travel the revolutionary road."

His voice was strong. He sang the song three times without accompaniment. Agnes thought the lament was for his wife, Wu Yu-lan, captured by the Kuomintang and murdered, her head mounted on the main street in the town of her birth.

The cave grew dark. Agnes covered the harmonium with a cloth to keep off the gritty dust, and led the way onto the terrace. Zhu De brought out two chairs, a sign that he wanted to talk. Agnes opened her notebook.

"Sun Yat-sen died in 1925," he began. "After that, nothing was the same." Agnes' pencil made a scratching sound on the thin paper.

"Chiang Kai-shek began to accept loans from Chinese and foreign bankers. In 1927 he found it necessary to please them by crushing the Shanghai Communist workers' coup."

Though the moon was not high enough to be reflected in the Yan River flowing slowly by the foot of the terraced hillside, it illuminated Zhu De's deep-set eyes and broad nose.

"The Chinese workers and peasants are the most revolutionary people on earth," he declared impulsively, extending one arm in a sweeping gesture toward the dark mountains that surrounded them. "All they need is good leadership, a sound program, and arms."

He pointed his finger at her. "Write this in your notebook: we choose our own battlefield and keep the mountains to our back. We draw the enemy where we want him, then cut off his transport columns, attack his flanks, surround and destroy him. We hold 'Speak Bitterness Meetings' with captured troops. We explain why they are poor and hungry, unpaid by the government that hires them. We invite them to join our cause. We offer freedom and military passes if they wish to leave."

"How many leave?"

"Few."

A dog barked from another hillside. Light from two cigarettes came and went on the river bank below.

"An old bandit of Chingkanshan taught me much about strategy," Zhu De said. "'You don't have to know how to fight,' he told me. 'All you have to know is how to encircle the enemy.'"

Agnes laughed.

"The Kuomintang," Zhu De continued, "learned tactics from the Japanese. Single column, front and flank guards. On the other hand, we Communists split up into small, swift combat units and cut the enemy into segments. The peasants in the villages capture transport for us, spy, destroy small enemy units and stragglers. The

Kuomintang is afraid to advance if they sight even one barefoot peasant watching from a distance."

"I have heard that you are called 'treacherous bandit chief,'" Agnes said. Zhu De did not answer. "There is a song about you," Agnes pursued. "The words tell that you carry rice to the top of a mountain, barefoot, without ever growing tired."

"That is not true," Zhu De said with an impatient, self-deprecating gesture of the hand. "I never go barefoot. I always wear straw sandals."

27
Xi'an 1936

Agnes awoke in the soft-seat accommodation of the train to Xi'an with a bad taste in her mouth. It was two years since a short visit to America, yet she came out of sleep with precise thoughts, fresh as yesterday, of her sister whom she'd visited in San Diego; of editors in New York; of various self-satisfied, amiable, ignorant, and fatuous Americans who had asked her questions, then listened suspiciously while she talked about the Russian Revolution and the coming revolution in China. Capitalism was dead, she informed them. But with joblessness and depression all about, they still screwed up their faces and disbelieved her.

She sat up and dampened her washcloth in the warm water brought to the compartment by a porter. Outside, mist rose from rice fields and hung, motionless and mysterious, in gray daybreak. Neither the man in the berth above her nor the two passengers on the opposite side of her compartment had stirred. She wiped her face and looked out the window at China, its crops, haystacks, grave mounds crowned with clay pots standing randomly in-between fields. Silhouetted against the sun breaking above the horizon, a barefoot man and woman, water carriers, balanced a bamboo pole between them.

Agnes got up to use the toilet at one end of the car. The fecal smell was heavy. In one part of her mind she recognized that she did not object to it, and that any American would. She squatted. Through the hole in the floor she watched the ground between tracks rush by.

The car next to hers was hard-seat. If it were not for her contact, Diu Ling, and the Chinese Communists paying for her trip to the Northwest, she would be sitting in one of those same hard seats that were nailed to the siding. The car full of peasants looked cheerful with a clothesline of brightly colored washcloths strung along its length. But with so many people crowded together, it would be impossible to write and meet her deadline.

Any American would expect a soft-seat as his due. Agnes did not. But then, Agnes no longer felt like an American. To the extent it taught her she no longer belonged in America, the trip home—no longer a home—had been instructive. An instructive mistake.

She could not find a newspaper job; the Depression was in full swing. Further, her sister, Myrtle, an elementary school principal by now, disliked her and wanted nothing to do with her politics. Myrtle, whom she had put through college, didn't want anyone to know they were sisters. She'd cringed when Agnes was written up in the San Diego newspaper. The right side of her face went into spasm, nervous paralysis, the doctor said, brought on by anxiety. Agnes understood that Myrtle's respected position in the community could be threatened by a sister's radical opinions. Even the liberal intellectuals in New York who should have understood what was happening in China were offended by the truths she brought back. They couldn't believe conditions among the poor were as bad as Agnes said they were. They couldn't believe Chiang Kai-shek was fighting the Communists instead of fighting Japan.

Her rich little friend from New York days, Florence, didn't understand the changes taking place in Europe, much less China. Agnes tried not to think about the money Florence had given her when she so desperately needed funds; Florence had saved her life, and now Agnes couldn't bear her.

She knew the intensity of her beliefs dazzled her friends and the small audiences she addressed. But though dazzled, electrified, they would not go the distance on behalf of the Chinese Communists who, almost alone, were fighting Japan. Her friends grew suspicious of her and she grew contemptuous of them. Her news was not entertaining; her radicalism was not easy.

She returned to her compartment. The woman across the aisle was sitting up in the lower berth, drinking tea from a glass jar. Through most of the night she had cracked pumpkin seeds between her long front teeth, and the shells lay all about the floor.

The landscape grew less and less flat as they left the coast behind. Hills changed to foothills, foothills to low mountains. The sun rose higher. Mentally she said good-bye to Shanghai and thought once more of her friend Ding Ling, kidnapped and murdered two years earlier. Silly girl. She should have left for the Northwest, not waited in Shanghai until it was too late. Agnes wiped away her tears with the washcloth. She made herself tea and opened the letter kept folded in an inside pocket of her trousers. It contained the address where she was to meet her contact this afternoon.

Diu Ling was waiting for her at the Forest of Steles, the museum of stone tablets located just inside the old Xi'an city wall. The upright monuments, taller than a person, with raised characters and illustrations, had been moved here in the eleventh century, by which time they were already ancient.

How different this part of China was from the coast! Here, Westerners were seldom seen. Most Northwest Chinese had never been to Shanghai or a treaty port. Perhaps no one in Xi'an had ever seen a Western woman pull up to the entrance of the museum in a taxi. Agnes hurried into the courtyard. Diu Ling, slim and high-strung, stood by the statue of the Emperor's favorite horse.

He did not greet her but turned and entered the high-ceilinged room of the first of several pagodas. Agnes followed between rows of stone steles. On through two more courtyards and more pagodas with elaborate eave tiles and red lacquered supporting posts, on through additional high-ceilinged rooms until she neared an unidentifiable sound: a fast thumping, like a hundred slaps to a hundred mounds of bread dough There was a sweet odor. Not jasmine, not perfume, but a gummy smell that began to cloy. When she'd plunged deep into the stone forest, Diu Ling suddenly stepped out from behind a tablet and motioned for her to follow him to a corner of the pagoda where he could see anyone who approached.

"You look well," he said in Chinese. She had last seen him in Shanghai when he was en route from the Communist soviet in Southern China to Xi'an and she'd hidden him in her apartment. "Your trip was comfortable?"

"Very comfortable. Soft-seat. Thank you."

"Please go to the compound of the German dentist, Dr. Wunsch," Diu Ling said. Agnes memorized the address. Still on the lookout for informers, he brought his eyes back to Agnes' face. "You will find old friends there. I, myself, will join you this evening."

"And Yan'an?" Agnes was eager to visit the Red Army base a day's drive over the mountains north of Xi'an.

"It will not be long now."

Agnes smiled. Already her eyes were brighter, her skin clearer. Northwest China was a tonic for revolutionaries. A brisk wind was blowing from the steppes of Russia and Central Asia. Unencumbered by Westerners and their spheres of influence, it freshened the bedraggled survivors of the Long March who had just ended their year-long walk from defeats in the South. It blew along the centuries-old pathway of the Mongols, into Xi'an, ancient terminus of the silk route.

But at this particular moment the sounds and smell coming from the far end of the pagoda interested Agnes more than the Revolution or any part she might play in it. She began walking. Her large, blue-gray eyes moved from stele to stele.

"Can you translate for me?" she asked, pointing to raised characters that ran in columns along the tablet.

Diu Ling snorted. "Ancient hypocrisies of a feudal society. I have other work to do," and he turned and left her alone among the steles.

The thumping increased. She proceeded toward the back of the hall. There, behind the last row of stones, dressed in loose-fitting trousers and tunics, two young men squatted before a stele covered with a sheet of rice paper. One of them took a long-handled brush from an ink pot resting on the floor and brushed the surface of a small paddle. The other was already in full swing, furiously slamming something like a bean bag against his inked paddle, then against the stele, paddle to stele, paddle to stele, faster and faster, punching out a rhythm, inking and pounding, sweating, breathing hard. The sweet odor of ink saturated the air.

The man stopped. Carefully he peeled off the rice paper. It had become a black-and-white tracing of a warrior from an ancient dynasty.

Agnes bought the paper rubbing. With the purchase rolled under her arm, she wandered among the cool gray stones, returning through several pagodas and courtyards until she came to a bench beside a camellia bush. Though unable to imagine ancient China or to penetrate the characters on the steles, she could imagine camellias in bloom a few months from now. Though winter still had to be lived through, though she was forty-five, she felt warmth and fertility surrounding her. She sat down on the bench, laid the rolled-up tracing beside her, and closed her eyes. Rarely did she allow herself to rest. Always she worked to achieve something, toiled, wrote, agonized, fought, dashed here, dashed there, rushed about because she was not sure of herself, activity covering the central doubt.

A deep, involuntary breath pushed her gently back against the bench. She felt as if a hand had passed over her head. She seemed to hear, around and through the steles, a gentle humming.

She picked up the rice paper tracing and walked toward the front of the museum where the shouts of rickshaw drivers and smells of hot oil and garlic replaced the transcendental hum and earthy thumps. Strangely, she thought of America and Mother. Mother had wanted her to get an education. Well, she hadn't done it. Not in America, not in Germany, not in China. She'd never even graduated from high school. She'd written one book about herself and one book about the Red Chinese Army. The rest, workable articles. Mentally she defended herself: I'm a daughter of earth, not heaven. My writing is useful, perhaps. Nothing as fine as Lu Xun's, Ding Ling's, Mao Dun's. I am here to toil for change. I am a toiler. Hours with writers are luxuries stolen from real work.

There was an imagined murmur of agreement from everyone in the family—yes, yes, the whisper sounded, *daughter of earth*—except Mother.

You are a writer, Agnes.

Agnes entered the street and climbed into a taxi. Through the narrow rear window she watched the Forest of Steles, library of heavenly wisdom, recede into the distance.

Dr. Herbert Wunsch looked after Warlord Zhang Xueliang's teeth. Long before Agnes left for the Northwest, she'd persuaded the German dentist to move from Shanghai to Xi'an where he now served as the last link in a smuggling operation she'd set up to bring medical supplies from the coast to the Communists recuperating north of Xi'an from their Long March.

"The Young Marshal has allowed his teeth to deteriorate," Dr. Wunsch said when Agnes returned from washing up in his Western-style bathroom.

"His teeth are just one of his problems," Agnes said, accepting tea from the servant girl. "He's rumored to be addicted to opium."

Dr. Wunsch stretched his legs out before him. "Was," he said in German. "Was addicted. He has recovered. There is much at stake for him and he's readying himself to fight Japan." He looked at Agnes as if he had secret knowledge. "We think he's also ready to fight Chiang Kai-shek. You will learn all this."

The servant girl stood at the door listening.

"More tea for Miss Smedley," Dr. Wunsch said in Chinese.

"Is your young assistant a student?" Agnes asked.

One of the dentist's gold-crowned bicuspids gleamed. "You could say so."

Agnes stood and walked to the window that faced the wall of the old city. She felt impatient. There was a great deal to learn in Xi'an and she wanted to begin immediately.

"You have just arrived," Dr. Wunsch observed, "and already you are tired of sitting." He seemed to contain some inner excitement. "To alleviate your restlessness I have planned a small surprise." Keeping his eyes on Agnes, he turned and called the servant in Chinese. This time when she entered the sitting room Agnes studied her.

"Closer to the window," said Dr. Wunsch. "Step closer." The girl moved until the afternoon light fell full on her face. Agnes gasped as Ding Ling tore off her dust cap and fell into Agnes' arms. They rocked back and forth, laughing and crying. Dr. Wunsch's gold tooth sparkled. He pulled out a large white handkerchief and blew his nose.

"They told me you were—" Agnes could not say "dead." Just before leaving for America, she'd written numerous articles about Ding Ling's kidnapping and placed them in Western publications. The publicity had intimidated the Nationalists and they had freed her.

Ding Ling knelt on the floor before her. "Because of you, I am alive."

Agnes pulled the young woman to her feet and crossed the room to the sofa where they sat with their arms about each other.

"You promised you would join me in Xi'an," Ding Ling whispered, "and you have kept your promise."

Dr. Wunsch tried to lighten the emotion. "Ding Ling has

given much thought to tonight's menu," he said.

Ding Ling nodded. "It will be a very special dinner." She stood and dried her eyes. "Come talk with me while I cook." Agnes followed her into the kitchen and sat down at the table. Ding Ling fetched three plucked chickens from the cooling room and laid them on a board. She lifted the cleaver and brought it down across their backs.

"Mr. Snow is coming for dinner."

"Edgar Snow!"

"He will read to us," Ding Ling continued, "from his book about the Red Army." She looked at Agnes' face and her own clouded over. She laid down the cleaver. "What is the matter, dear friend?"

Agnes turned her head sharply. The book should be hers. She was the one who had urged Ed Snow to visit the Communists north of Xi'an. It was she who had arranged contacts for his travel to the army base. She picked up a green onion and pretended to study its white head and root hairs.

Perhaps Mao Zedong wanted a nonpartisan writer to tell the world about the Long March. She, herself, cared too much. She was known as a writer of the international left, and might not be believed. She hadn't been productive these past two years in Shanghai. Bogged down in living, she'd worked on political causes to the detriment of her writing. She put down the onion. Perhaps it was because Ed was the better writer.

But Mao Zedong couldn't know that. Or was her lack of education obvious to everyone? Could the Chinese, too, see that she was a toiler, a daughter of earth, not of heaven? Ding Ling must know it. With the girl's talent and intellect, she must surely know it. Within the space of a minute Agnes grew jealous of almost everyone she knew.

"What is the matter?" Ding Ling asked twice.

"Ed Snow got to the Red Army before I did!"

Immediately Ding Ling understood. In her black eyes was an admission of her own: "I can never be a Westerner, free to the degree you are. In me will always be a remnant of China, a remnant of feudalism." The two women gazed at each other. Love and rivalry bubbled richly between them.

Agnes crossed the hot sulfur pool in five strokes. Steep green crags looked misty through the steam coming off the mineral springs. She shook water out of her eyes and submerged to her chin. Every day she waited for Diu Ling to come and tell her to pack her suitcase and portable typewriter, that it was time to leave for Yan'an where she would see the Communist base for herself.

In the meantime she took the baths, worked on another book about the Red Army, and studied Chinese history. Often she rode horseback to the tomb of Emperor Qin Shihuangdi, builder of the Great Wall one hundred miles to the north. She tied up her pony at the foot of the small, manmade mountain under which the Emperor occupied himself during death among fabled temples and rivers of quicksilver flowing through copper floors. Like the mountain rising over him, he had seen farther than those before him. He had tried to bring his kingdom out of feudalism. Agnes climbed hundreds of steps leading to the hilltop where she looked out over flat wheat lands; villages in the distance; long, dirt roads leading to the heart of China or outward to the world of non-China.

Now she side-stroked around the edges of the pool. Among the baths, temples, covered walkways and lotus ponds of Lington, ancient resort of kings and courtesans, she was waiting to report to the Western world what Diu Ling promised would be a historic agreement between Chiang Kai-shek and his semi-loyal warlords of Northwest China.

The Generalissimo was coming to Xi'an for a conference. He had hoped the armies of the Young Marshal and Yang Hucheng would drive out the Japanese, then kill each other. However, the Japanese had refused to be driven from Manchuria. In fact, they were now very close to Beijing. And far from killing each other, the two warlords were beginning to cooperate, thanks in part to Communists such as Diu Ling who had infiltrated their organizations and tried to reconcile their viewpoints in favor of unified war against Japan.

Agnes let her feet rise. She floated, partly exposed to the cold air, partly cradled by the mineral springs. Through wet eyelashes she looked at the temples and pavilions set like gems in the terraced mountainside rising straight up from the baths.

While Agnes was staying with Dr. Wunsch, Edgar Snow had visited them and read parts of his manuscript aloud. The book was superlative. She recalled a bit of it: "... there had been perhaps no greater mystery among nations, no more confused an epic, than the story of Red China. Fighting in the very heart of the most populous nation on earth, the Celestial Reds had for nine years been isolated by a news blockade as effective as a stone fortress ... their territory was more inaccessible than Tibet. No one had voluntarily penetrated that wall and returned to write of his experiences ... ."

"His experiences." Agnes kicked lightly and propelled herself across the pool again. Edgar Snow was a man. Mao Tse-tung and Zhou Enlai were men. She let her mind drift over an imaginary Central Committee composed of women. Mentally, she played with the implications for a woman reporter.

Apart from the real difficulties in competing with men, she had a jealous, insecure nature. She knew that, and struggled against it. Like steam hanging over hot springs, her self-doubt rose and drifted away, to form again and dissipate. She would think it had blown over for good, and then a certain weather condition would return, bringing the steam again.

Ed Snow wrote better than she did. Like herself, he was born in Missouri, but his family had money, stability, education. When he first met her, he'd tried talking about a past he thought they shared. But she had no intention of discussing her childhood or exchanging fond remembrances of the Midwest.

She had no summer camps and college to talk about. He would never understand a father in the coal mines; a mother who dies of overwork and malnutrition; an aunt who is a prostitute. She'd shocked him, she knew, by her bitterness. Too bad. In her experience, the middle class was easily shocked.

"In working overseas you are bound to notice that fifteen of every sixteen people on earth are not Americans," Ed said once. She'd laughed. He was clever. He was talented. But he did not feel poor. He did not feel Chinese. Agnes felt both. For her there was never a curtain, not even a transparent curtain, between herself and China. She saw herself in every girl child's eyes. Her parents were everywhere she looked.

In Xi'an, in Dr. Wunsch's compound, she'd gained perspective on herself. It was partly the simple act of confessing her jealousy to Ding Ling. But mostly it was Ed's writing. She was a worker who happened to be a writer; Ed was a writer. When he'd finished reading to the party gathered in Dr. Wunsch's living room, he'd closed the book to silence. No one applauded. They were too close to the Revolution, too overcome, to break the stillness immediately. Dispelling his own self-consciousness, Ed had turned to Diu Ling.

"You must tell me of developments in Xi'an," he said quietly.

Diu Ling nearly trembled with intensity, shifting his position where he sat on the floor near Dr. Wunsch's chair. As he spoke, he touched the fingertips of his hands together.

"I brought Zhou Enlai to the Catholic Church in Yan'an for a meeting with the Young Marshall." Agnes had scarcely breathed as he described the conference between the Central Committee member and the powerful warlord who had been pushed out of Manchuria by the Japanese. At that point Diu Ling had turned and looked at her.

"We want you to report an expected agreement between the warlords and ourselves for the defense of China. And we want you to report the warlords' conference with Chiang Kai-shek. Whatever the results, we want the world to know that Chiang is losing control in the Northwest."

Ed Snow had smiled at Agnes. She bowed her head.

"And we are isolating you at Lington," Diu Ling added with rare humor. "If your presence in Xi'an becomes known, the Kuomintang will suspect something newsworthy is about to occur." Agnes lit a cigarette and joined in the laughter.

Now she pulled up out of the pool and dried herself. The climb up the wide stone steps to her room in one of the small temples chilled her in spite of the pink flush she carried away from the mineral springs. She opened the intricately carved door to her room and closed it behind her. The fire in the fireplace had nearly gone out. She stirred the coals and added a log. As she stepped out of her wet bathing suit, she saw a letter that one of the servant women had laid on the sleeping platform. She crossed the room and saw Myrtle's handwriting. She opened it and read the single sheet. Shaking with cold, she pulled on long wool stockings, wool undershirt, riding breeches, and red sweater.

Father had died. Myrtle blamed Agnes for leaving the family after Mother's death. Agnes, the letter said, should have stayed home to care for her younger brothers and sister. If she'd stayed home, Father would have found work and remained sober the rest of his life.

Agnes sat down at the table and stared at the wall. She started a letter but couldn't finish it. She sought desperately for something to do.

The Emperor's tomb. She would ride to the Emperor's tomb! But she found she could barely stand. Trembling, she lay down on the platform and cried. Years of misery passed before her eyes, the misery of a man who failed at everything he tried, the misery of an exhausted woman attached to failure. Now that Father was dead, she cried for both her parents.

The next day her desolation mysteriously lifted. This room in the temple, the very room that had belonged to Yang Kweifei, favorite courtesan of ninth-century Emperor Hsuan

Tsung, bestowed its gift upon her. Agnes heard music and lovemaking. Not the rough sounds of her parents at night that had so frightened her as a child, but simple, dove-like sounds. Unexpected beauty and quiet joy.

An old musician once played for her "Song of Unending Sorrow" on his five-stringed lute. The words told of the Emperor's grief when Lady Yang died and how her spirit sent him messages from the enchanted isle where she lived among the immortals. Waiting in this beautiful place for the signal from Diu Ling to travel to Ya'nan, Agnes felt that she was receiving a life-giving message. Perhaps it was from her mother and father, transformed. Perhaps it was from some part of her own mind growing stronger.

From where she sat on the steps of the temple, regarding the swirling red and gold leaves blowing down from the mountainside, skittering and popping against retaining walls, Agnes watched the figure of portly Dr. Wunsch advance toward her from several terraces below. She was run through by yearning. Father! Underlying the sharp need was a generalized longing for a man, for maleness, for mental coolness, the analytic edge, height, weight, the flat male chest against which to lay her breasts.

The figure seemed to move in slow motion while she endured a long moment of self-revelation. She lacked. Lacked love. Lacked family. It came down to something quite simple: a husband and child. Family, which she held in contempt—bourgeois anodyne for pain, prettifier of reality, exploiter of women—suddenly seemed truth itself.

"Dr Wunsch!" She stood and ran down the steps to meet him. Breathing heavily from the climb, he opened his strong arms and caught her up in a hug. She pulled away and looked into his faded blue eyes spilling tears. "What is it?"

He took her hand and spoke in German. "I'm afraid I have bad news. Bad news for all of us."

No more bad news, she silently begged.

Dr. Wunsch withdrew a clean white handkerchief from his breast pocket. "Lu Xun is dead."

The terrace dropped away. Agnes whirled and faced the mountainside. She saw that the colors of blowing leaves were no longer ruddy and gold, but brown. Winter. Wordlessly she and Dr. Wunsch sat down on one of the steps. He forgot to offer her the handkerchief. Instead, he wiped his own eyes.

"Good is fragile, evil so strong," he said brokenly. He was, she knew, thinking of his native Germany as well as of China. He opened his mouth. She concentrated on the gold bicuspid. "China has fallen silent," he said in a near-whisper. "Now there is no one to speak for her."

Agnes bowed her head in the sorrow of a great man's death. Yet the loss was so personal she felt physically bruised.

Dr. Wunsch gained control over himself and pulled out another of what seemed an endless supply of white handkerchiefs. "My dear, let me buy you tea." They stood and carefully descended the terraces and flights of stairs, as many-leveled as the consciousness of Lu Xun.

Tuberculosis. How could such a common disease exist in a man devoid of commonness?

They reached the teahouse nestled against the dragon wall.

"I had trouble getting here," Dr. Wunsch said as they seated themselves. The waitress set a basket of small meat dumplings and a teapot and cups on the turn-table tray in the center. Dr. Wunsch rotated the wheel so that Agnes could serve herself.

"Did you come by Army truck?"

"Yes, but the blockade has tightened. Everyone is being questioned. Chiang Kai-shek's train arrives soon in Xi'an."

Agnes paused, her chopsticks poised a few inches above the dumpling.

"Even Chiang Kai-shek cannot help but notice," Dr. Wunsch continued, "the profound grief that all of China feels for Lu Xun."

Agnes picked up the dumpling with her chopsticks and bit

into it. Hot grease ran over her hand and down her wrist.

"Lu Xun compared China to a nation of cannibals devouring each other." She pointed to the dumpling. "Now I compare him to the food we eat, nourishment for the body of China." She sounded insincere to herself. A poor attempt to dignify death.

"You will be asked to leave soon," Dr. Wunsch remarked. He ladled soup into a small bowl. "Chiang Kai-shek will be staying here in Lington."

Agnes gave the tray a turn.

"You must come back with me and stay in Xi'an until you are transported to Yan'an."

Security measures were strict between Lington and Xi'an. After the ride in Dr. Wunsch's automobile through roads glutted with refugees being evacuated from their villages along the route Chiang Kai-shek was to take, Agnes asked the dentist to drop her off at the Xi'an Guest House. As she was signing the register, she overheard several men in Nationalist uniform.

"Now that we're here," bragged a middle-aged officer with acne scars and a florid face, "we'll straighten them out. They're spoiled kids."

Early the next morning, after photographing protest marches from the side of the unpaved road, Agnes was sitting in a tearoom writing shorthand notes when shots rang out. Buoyed by Chiang's presence in the Northwest, the local Xi'an police had fired into the Communist demonstration and killed nine protesters. So quickly did the owner of the tearoom slam shut his door that Agnes barely got out of the little building before being locked inside.

In the middle of the street lay the body of a student, the face unrecognizable as a face; its brains moistened the dirt. Nearly fainting, Agnes fumbled with her small box camera. In the lens she saw her brother—it might have been John crushed to death in a ditch in Oklahoma. She could not take the picture.

That night she couldn't sleep. Pacing about her room, she heard shouts outside the Guest House. Her first act was to turn off the ceiling light, but the string snapped in her hand. She climbed up on the bed and unscrewed the single bulb. In the sudden darkness, hectic flashlight beams played across her window. She climbed off the bed and heard a great blow. Downstairs, the thick front door of the hotel splintered and fell. From the middle of the room she tried to separate the sound of running footsteps from her own pounding heart.

"Come out, Japanese!" someone shouted. It was a ludicrous command from a soldier who didn't know what army he was fighting. The footsteps drew closer, past the manager's apartment, on toward her own door, where they stopped abruptly.

"Japanese!"

"I'm not Japanese! I'm an American!" Agnes shouted.

Men in gray uniform broke her door down and rushed in. The leader shoved his rifle butt into her stomach and pushed her against the wall. When they saw her purse, camera, eyeglasses, fountain pen, they lost interest in her nationality. The man withdrew his rifle. Gingerly she touched her bruised abdomen.

"Who are you?" she asked. For an answer he tore the wristwatch from her arm. The others pawed through her belongings until, loaded down with loot, they swaggered out of the room, bedding draped around their shoulders. Shots, shouts, running footsteps sounded in the hotel and in the streets outside. Agnes thought of a phrase: the roar of soldiers gone amok. She went to the manager's apartment next door and called to him in a low, urgent voice. He crawled out from under his bed and followed her back to her room where he nailed a piece of blank paper to the broken door. With a flourish he wrote: "Anyone who enters this room will be shot."

Agnes laughed out loud. "It will probably be me." She sat down on the edge of a straight chair, intending to rest for only a moment. But when she looked up it was daylight and she was listening to Dr. Wunsch's German-accented Chinese: "Let me in! I have an appointment!" Dr. Wunsch had come to see if she was all right. She moved to the window to be closer to him.

"An appointment!" he shouted. His tone was angry. After all, he was the Young Marshal's dentist! Agnes heard a brief, intense argument.

The single gunshot was like the crack of a whip. She ran out of her room, down the hall, and to the front entrance. There on the sidewalk, his legs twisted under him, lay Dr. Wunsch. She made no sound, but walked slowly toward him. The dozen soldiers standing in a knot eyed her as she knelt and felt for a pulse. Held in the soldiers' hostile gaze, she stood. The air smelled sulfurous. Gunfire popped in random bursts throughout town. She walked away from the hotel, toward the headquarters of the Young Marshal, Zhang Xueliang. Someone there must help her bury Dr. Wunsch.

With Diu Ling, Agnes pieced together the pre-dawn events of December 12th, 1936 that had instigated the warfare. The infuriated Young Marshall and Warlord Zhang Xueliang had demanded immediate release of the captured Communist demonstrators, to which Chiang Kai-shek responded by issuing an ultimatum to both of his warlord generals: attack the Communists or lose your command. But the warlords surprised everyone and kidnapped Chiang Kai-shek instead.

Diu Ling paced back and forth in front of the shattered mirror that still hung in Agnes' room. "The Young Marshall kidnapped Chiang Kai-shek in the middle of the night!" He grinned. "In his nightshirt! They found him in a cave behind a temple in Lington."

"Where did they take him?"

"They brought him here to Xi'an and have put a guard at the door of an unknown location."

"The troops who looted the hotel—"

"Belonged to Warlord Yang Hucheng," said Diu Ling. "They were looking for Nationalists."

Agnes massaged her forehead with the fingertips of both hands. The armies were confused, and no one knew who the enemy was. Agnes knew the real enemy was not here. The real enemy was Japan.

"When can I go to Yan'an?" she asked. Yan'an was now the headquarters of the raggle-taggle Red Chinese Army.

"Soon. Yesterday I flew Zhou Enlai into Xi'an. The conference with Chiang Kai-shek will continue until he agrees to fight with us against Japan." He stopped pacing and faced Agnes. "Zhou Enlai wishes to speak to you. The Kuomintang has erected a blockade around us, and we want you to begin broadcasting over Zhang Xueliang's transmitter. It will be picked up in Shanghai and sent to the West."

Within days Agnes was broadcasting forty-minute news bulletins and interviews to Shanghai from the warlord's headquarters, the only daily news of the Xi'an Incident to reach the outside world.

Agnes met her first Communist foot soldiers, not in Yan'an as she'd expected, but in Xi'an, in jail. They were political prisoners captured months earlier in skirmishes with warlord and Nationalist troops. Now that they had been granted freedom, many were too ill to leave prison. The Baptist hospital gave her bandages, the hotel manager gave her small bottles of cognac, and she bought iodine and alcohol with money the looters had not found. The young Red soldiers watched her without expression as she moved about the cells performing first-aid. Sometimes in the evening before she returned to her room for strong coffee brewed on a hot plate, they sang softly from the straw pallets where they lay:

> *The crescent moon casts a long shadow.*
> *The pine trees mourn their mournful sigh.*
> *The autumn winds cry to the sky.*

The war spreads far, the nights grow dark.
Our hearts bow down in loneliness.
The very seas sigh wistfully.

The doves plane homeward to their nests.
The grasses bow down into the dust,
Weary with sorrow, seeking rest.

"I admire your courage," Agnes said to a young soldier when the song ended.

He nodded. "I like the army."

"Why do you like the army?"

"I like it because I learn many things."

"Tell me exactly—one, two three, four, five—what have you learned that you did not know before?"

"We learn more than five things. We go to school."

"What do you learn?"

"We learn about the world."

"What shape is the world—flat, round, square—?"

"Well, around here it's both flat and has mountains."

"But the whole world?"

The soldier's dark eyes never left Agnes' face. "I don't know," he said. "I haven't been in the army very long."

28

Yan'an 1937

In January Agnes sneaked through the military blockade around Xi'an and caught a ride to Yan'an in a Red Army truck. From the canopied truck bed she stared backwards at the narrow road unwinding behind her, a reddish-brown ledge clinging to the mountainside. The vast, lonely landscape of Shaanxi Province reminded her of peaks and plateaus of New Mexico and dry brush and roiling creeks of Arizona. She was at home in the mountains and red dirt; in the poverty and hope of the place. Though it looked barren, this soil was generative. Agnes understood it and mixed with it, for after all, she was as she had written, daughter of earth.

The truck had to stop for peasants herding scrawny goats. Chickens squawked, teetered, and tacked just ahead of the wheels. Trees with angled trunks looked jointed, as if they were giant, bizarre, walking vegetables. An enormous hairy pig, built low to the ground and with a head the size of a vat, slung himself along the side of the road.

They stopped in villages to organize the peasants into Communist soviets and anti-Japanese associations. They slept in deserted buildings and ate outdoors.

"We will be in Yan'an by sunset," Diu Ling said over ten o'clock breakfast, fringes of egg white cooked in a sweet broth. The soup steamed in the winter air.

Agnes pointed with her chopsticks to the numerous caves that hived the mountainside. "Are they natural?"

"They were dug centuries ago to store grain and to live in." Diu Ling smiled his quick, intense smile. "You will see the inside of a cave soon enough."

Agnes lit a cigarette and sat back to study the woman who

served them breakfast. The Northwest Chinese, with their ruddy cheeks and large eyes, reminded her of American Indians or pictures she'd seen of Eskimos. This woman, Agnes' own age, cooked in a lean-to attached to a deserted mission church where the Red Army workers slept. Already she had a mouthful of bad teeth and her face was as ravaged as the landscape. She carried bowls of soup, baskets of steamed bread, back and forth, serving without question.

"Come sit with us and eat," Agnes said in Chinese. The woman looked shocked, then embarrassed for the foreigner with bad manners. Diu Ling, too, looked embarrassed. Agnes fixed him with her gaze.

"What about the Communist principle of equality for women?"

"At the present time fighting Japan is more important than equality of women." Diu Ling tipped the bowl until only his black eyebrows showed above the rim, hiding, Agnes suspected, a contempt for women. He finished off the broth. "Tonight you will see equal women." He set down the bowl, wiped his mouth, and left the table.

"Lily Wu is an actress from Beijing," Ding Ling said to Agnes when the Red Army truck rolled into camp. She had preceded Agnes to Yan'an, and was, presumably, one of the "equal women" Diu had grudgingly referred to. "You're in time to see the play."

Agnes left her portable typewriter in the truck and followed Ding Ling toward the river. A cleared area had been given over to the Anti-Japanese Resistance Theatre. The large audience sat in a circle around a bare dirt stage. Below flowed the Yan, at this time of year a narrow ribbon of water. Red light from the dying sun touched the young soldiers seated on the ground and turned their caps and padded jackets pink. The mountains were enormous velvet shadows that stanched the bleeding sky, held off the Japanese, averted the hemorrhaging of China for a while longer.

On stage a character in a long Mandarin robe spoke to a soldier wearing the Red Army uniform.

"I cannot attend your people's meeting because I am busy." The Mandarin adjusted his false beard.

"Why cannot you attend the people's meeting?" the soldier asked in a stilted, sing-song voice.

"I cannot attend the people's meeting because I have to trim my beard." The audience laughed.

"If you trim your beard quickly, you will be able to come to the people's meeting."

The Mandarin paused in stagy thought. "My daughter trims my beard and she is not here."

"Where is she?"

"At the people's meeting." There was a roar of laughter. Agnes looked about the open-air theatre to see if she could recognize any of the Red Army leaders. She expected them to be in special seats set apart from the rest of the audience.

"Is Mao Zedong here tonight?" she whispered to Ding Ling.

"There." Ding Ling indicated one of the middle rows. Agnes saw him next to Zhu De. Both sat among the ordinary soldiers, no difference in seating, no difference in uniform. They concentrated on the play, like the others, as charmed as children.

"Here is the actress Lily Wu," Ding Ling whispered as the Mandarin's daughter approached the old man on stage.

"Father," Lily said in a sweet, clear voice that reached the last rows, "I have come to trim your beard." In one hand she carried a pair of scissors. She opened them wide and extended them toward her father's face. The audience did not laugh. The Mandarin backed away.

"Bring me a chair," he said. "I do not like to stand while my beard is being trimmed."

"Here is a chair, Father." Lily Wu moved to one side of the dirt stage and picked up a straight chair. She walked with lithe grace, and her long black hair swayed like silk.

"Tonight I will introduce you," Ding Ling whispered. "Your cave is next to hers."

Your cave. Agnes flushed.

"This is the last scene," Ding Ling murmured.

"How do you know?"

"I wrote it."

Agnes turned to Ding Ling in surprise. The writing was primitive.

"I write plays for a purpose," Ding Ling whispered. "The needs of China are more important than style."

Lily Wu placed the chair behind the old Mandarin, but he refused to sit.

"You do not wish to sit, Father?"

"I have changed my mind. I do not wish to sit."

"Why do you not wish to sit?"

"I do not wish to sit because I am displeased with you." The audience leaned forward.

Lily Wu lowered the scissors. "How have I displeased you?"

"By attending the people's meeting and by mingling with Communists."

"At the people's meeting we learn that all classes must unite against Japan."

The old Mandarin lifted the chair a few inches off the ground and set it down hard. "Daughter, I forbid you to attend the people's meeting."

The audience sat tense and still, waiting for Lily's response. She stood immobile, arrested in a painful choice between love for old and new China. Still holding onto the scissors, she finally walked, crying, away from her father and off the stage. The audience of young soldiers, Agnes could tell, was deeply affected. Tears ran down Ding Ling's cheeks. Grief was palpable. Disruption between child and parent was a crisis in Chinese families. Agnes, who had spent most of her life rebelling, was struck again by the deep sense of obedience Chinese felt for their elders. In Agnes herself the play evoked a remnant of feudalistic feeling she usually denied: the impulse to please one's parents and to obey, even when disobedience becomes necessary.

The Mandarin gave a speech in which he brought into clear relief what China was giving up and what she was gaining in social change. But Agnes was more interested in watching Lily Wu circle around behind the audience. Someone draped a coat over the actress's shoulders. This woman was to be her next-door neighbor. Mentally she fidgeted for pencil and paper. The old Mandarin finished his didactic monologue and the audience began a rhythmic clapping. They turned to look at Agnes in the last row.

"They want the foreign woman to perform," Ding Ling said, her color high.

"I'm not an actress."

"But surely you can perform something!"

Agnes, edgy with stage fright, started down the aisle that the soldiers opened up for her. Someone fixed her in a flashlight beam. In the center of the bare dirt stage she began to sing "Streets of Laredo." As she cast the American tune out onto the Chinese night, the mountains of Colorado seemed as near as Shaanxi Province. Lit by music, time, and distance, her youth now felt happy and luminous. She sang all the verses. When she finished, Ding Ling came down the aisle.

"They want a speech!" she said. "They want to hear you talk!" Agnes was now into the swing of things. She addressed the audience—most had never seen an American woman before. With Ding Ling translating, she told them about her own country, about the American Revolution, the nationalist struggle in India, about fascism in Germany, Japan, China. She ended with something she knew well: tenant farming in Missouri, and coal mining in Colorado.

"Your speech was very fine," Lily Wu said in fluent English later that evening. She had invited Agnes to her cave. "Everything in China is confused, but you are not confused."

In the lantern light she rose and poured tea. Agnes was opening her notebook to record the conversation when footsteps sounded outside on the narrow terrace that snaked up from the river bank, passed the caves of Zhou Enlai, Zhu De, Mao Zedong, went into a hairpin turn, and continued on to the second level which held more caves, Lily's and Agnes' among them.

"It is Mao," Lily breathed. "He wants to meet you."

The footsteps stopped. "Miss Wu?"

Lily stood and pulled back the padded cotton drape that fit over the mouth of the cave. The moon seemed exactly suspended above the mountain, and the night sky was bright with stars. There was a smell of snow in the air. A tall man in a great coat stood in the darkness. He bent his large head, stepped into the cave, and looked at Agnes with still, distant eyes.

"How do you do," she murmured in Chinese, omitting any title. "Thank you for the opportunity to visit the Red Army."

Mao Zedong reached for both her hands. His own were long and slender, like a woman's. His lips were full, and the small brown mole just above the upper lip looked oddly like a beauty spot. Lily pulled a straight chair toward him. He motioned for the two women to sit first. When they had settled themselves at the table he loosened his great coat, sat down, and looked into space with a remote expression on his large face, as if he gained nourishment not from food but from his own thoughts. Agnes waited for him to say something. When she had studied his sensitive face, studied Lily Wu's pretty features again, studied the white-washed walls of the cave upon which the flickering lantern light projected Mao's profile, she spoke.

Lily translated. "It is not easy to reach Yan'an." Mao looked mildly interested. She continued. "The military blockade and the news blockade are both effective."

There was a long silence that she was just getting ready to break when he said, in a voice that was higher than expected, "It appears there are few blockades that can stop you, Miss Smedley." He smiled coolly and continued. "The blockade does us great harm." As soon as Lily translated he looked directly at Agnes. "We welcome our journalist friends to Yan'an. We welcome the end of the blockade. I solicit help from the West for China." He moved his head slightly, as if to affirm his own statement.

"I will write letters and articles," Agnes said. "We will take the story of the Red Army to the world." She knew several writers who would come to Yan'an if safe passage were offered. "Can you provide an escort from Xi'an?"

"We will provide an escort." He turned to Lily Wu. "The American woman is far from home."

Agnes understood without translation and answered quickly, hotly, "My home is wherever people resist oppression."

Mao seemed unmoved by her emotion. "I believe you have spent several years in Shanghai."

Agnes nodded.

"You were in Germany."

"I have lived in Berlin."

"Many of our comrades have studied in Germany," he said thoughtfully. "I, myself, have never been outside China. I understand my country. I talk to the people about China, not about Marx and Lenin." He studied Agnes more openly. "You have been away from America for many years. Do you still understand your country?"

"Yes," Agnes said. "I understand that America gives aid to Chiang Kai-shek. I understand that she sells scrap metal to Japan." She looked into the lantern, eyes narrowed against the direct light. "But there are many Americans who would understand your reform movement if they knew about it." She leaned forward and looked closely at Mao. She was not sure she liked him. There was something soft, almost effeminate, about him. She liked men who were physically tough. Men who had their feet on the ground, like the cowboys she remembered from Colorado and Arizona. Like Big Buck and other men her father had known.

"There is another great country struggling for independence and unity," she said. "Do you know India? Do you know Nehru?"

"I do not know this great leader."

"I became acquainted with him in Berlin. I will write him a letter of introduction to you. Perhaps India can contribute to China's efforts."

"Have you been to India?"

"No, but my husband was Virendranath Chattopadhyaya." She waited for recognition. "Perhaps you have heard of the Indian nationalists who lived in exile in Berlin?"

Mao made a noncommittal gesture with his slender hands. "You are an internationalist, I believe."

"Yes. Oh, yes."

"Your speech interested us tonight." He wrapped the skirt of his great coat closer about his knees and studied her. "Like the poor of China, you are turning your weak position into a position of strength."

Agnes was stunned by the insight. Did he guess that she hadn't finished grade school? That her family was the poorest of the poor? She looked into his face. This man knew too much. He seemed to know that she, like his soldiers, had no home. That she lacked what they had: the Red Army for a family. She stared down at her notebook. When she looked up again, Mao and Lily were talking. The expression on his face was animated.

"Ask Miss Smedley if she is married," Mao said. Agnes waited for the translation.

"No," she answered. "I have been married in the past. But I do not believe in marriage."

Mao frowned.

"The benefits go to the husband. He can love other women, but the wife must remain faithful."

"I have read of love in Western novels," Mao said after a silence. "Have you experienced this one, true love?"

"My Indian husband was the love of my life," Agnes said,

surprised at herself for saying so, and knowing it to be true. Surprised, too, at Mao's childish curiosity about men and women.

"Why?" he asked.

"We combined work and love," she answered. "Still, I suffered."

"How did you suffer?"

"He wanted to control my thinking."

Mao sat in silence for a moment. "In a marriage of equality," he said, "who makes decisions when there is a disagreement?"

"Whoever can marshal the best evidence."

Mao smiled slightly. "Political theory." In the flickering light he turned toward Lily again. Longing was in his face. Agnes hoped Mao's wife was not sitting in a cave waiting for him to return. She hoped the wife was visiting a lover this very moment. The lover would be wearing Red Army fatigues. He was probably shorter than Mao. Most Chinese were shorter than Mao. The two of them would be sitting in a cave, talking, like Mao and Lily. There would be a bed in the shadows. Agnes' eyes wandered to Lily's bed. She wondered if, when she left tonight, Mao would stay.

"I received a Victrola from an American friend," Agnes told Lily Wu and Zhu De as they sat outside drinking tea in early spring sunshine. The American friend was Margaret Sanger. She'd sent records, too, western songs Agnes had requested: "On Top of Old Smoky," "Streets of Laredo," "Red River Valley," "She'll Be Comin' Around the Mountain When She Comes." Below the terrace, the river cracked and thawed, and soldiers drilled on the parade ground on the opposite bank. "The Victrola arrived yesterday with the trucks. Shall we have music tonight?"

Zhu De grinned. His teeth and gums showed. Laugh lines in his leathery face were deep. "We will have an American party."

"I'll teach you to square-dance," said Agnes.

"I am eager to learn."

"And Mao and Zhou Enlai and the others?"

"We will see if they have two feet or three." Zhu De's smile was broad, like his stance when he stood in the center of a circle of seated soldiers, broad as the space he filled when he rested his fists on his hips and turned this way and that, seeming to address each soldier individually. His soldiers loved him and he loved them. They came from poor farms, poor villages. Their talk was earthy They understood their Commander and their Commander understood them.

On a particular night in late March when he arrived for his daily interview with Agnes, he stepped into her cave and began with a question: "Can you help me solve a problem?"

Agnes looked up quickly from her notebook. He was speaking a simple Mandarin that she could understand. Somehow she knew he did not want Lily to translate.

"The wives of my square-dancing comrades"—he hesitated—"ask why the leaders of the Red Army spend their evenings dancing with the American woman."

"They are free to join us," Agnes said. "Isn't it bourgeois to think that there is only one thing men and women are interested in when they are together?"

"I do not think they wish to dance with their husbands."

"Why not?"

"Husbands are not for dancing with."

Agnes' eyes narrowed. "Marriage is"—she did not know the Chinese word for "confining," and so she demonstrated by putting her hands around her neck and squeezing.

"In America is marriage…?" Zhu De put his hands to his own neck.

"Oh, yes," Agnes said decisively. "Marriage is the same all over the world."

"I see you are a worldwide expert," said Zhu De. He returned to the local matter. "My wife asks why I talk to you every evening and what you are writing on your typewriter keys which everyone hears day and night."

"News reports to the West." Sensing a delicate problem behind his words, she laid her pen aside and waited for him to get to the heart of the matter.

"Mao's wife is unhappy," he said.

Agnes' distaste for the institution of marriage overrode feminist sympathy. "If the Red Army leaders cannot free themselves from the control of their wives, how can they free China?"

Zhu De laughed outright. Agnes thought he was going to slap his knee.

"That is a good observation, but I will not tell Mao what you have said." He added more quietly, "The women have had a difficult life in the Revolution. They endure great physical hardship. They want to make homes here for as long as possible."

"It is a historic time," Agnes said with feeling. "We are part of a movement which is changing the world. It is not a time to follow the old wisdom. Perhaps Mao can solve his problem," she added pointedly, "by showing less interest in Lily Wu."

She picked up her pen and began the interview, made restless by the mention of wives and of Lily Wu. Later, it was she, not Zhu De, who cut short the session. She wandered outside. It was still light; the days were growing longer. She followed the terrace down to the river where the water ran faster each day now, gurgling sluggishly as it ate into the thick plate of ice at the center. Spring was a moist, fresh scent in the air.

She crossed the footbridge and set out across the parade ground. A warm wind from the south and southwest, from the gorges of the Yangtze, from the South China Sea, perhaps even from India, blew through her hair. She felt as if a lover's hand, Chatto's, or perhaps the hand of a man she didn't yet know, was stroking her. She experienced a startling desire for unity with him and with China. She was tired of knocking about the world on an individual basis, freelance revolutionary, depending on her personal energy alone to thaw, like the warm water at the river's edge, the thick ice plate of the world's troubles.

"I have applied for membership in the Chinese Communist Party," she told Zhu De the next evening when they met again. Her face beamed. There was a soft expression of fulfillment in her eyes. "I appeared before the membership committee. They will give me their answer in a few days."

Zhu De took a soiled photograph from his pocket.

"Do you think I will be accepted?"

Zhu De fingered the photograph and said nothing. Agnes turned to light the kerosene lamp. "Who is the woman in your picture?"

"My wife who died."

Picking up a pocketknife, she began to sharpen her pencil, collecting the shavings in a neat pile on the open notebook.

"It is pleasant here in Yan'an," he said. "It is not often so pleasant." He began to speak of sons and daughters disobeying their parents to join the Red Army. Of the death of husbands, wives, brothers, and sisters. Agnes listened and made notes.

Twilight came, then darkness fell. Zhu De left. Agnes lay down for the night, lulled by the soft running of the river and the distant laughter of soldiers smoking at the footbridge.

A few days later, compelled by the procedures of Party membership, by signs of spring all around, by the power of her own personality, Agnes appeared before the membership committee. The meeting was held in the open air. Wild apple trees had put out leaves, and soon they would be in full blossom; the river was rising in its banks from melting snow higher up. Agnes approached the committee like a bride, like a girl at her first communion. She should have been wearing white instead of clean army fatigues. Her hair, freshly washed, lay softly on her wide, pale forehead. The committee spokesman said a few words to her. It took a moment for Agnes to understand.

"We believe you will be more persuasive to your fellow countrymen if you are not a member of the Party," he said. "You will not so readily be accused of partisanship."

Agnes stared stupidly at the spokesman's mouth, as if the words had not been said and she was waiting for his lips to open. When she understood, she turned her back on the committee and began walking away. She reached the footbridge before stumbling. Her legs didn't work correctly but her heart made up for it by pumping too hard. She leaned against the bridge's rail and looked down at the narrow, now deep, river. The committee had not been honest with her. It was not a question of unbiased reporting. It was a question of trust. They thought her impulsive, individualistic, uncontrollable. She was being used without being accepted. She wanted to drown.

Agnes fell on the terrace at the hairpin turn and began to cry. She could not stop. She knew someone was crying too loudly, and suspected the sounds were coming from herself, but it did not feel worth the effort to try and stop. Even when Lily came running, with another woman behind her, and then Zhu De, still she didn't quite realize she was the only one who could bring an end to the embarrassing shudders and cries.

Finally Lily shook her and she stopped abruptly. Lily, Zhu De, and the others gathering around looked like strangers. An hour before, they had been her brothers and sisters. But within a moment her family dissolved. She had lost her place. She'd been put outside the warm circle to make her own way again, alone, thawing the world around her with nothing more substantial than her wit, personality, and typewriter.

Lily helped her inside. The cave was dark. She asked Lily to leave and pull the padded drape across the mouth of the cave behind her. By herself she must become reacquainted with the absence of light. She would never be permitted to join in comforting assumptions. She was doomed to be an outsider.

On a late June night, shortly before outright war with Japan, Agnes lay on her sleeping platform listening to the sounds of children's voices down by the river. Her *Xiaogui* — Little

Devil—one of the young boys adopted, trained, and educated by the Red Army wherever it went, was still out playing. During the day her *Xiaogui* took his pet duck to swim in the river. Now the duck slept not far from the boy's cot at the back of the cave, stirring occasionally. Agnes turned on her bed. She was careful about what thoughts she allowed to occupy her. It was permissible to think about writing, to think about the Lu Xun library she stocked with foreign books and publications, to think about her garden and about her *Xiaogui*. She forgot, for short periods, that she was not Chinese after all, that she was not American. That she was really nothing at all.

She considered whether to step onto the terrace and call her X*iaogui* to bed. She enjoyed playing mother. However, the boy had been without mother and father for most of his eleven years and hardly needed to be called in for the night. In his harsh young life he had slept on the ground, in strange beds, sitting up, perhaps even standing. Still, like the other Little Devils, like the peasant soldiers and leaders themselves, he had a ready smile and a certainty of purpose. He was happy.

Agnes heard running footsteps on the lower terrace. They paused at the hairpin turn, continued, passed her own doorway, and stopped in front of Lily Wu's cave.

"Come out, bourgeois bitch!" a woman screamed in Mandarin. Agnes shot up from her bed, threw on her khaki jacket, ran barefoot along the terrace, and rushed past the guard at the entrance in time to see Mao Zedong's wife lift a long-handled flashlight over her seated husband and come down hard with it again and again. Mao shielded his large head with his hands. The guard ran to his side, unsure how to handle the domestic fight. Finally, after what seemed an eternity, Mao stood.

"Be quiet, Zizhen," he said. "There's nothing shameful in the friendship between Comrade Wu and myself. We were just talking. You are ruining yourself as a Communist and are doing something to be ashamed of. Hurry home before other Party members hear of this."

Lily had backed up against the wall of the cave. Mao's wife, a big, flaccid woman, now turned her attention to the actress.

"Dance-hall bitch! You're making a fool of the Chairman!" She raised the flashlight, but at the last minute dropped it in favor of scratching and pulling hair. Lily tore herself loose and ran to hide behind Agnes, who stood amazed in the center of the cave.

"Imperialist bitch!" Mao's wife shrieked. She picked up the flashlight from the ground and struck Agnes over the head. Agnes reared back and punched the Chairman's wife in the nose. Zizhen lay screaming on the cave floor. Mao ordered the guard to get her on her feet.

"You're acting like a rich woman in a bad American movie!" he said. But his wife refused to leave until he called for two more guards who came and led her down the hill. Mao followed in silence.

Weeks later when the Japanese attacked Marco Polo Bridge near Beijing, the Central Executive Committee of the Party granted Mao a divorce. Zizhen was sent to Moscow for political study; Lily Wu was banished from Yan'an.

"I will miss you," Agnes said as Lily padded about the cave, crying softly and gathering up papers. Agnes, who had escaped formal censure, lay on Lily Wu's bed, easing her injured back. She'd fallen off her pony, Yunnan, that Zhu De had stolen from a rich landlord during the Long March and given to her. "Where are you going?"

"I've been assigned to a theatre group at the front."

Agnes brightened. "You can see the war firsthand."

"I don't want to see the war firsthand," Lily sobbed. She wadded up papers, set them in the dirt just outside her cave, and touched a lighted match to four corners.

"What are you burning?" From the bed Agnes watched the

small flames waver, catch, and burn brightly.

"Poems from the Chairman."

Love poems, Agnes thought. October to July had been a brief respite from battle, and Mao Zedong had permitted himself the luxury of writing poetry and exploring romantic love. She was not surprised that Lily and Zizhen were being punished—in her experience it was women who paid for men's pleasures. But now Mao's months of personal indulgence were over. Chiang Kai-shek had finally declared war on Japan.

With Lily departing and Zhu De already at the battlefront, Agnes would have no close friend in Yan'an. She packed her bag and typewriter and, looking back once at the cave which had been her home from February to September, limped down the terrace to hitch a ride into the village.

In town, Red Army soldiers explained the war to civilians gathered in the dusty streets. On maps printed by Kang Da, the Anti-Japanese Resistance University, or drawings hastily scratched in the dirt with a stick, they pointed to China and Japan, to Shaanxi Province where the peasants had lived all their lives with only the vaguest concept of Asia and the world.

Agnes sat down gingerly on her suitcase near the old city gate and took a final survey of Yan'an and the past seven months of her life. A solemn gong sounded and a bugle played from the ancient pagoda overlooking the town and the Yan River. A line of peasants in blue-gray uniform came walking down the road. There was no cheering. The people knew great hardship lay ahead. Their faces were serious. There was a peaceful, fatalistic certainty about them. By contrast, Agnes' life seemed anchored in nothing more than struggle and rejection.

29

Red Army Headquarters 1937

Marine Captain Evans Carlson smelled coffee. Immediately he embarked upon a reconnaissance mission through the abandoned Presbyterian schoolhouse that served as Eighth Route Army headquarters. He went from room to room, an American intelligence officer turning away from every pot of tea he saw, consumed by the smell of the coffee bean and home.

The smell grew stronger. He peered into the anteroom outside Zhu De's office. A slender, grim-looking Western woman in a military uniform and muddy puttees, her short, straight hair pushed back off her high forehead, stood at a small charcoal stove boiling coffee. On the table behind her he saw a handwritten list on lined paper: "Carbolic acid, gauze, medical cotton, dressing instruments, bullet probes, large and small scissors, artery forceps, camphor ampules, morphine tablets, codeine tablets, bleaching powder, salves." There were shorthand notes beneath, which he could not read.

"I haven't smelled coffee since I left Hankow," he said. Agnes turned to face him. When she saw his American military uniform she turned back to the coffee and ignored him.

"I'm Evans Carlson," he said. "It's a pleasure to meet you."

"It's not a pleasure for me," Agnes said. Evans stared at her back, dumbfounded. The only American within hundreds of miles, and she wouldn't introduce herself.

"I haven't *smelled* coffee since I was in Hankow, and I haven't *tasted* it, either."

"Here," she said, and poured out a cup. He slurped noisily, making a show of enjoyment. Then he forgot about making a show because it was so good and he was so damn tired of tea.

"Wonderful!" he said, and walked out of the room.

"What's so wonderful?" the woman growled. "A little coffee. A little boiled water." He was already out the door.

She was weatherbeaten, and you seldom saw a face with so much suffering in it. But the eyes warmed to him when she at last decided he wasn't trying to get her kicked out of China as, she later told him, so many Westerners wearing uniforms and sporting titles had tried to do over the years. It didn't take her long to realize he wasn't going to ask her what she saw in the Communists, or if she wanted protection, or if she wanted to leave the field and go live with missionaries, or if she wanted to go to Hong Kong where it was safe. Since living in the Yan'an cave for seven months, she'd been knocking about China, sometimes asked to help, sometimes not. The Chinese admired the foreign woman, while keeping their distance. Westerners in China mistrusted her or pitied her for her misplaced sympathies.

Every evening Agnes carried the little stove to her room, partly for warmth, mostly for coffee. Evans began to join her, at first drawn by the coffee, gradually drawn by her. Huddling over the hot charcoal, they talked about China and America and themselves.

"Why were you so interested in the freedom of India?" he asked when she'd caught him up to the year 1919.

"I'm for the underdog," she said. "Why should one country dominate another? India was my family. Now it's China. I am Indian. I am Chinese."

Evans Carlson was the son of a Connecticut minister. All his life his friends had told him he was a romantic. Simple-minded in his patriotism, they said, simple-minded in his admiration for integrity. And now, in this grim woman who seemed less grim all the time, who laughed and sang and had a wide grin that illuminated the tough face, he sensed a unique lack of self-interest. She claimed to be an atheist, yet she sacrificed herself in what he thought was almost a Christ-like manner.

"You don't sound like an atheist," he'd said once, studying her.

She looked at him intently. "I revere great men and women, particularly if they're despised. I hold Jesus and his twelve conspirators in the highest esteem." She looked defensive, waiting for an attack.

But Evans was not on the attack. "I have never met anyone like you, Agnes."

She flopped onto the bed. "I'm chronically unhappy," she admitted. Her eyes were large and unguarded. "Why do you think that is?" But she didn't wait for an answer. "All my life I've been an outsider. And I'm still an outsider." She looked mournful, not at all tough. Evans drew up his long legs, went over to sit on the bed beside her, and took her in his arms.

It had been a very long time since Agnes had touched a man. His cheek with its two days' growth of beard electrified her. How had she lived without a man's beard, a man's height and weight, arms and hands? A man's mouth? She reached up and touched his hair. He kissed her and she took in his strength, his fighting spirit, his tenderness. When his hand moved to her breast it was because she moved it there. And with that signal his kisses grew hungrier and she gave up all the love collected within herself from years of loneliness and outrage.

The next night he came to her room again. While the charcoal stove glowed, they sat close and talked. "Yesterday I saw a bamboo thatch structure with posters on the walls, pictures of Chiang Kai-shek, Sun Yat-sen, Benjamin Franklin, Thomas Edison, and Madame Curie. How do they know about these Westerners?"

Agnes looked smug but said nothing.

"I saw soldiers who can read teaching others who can't. Newspapers plastered to walls. And wall writing"—he fished in his jacket pocket for several slips of paper. "For example: 'Purpose of guerrilla warfare is to turn enemy rear into Communist front,' and 'Civilians must gather up dropped weapons of retreating enemy.'"

He stood. The Reds' disciplined behavior and comprehension

of the goals they were fighting for was what American troops needed, he told her excitedly. It was ethical indoctrination and he wanted the same thing for the American military. "We've grown flabby, unwieldy, bureaucratic."

Agnes gazed at him in passionate agreement that turned to softness when he touched her hand. He guessed she had not always been so tender and soft with other men as she was with him. He sometimes forgot that he would have to leave soon.

They spent Christmas Eve together, 1937, far from carols and lighted trees and the English language.

"I brought you a present," he said, and handed her a half pound of roasted peanuts. She hugged him.

"My gift is more coffee." They stepped back to look at each other. Their separate breaths steamed in the cold room.

He took a harmonica from his pocket. "Do you know any carols?"

"Silent Night," said Agnes, and began to sing softly while he played a simple accompaniment. Since she couldn't remember the words to the second verse, she sang the first verse twice.

"How about a spiritual?"

"When Israel was in Egypt. Let my people go," she sang, and began to cry. Evans pulled her to him. "I'm losing my revolutionary edge!" she bawled into his large handkerchief. He threw back his head and laughed.

"This won't sharpen any edges," he said, "but it will dry your tears." And he rendered a wheezy version of "From the Halls of Montezuma." When he finished, Agnes asked for "My Country 'Tis of Thee." She stood beside the stove, took off her soldier's cap, and sang with it held over her heart.

At the end of the song she broke into more sobbing, then slammed the cap on her head. "I don't understand all this damn emotion!"

Evans brushed away her tears with the back of a finger.

"You're starved for a home and a country," he said. "Whether you know it or not, you're a fine American, Agnes."

"I'm not an American," she said. "And I'm not Chinese." She told him about being rejected by the Communist Party. She looked pale, and the circles under her eyes were dark. Without comment he led her to the bed and began massaging her shoulders and back. He lay down beside her.

"You don't fit into an organization," he said. "You would be a brave soldier but not a good soldier."

"What do you mean by that?"

"You don't follow orders very well."

"Such as?"

"Such as: Give me a kiss." She refused. He planted one on her stubborn mouth. "KP duty for you." She struggled. He pinned her down with one leg. "Stop laughing," he said, "and take your punishment."

When, a few days later, he prepared to return to his intelligence work, she was disobedient again. Zhu De ordered her to remain at headquarters rather than accompany Evans to the front lines.

"I must go with Captain Carlson," she said, and stomped her foot. She even cried.

But Zhu De said she was more useful writing and organizing than fighting on the battlefield. "I am requesting you to go to Hankow soon. There you can raise funds from the West for medical supplies."

"The West may not give me funds. I am not so popular with Westerners," she retorted, still stung by his refusal to let her accompany Evans. "Some of them call me immoral. They say I'm a camp follower, a prostitute. And worse: a Red." She grinned and Zhu De grinned with her.

"It is not only Westerners I want you to meet," he said. "You must tell Dr. Lin about our needs."

"Who is Dr. Lin?"

"The founder of the Chinese Red Cross."

She turned away from him and left the room. Mentally she argued: I don't want to meet the founder of the Chinese Red Cross. I want to stay with Evans Carlson. It's hearing English spoken without an accent. It's having a friend who drinks coffee. But mostly it's the man himself. I do not want to be separated from him.

But she would not say such things to Zhu De. If one American male, if the English language, if homesickness for a home could call into question all that she had devoted herself to for the past eight years, what kind of woman was she?

30

Hankow 1938

She met Dr. Lin in the lobby of the YMCA in Hankow. Agnes was noticeable in her slacks and mannish haircut, and Dr. Lin, too, stood out: a short, slight Chinese man who wore knickers and carried a cane.

"How do you do," he said in precise English colored by a Scots accent. He had been educated in Edinburgh. "There is much work to be done in caring for China's wounded. You are a great foreign friend. On behalf of China, I thank you."

"I understand you are a friend of Chiang Kai-shek," Agnes said.

"We are acquainted."

"I do not like Chiang Kai-shek but I am prepared to work with you and with the United Front." It was 1938. The Kuomintang and Communists were, for the moment, cooperating in the defense of China.

Dr. Lin bowed courteously. "We must all work for the greater good of China."

But it would take more than courtesy to hold the United Front together. Disharmony extended even into the workings of the Red Cross. Agnes began receiving negative replies to her solicitations for funds.

"Madame Sun Yat-sen reminds us that any monies sent to the Chinese Red Cross and Dr. Lin," read one letter, "will unavoidably fall into the hands of the Generalissimo and Madame Chiang Kai-shek. We, of course, cannot run the risk of helping to sustain the Kuomintang in any way. Henceforth our contributions will be made through Madame Sun Yat-sen."

Agnes stormed into Dr. Lin's office in the temporary structure that housed the new medical school in Hankow.

"Look at this!" she said, and thrust the letter in his face.

Dr. Lin read it and looked up with a whimsical expression. "The two sisters are struggling over China."

"Madame Sun Yat-sen has no right to interfere with our fundraising!" Madame's rejection years earlier intensified her fury. "We're laying the foundations for socialized medicine! It's part of the reform that will isolate her brother-in-law after we lick the Japs! Why can't she understand that?"

Dr. Lin donned his Tam O'Shanter. "Aye, lassie," he said gently. "China is divided against itself." With a melancholy expression he twirled his cane and walked away. He had been warned about Agnes Smedley's emotionalism, but this was the first time he had seen the blaze for himself.

For the next year and a half Agnes burned brightly. In make-shift hospitals on the Central China front she organized medical service and supplies, tended the wounded, and wrote news reports at night for the *Manchester Guardian*. But the hot flame used her up, as if her health were a too-small draft in a large furnace.

"I don't sleep well these days," she admitted to Evans on one of their brief visits together. They were spending the night at a guest house in Chongqing, the relocated Chinese capital. She felt the chest pains again.

"I am so sorry," she whispered as they lay together in bed. "I don't feel well enough to make love."

Evans kissed her on the cheek, then rolled onto his back and stared into the darkness.

"Very few Americans have spent as much time at the front as you, Agnes."

She supposed he might be right.

"How long have you been in the field?"

She didn't know. Over a year. Months and months. She eased herself onto her right side. Someone had told her that, in bed, the heart works best with the chest's weight beneath it. Evans had fallen asleep. He pulled air deep into his rangy body and let it out in slow expulsions that sometimes alarmed her because they were so long in coming.

She had grown terribly insomniac. She returned to her left side, toward Evans. Bugger her weak heart. She nestled against him and was comforted. She slept, but awakened to the sound of a single airplane engine overhead. The buzz hovered, circled Chongqing as if it were lost, then retreated into the distance. She lay in uneasy wakefulness.

Evans loved her in China, but what about after the war? Would he love her in America? Would she even want to return to America? His parents were high-class New Englanders, and they would sniff at her lack of education, be appalled by her reputation in politics and sex. The more she thought about them, the worse they became. By the time the Upper Yangtze fog had lifted enough to let moonlight shine through the small window—and with it, the risk of Japanese bombers—she was convinced that the Carlsons didn't deserve their wonderful son.

It was silly to imagine being married to him, she who didn't believe in marriage.

"Agnes," Evans said, covering her, "you're having a bad dream." She put her arms around him and clung.

31
Hong Kong, early morning, August 26, 1940.

Agnes disembarked from a small mail plane. She and the pilot had flown all night over Japanese lines. Even before she reached the taxi waiting for her, two immigration officials walked up and took her into custody. The British Secret Service had been tracking her activities for the past twenty-two years, they said, ever since her work with Indian nationalists in New York. She would not be permitted to incite the Indian population in Hong Kong to rebellion against Great Britain. The next day a bewigged judge asked her about past Indian activities and accused her of being a loose and immoral woman.

"I have slept with many men," she answered the representative of the Crown, "but if any were English, I cannot remember, for they made very little impact upon me." She was released, not because of her cocky humor, but because there was not enough evidence.

Agnes was in Hong Kong, safe and remote from action, when fighting broke out within the New Fourth Army between the Communists and Chiang Kai-shek's forces. The United Front immediately disintegrated. Agnes spilled out her unhappiness in a long letter to Evans Carlson. The New Fourth Army was *her* army. For months she had marched with them. It was *her* story and she wasn't there to write it.

She admitted to him that it might be time to leave China. Did not everyone's usefulness sometime come to an end? Had not Evans, himself, resigned from the military to protest the complacency of superiors who refused to believe the United States should prepare for war in Asia, should study the strategy and methods of the guerrilla fighters in Northwest China?

Agnes booked passage for America on a Norwegian ship.

Three days before she left she wrote a speech in shorthand, fast and with passion, to deliver at a fundraising banquet in Hong Kong. She wanted to give the audience a taste of what it was like to cross the Yangtze in Japanese-held territory. And she wanted to remember what it was like to fight for China at the front.

Now I want you to come with me with a band of these guerrillas and see how they organize and carry out a night march. We are going to cross the Yangtze River between Japanese garrison points. The Yangtze is patrolled by Japanese gun boats...

...we pass through the night and come to a small village at dawn. On the surrounding hills we can see figures of civilians with guns, standing guard. The guns are often not much—old bird guns, some of them. But that is something. We rest in the heart of the people...

...as we pass through the poor villages of mud walls and thatched roof, we always hear sounds of moaning. It is a malarial region, and there is no medicine other than what our army has...

No talking, no coughing, no smoking, no matches lit. Carriers, test your burdens so that no squeak sounds. Stick leaves or grass in places of friction...men with white face towels must tuck one end inside their collar at the back and let the towel hang down so men behind can see...

Once, we come near a village and rest at command. Right under the bushes I see a small temple to the Earth God, and a bright new candle burns in the little alcove. It is a signal that all is well. This is the last stop before we pass through the enemy defense positions. The whisper comes: 'March quickly.'

...I hear the night birds, the wind through the trees, and the stars are very bright. Once, from our left, far away, I hear a faint blast on a horn, like the bellow of a water buffalo calf. Then I hear a long, low blast of another horn. They come from near the enemy and our troops are telling us that all is well. I love our troops that night. I love the civilians. I love them with all my heart...

As we near the Yangtze, we come out on top of the high mud dikes that rise fifty feet in the air to hold back the river at high tide. Dark lagoons lie on either hand, breeding places of the malaria mosquito. Then a traitor appears. It is the moon, rising over the mountains back of us. We curse under our breaths, and begin to run. We crouch and run and our carriers drop into a slow dog trot...

Then, ahead of us, we see a light suddenly flare up, and we see the gate of the village ahead of us outlined. It is directly on the Yangtze...

On a short tributary...lie two big river junks, with sails up. Two gang planks run up the side of each. Our carriers run up one plank, silently drop their burdens in the hold and run down the other plank. And within five minutes the junks are loaded and we have run up the planks, the planks are drawn up, and the big oars begin to work. Soon we come out upon the Yangtze, now a sheet of silver in the moonlight. It is misty and we cannot see far. We know a gun boat is down to our left at Kikang, and that it could reach us within seven minutes—and it takes forty-five minutes to cross the Yangtze...

We approach the north bank of the river and see the outline of soldiers standing watching. We touch land, and then leap out and run to meet a large number of people waiting for us. The local government official comes toward us laughing, welcoming us. And since the Japanese have never even been once to this village, we are safe, and we begin marching inland, singing the guerrilla marching song. After about ten miles, we come to the great sprawling home of a big landlord. This landlord is a remarkable creature, for he and his three sons are guerrilla leaders and the entire income from their estate helps finance the guerrillas.

In this way we crossed the Yangtze.
Wanla.... Finished.

32
Ojai, California 1941

"So many white buildings make perfect bomb targets," Agnes said to Aino Taylor as they walked down the main street of Ojai, California.

"Then let's stick to the woods," said Aino, a young housewife whose mother gave Agnes massages and treatments for her injured back. They cut through the oaks that separated Agnes' rental cottage from Aino's house. Somewhere in the woods a mourning dove cooed. Such a beautiful little town, set in a valley of orchards north of Los Angeles and inland from the Pacific Ocean. Friends had directed her to this peaceful place to finish her book. Like everyone else in town, she paused for "the pink moment" when the sun touched the top of Topa Topa Peak and rendered the valley magical. But the light and fragrance were tenuous. And there were all those white buildings. Peace felt like an interval in war. It was May 1941.

Every day she worked on her book. When she couldn't write any more, she called Aino. "I've got to get away from 'The Odyssey.'" She meant *Battle Hymn of China*.

"I'll meet you in the oaks," said Aino.

These oaks discouraged gardening. Agnes' cottage was so shaded that she'd decided against planting. It was just as well. The book required all her effort—there was not much time left to tell Americans what she knew about China.

Agnes was already out of the oaks and beside an orchard. The late afternoon was fragrant with orange blossoms, almost too sweet. She slowed her pace—she was still accustomed to marching with men—and stopped to look at a hollyhock beside the road. The plant was as tall as she.

America seemed very different to her than it had the last time she'd lived here, twenty-three years earlier. Enough time had passed for an entire new generation to come of age. Everyone seemed to think about money, and a constant barrage of advertising poisoned the airwaves and the air. There were some fine changes, though. Labor unions were admitting Negroes. The New Deal helped equalize wealth.

Mostly as she walked, picking wild poppies for Aino, pausing at a patch of sage to kneel and smell the lemony scent, she missed China. China's history was her history. Away from China she was only half herself. Quantities of food, hot running water, a warm bed were nothing compared to righteous struggle.

She saw that luxury weakens people. Here in Ojai there was a cult of Theosophists who sat at the feet of an Indian religious leader, Krishnamurti. These spiritually hungry Americans with their great wealth had not the slightest idea of India's poverty and mistreatment under Great Britain. This Krishnamurti preferred being adored in a comfortable setting to struggling with Gandhi and Nehru for the release of his country. He could not hold a candle to a man like her ex-husband Chattopadhyaya.

Agnes felt deeply alone in America. No one she knew had the faintest idea of what life in Asia was like. And yet there was that American openness, a willingness to listen and question, a sense of fair play. There were the Aino Taylors. Aino might not understand from experience what Agnes talked about—she was, after all, a young housewife and Agnes felt slightly desperate when she thought of this bright and efficient woman spending her life washing and ironing and looking after her husband—but she intuitively understood all that Agnes tried to tell her.

"I don't know if I can write this book!" Agnes said, seated at Aino's kitchen table. Unexpectedly, she broke into tears. "I must write about a boy who was wounded in the fighting. I can't forget him." Her hand shook. Coffee slopped over into the saucer. She poured it back into the cup. "He was sitting against the wall of the mud hut which was our hospital. His head was bandaged. I asked him to tell me how he was wounded.

"'It is such a little thing,' he said. 'It is for my country.' His head sank onto his chest. I lowered him onto the pallet and he died."

Aino sat, still and electrified. "I am too tired to go on," Agnes whispered. She had left China in a daze, afraid that when she returned to Asia, all her friends might be dead. When she came back, China might belong to Japan.

Aino leaned forward. "You need rest."

Rest. That is why she had come to this pretty little town. But it is hard to rest after forty-nine years of not resting. She looked down at her hand on the table beside Aino's. The fingernails were just beginning to grow in again. She had lost them from malnutrition. "Malnutrition" was a serious word, a dangerous word. Agnes had not died like Mother, but she was struggling for stability. She'd been eased out of China, she knew. She'd come close to being Chinese, yet failed in essential ways to *be* Chinese.

Aino, this blond-haired, blue-eyed woman of Finnish descent, slender and light on her feet, was looking at her intently. Aino's maiden name was Haanapa. Agnes liked the name. It was cool, fresh, useful, like Aino herself. Aino listened to her stories without shock or a sense of foreignness. She did not have the look Agnes had seen in her sister Myrtle's eye on a recent visit to San Diego: distrust. Myrtle had worked herself up to superintendent of schools in San Diego and didn't want her fellow teachers to know her sister worked with the Communists. She did not want to hear about life in China.

Ernest, her ex-husband, had called her. Dear Ernest and his sister and his wife wanted to see her—wanted to see the damage, perhaps. Because there *was* damage. She looked far worse, was in poorer health, she was sure, than any of them.

She turned toward Aino for distraction. "Tell me something amusing. Tell me about your actor friend."

Aino went to the stove and opened the oven door. Agnes

breathed deeply. Heat and fragrance rolled over her.

"He lives in the country in a fieldstone house topped by a round tower." With a toothpick Aino pierced the center of the cake. "He's Austrian. His name is Norbert Schiller. He plays Nazis in the movies."

"Have you visited him?"

"Of course," said Aino. "He has a goat named Helena. He drives her around with him in his red convertible." Aino took the cake out of the oven. When she stood, her face was pink. "Once I saw Helena go to the bathroom on a small round table in the house. She deposited her turd nicely and kept her feet together while doing so, like the delicate lady she is. Norbert swept it up as if it were nothing."

Agnes laughed and felt better. The mood would last, she knew, until she was alone again with her manuscript. Then she would miss China so intensely that life apart from its simplicity, fatalism, humor, seemed unendurable.

Agnes knew a failed night when she saw one. From bed, she watched Evans Carlson. He'd tossed his pillow onto the floor, preferring a flat surface under his back, a man as used to hardship as she. Under a day and night's growth of beard, his face was strong and bony. The night before, they'd talked about China like two homesick children. There were no other Westerners who knew where the Eighth Army headquarters had been, what Zhu De said to his troops, how a small charcoal stove glows in the night. But a hotel room in San Diego has no charcoal stove and they had created no blaze of their own. Though he'd invited her to meet him for a few days, she knew he was sorry he'd asked. Now, sensing her wakefulness, he stood up from the floor, leaned over her bed, and touched the tip of her nose. After a few minutes in the bathroom, he was washed, shaved, and dressed.

"Ready for breakfast?"

Agnes, who'd stayed in bed in hopes of rekindling even a small fire, got up and began to dress.

"I'll meet you downstairs," he said. "I want to get a newspaper."

At a patio table beside a swimming pool, Evans dug into his ham and eggs. Agnes played with her toast.

"Roosevelt and Churchill have signed the Atlantic Charter," he said from behind his newspaper. "The end of imperialism."

Agnes snorted. "The end of *white* imperialism. The Japanese want the same opportunity. We taught them how."

Evans looked up. "Not hungry?" He pushed the jelly dish toward her.

"I can't eat beside a swimming pool."

"Too much luxury," he agreed. "Not good for people." Still, she noticed, luxury hadn't damaged his appetite. He reached across the table for her hand. In the past, his touch had always restored her.

"Shall we see each other soon?" she asked at the train station. He was returning to Washington to form a Marine battalion modeled on the Chinese guerrillas; she was returning to Ojai and her book; both would rather be in China than America. He kissed her and held her close so that she would know he loved her. But she was afraid he loved her now as a friend, not as a lover. It was, Agnes thought, a hell of a time to find the one man you wanted for the rest of your life.

Ernest, Elinor, and Thorberg arrived for their visit in a comfortable American car. And what other car should they arrive in? They were comfortable and they were American. Ernest parked in front of Agnes' redwood cottage and walked toward her with the light, slow step she remembered. He put his arms around her, then moved away and opened the car door for his wife.

"How are you, Elinor?" Agnes said bluntly, without waiting

for an introduction. The woman looked surprised, even alarmed.

"Thorberg!" Agnes hugged the tall, calm, blonde woman who emerged from the back seat. They pulled away to look at each other, and hugged again. For the rest of the visit, Agnes ignored Elinor.

"She didn't like me," Agnes told Aino after the visit. "Elinor and I can never be friends."

"She didn't seem to *dis*like you," said Aino.

"Oh, she's got good manners. She knows how to hide her feelings."

"Well, it's obvious that Ernest and Thorberg are crazy about you. I thought the visit was grand. And when you and Thorberg and I sat listening to Beethoven—"

Agnes' face softened. Nourished by friendship with Thorberg and Aino, she'd relaxed into quietude. "Beethoven," she mused dreamily. "And the cactus flower in its vase on the white mantel. It was a moment I'll never forget."

"Nor I." Both women fell silent.

"Our ride to Pomona College was not so peaceful," said Agnes, breaking the mood. "I was terribly nervous in the back seat before my speech. I couldn't carry on a conversation. I'm afraid I groaned."

"All the way to Pomona?"

Agnes nodded. She laughed behind her rough hand. Sometimes she delivered herself of this dainty, almost coy laugh which she half-hid, a gesture Aino associated with Asian modesty.

"Was your speech a success?"

"The audience seemed to like it. On the way home I felt wonderful. We sang in the car. Ernest spun a story about how he, Elinor, Thorberg and I will retire together on Thor's farm. I'm to do the plowing with one mule and Ernest will help me. Thor will lie in a hammock and recommend books for us to read."

"What will Elinor do?"

"He didn't say. She took no part in the conversation. But then"—here Agnes' eyes grew dark and she pressed her hands to her forehead—"the car ran out of gas, miles from anywhere. Ernest and Thorberg went for help so I had to sit in the parked car with Elinor, and it was such a terrible come-down from my speech—I was furious." She looked up at Aino. "I ranted and I cried. I just fell to pieces. I could tell by Elinor's face that I was behaving badly." Agnes didn't look particularly sorry for behaving badly. "I think she was shocked. But I knew she disapproved of me, anyway. Didn't want me there. So I might as well do what I felt like doing."

She stood up suddenly. "Comfortable people make me sick. I don't trust them. All except you," she added, for Aino at that moment was sitting comfortably at her kitchen table, dinner in the oven, her young daughter playing in the back yard.

"Elinor is like so many American women I've met. Comfortable, vacuous, unhappy, narrow. They have less to do with their country than the peasant women of China. At that moment in the car, when people all over the world are starving and dying"—Agnes was trembling now—"well, I just misbehaved, and I didn't mind upsetting that comfortable American woman at all. And I didn't mind yelling at Ernest."

Aino came over and began to massage Agnes' shoulders.

"The Communists don't want me and neither do the Capitalists," Agnes said bitterly. Aino worked in silence. Agnes dropped her head and stopped thinking.

Excessive devotion to home alarmed Agnes. In her opinion, Aino took more time with her daughter's clothing than necessary, paid too much attention to her husband's comfort, and was so excellent and thorough a homemaker that she lost impetus for creative work; Aino had confessed to Agnes that she had a secret longing to sculpt and to write.

From New York where she was working with her editor on *Battle Hymn of China*, waiting for the publication date and a paycheck, Agnes wrote Aino, "Just because you have a husband and a home you love, with a secure income, the danger of drifting is all the greater. I wouldn't want to see you without some security," she added, "but you should use it and use it hard. Shake yourself daily and try to write and model. Don't be a mediocrity, nor just a 'nice woman.'"

John Taylor defended his wife. To Agnes he wrote a letter, reminding her that she relied on the very home Aino created; the very home she was criticizing. Though she might not know it, he said, Agnes needed family, maybe more than most, and that's exactly what the Taylors were to her. She would always be welcome in their home because they loved her, he said.

Agnes replied that she loved them, too. She admitted she did not know of any place in the world that had discovered a substitute for family, but she would continue to look.

She was also continuing to look for publications where she could place articles about China. She needed money, but high-paying magazines like *Reader's Digest*, though they led her on for a while and even talked with her about projected work, backed off when they discovered it was the Reds she wanted to write about. The Reds were material for a book, perhaps, but not *Reader's Digest*. The editor asked her if America would eventually have to feed China, "the yellow peril," he called it.

"Oh, they have been feeding themselves for centuries," Agnes told him. "It would, however, be nice if America stopped selling scrap metal to Japan."

She felt unwelcome—no, not unwelcome so much as caricatured—by the Press Club in New York. At a banquet honoring some newspaperman or other, wives of reporters she knew from China looked her over while their husbands hugged and glad-handed her. Apparently she was considered to be some sort of *character*. The worst part about being a character, a revolutionary, a sexually free feminist, is that a lot of people didn't take you seriously.

At times even *she* didn't take herself seriously and thought her critics were right. She went even further and thought herself ludicrous. "What a rotten life I must have led …" she wrote Aino. "If only I could meet one man whom I could be proud of, and say, 'I slept with him!' But I have to creep off in some corner of myself and contemplate such things in shame."

For all her efforts, she had not loved nor been loved as she would have liked. She had sought to overcome her fear of sex the only way she knew how: practice. Once she got the hang of it, she'd considered it her right. Love, though, had proved to be more than a collection of rights. It had proved almost unobtainable.

Battle Hymn of China received good reviews. She took advantage of her growing reputation as a China expert and booked herself on a public speaking tour. The trips made her nervous. She never felt equal to the people she was addressing. She practiced her speeches ahead of time and underlined certain words and phrases to be emphasized. She marked pauses and tried to keep her voice from rising. She developed chronic indigestion from the meals she ate at head tables.

But when the speeches themselves were over and questions came from the audience, Agnes forgot about herself and her performance and engaged wholeheartedly with the Americans who questioned her. She bound them to her by her sincerity and wide experience.

"What made you go to China?" a girl asked after a lecture at a private church college in Mississippi. The auditorium was small. Polished railings, dark oak wainscoting, a mural painted by a regional artist. It was an auditorium of the type to be found in hundreds of small American colleges. An auditorium where young people's minds were sometimes ignited, sometimes put to sleep.

Agnes looked up into the balcony at the questioner. The tall, thin girl sounded passionate, and her question seemed to carry a charge, as if the answer might have an effect on a choice being made that very day.

"I went to China because"—Agnes paused—"because it was my destiny." There was a hush. "A bridge was needed between the two halves of our globe. I am a thin cable in that structure." She wanted to make sense to these boys and girls, for boys and girls they seemed, not college men and women. Limited by a comfortable life, they were just now stirring into wakefulness. Many of them would be fighting in Europe or Asia soon. Some would die for America.

"We are here for a short time," she said to the girl in the balcony. "Some of us are placed in positions of risk." No one coughed. Not a hinged seat creaked. The stained glass window above the speaker's platform, Jesus' blue gown, the red robe of a disciple, an orange sun, cast colors out into the audience.

"All my life I have followed my heart and sought knowledge. My search led me to people whom I admired greatly. Those people led me to tasks which needed doing. I am a writer. I had to earn a living, so I went to a continent where there was a great deal to write about." Instead of exhorting the young audience to action, she found herself summing up her life.

"I believed I could break out of my limitations and help China break out of hers. I did not resist change. I welcomed it. And I took responsibility for what my country was doing. It is not enough to live only for oneself or one's family."

She straightened the papers in front of her and looked up at the girl. "I did not know it would be so difficult to live for an elusive ideal." She sat down in the speaker's chair. At first there was no sound. In the moment of silence before applause began, she knew she was one of those who is strong enough to do necessary work. One of those who knows what her work is. About that she had no confusion.

Pearl Buck studied Agnes across the luncheon entrée in the

dining room of the Waldorf Astoria. "Madame Chiang Kai-shek," she said, her eyes gentle but disturbed, "has told others that you will never be allowed to enter China again."

Agnes laughed a quick caw of a laugh. "Her sister says the same. I've earned the enmity of the Madames, both right and left."

Mrs. Buck rested one arm on the edge of the table and brought her maternal face closer to Agnes. "I can understand Madame Chiang Kai-shek's feelings," she said, "but what happened between you and Madame Sun Yat-sen?"

Coming from Pearl, the question didn't seem like gossip. It was more like a frank inquiry into human nature. Agnes took no offense at the famous author of *The Good Earth*.

"I'm not Chinese enough," Agnes said. "I think I talked too much. And one of Madame's friends told me she was annoyed because I always ran up her staircase instead of walking. And she accused me of mishandling funds, which I didn't." Agnes still felt shamed by the whole episode. To have met a great lady, a great humanitarian, Sun Yat-sen's widow; to be rejected because you failed in some way you didn't understand—it was unbearable, even after all these years.

"I'm low-class," Agnes added. "Madame Sun Yat-sen isn't." She forbade tears to come to her eyes. She did nothing but cry in America, it seemed. She looked up and saw that the only tears being shed were Pearl Buck's.

Agnes put her hand quite close to Pearl's on the white linen tablecloth. "What is it?"

"You don't bother with appearances. Therefore I don't need to."

"You miss China, too," Agnes said hopefully. It would be a bond between them.

"That's not why I'm crying," said Pearl.

"What, then?"

"It is you."

Agnes abhorred pity. To be accurate, there were times when

she enjoyed *self*-pity and indulged in it quite readily. But she would not allow anyone else to feel sorry for her. She brought her hand back to her knife and fork and began to toy with the elegant lunch.

"I'm actually crying for my daughter," Pearl said. "And for myself."

"Your daughter?"

"You make me think of my child. She is as vulnerable as you, but without your gifts. She cannot learn and it breaks my heart." She looked deeply into Agnes' wide eyes and whispered, "Sometimes sadness washes over me and I can't stop it. At such times I feel it is my fault that she is retarded."

"You haven't failed your daughter," Agnes said. Pearl Buck didn't know how to fail a child, didn't know how to abandon someone. She would have found Agnes' abandonment of her family after Mother died shocking. But Pearl would never know because Agnes would never tell her. Pearl was from another class, a class so beyond Agnes that abandonment would never occur to her.

"I abandoned my first husband," Pearl blurted out.

"You mean you divorced him, don't you?" But Pearl wasn't going to elaborate. She sat stricken, as if she could not believe anyone would divorce, certainly not herself. She wiped her eyes with a handkerchief whose edging looked as if it had been embroidered in China. Agnes tried to sympathize. It was one of her failings that she couldn't comfort people who she thought already had so many reasons to be comfortable.

"Where are you living now?" Pearl asked after a bit.

"A little hall bedroom on the west side of Manhattan. There's a chance I may go to an artists' colony in upstate New York and finish a writing project."

"Yaddo?"

"Yes. Malcolm Cowley is on the board of directors. He's an old friend. He suggested Yaddo. But first he has to get approval of the board." Agnes reached for a roll. "I'm not often approved of." She helped herself to butter. "I would worry if I were approved of."

Pearl signaled the waiter to remove the plates. "Tell me what you're working on."

"A play. I've never written a play before. It's set in China. It opens during a flood. A brother and sister are walking along a railroad track that runs beside the Yellow River." She had a sudden memory of the flood in Colorado where her family's tent had been washed down the Purgatory River. "After their parents are drowned, the children go to Shanghai where they see great luxury, but they have to work in a metal-polishing shop for long hours under terrible conditions. In the same building is an office where a revolutionary writer and artist are making lithographed notices for political work. And then they go to a chocolate shop in Shanghai where they beg for candy… "

Pearl was listening with good manners rather than interest. Even if the play were the best play in the world, Agnes thought, even if she were explaining it brilliantly, Pearl wouldn't find political drama palatable.

It wasn't the best play in the world, she acknowledged to herself. In fact, it was probably one of the worst.

"You write well about the realities of war," Pearl said quietly. "I've read *Battle Hymn of China*. It is very fine. You're knowledgeable about a China I don't know. I'm the daughter of a missionary, but you march with soldiers."

"The Army has asked me to speak before an officers' training school at Harvard," Agnes said, rather proud of being asked to help educate the establishment.

Pearl leaned forward. "Do you think the Communists will take over China?"

"Oh, yes." Agnes didn't say, "I hope so." She'd never heard Pearl call for redistribution of the land. Never heard her say the upper classes must be stripped of their excess wealth so that everyone's children would have enough to eat.

"Are you willing to address a church convention in

Philadelphia that has asked me to find a speaker?" Pearl asked when they'd finished their lunch.

Certainly Agnes would. She would do it out of passion for China. And she would do it because she needed money.

"Do let me know when you leave for Yaddo," Pearl said. She called for the check. "And best of luck with your play." In front of the hotel Pearl pulled on kid gloves. The doorman hailed a taxi.

"Can I drop you somewhere, Agnes?"

Agnes shook her head. As she set out for the subway she put her hand in her coat pocket and felt the roll and cutlet she'd smuggled out of the hotel in a linen napkin. It would make a fine sandwich. It would do for another meal.

33
Saratoga Springs, New York 1944

Moonlight and white snow made midnight bright. Agnes saw her own breath, listened to her boots break through the white crust. Quite regularly snow crashed to the ground somewhere in the woods and a creaking pine bough, released, sprang slowly back to position. Agnes walked toward one of the lakes of Yaddo near Saratoga Springs, New York. She imagined speckled trout moving slowly beneath the ice, stoically swimming through winter. She loosened her hood. The cold almost had a smell. Perhaps it was the crisp absence of smell that gave the snowy night something like a fragrance.

She looked up at the stars. In China it was day now. The personality of Zhu De shone on the daylight side of the earth. She, herself, filled this dark half. And Evans Carlson—she didn't know where Evans was. In China, in the United States, perhaps somewhere between. Wherever he was, he filled both halves. Until today she hadn't heard from him in a very long time.

To be accurate, she hadn't heard from him today, either. But in the morning mail a friend sent her a copy of a newspaper article Evans wrote. It was a review of her book *Battle Hymn of China*. After dinner she'd left the great dining room of the Yaddo mansion and run upstairs to her bedroom where she kept the scrapbook of his press writings. She'd grabbed scissors and paste pot and set out for the one-room cabin in the woods where she worked.

She smiled now and bent down to pack a snowball between her gloved hands. Evans' article had actually praised *her* more than her *book*. It almost seemed that he had written a love letter disguised as a review. On the pages of the *New York Herald*

Tribune, for all the world to see, he described their reunion in Central China after several months' separation. She had thrown aside, he said, "the barriers she had erected to shield a sensitive soul. The air of belligerency disappeared… "

She hadn't known she was belligerent. All she knew was that Evans didn't question her presence in China. He'd asked her what she knew about China and listened when she told him. And she was not belligerent around someone who cared for her.

The snowball hit the tree and broke apart soundlessly. Agnes pulled up her hood and returned to the cabin. The fire had almost gone out. She added a log to the woodburner and knelt in front of the hearth to watch sparks fly up in the draft. The sweet piney smell of unburned wood stacked beside the fireplace mixed with smoke and sent out an incense from Yaddo to the winds of heaven where it was blown—how high? How far? She reread the review.

"…a dispatch from Chongqing announced her arrival in an emaciated condition. In the interim she had traveled with troops of the Chinese Communist and Kuomintang armies on both sides of the Yangtze, the only foreigner to witness operations in Central China during the years 1938-'39-'40."

Evans understood her. He praised her privately and publicly. He loved her; she loved him. For more than a year now she had read the war news, specifically all the news of him she could find. She read right through the procession of natural beauty here at Yaddo, read while leaves turned red and dropped, while rain fell through bare boughs and ran off the roof, while pine needles rattled down in a wind.

It had not taken her long to lay aside the play and settle into something she knew better: the life of Zhu De. Her shorthand notes from Yan'an were harder to bring to life in America than they would have been in China. She could have written the book with ease in China. The materials that she needed, the people that she needed, were on the daylight side of the earth.

She closed her eyes and pictured the caves of Yan'an, the

terraces, the footbridge. She could see the uncomplicated smiles of the young peasant soldiers; Zhu De's intelligent eyes and earthy stance. He was as near as the pheasant and deer who came to watch through her single window each morning. He was as deeply rooted in her life as the blue spruce and silver-green poplars were rooted in Yaddo soil.

She exchanged her winter jacket for an old sweater, sat down in the rocking chair, and ruminated. Last night after dinner, Carson McCullers, the talented, intense, long-legged, boyish girl-woman in residence at Yaddo had come into the mansion's library and stunned everyone by crying out, "I've lost the presence of God!"

Agnes understood. She understood the difference between losing a thing and losing its presence. She had lost China, but not its presence. It would be far worse to lose the presence than the thing itself. It is important to keep God or China or an idea or someone you love alive by the force of your imagination.

Just this afternoon Agnes had wandered into the enormous kitchen of the mansion for a cup of tea and come upon Carson and Mrs. Ames, the director of the artists' colony, bent over a manuscript. At first they hadn't seen her. She'd filled the kettle with water and set it to boil. Mrs. Ames, a brusque woman who ran Yaddo with a firm hand, looked up. Her smile, bathed in the snow-filtered light coming through the bay window, was rare.

"We're going over a thorny section," she said, returning to the manuscript and applying her pencil to the margin. Carson read hungrily, tapping ash off the end of her cigarette and taking a quick swallow of sherry from the thermos at her elbow.

"My sister has been asking for you," Mrs. Ames said to Agnes.

"Would you like me to read to her now?"

Mrs. Ames laid down the pen and brushed Agnes' arm with her large, liver-spotted hand that could wash a dish, cook a meal, knock smartly on the door of a resident who wasn't following rules, nurse an invalid sister, improve a manuscript.

"Could you? She so looks forward to seeing you."

Agnes had been helping Mrs. Ames with her ill sister for months. The sister was from Carson McCuller's hometown in Georgia, and thus there was a bond between the three women. For Agnes, it was family.

"Shall we take the station wagon to town tomorrow?" Carson said through a cloud of smoke. "I want to spend the entire afternoon hearing about China. And playing pool, of course."

Agnes shook a cigarette out of its pack. "Around four?" It was agreed. Agnes watched Carson through her own cloud of smoke. Such talent. Here at Yaddo she was surrounded by talent. Langston Hughes, for instance. She admired him more than she could say. A very American man. Practical, but able to reflect on vast subjects. She felt pedestrian by comparison.

"Only certain things penetrate my hard soul," she would tell Carson tomorrow. "I have standards and principles and prejudices and weaknesses. But Hughes looks on and listens and absorbs everything. That makes him an artist." The play she'd started, then stopped, sputtered and dimmed each time she tried to present the *truth* of a character on stage.

"Let the characters grow naturally," Mrs. Ames had said, laughing at Agnes' headstrong plunge into a scene. For weeks she'd returned from the main house to her cabin in the woods where she bent herself double trying to write a literary play, when what she really wanted to do was tell the audience straight out how things were in China.

Now she was writing a biography of Zhu De instead. It wasn't easy handling historical material. She should be a better researcher. She should have gone to college. Should have gone to high school, for God's sake.

Carson was so pale. The girl drank too much and didn't eat enough. If Agnes had a daughter, she might be Carson's age. Might be just like Carson. She rocked and half-closed her eyes, pretending for a moment that Carson was her daughter. Brilliant. Unsure of herself. Then she pretended that Lily Wu and Ding Ling were her daughters. Or perhaps she would have had a child like Pearl Buck's little girl—eternally a little girl. Even a handicapped child would be your own flesh and blood; someone to love and care for.

Tomorrow she would see that Carson ate properly before they went to their favorite bar on sleazy Congress Street.

"Thank you, thank you, thank you," Carson murmured as she stood and gathered up the pages of *Member of the Wedding*. She reached for Mrs. Ames and pressed the stern face dramatically to her flat chest. Agnes kept a sharp eye on the ash at the tip of Carson's cigarette that threatened to fall into Mrs. Ames's hair.

They left and Agnes remained alone in the kitchen, drinking tea. The world outside the bay windows was white. White snow as slow in its fall as history itself. Movement so repetitive, so disinterested and faceless, that motion took on the quality of stillness.

Agnes was comfortable with action, purpose, heat, light, risk, conclusions, but here in winter there was no beginning or end, and no purpose. She thought of China. Peace had come to America and Europe, but not to China. If Chiang Kai-shek won the civil war now raging, China would be plunged back into corrupt elitism, with perhaps another revolution required, like the snow falling slowly, slowly, no beginning, no end.

But snow falls bloodlessly.

All morning in the little cabin in the woods the letter felt like a heat source over her heart. Warmth traveled down her arms and hands and emptied in an igneous flow of words onto the keyboard of her old typewriter. At noon, pleased with the half day's work, she paused and pulled the letter from her pocket. She slit the envelope with her index finger. Sitting down in the rocker, she began to read, savoring Evans' personality and his reach for her.

But the reach today was short. She stopped rocking. Her heart, moments earlier so warm, now cooled and nearly stopped.

Evans had recently married. He'd married a young woman named Peggy. He called her Peg. He said she was a "grand companion."

The fire in the wood stove burned out, and still she sat. The rocking chair became a straight chair, without movement or rhythm. The day became night, without stars or moon. Her inner voice died. She had no thoughts.

When her mind came back to life, she felt mortally wounded. "Grand companion!" The words split her heart open because they hid so much. She got out of the rocker and walked to the small window of her cabin. "Peg shares my inner life," he should have said. "No secret is too small. In bed, I find my home." Why didn't he say that? "Grand companion" was a lie. *Agnes* was his grand companion! His pal. Only a companion and pal.

She tore up the letter. She would have taken it outside to bury under the snow except for the pain of finding it next spring. She threw it in the fire. She laid her lunch out for birds or deer or any animal who, unlike herself, could still eat. She put on her coat and gloves and set out to walk away the rest of the day and night. The tears running down her cheeks would freeze. She would leave them there. She would never chip them off. Perhaps, if spring never came, she would find peace within this brittle casing.

Afterword

It is respectfully requested that Agnes Smedley, of Yaddo, Saratoga Springs, New York, be placed on the regular Censorship Watch List, and submissions of all communications and telephone conversations to, from, or regarding her be forwarded to the Bureau.

Purpose: Agnes Smedley is recognized as one of the principal propagandists for the Soviets writing in the English language. Agnes Smedley is considered an authority on Communist activity in the Far East, and as the operations of the United States Army and Navy come closer to the Asiatic Mainland and the Japanese home islands, Communist activity in those areas will be of increasing importance to the Bureau.

*J. Edgar Hoover, Memo to Albany,
New York office, October 24, 1945*

[*Battle Hymn of China* has been offered by the Book Find Club, which], according to information available locally, [is] a Communist Book of the Month Club.

*Agnes Smedley File, FBI
Boston office, 1946*

The subject was reported to at all times carry a sidearm of heavy calibre.

*Agnes Smedley File, FBI
Boston office, 1946*

Smedley, Agnes: Native Born Communist.

*Caption,
FBI Security Watch Index,
July 1946*

The Subject's name is being deleted from the Key Figure List of the Albany Division. In view of SAC Letter #44 dated April 17, 1947, it is not believed this subject warrants active investigation. It is requested that the Subject's name be removed from the Bureau's Key Figure List. This case is being closed in the Albany Office.

Agnes Smedley File,
FBI Albany, New York office
May 1947

…everyone knows that she is a Communist.

Whittaker Chambers
December 1945

I had no information that [Smedley] was a CP member, but gained the impression that she was at least a CP sympathizer.

Whittaker Chambers
March 1947

American Woman Involved in Spy Disclosure.

Agnes Smedley, an American writer, described as a native of a Missouri farm, shown in a camera study made today before she conferred with her attorney in New York. The United States Army had released a report on the amazing Russian spy ring which operated in the Far East before the Pearl Harbor attack. The report links Miss Smedley to the ring as its Shanghai operative and states she is 'a spy and agent of the Soviet government.'

Kansas City Star
February 10, 1949

MacArthur Says Remnants of Ring Could Be Active in World Capitals.

Kansas City Star
February 10, 1949

General MacArthur proposed no action against me. He knows I am not guilty of the charges brought against me. He makes his charges while hiding behind the protection of a law which says that he, as a top Army official, cannot be sued for falsehood. I therefore call him a coward and a cad. I now say to him: waive your immunity, and I will sue for libel.

Agnes Smedley
Mutual Broadcasting System radio program
February 10, 1949

[The] report contained several opinions that are now embarrassing the Army here… .

[It was] believed that Miss Smedley should not have been mentioned by name until the appropriate authorities had investigated her.

Army spokesman
New York Times
February 16, 1949

The Army acknowledged publicly tonight that it had made a 'faux pas' in releasing a 'philosophical' report of Communist spying in Japan and China, and said it had no proof to back charges that Miss Smedley, U.S. author, had been a member of the alleged spy ring… . Colonel Eyster said it was not the policy of the U.S. government to 'tar and feather people without proof.'

New York Times
February 18, 1949

...the Albany office determined that subject still remained at the estate [Yaddo] and was doing nothing inconsistent with her occupation as a writer. She seldom left her residence and according to the informant [Mrs. Ames' secretary], she made no trips of any consequence... Furthermore, investigation by the Albany and New York offices had failed to disclose current espionage activity on her part.

Agnes Smedley File,
FBI Albany, New York office
1949

It is our impression that Mrs. Ames is somehow deeply and mysteriously involved in Mrs. Smedley's political activities.... She is totally unfitted for the position of executive director.

Robert Lowell, Poet
Yaddo, Saratoga Springs
February 26, 1949

The guests departed, vowing to blacken the name of Yaddo in all literary circles and call a mass meeting of protest...then I left too, feeling as if I had been at a meeting of the Russian Writers' Union during a big purge. Elizabeth [Ames] went to a nursing home. Her secretary resigned. Yaddo was left like a stricken battlefield."

Malcolm Cowley, Writer
Board member, Yaddo
February 26, 1949

...even if I wrote you a long letter I couldn't begin to tell you how angry I feel at the s.o.b.'s who so casually smear a person of your record. Somehow you and I and a number of others seem to have lived through a period when the spirit and the will counted; and are now caught up in the hands of mechanical men who measure faith by the yard and loyalty by lead counters.

Theodore White,
letter to Agnes Smedley,
March 1949

My friend, why didn't I go to China and become a Chinese citizen months ago? I could have worked in peace there. But this country is no place for anyone who loves liberty. A general can simply say 'A.S. is a spy and an agent of the Soviet govt.' because she defends China.

Agnes Smedley, letter
February 1949

Miss Agnes Smedley, author and former newspaper correspondent…appealed today to President Truman as commander-in-chief to intervene with the Army and help clear her name and reputation. Miss Smedley, who has denied the charge, described MacArthur and his aides as having engaged in 'privileged smearing.'

She… called on him to make General MacArthur either apologize or else waive his immunity so that she could sue him for libel.

New York Sun
February 11, 1949

The charge against me took many weeks out of my life and cost me $1,500 in legal and other expenses. Though the charge was called a faux pas, it stuck to me so that I was thereafter never again able to get a lecture engagement or sell an article. I could, of course, speak before radical meetings for nothing, which I did… .

Agnes Smedley,
letter to Zhu De,
1949

They won't give me a passport for Europe because I might go on to China.

*Agnes Smedley,
letter to Zhu De,
1949*

The news from China fills me with great joy and I feel at peace at last. Here I sit in this God-forsaken country when I should have been in China. I have missed the greatest revolution in human history.

*Agnes Smedley,
letter to Zhu De,
1949*

Anna Louise Strong also will have a new book, *The Chinese Conquer China*… Edgar Snow gave me the proofs of her book… She is now lecturing on China through the country. She can get lecture engagements, but I cannot.

*Agnes Smedley,
letter to Zhu De,
1949*

Day before yesterday I saw the Italian movie 'Bicycle Thief.' I went alone and stood in a queue for two solid hours to buy a ticket. It was worth it. That little child sits enthroned in my heart. God of gods, but the human animal is savage! On every hand, everywhere, the human being can look on the most appalling injustice, the most blatant poverty due to the ownership of the earth by a few, without rising in their wrath. I can never understand that, and it fills me with despair.

*Agnes Smedley,
letter to Edgar Snow
January 9, 1950*

Thanks, Aino, for parcels. They are desperate for clothing and other supplies in England.... Basic foods are rationed. We get one-fourth pound of butter each a week, with a little more than that of margarine... .

*Agnes Smedley,
letter to Aino Taylor,
London
February 11, 1950*

I regard myself as a kind of political exile, and I find that Europe now has many American exiles who cannot earn a living in America because of the political reaction... I hope I never again have to return to the USA. I have no love for fascism, the American brand or otherwise.

*Agnes Smedley,
letter to Aino Taylor
London, 1950*

I've had a terrible cold for days—inflamed throat and eyes and God knows what. I have sort of disintegrated.

*Agnes Smedley, letter to
Aino Taylor, London
January 21, 1950*

My dear Margaret, I don't expect to die under the operation before me, but in case I do, I'd like to inform you of a few things and ask you to do me a favor or two.

...I own no property. All I possess is with me: $1,900 in Government Bonds (in my purse) and a book of Thomas Cook's Travel Checks, also in my purse... I do not recall the exact terms of my will, but I think I left $1,000 of my Government Bonds to my little niece, Mary Smedley. All income from my books, everywhere, all go to General Zhu De, Commander-in-Chief of the People's Liberation Army of China, to do with as he wishes…which means the building of a strong and free China… .

I am not a Christian and therefore wish no kind of religious rites over my body—absolutely none. I have had but one loyalty, one faith, and that was to the liberation of the poor and oppressed, and within that framework, to the Chinese revolution as it has now materialized. If the Chinese embassy arrives, I would be thankful if but one song were sung over my body: the Chinese national anthem, "Chee Lai" ["Rise Up"]. As my heart and spirit have found no rest in any land on earth except China, I wish my ashes to live with the Chinese Revolutionary dead.

Agnes Smedley,
letter to Margaret Sloss
April 28, 1950

On Monday I enter the Acland Nursing Home to have this old duodenal ulcer cut out… . I'll be coming out from under the anesthesia by the time this reaches you… .

Agnes Smedley,
letter to Aino Taylor,
London
April 28, 1950

A memorial meeting will be held for Agnes Smedley on Thursday afternoon, May 18, 1950, six o'clock, at the meeting house of the Religious Society of Friends, 221 East 15th Street, New York. You are invited to attend in person, or if that is not possible, to send a message, Room 567, 11 Broadway, Hanover 2-5845.

Announcement of Memorial Service for
Agnes Smedley following her death
on May 6, 1950
Age 58

There is no vanity in this woman. Absolute honesty in thought, speech and action was written all over her. She was grand, attractive, alive, animated, wise, courageous, a wonderful companion—impetuous and wants things done right away!
Evans Carlson,
Diary

In memory of Agnes Smedley, American Revolutionary Writer and Friend of the Chinese People.
Chinese characters inscribed by Zhu De on
Agnes Smedley's gravestone in the
Cemetery for Revolutionaries
Beijing,
China

ABOUT THE AUTHOR

Marlene Lee has worked as a court reporter, teacher, college instructor, and writer. A graduate of Kansas Wesleyan University (BA), University of Kansas (MA), and Brooklyn College (MFA), she currently lives in Columbia, Missouri and New York City. After graduating from Kansas Wesleyan, she taught English at Salina Senior High School. Her poems, stories, and essays have appeared in numerous publications.

Other books by Marlene Lee:

The Absent Woman
Published by Holland House April 2013

Virginia Johnstone doesn't need a rest, she needs a change; not comfort, but purpose. Divorced, and a visitor in her children's lives, she decides to leave Seattle and spend three months in the harbor town of Hilliard. There, on the edge of Puget Sound, she sublets rooms in an old hotel, rooms belonging to a woman who has vanished without explanation. In search of someone who can take her piano-playing to the next level, Virginia encounters Twilah Chan, an inspiring teacher and disturbing presence. Twilah's son, Greg, an exciting but also disturbing presence, re-awakens Virginia's romantic life. When she discovers a connection between the absent woman of the old hotel, Twilah, and Greg, she must decide whether to pursue the uncertain course she has set for herself or return to the safety of Seattle.

In a novel which is both elegiac and passionate, insightful and wryly humorous, Marlene Lee explores the need for change and the emotional consequences of leaving an old life in order to embrace a new one.

Praise for *The Absent Woman:*

> *"I couldn't put down The Absent Woman. I relished every scene, every word. It's one of the most compelling novels that I've read..."*

Ella Leffland, author of *Rumors of Peace; The Knight, Death, and the Devi*l, and others

"Lee writes quite beautifully, with grace and wit and precision. I thought it was a very brave book, and very honest. Virginia's feelings about leaving her boys were especially resonant. And she writes about music wonderfully. The book will stay with me for a long time."

Alex George, author of A Good American

Limestone Wall
Published by Holland House November 2014

Evelyn Grant, newly widowed, returns to her hometown of Jefferson City, Missouri, where she rents rooms in her old family home across the street from the Missouri State Penitentiary. Then Evelyn sets about trying to see her mother for the first time in forty years. She knows where to find her – across the street, behind the limestone wall: Mabel Grant is serving a life sentence in the penitentiary for murdering the twin babies of a neighbour.

Evelyn makes the acquaintance of Roz Teal, who has befriended a condemned prisoner soon to be executed. Through Roz, Evelyn meets Ezekiel, lifetime convict, who leads Evelyn to her mother.

A novel about loss and healing and unexpected bonds. Moving, poignant, Limestone Wall explores the tragic and the absurd in one town, one prison, and one person's past.

> *"Limestone Wall is a slim novel that nonetheless contains worlds upon worlds--in its wonderfully knobby, authentic characters, and in its elegant meditations on childhood, marriage, death, and the passage of time. Each page is a gift of beauty and truth. Fans of Marilynne Robinson and Paul Harding will find much to admire in Marlene Lee's books."*
>
> Keija Parssinen, the author of *The Ruins Of Us*